****

Into the Reckoning

Book Ten of Rise of the Republic

By

James Rosone and Miranda Watson

****

Illustration © Tom Edwards
Tom EdwardsDesign.com

****

Published in conjunction with Front Line Publishing, Inc.

Manuscript Copyright Notice

ISBN: 978-1-961748-39-2
Sun City Center, Florida, United States of America
Library of Congress Control Number: 2024904096

Table of Contents

Chapter One
It's a Trap, Captain

September 2113
Task Force 22
Lyrius Star System
RNS *Vanguard*

Rear Admiral Amy Dobbs looked on in abject horror as the ambush against her reconnaissance force continued to unfold. The handful of frigates and cruisers escorting what their sensors had identified as a convoy of giant freighters heading toward Corusca had morphed into something more dangerous. Nearly a dozen Pharaonis cruisers and destroyers broke formation, advancing away from the freighters they had been using to shield themselves from Republic sensors. With the initial escort having decisively engaged her reconnaissance force, there was little she could do to intervene other than to push the ships of her task force to use all available thrust to shorten the time to contact with the enemy and hope they weren't too late.

I knew something wasn't right about this convoy the moment we detected it, she lamented.

Shortly after the alliance fleet had entered the system, they'd detected the main Pharaonis fleet forming near Corusca, one of two habitable moons in orbit of the gas giant Aiolia. It was the only inhabited moon or planet in the system, making its capture by either side a strategic win. Since its takeover, Corusca had become a logistical staging point, allowing the Pharaonis to launch raiding missions into Ry'lian and Tully space. It was only when the alliance moved further into the system toward the enemy fleet that they detected something else—a convoy of freighters moving towards Corusca. That was when Task Force 22—Dobbs's task force—was ordered to engage and eliminate it.

I should have sent more ships, she thought, second-guessing herself as she studied each update of the battle unfolding just beyond the range of their weapons.

After directing her former XO, Captain Joseph Wright, to lead a reconnaissance force consisting of his ship, the battle cruiser *Teddy Roosevelt*, a heavy cruiser, a pair of frigates, and a single corvette, she was upset with herself for not sending more cruisers, especially with the appearance of those new destroyers the Pharaonis had recently begun fielding. Now, as her reconnaissance element was decisively engaged, unable to break free from their quarry, it was a race against time to see if her ships would come to the rescue or if she would be left to watch helplessly as they were destroyed, one by one.

Damn this jamming—why the hell are we only learning now of this new capability they seem to have acquired? she questioned, wondering who had dropped the intelligence ball on this one.

From the moment the Pharaonis had sprung their trap, one or more of their newer vessels had succeeded in jamming the targeting sensors of her ships. Normally, this was something the Republic was known for doing to its adversaries, not the other way around. Being on the receiving end was an entirely new experience and one she did not enjoy.

She cursed under her breath, frustrated beyond belief. She watched helplessly as Pharaonis warships continued to pummel the *Teddy Roosevelt* and the heavy cruiser *Oceanus*. Seeing the pair of Republic ships firing back at the enemy, impressively scoring hit after hit against the Pharaonis, felt good. But it still irked her that five of her ships were in grave danger of being destroyed, and there was little she could do until her ships could burn through the electronic jamming or get close enough for their targeting sensors to overpower the jamming. For now, all she could do was watch and wait and hope her ships could hold out a little longer.

"Admiral, I think we're almost through the jamming. I'm starting to get targeting data on those large contacts we identified as freighters. It shouldn't be long now until we can target the rest of them," Lieutenant Michael Luther announced excitedly.

Dobbs turned to look at her electronics warfare officer, hope in her eyes. "Outstanding, Lieutenant! Keep doing whatever you can to figure out which one of those ships is blinding us," she replied encouragingly. "Weps, the moment Lieutenant Luther identifies the source of the jamming, I want all our guns and ASMs targeting it—delete that ship from existence!" she ordered with cold precision.

"Aye, Admiral. We're on it," replied the lieutenant as he began coordinating with gun crews.

"Holy hell, that's a lot of missiles!" Lieutenant Commander Thomas Hill exclaimed suddenly from his tactical action station near the

TAMs or tactical action map table. The battle's holographic display now showed dozens upon dozens of tiny red lines streaking toward her recon element.

"Get the TAMs readout displayed on the main monitor now!" barked Captain Brian Wiirre, the *Vanguard*'s skipper, before Dobbs could.

In seconds, the desperate battle being fought from afar was now playing against the backdrop of the floor-to-ceiling main bridge monitor. Seeing the expanse of the battle like this was almost too immersive for some, but for Dobbs and her new ship captain, it was perfect.

What they saw on the display felt like a punch to the diaphragm, and Dobbs reached a hand out to steady herself. The detailed, zoomed-in display of the battle showed the RNS frigate *Havana* taking some hits while doing its best to evade and throw off gunners aboard the Pharaonis ships targeting them. That was when they saw it. One of the Pharaonis' new destroyers emerged from behind one of the giant cargo ships. It didn't take long to see that the destroyer had found its prey and was angling in for the kill.

"Weps, tell me you can get a lock on that destroyer. It's heading right for the *Chennai*," Captain Wiirre said, his eyes still affixed to the already heavily damaged Republic frigate.

"Eh…it's risky, sir. We're almost as likely to frag the *Teddy* or *Havana* with a barrage of magrail slugs as we are that destroyer. The jamming is still scrambling our targeting computers," replied Lieutenant Bullard before offering an idea. "Captain, there is another option we can try if you'd like?"

Without waiting for Wiirre to respond, Dobbs jumped in. "What is it, and will it work?"

"We can fire a couple of dozen ASMs in the direction of the enemy fleet and hand off the final targeting of the missiles to Commander Mitsu and his squadron," Bullard suggested, referring to their Havoc-II antiship missiles. "They've got to be getting close to burning through the jamming on their end."

Captain Wiirre turned to face Dobbs. "I think it's worth a shot, Admiral. If Kenji's bombers aren't able to get a lock on the destroyer, then I'd wager they could find us other targets worth some rapid disassembly."

Dobbs thought about that for a moment. Then, reaching for the comms headset next to her chair, she connected to Commander Mitsu aboard one of the B-11 Valkyrie bombers. "Shogun Actual, Athena Actual. I'm not sure if you've managed to break through the enemy jamming or not, but if the *Vanguard* sent a few dozen ASMs for your bombardier to take control of, do you think you guys could get 'em locked onto those destroyers or at least some kind of target for us? We're still having a devil of a time burning through this jamming right now."

There was a pause as she waited for the time delay and Mitsu's response. Then the radio crackled with static, another side effect of the jamming. "Athena Actual, Shogun Actual. Good copy on request. We are a go for ASM assistance. We'll find a home for them. Out."

Smiling, Dobbs looked at Wiirre. "He's good. Let's get some ASMs on the way and do what we can until we're able to burn through this noise."

As the *Vanguard* fired its missiles, the only thing she could do was watch and wait as her task force continued to close the gap between the enemy force that had ambushed her recon element and the battle continued to unfold. *Come on, Mike, find a way to burn through this jamming so we can help*, she urged privately.

"They're firing another barrage," Lieutenant Commander Thomas Hill exclaimed from his TAO station. "I'm showing forty-six missiles heading for the *Chennai*. They're from that destroyer that was hiding behind the freighter."

Dobbs heard him but didn't know what else to say for the moment. Like some of the others on the bridge, she watched in alarm as the swarm of missiles raced towards the *Chennai*, towards *her* spacers. In seconds, the frigate's point-defense guns, or PDGs, responded, firing near-constant strings of 30mm exploding projectiles toward the incoming threat. Observing the battle from afar was both spectacular and frightening as the spacers aboard the *Chennai* were in a desperate fight for survival.

"Hot damn! They've nailed eleven of them so far—make it seventeen now," exclaimed Commander Hill as explosions continued to occur in what was becoming an obvious line directly toward the ship.

They're out of time…, she realized as the first missile impacted *Chennai*. Before her brain had a chance to process what happened, nearly two dozen more slammed into the vessel along its entire length. Fractions of a second later, the frigate blew up—separating into two pieces, the forward momentum of the ship now pushing the two parts further away from each other.

Dobbs wanted to scream in frustration at the destruction of one of her ships and the loss of its crew. Barely containing the rage building within her, she turned to face Lieutenant Bullard. "Weps, tell me you've got some firing solutions by now."

Looking up to meet her eyes, Bullard smiled. "I sure do."

Dobbs smiled like a predator. "Get us a lock on those destroyers and fire everything we've got at them. It's time to end this fight."
****

Eighteen Hours Earlier
Task Force 22
RNS *Teddy Roosevelt*
Tau Sagittarii System

Captain Joe Wright stood on the bridge of the battle cruiser *Teddy Roosevelt*, waiting like everyone else for the Altairian star carrier to officially open the bridge to the Lyrius system in Pharaonis-controlled space. During the mission brief for Operation Orion's Hammer, Admiral Pandolly had explained that the system had once been part of the Ry'lian territory. It had been lost to the Pharaonis just prior to the end of the First Zodark War in a brutal multimonth campaign that had seen the system change hands several times. In the eight years since they had wrested control of it from the Ry'lians, the Pharaonis had turned the system into a staging base for further incursions into Ry'lian and Tully space near the Serpentis system. While the alliance continued to grow its fleets and train its ground forces for the eventual invasion of the Zodark Empire, the alliance force that had defeated the Orbots was now being directed to go after the Haven—a pair of systems the Pharaonis called home.

"Captain, we're receiving a message from the *Digimon CS1*," announced Lieutenant Levi Baker from the tactical action station. "It's the five-minute warning, sir, before they open the bridge."

Wright saw the faces of the bridge crew staring at him, waiting for him to issue the orders that would set them in motion as they readied the ship to cross into a hostile system. "Very well, Lieutenant. Why don't you go ahead and open a ship-wide channel so I can address the crew?" he replied.

As Wright was collecting his thoughts before speaking to the crew, his Chief of the Boat, Master Chief Petty Officer Bill Walters, walked up and whispered, "Just give it to them straight, Skipper—they trust you."

"Thanks, COB; you're right. They should know what we're up against," Wright whispered back as he readied to speak.

Taking a breath in as he steadied his thoughts, he exclaimed, "This is the captain speaking. In the next couple of minutes, the Altairians will open a bridge connecting us to the Lyrius system—starting Operation Orion's Hammer. I would expect to encounter enemy warships shortly after our arrival. It will be important for everyone to remain sharp and be ready to react to whatever the enemy throws at us. You know what to do, people. I'm proud of you guys. Now let's kick some ass," he said, ending with the official battle cry of the Republic: "To victory!"

Moments after his pep talk was finished, the Altairian ship opened the bridge that connected the two systems—allowing the alliance ships to cross the vast distance in mere seconds.

Captain Wright looked to Ensign House. "Helm, take us in, let's do this."

As the ships of the combined allied fleet crossed the bridge, the vast emptiness of space blinked away before returning, this time in an entirely different region of space as the fleet exited the bridge. The moment the first ships appeared in the Lyrius system, bridge crews across the fleet snapped into action as they prepared their warships for battle.

"TAO, get our active sensors going and get us a view of the situation around us," Captain Wright called out the moment they were through. "Weapons, start charging the magrails and the turbo lasers. I want our guns ready for action the moment we spot the Pharaonis."

"Aye, Captain," came the affirmative calls as the bridge crew reacted to the flurry of orders.

While the crew waited for the active sensors to populate the TAMs and radar scopes, the forward-facing cameras filled in the immediate gap in their situational awareness, feeding images of what was happening around them to the bridge. They painted a scene with a mixture of silhouettes of formidable battleships, their engines lit hot as the metal beasts got underway to form a battle line with which the fleet would eventually advance into the system.

As the lumbering giants of space warfare methodically moved into position, the faster, more nimble corvettes zipped ahead of the formation and to the flanks of the battle line as they scouted for any immediate threats. After the corvettes took off, the frigates were the next ships to advance, establishing the screening force and picket line to intercept potential missiles or small attack craft intent on finding a gap in the line to exploit with their missiles and plasma torpedoes.

The Pharaonis were known for spamming battle lines with swarms of missiles and torpedoes as their capital ships maneuvered to get in close, where their hard-hitting lasers could deliver devastating blows. Thankfully, their laser batteries were slower to recharge than those of the Republic and its allies, negating their potency a bit. With the corvettes and frigates moving into their positions, the heavy cruisers and battle cruisers began forming their protective barriers around the capital ships—the carriers and battleships that comprised the bulk of the fleet's firepower.

"It's impressive, isn't it?" Wright commented to his XO, Commander Weber, as the two of them stared at the display of raw firepower on the giant bridge monitor.

"It sure is. I wonder what the Pharaonis must think."

"Probably crapping their pants if I had to guess. They've relied on the Orbots to protect them as they nip at the edges of Ry'lian and Tully space. Now they get to deal with the full attention and might of the alliance," Wright countered, then added. "Let's just be thankful, Jeff, that our fight in this war is out here—among the stars in these giant warships. I'd hate to have to battle this enemy on the surface."

Weber grunted in agreement. "Amen to that, Skipper. Their faces—my God, they look like demonic figures, and those ant-like bodies of theirs give me the heebie-jeebies."

"Captain, we're receiving returns from the active scanners," exclaimed Lieutenant Baker excitedly. "It's the Pharaonis, sir. We're detecting a large formation of warships in the direction of the planet Aiolia."

Wright turned to face his tactical action officer standing next to the holographic display on the TAMs table. "Very well, TAO. Continue monitoring the situation, and stay tuned for further orders from the Fleet. Helm, stand by to receive a revised course heading from carrier *Sirius*. I suspect Admiral Rosentreter will issue a revised battle order to advance on Aiolia."

"Aye, Captain. Standing by," acknowledged the helmsman, giving a curt nod.

As the data from the active sensor arrays continued to flow into the CIC, populating the ship's tactical action map, a clearer picture emerged of what exactly the fleet was facing. Interlaced among the rings encircling the gas giant Aiolia was a formation of two separate Pharaonis fleets. One was positioned near Serenea, the other closer to Corusca, moving slowly amongst the cosmic dust, debris, and countless floating ice particles towards Serenea.

When the order to advance was given, Admiral Rosentreter detached part of the fleet to head towards the smaller grouping of warships that looked to be escorting some giant cargo vessels en route to Serenea. Until they got closer, or the probes returned more accurate information, their knowledge of the exact types of Pharaonis ships they were facing was limited. The Republic's experience with this adversary was limited to their brief encounters during the Serpentis campaign, but the Altairians, Ry'lians, and Tully had shared the types of ships they had encountered during their many conflicts.

Like most spacefaring species, the Pharaonis had created their own versions of ships that the alliance had classified as Blacktips for frigates, Makos for cruisers, and Threshers for battleships. But the introduction of a new ship, a destroyer the alliance now called Hammerheads, was causing some angst. Like many Pharaonis ships before it, its primary weapons were missiles and plasma torpedoes. But unlike the other ships of their fleet, the Hammerheads were purpose-built for head-on fights and charging into enemy battle lines. The front of the destroyer had extensive armor plating that extended another forty-five degrees around both sides of the ship. This meant the ship could absorb tremendous levels of damage beyond what even many of the larger vessels could sustain, making it a deadly new addition to their fleet.

The Republic had used destroyers in the early years of the Zodark war before phasing them out in favor of the Altairian-Human hybrid *Decatur*-class frigates and the *Neptune*-class corvettes.

What little the alliance knew of this destroyer came from a battle that had occurred a few months back when the Pharaonis had tried once again to reclaim Serpentis. A superior Altairian fleet had repulsed their attack, but not before this new ship was able to inflict some serious damage against it. During the battle, the new vessel had severely damaged an Altairian *Berkimon* battleship and destroyed a *Trilimon*-class cruiser—a smaller version of the Type-002 Altairian-Human hybrid heavy cruiser.

"Captain, we're receiving an encoded message from Admiral Dobbs for you," Lieutenant Commander Becerra announced.

"Thank you, Becerra. Send it to my station," he replied, suspecting this was the order they had been waiting for as the fleet got underway toward Aiolia.

As Wright returned to his captain's chair, his frame gently depressed into the overly comfortable ergonomic chair. He still felt a weird sense of guilt about how much attention had been paid to the comfort of seats aboard these new classes of hybrid warships. It wasn't that he believed a person should have to be uncomfortable while seated at their workstation, but, like some other long-in-the-tooth officers, he felt that maybe a little too much attention was being paid to such creature comforts as opposed to other equally important MWR needs aboard a ship.

A video image of Admiral Dobbs appeared on Wright's terminal. "Ah, there you are, Joe. Is everything good on the *Teddy*?"

Smiling, he responded, "Always, Admiral, you know that. So let me guess, we've been detailed off for an assignment?"

Now it was her turn to smile. "You know it, and enough of that admiral stuff when it's just us. We've got too much history to bother with formalities. But, yes, the fleet commander wants our task force to deal with this second grouping of ships near that moon Corusca. We've been getting some strange electromagnetic interference that may be originating from them or might have something to do with Aiolia. In either case, we haven't been able to nail down the specifics of what kinds of ships we're up against just yet."

Wright nodded along as he listened, then commented, "I'm sure we'll burn through whatever it is as we move closer. What are your thoughts on how you want to deploy our battle line as we approach 'em?"

He watched her contemplate his question before answering. He liked that about Amy. She took the time to think and wasn't quick to rush into battle like some officers they had served with in the past.

"If I'm being honest, Joe, I don't like not knowing what kind of ships we're up against before we have a chance to decelerate and readjust our approach. It's one thing to encounter a squadron with a couple of battleships, cruisers, and frigates. It's another thing entirely if half those ships are those new destroyers the Altairians ran into in Serpentis. If you ask me, if the Pharaonis had deployed a handful more of those ships, it might have cost the Altairians and Tully control of the system again," Dobbs replied, sharing her concern with him.

Then an idea came, and he asked, "That's a good point about not rushing their position before we know what kind of ships we're up against. What if we do this—I burn ahead of the task force with the *Teddy* and a pair of frigates and corvettes? Call it a recon in force. That should get us the intel on what kind of ships we're dealing with."

Dobbs bit her lip as her mind raced through whatever scenarios she was running, then looked at him. "All right. I'll let you take the frigates *Havana* and *Chennai*, and the heavy cruiser *Oceana*, but only one of the corvettes, the *Naiad*. This is a recon mission, Joe—not a fight. That'll come once we have a better picture of what we are up against. Good?"

Smiling, he responded, "Yes, ma'am. Recon, no fighting. Got it."

Dobbs snorted at what must have been his failed attempt to conceal his excitement about the pending battle. She shook her head and then disconnected the call.

"New orders?" Weber asked mischievously.

"Yup, we're going hunting. Helm, advance engines to full and begin to pull us away from the task force," Wright declared as he stood from his chair. "Comms, send a message to the *Havana*, *Chennai*, *Oceana*, and *Naiad* to form up on us. Let the skippers know I'll be contacting them shortly to apprise them of the change in orders."

"Aye, Captain," came the quick replies from the two stations.

"Come on, XO. Let's look at the situation on the TAMs and go over our new orders," directed Wright before he led them to the holographic table, excitedly discussing his idea.

****

Three Hours Later
RNS *Teddy Roosevelt*

"Brace for impact!" shouted Lieutenant Baker as more missiles impacted against the ship.

Boom, boom, boom.

Captain Wright gripped the armrest of his chair tightly, grimacing as the ship took another pounding. *Come on, Amy, where the hell are you? We're getting picked apart out here.* His mind raced with thoughts of what he could have done differently to avoid this apparent ambush. *Deal with that later...focus on the here and now*, he reasoned with himself as he pushed aside the distracting thoughts and the fear and anxiety he felt growing inside him.

When he returned his gaze to the bridge monitor, taking in the situation of the battle, he saw a magnified real-time image of the lone corvette under his command, the *Naiad*, taking a pounding from a pair of Pharaonis frigates that looked to have bracketed them to either side. He could tell even from this magnification level that most of the corvette's guns and PDGs had been blown apart or melted to useless slag by enemy laser fire. He felt helpless at that moment, knowing the ship was going down and there was nothing he could do to stop it.

"Damage report?" he barked aloud to his bridge crew.

"Captain, Weps. Damage reports are coming in now," Lieutenant Baker announced. He paused for a second as he read the report, his eyes widening as he did.

Whatever the report was telling Baker, he was having a hard time coming to grips with it, Wright saw. Interceding before his junior officer lost hope, he interjected, "Lieutenant Baker, put aside whatever it is you're feeling right now and just focus on the facts. Don't sugarcoat something or make it sound better or worse—just give it to me straight. Did we lose any additional guns, and what's the status report on the ones already down?"

Baker seemed to stiffen his back in response, explaining, "Yes, Captain, you're right, just the facts. On the port side, solely focusing on the large turbo laser batteries, turrets one and four are down, along with the three others from the previous attack. That leaves us with three operational turrets until we can get power restored to turrets two and three. Staying on the port side, another four medium laser batteries are down. I'm still waiting for an ETA from Damage Control and Engineering on when those turrets will be operational again."

Good grief, we're going to be toothless by the time the rest of the task force gets here, Wright grumbled to himself before replying, "Thank you, Baker. How are we doing along the starboard side?"

The weapons officer glanced once more at his screen for a moment before looking up. "Sir, Commander Mertes provided an update just seconds ago. He said they found a workaround to get power to the large laser batteries three and six, but he said they're being held together with duct tape and superglue, so it may not last more than a shot or two. He also updated the status of VLS three—it's toast. Nearly half the missile caps appear stuck in the closed position. Short of sending repair bots outside the ship to cut them open, there isn't anything more his people can do," explained Lieutenant Baker, a bit more confidently than before.

Captain Wright grunted at the idea of having his engineering Synths standing outside the ship while they were actively fighting other warships. Looking to his helmsman, Wright ordered, "Helm, increase engines to fifty percent and bring us about eighty-one degrees to our portside."

"Aye, Captain," replied Ensign House, increasing the power to the engines as he turned the giant warship, bringing to bear the majority of the ship's firepower.

Once the ship turned, twelve of the twenty-four turrets housing the ships' main guns, the twin-barreled twenty-four-inch magnetic railguns, would now have a clean field of fire. This would also give the enemy a much larger target to shoot at, exposing the broadside of the *Teddy* so its main guns could be brought to bear.

With the main guns' field of firing widening, Captain Wright turned to face Lieutenant Baker. "TAO, once the starboard turrets have a clean line of engagement, I want whatever primary and secondary laser batteries are still operational to focus on destroying those frigates pounding on the *Naiad* and those two cruisers hammering the *Chennai* and *Havana*. But the moment our magrail turrets have a clean shot at the big-ass freighters those destroyers keep ducking behind for cover—I want them gone. You hear me, Baker? Rapid disassembly, gone. We can't allow their ships to keep ducking behind those monstrosities for cover. I

16

have no idea why *Oceanus*'s sixteen-inch guns haven't been able to take 'em out, but we'll see how they work against ours."

As the seconds turned to minutes, Wright continued to watch how the enemy was reacting to their course and speed changes—they seemed like they had expected his reaction and were already moving to counter it. Glancing to the bottom-right corner of the main display to see where the rest of the task force was, he realized they were much closer than the last time he'd checked. He'd bet Admiral Dobbs was pushing the ships of her task force pretty hard—hopefully not hard enough to burn out a reactor.

Just then, he heard an audible gasp and some choice curse words as the main display showed what had just been the *Naiad* splitting apart into three sections. The corvette was down, leaving him with just a pair of frigates and a heavy cruiser to augment his ship.

"Captain, we're receiving a distress call from the *Chennai*. It's the XO—he said the skipper's dead and his ship's done for. They've lost control of the reactor, and it's going to go critical soon. He's ordering the crew to abandon ship," Commander Becerra from Comms alerted him.

"Stand by. Main guns preparing to fire—firing," his weapons officer, Lieutenant Van Vleet, stated moments before the twelve twin-barreled twenty-four-inch magrail guns fired, shaking the ship. Despite the blasts of compressed air from the stabilizing nozzles that followed, they could still feel the ship slide slightly to the side from the recoil.

Captain Wright watched in awe as two dozen of the twenty-five-hundred-pound projectiles were fired into the broadside of the giant freighter behind which the Pharaonis destroyers had been ducking for cover. When shells reached the inner guts of the freighters, they went up in a series of independent explosions that, seconds later, combined to create one giant blast that blew apart the giant ship.

"Captain, CIC, I'm not sure what ship you just blew up, but whatever it was, it just halved the intensity and power of the enemy jamming. If you can find another ship like the one you just blew up, I'd wager the ships of the task force could start targeting these bastards and help us take them out," alerted Commander Little from CIC, the ship's nerve center located on the deck just beneath the bridge.

Tapping the side of his comms device, Wright transmitted, "Maggie, it's Joe. We just blew up one of the three freighters those destroyers have been hiding behind. You think it's possible they jerry-rigged them with jamming equipment?"

There was a momentary pause before she responded, "They must have. I don't see any reason why the intensity of the jamming would have changed if the ship hadn't been outfitted with jamming equipment. I mean, Lord knows it's certainly large enough for it."

"Thanks, Maggie. We'll target the other two freighters and see if that makes a difference. Out," he finished, then directed his weapons officer to target the other two freighters with the ship's remaining laser batteries while the magrails continued to recharge.

"Alert, alert, brace for impact, brace for impact!"

The warning barely had time to echo through the bridge before chaos ensued. A thunderous *BAM, BAM* resonated through the ship, cascading through the bridge like an unexpected shockwave.

Wright watched as the bridge transformed from a hub of controlled military precision into a scene of devastation. Before he could react, he felt himself being knocked along the side of his body and grabbed for something, anything, to keep from falling to the ground. Just as he felt like he was about to fall or black out, allowing the pull of the darkness just to consume him, his hand caught the side of a chair from one of the stations near his captain's chair. Holding on to it, he felt a heaviness fall across his body, like he wanted to lie down and take a nap.

Forcing his eyes to stay open, he saw the overhead lights flicker briefly before succumbing to the darkness. Their absence was quickly followed by the violent arcing of electricity from exposed wiring. It created a hazardous light show of sparks that zipped across parts of the bridge, dancing with lethal grace.

The ceiling panels, unable to withstand the ship's violent shuddering, detached and plummeted downwards, one of them whacking him across the side of his body, his head, as he fell to the deck. The thunderous noise as they crashed onto the floor sounded like gunshots, adding further chaos to the situation.

Then a new sound rippled across the bridge—the creaking of metal as support beams groaned under the unseen pressure above them. A fraction of a second later, the beams bent, bowing until they buckled and collapsed across workstations and people alike. Wright panicked, wondering if the bridge would be exposed to the vacuum of space. Thankfully, the only noise he heard following the crashing of metal against the workstations of the bridge was the cries of the wounded, those crewmen who found themselves trapped beneath the debris or too grievously wounded to move.

Blinking his eyes in the quasi-darkness, Wright tried to regain control of his mind, pushing away the force he felt was trying to lull him into sleep. The first coherent thought that came to mind was *Oh…what the hell happened?*

He lifted a hand to touch his forehead, wincing briefly and gently opening his eyes. He realized he was surrounded by darkness, the lights of the bridge having been fully extinguished, but only for a moment before the emergency lights flicked on, illuminating a chaotic mess that had once been his bridge. Attempting to walk towards a wounded comrade, he felt lightheaded and grabbed for something to steady himself.

"Help, please help. Someone…please help me," Wright heard a voice call out somewhere to his right.

Turning to look in that direction, he couldn't believe what he was seeing. The workstations, once alive with the hum of activity, his crew directing the activities of the ship, were now a broken mess of twisted metal, shattered screens, the arcing of loose wires hanging from the ceiling. A small electrical fire burned about ten feet from him.

He tapped the comms unit still affixed to him. "Sickbay, this is the captain. We need medical help on the bridge. I've got dozens of urgent critical patients. Please acknowledge," he stammered as a wave of nausea and dizziness washed over him.

"Sickbay to bridge. Affirmative on the last transmission. Medbots and medics are en route. Hang in there, Skipper, I've got help on the way—out." replied Commander Kenny "Doc" Hamlin over the sound of organized chaos in the background.

Wright was about to call Engineering to see what the holdup was in getting some damage control parties to the bridge when his engineering chief beat him to it. "Captain—it's Pete. I've got a damage control party approaching the outer door to the bridge as we speak. Joe, are you OK? That was a bad hit we took. How badly damaged is the bridge?" Commander Mertes asked with genuine concern in his voice.

Coughing a couple of times, Wright replied, "It's bad, Pete. The support beams buckled and collapsed on us. I can't see too well. The smoke is getting bad. I think the HVAC system is down." He coughed a few more times as smoke from the fires continued unabated. "Don't worry about me or the bridge, Pete. Maggie in CIC should have had the alternate bridge up and running the moment we went down. That's why the CIC was built beneath and behind the bridge, for situations like this." He coughed some more, then asked, "Pete, how bad are we? Do we have guns still firing?"

If we lose the guns—the turbo lasers or the magrails—we're toast.

"I'm not going to sugarcoat it, Joe—we're in bad shape. That last hit tore a gash in the hull, and now the bastards are trying to hit us with more missiles right into that chink in the armor. On a good note, we still have most of the guns firing. In fact, we took out one more of those transports and severely damaged the third one," Pete explained. "Joe, if you're mobile, I'd get down to the CIC and take charge of the ship. It's nothing against Maggie, but she's no skipper. That last missile that hit us—it was a doozy. It blew out the two decks above yours—the command deck. If those support beams fail, it may just be a matter of time until the decks collapse into each other. When that happens, Joe, it'll expose the command deck to the vacuum of space. We'll lose access to at least a third of the ship, damn near all the gun turrets and the munition fabricators—"

"Whoa, Pete, if we lose control of the command deck and it opens to space, we may lose the entire ship!" Wright interrupted, the sudden seriousness of the situation pushing away the brain fog he still felt.

"I know, I know, it's bad. I get it. I've got every maintenance bot and Synth working on trying to reseal the ship. It's a little hard right now, given we're still in the enemy kill box," Pete responded, exasperated by the situation.

The door to the bridge finally opened, and a handful of damage control personnel rushed in, making their way toward the fires that needed to be put out. Tapping the communicator, he said, "Pete, your team's here. I'm going to check on a couple of people here on the bridge and then head down to the CIC and help Maggie. Just do what you can to keep us in the fight, and whatever you do, keep power flowing to the guns. They're the only thing keeping us alive."
****

"They did it! That last ship, the one the *Teddy* blew up—it must've been how the Pharaonis were jamming us," exclaimed Lieutenant Luther excitedly. "I'd wager they packed the insides of those freighters with all sorts of jamming equipment."

Lieutenant Bullard hooted and hollered with excitement. "Captain, we're generating targeting solutions for the enemy ships," he declared loudly. "Our main guns are charging. They should be ready to fire within two minutes. The primary turbo lasers are spooling up now and will be ready to engage targets within sixty seconds."

"Excellent work, people. This is what I'm talking about: everyone staying on top of their sections and being ready to react the moment the situation changes," replied Captain Brian Wiirre, who had replaced Captain Wright as skipper on the *Vanguard* when Wright took command of the *Teddy*.

Admiral Dobbs heard the excitement but kept her eyes glued to the monitor of the workstation she was sitting at. She was reading the status reports coming in from the *Teddy Roosevelt*, the *Oceanus*, and the *Havana*—they were not good. All three of the ships had sustained various levels of damage, with the *Teddy* and the *Oceanus* the most severe. The frigate *Chennai* and the corvette *Naiad* had been lost earlier in the battle when her task force had been unable to fire their guns on the enemy in support due to the intensity of the surprise jamming they'd encountered the moment the enemy had initiated their ambush.

"How's the *Teddy* holding up, Admiral?" asked Captain Wiirre, a look of concern on his face.

Dobbs grimaced at the question before answering, "If these status reports from the ship are correct, they're in trouble. They've got a hull breach in two separate locations—decks two and three had to be sealed off. They lost eighty spacers because of it, and they're in danger of losing structural integrity on decks one, six, and seven."

"Oh jeez, that's bad," Wiirre commented. "Anything we can do to help?"

"Destroy those enemy ships before they can finish the *Teddy* off. That's about it."

Chapter Two
Mountain Home, Idaho

Space Command Headquarters
Future Republic Capital
Mountain Home, Idaho
Earth, Sol System

Viceroy Miles Hunt stood at the edge of the hangar bay, staring in awe as the shuttle carrying President Gudea, the leader of the Humtar Federation, taxied gracefully towards the giant doors. This was no ordinary shuttlecraft; it was the first time anyone had seen one of the newer Humtar vessels. Unlike the historical model that had been unearthed at Lab Site X, this shuttle was well maintained, with a sleek and elegant design that embodied the Humtars' mastery over technology. It left Miles momentarily breathless. The metallic surface seemed to ripple with colors, reflecting the hues of the leaves nearby that were beginning to change to autumn shades.

Even as it maneuvered silently along the parking ramp, the ship exuded majesty and purpose. The shimmering silver-blue body appeared seamless, molded by some advanced technique currently unknown to Earthers. It was unlike any spacecraft Miles had ever seen before, outshining every advanced ship of the Republic.

The subtle thrum of its engines vibrated gently through the air as it came to a halt, poised before the immense hangar doors. Nearby was the ceremonial color guard and band that the base had cobbled together to greet someone of President Gudea's stature on such short notice. The ramp extended smoothly from the belly of the shuttle, and moments later, the leader of the Humtar people emerged.

Upon seeing the President, the Commanding Officer of the Guard called the nearby Republic Army soldiers to attention as the band began to play the anthem of the Republic. The Humtar President stopped briefly as the band played. A big smile spread across his face; he was clearly impressed and enjoying the ceremonial greeting.

Miles watched him as he stood there, taking in the music. Then Gudea looked around at the surrounding landscape with an expression of childlike wonder. Miles felt the same way as he studied the man walking toward him. The Humtars were humans, to be sure, but as Miles watched this Humtar and his entourage walk toward him, it was as if Gudea was the embodiment of perfection, a specimen of humanity almost touched by the hand of a divine being. His features were strikingly symmetrical, his physique lean and muscular, and his movements fluid and graceful. His presence radiated a sense of power and intelligence—it was almost intimidating.

I wonder what his diet and exercise routine is like, thought Miles as he stepped forward to shake President Gudea's hand. As their hands were about to touch, Miles felt a sense of horror, and he pulled back his hand. "Excuse me, President Gudea. Do you want me to go through your decontamination process before shaking hands?" he asked.

Gudea laughed at his awkwardness. "Thank you for asking. No, you do not need to concern yourself with this, Viceroy. I will follow the procedures of our medical personnel when I return to my ship."

Miles let out a deep breath, realizing he hadn't created a major breach of protocol in the first thirty seconds of this anticipated meeting. He had long dreamed about this day when he might be able to meet the long-lost Humtars, and he did not want to mess it up.

President Gudea remarked on the beauty of their surroundings. "This planet is not too dissimilar to Etlu, where I live," he explained.

"Yes, you are right. Planets such as ours are rare to find. These mountains offer a fantastic view of what will become our new capital city once the construction is finished," Miles agreed.

Gudea's expression then became somber. "Yes, I was briefed on what happened here and within this star system. We saw the expansive destruction wrought upon the Earth as we approached...the scars of war are still fresh and not fully healed."

Miles nodded. As they walked slowly together toward the meeting room that had been hastily set up, the two leaders talked about the recent battle with the Zodarks. This naturally led to a lesson about the Galactic Empire and the Dominion and the current state of the ongoing war between the two groups.

The two men had been chatting for some time when President Gudea leaned back suddenly and smiled.

"What is it?" asked Miles.

"My people have dreamed that maybe the people here on this planet, which you now call Earth, survived—maybe even restarting our civilization. We had not connected this system to the stargate network, which meant the colonists would remain accessible only through the use of our wormhole technology. We had hoped your world would survive the virus that ravaged our people—and it appears it has. Miles, I must confess something. It feels surreal to be speaking with you—like something out of a dream."

Miles chuckled. "If it's surreal to *you*," he replied, "imagine how *we* feel. I can't even begin to explain just how many questions our people have about the history of our own ancestorial origins, especially in light of the revelation that our planet, Earth, was a part of a colony—small and insignificant.

"After our first official contact with an alien species that wasn't trying to actively enslave us—the Altairians—they told us the reason humans could be found on other planets and moons besides our own was largely due to their own intervention when a meteor was on a collision course with Earth. This was when they told us they had brought as many humans as they could to the Rhea system, to a planet we now call New Eden. But the Altairians have also altered their story over the years, and that still doesn't explain why we as humans survived here. Frankly, speaking with you today is like finding another half of a puzzle that we didn't have before."

Miles paused, conflicted. "Mr. President, if I may ask something of you—if we are descendants of yours, a Humtar colony, what is *your* origin story? Who created the Humtars?"

President Gudea laughed. "These are good questions you have asked, Miles, and they deserve a proper and thorough answer. However, this is not the time or the appropriate place for you and me to have *that* discussion." Gudea leaned forward. "Today, Miles, is like two long-lost family members discovering they lived in a nearby city all these years. We will continue to have this discussion—and provide each other with answers to the questions I know are swirling about in your head as they are in my own. For now, as respective leaders of our people, we must place these matters to the side and discuss the more time-sensitive and pressing matters that necessitated my presence on this trip."

Miles nodded at the reply. He felt a strong sense of disappointment, but ultimately, he knew Gudea was right.

"Miles, please do not be offended at my bluntness," said President Gudea. "In view of the obvious destruction we saw on our way to this meeting, it is understandable, given your stature and position, that you would like our help or technological assistance against this Dominion Alliance.

"We have been living in relative peace on our side of the stargate for millennia. The ways of large-scale war are not as familiar to us as they appear to be to your people."

"I could certainly see that perspective," Miles acquiesced. "However, there is a part of your history—the 'stripping,' I believe you called it—another species, the Amoor, replicated it. They not only found a way to separate their consciousness from their physical bodies, but they networked themselves into one single cohesive consciousness. Imagine if you could instantly harness all of the world's most brilliant minds for a single purpose—that is the power this Collective yields. Each planet that the Collective visits, they completely devastate. Either a being willingly submits to join the Collective, or they are forced to die and their consciousness becomes a part of Legion, in a sort of eternal hell of servitude to the Collective.

"This enemy is more than just another warring faction, which may be here today and gone tomorrow. The Collective threatens the very existence of all living beings everywhere. If they conquer us, I'm sure that they will find a way to uncover the knowledge of your stargate…and then it will be only a matter of time before they also conquer you."

President Gudea stroked his chin, deep in thought. "I must say, this information is disturbing. This changes our risk-to-benefit calculations, to be sure," he offered. "So, Viceroy Hunt, what sort of help would you be asking of us exactly? We could certainly help you in terms of technological knowledge. Dr. Katherine Johnson explained to me that you had only recently discovered the power generators at Himzurleppak, which are more advanced than your current options—but we have improved our capabilities since then."

Miles found himself imagining what advancements could have been possible with thousands of years of relative peace, starting at the point of what was available on Lab Site X. The potential was astronomical.

"President Gudea, as much as I might want to negotiate with you myself about what you would be willing or able to provide to the Galactic Empire, I'm afraid that there is someone above me with whom you really should be having this conversation," said Miles in deference.

"Above you?" asked Gudea. "Are you not the Viceroy of the Republic? Were not the Gallentine ships sent on your orders as well?" He scrunched his eyebrows. Miles couldn't tell if he was confused or simply suspicious, trying to determine if there was any reason not to trust this new possible ally.

Miles smiled disarmingly and calmly explained the intricacies of the Galactic Empire and their current arrangements and power dynamics. When he'd finished, he invited President Gudea to meet with the Emperor at Alliance City on New Eden.

"I would be willing to meet with this Emperor if you were also present. Your role is pivotal enough that your absence will make negotiations a moot point. However, I would like to change the location of the meeting to our original home planet."

"Humtar?" Miles asked, confused. "But the planet has been uninhabited since your people lived there. Why do you want to go there?"

"You have been searching for the origin of your people, and we have our own quest. You see, on Humtar, there are devices similar to what you would call a 'black box.' Even now, they would be able to tell us more about what happened to our people in those final days. I am particularly interested in what the Ministry of MedTech had been up to at the end."

"Do you think the virus that ravaged your people was somehow created *on purpose*…to wipe everyone out?" Miles asked, subconsciously tapping his foot slightly as he nervously considered the Zodark project he had axed.

"I don't know," President Gudea replied. "But I don't want to leave this side of the stargate until I find out."

Miles thought for a moment. "If I may…I would be interested in coming with you to learn more about the origin of the Humtars myself. However, I cannot imagine the Emperor leaving the comfort of his palace to travel to an uninhabited planet, and certainly not to have serious discussions about our potential future military collaboration. Would you be willing to collect your data on Humtar and then travel to Alliance City, as I originally requested?"

"If you will accompany me, then yes," said President Gudea.

"Very well," Miles answered. "I do have a few pressing matters here that I will need to arrange before I leave with you, but I can be ready within a few hours. Does that work?"

President Gudea stood, extending his hand. "I very much look forward to traveling with you, Miles, and learning everything I can about your people, culture, and history. We have a shared ancestry; we could even be long-lost cousins. Come, we have much to talk about, and I am eager to learn everything about your people and your family."

Chapter Three
Tell Me That's Not a Chickenhawk?

September 2113 – Lyrius Campaign
Echo Company, 2nd Regiment, 4th Ranger Division
Silvanea Outpost
Serenea, Tau Sagittarii System

Splashing cold water on his face, Captain Paul "Pauli" Smith stared into the mirror, hardly recognizing the man staring back. *It was supposed to be a four-month senior leadership course.* He recalled how four months had stretched into more than two years. He was thankful for the short reprieve at Darby, the train-up period before the start of the Sagittarius and Lyrius campaigns. *These wars have to end eventually...*

The door to the bathroom creaked, and a familiar voice called out. "Hey, Pauli, they're ready for you," Lieutenant Yogi Sanders announced, a concerned look on his face.

Staring into the mirror, he responded, "Thanks, Yogi. I'll be out in a moment. Just needed to collect my thoughts before putting my war face on for the troops."

His friend snickered in response. "Hey, don't let me intrude on your ritual, Hoss. You know I'm here if you ever need anything."

Yogi closed the door, leaving him alone a minute more before it was time. Time to go brief his men on the mission ahead, a mission that would place them one step closer to securing the planet, one step closer to defeating the Pharaonis and the Dominion Alliance.

All right, soldier, it's time to Ranger up and kick some ass. You got a planet to conquer, he thought, psyching himself up. Preparing his mind to lead his soldiers into battle.

In the aftermath of the orbital assault against the Orbot planet, Astrionis, Big Army and Special Operations Command had hastily reorganized the surviving units into something resembling a cohesive fighting force. During the reshuffling of units, Pauli's 4th Ranger Regiment found themselves reorganized into a new regiment. Having sustained a fifty-six percent casualty rate during the previous campaign. Fox Company, like the 4th Regiment, had been disbanded and reformed into the Echo Company "Brawlers," part of the 2nd Regiment. Until there were enough replacements to reform the 3rd and 4th Regiments, the division would function with half its normal complement. "When life gives you lemons…make lemonade," his mother used to say. He liked that about her. She didn't complain about the cards life dealt her. She learned to play the ones she had and was good at it.

Stepping into the partially destroyed building their regiment had taken control of, Pauli looked at his platoon leaders and senior NCOs with pride. They were survivors, and now they were also veterans— leaders who had experience under their belts and knew how to lead and keep their people alive.

Walking toward them, he jovially exclaimed, "All right, Rangers, break time is over. It's been a pleasant break—the brass letting us catch some z's and take a break after capturing this spaceport. But, all good things eventually come to an end. So gather around and let's go over what kind of giant turd they've given us, 'cause it's a bit of a doozy." Pauli pulled his tablet out, activating a holographic map display that floated above it. A few of the NCOs groaned, already sensing it was going to be a tough mission.

"This place right here"—he pointed to a few red icons several kilometers inside a forested area—"the brass is calling this Skyfall. It's part of a network of fortified military outposts the Pharaonis constructed along the equator. These outposts have been placed every thirty-eight hundred kilometers along the equator, with more outposts positioned at the halfway point, approximately fifteen degrees above and below the equatorial line. Skyfall is one of these outposts that's been positioned above the equator, and it's our primary target—"

"Excuse me, Captain. These outposts—is this why the Fleet had us enter the planet from the north pole before moving south to seize the Silvanea spaceport?" interrupted Lieutenant Yassin, a few others next to him nodding in agreement.

"Yes, it is. In a way, it's pretty clever. The outposts along the equator can provide each other with two hundred kilometers of overlapping aerial coverage. The other set of outposts could provide even greater coverage, making it extremely costly if the Fleet had opted to attack them directly. Gentlemen, these outposts are the reason why the Fleet hasn't reduced the enemy to dust and why our regiment and the orbital assault divisions haven't been rotated off-planet in place of RA units. The brass knows this is going to be a fight, and because of that, they want their best units working with the RA in clearing these forts out," Pauli said.

For the next hour, Pauli discussed the Army's plan to attack Skyfall from the north and west with the 9th Infantry Division while two other regiments from the 11th ID would press the fortress from the east. This left the Rangers with the southern approach, right through a densely packed forest and bog. The move to get in attack position would suck beyond words, but since the enemy would be unlikely to expect their approach from this path, this side of the fortress perimeter would probably be lightly guarded, especially once the RA units began their main attacks.

"Hey, one other thing I want to make you guys aware of. We won't be making this journey through Helm's Deep alone—the 24th Spartan Infantry Regiment will be joining us," Pauli explained, to the chagrin of more than a few NCOs. Not everyone understood his nerdy references to J.R.R. Tolkien or would appreciate the crucible that Helm's Deep represented. Pauli was unfazed.

Yogi stepped forward, jokingly asking, "Cap'n, if the Spartans are tagging along with us for a hike through the woods and marshlands, does that mean we'll have access to that crazy-ass Korean artillery regiment, or is Spartacus still not playing nice with others?"

This question elicited a raucous laugh from Pauli's platoon leaders and sergeants. The 24th Spartan Infantry Regiment belonged to the 11th Infantry Division, sometimes called the Spartacus Division. Its commander, Brigadier General Spartacus Varinius, was a bit of an eccentric man who very much lived up to his name—rising from the ranks of private at the outset of the First Zodark War to eventually earning a battlefield commission during the Intus campaign. During the battle for Alfheim, his battalion was among the many others who'd found themselves trapped on the planet when the allied fleet had been forced to withdraw from the system. He'd gone on to lead one of the more effective insurgent groups during the Zodark occupation until the allies returned and the war ended.

Pauli smiled as he shook his head. "Yes, yes, it means we'll have access to K-pop, but before you all get too excited, they're also supporting the 23rd Texas Mechanized and the 11th Guards Tank Regiment, which are attacking Skyfall from the east. Once I've gotten a chance to confer with the Spartans, I'll find out what kind of RA support

we should have, but given that a division and a half of RA units are involved in this attack, we should have plenty of conventional army support—which is something we don't usually have, so don't get used to it. Now, I've got other 'officer duties' to attend to." Pauli used air quotes as he made a sour face. "Oh, one other thing." He pulled something from his pocket before tossing it to Master Sergeant Drew Tinker. "Go ahead, put 'em on. Drew's promotion to sergeant major came through—congratulations, Sergeant Major. Now get the company ready. Our battle taxis are arriving in three hours."
****

Echo Company "Brawlers," 2nd Regiment

Standing not far from the edge of the tree line, Pauli could hear the sound of transports as they approached. He turned to look in the direction of the empty field not far from the tree line behind which his platoons had taken cover. Checking the time as he looked off into the horizon, he noted they were late—nineteen minutes, to be precise.

"It's about time those Chickenhawks arrived," Sergeant Major Tinker commented, unimpressed with the tardiness of their Republic Army counterparts.

"Hey, did you hear that, Sergeant Major?" Pauli said, the faint sound of an explosion rumbling in the distance.

Tinker grunted. "Yeah, sounds like K-pop is starting the show. You know, sir, I gotta admit, it's going to be nice having some dedicated artillery support. That's not something we usually have."

Pauli chuckled. "Yeah, well, usually, we have control of the high ground and can just call for an orbital strike."

"True, but anytime you're within five hundred meters of that strike, it's danger-close. If those Fleeters are off by even the smallest margin…," he responded.

"Yeah, I get it…splat. Hey, so back to the here and now, Sergeant Major. Pass the word we're pulling out once I've made contact with whoever's the OIC for this chalk that's landing. I want to make sure they know to start following behind us within thirty mikes of us leaving. That should give them enough time to get their people sorted and us a bit of a head start," Pauli explained, then started walking towards the edge of the tree line.

As he got closer to the LZ, he had to marvel at how quickly this place was going to be transformed into a combat support base. Once the 11th Lugano Logistic Support Regiment's Mongooses began arriving, they were going to call it CSB Salerno. Pauli had to remind himself that the conventional army fought differently from how SOF was trained to fight. They were scalpels—surgical tools for precise jobs. The RA was the Republic's broadsword—a giant blade to be wielded against large, entrenched targets.

"Damn, those Chickenhawks are something else, aren't they?" commented Lieutenant Yogi Sanders as the second wave of Chickenhawk troop transporters or T2s touched down just long enough for the troops to get off before climbing back into the air.

"They're no Ospreys, that's for sure," Pauli countered.

The T2s were smaller than the larger Osprey assault transports used by SOF and the orbital assault divisions. While the T2s could fly into low orbit, the conventional force mainly used them as their dominant mode of transportation once planetside. They were a fraction of the cost of an Osprey and could still carry two squads of soldiers and some weapons to clear a landing zone if needed. The design wasn't too different from the Mongoose or Goose logistic support transports or LSTs. The LSTs were phenomenal VTOL ships for moving prepacked cargo units, or PCUs for short. They'd fly in, drop a PCU, and dart back into the air to head back to base.

"Excuse me, are you Captain Smith, the Ranger CO?" a soldier called out as he approached them.

Pauli turned to see who had asked about him. Spotting the gold oakleaf rank insignia, he guessed this was the guy he had been waiting to speak with. "Yes, Major. I'm Captain Smith—everyone just calls me Pauli. I take it you're the CO for the 24th Spartans?"

"I am, Major Tom Bacich from the 24th Infantry Regiment. Although sometimes we just call ourselves the Spartans—it's a long story best told over a beer," the major joked naturally. "So, Captain, what's the plan of attack here?"

Pauli smiled at the man's directness. *I think I'm going to like this guy. He's straight to the point.* "Well, that depends on how much you've been told about this objective and what kind of support units the 11th ID sent along with you guys."

The major smiled in response. "The division intel weenies said we're attacking an enemy stronghold they've labeled Skyfall. Supposedly, once we clear this base, it should create a gap in the enemy's planetary defense network. In support of the Rangers' assault on this place, my regiment, the 24th, is here to help in whatever manner you need us to. Now, as to other division assets we can draw from, we've been granted a few.

"Two companies from the 11th Lugano Logistic Support Regiment are starting to arrive, as you can see. The LSR will handle our supply and logistics needs. As to arty support—we've got Alpha Battery from the 11th Korean Artillery Regiment, which should start arriving in the next thirty or so minutes. They'll have four 320mm howitzers set for indirect fire support, which you'll be able to leverage along with two 40mm antidrone aerial denial systems," the major explained, Pauli doing his best not to show too much excitement at the level of support his Rangers were being given.

"Major, this sounds great. What about the Dubliners? Are they still coming?" Pauli asked.

Major Bacich paused a second before answering. "The last update from five minutes ago shows they'll start arriving sometime in three hours. I was told the priority was to get the artillery guys in place before more troops arrived. Why, when are you hoping to start your attack on this place?"

"Major, how close do you think this place is?"

"Um, ten or so kilometers?" replied Bacich hesitantly.

"You're close. It's about nine klicks in that direction," Pauli said, pointing into the forest, noticing perhaps for the first time just how dark and ominous it looked. "So, here's how I'd like to play this, Major. My unit's going to set out and head towards this base, Skyfall. The other Ranger units in our regiment will be starting their attacks in a few hours from now, once they've let the artillery work them over a bit. Once the arty and drones have wrecked the place as best they can, then it'll be our turn to breach our way into the fortress, where I suspect the heaviest fighting will take place. Now, given this place is not exactly close to our present position, I highly suggest working with some engineers to begin clearing the path as close to the fighting as possible. We're going to take casualties, so we're going to need a means to evacuate them—"

"Yes, exactly," Bacich interrupted, then added, "I'm not sure if you were told or not, but Major General Varinius is going to deploy the division's combat support hospital. I'll relay your request and suggestion to both the CSH and Lugano J3s so they can prioritize getting this path cut through those trees for you. When are you thinking you'd like to start having our infantry units move forward to link up with your Rangers?"

Wow, access to a division hospital this close to the fighting is going to save lives—I like this general already, Pauli thought as he took in the information.

"Thanks, Major, for letting me know about the med unit. This is great. Circling back to your question—give us about thirty minutes lead time. Then start having your regiment follow behind us, one company at a time. Whatever you do, don't let your units get bunched up. We're already playing at a disadvantage, having to trek through kilometers of dense forest before we even reach the base. Let's not give 'em a juicier target because we got cocky or lazy or both.

"Once your first echelons begin to arrive, that's when we'll start looking for ways to punch some holes in their defensive works. When we start creating some breach points, I need your company COs to push their units through them. My Rangers are great at causing lots of chaos and confusion, but that's only beneficial if you have forces to punch through the newly created vulnerabilities. That's where your units come into play and will be pivotal to the success or failure of this mission. Makes sense? Do you have any questions?" Pauli asked, pausing long enough to let him think about it before moving on.

Bacich slowly nodded. "I like it. I have no questions. We'll reach out if we think of any. I'll pass the word to my company commanders to stay in contact with you and keep you apprised of their locations. Good luck, Captain, I'll see you up."
****

Two Hours Later

The alien forest loomed like a citadel as Pauli and his company of Rangers trekked deeper into it—the sounds of battle becoming louder the closer they got to the Pharaonis fortress. The sooner they cleared the planetary defenses of their ion cannons, the sooner allied battleships could move safely into orbit to pound the remaining enemy formations into dust.

"Hey, watch out for those vines," a soldier ahead of Pauli warned. Seeing the tangled cluster of bioluminescent vines hanging near chest level from the banyan-like alien trees, he brushed them aside, doing his best not to get tangled up in them.

It had been just over two hours of trekking through what Pauli believed had to be one of the strangest, most peculiar alien forests he'd seen. From the moment they'd set off from the newly created combat support base, Salerno, they had been fighting their way through the oddest-looking vines, which almost seemed like they were sentient beings. Putting aside their bioluminescent colors, they were unlike anything he had seen on Earth and the other worlds the Rangers had taken him to. These vines looked to be wrapped in some kind of tiny hairlike prickles that, as something got closer—reacted. They would almost come to life as they went from hanging from the vine like hair to magically standing straight up, attempting to snag whatever passed nearby. More than one of his Rangers had found themselves entangled in them, requiring them to cut themselves free.

The entire forest was strange, full of colors, noises, and odd-looking animals and birds. The deeper they trekked into it, its single- and occasionally double-canopy tree cover would darken their surroundings. It created an interesting contrast between some plants and vines that had an odd glow to them when in the shadows versus when they were in a brighter setting.

"Brawlers, Brawler Actual. Stay frosty, people; there are a lot of distracting things around us. I need you to stay sharp. Stay focused on the mission. We should be coming into visual range of Skyfall shortly," Pauli announced across the company net. *If I'm having a hard time not getting distracted by all this, then I'm pretty sure the others are as well*, he reasoned.

They pressed forward, the sounds of battle becoming louder with each step. On more than one occasion, they stopped advancing, taking immediate defensive positions when their point man thought he saw something. The phrase "slow is smooth, smooth is fast" wasn't just a motto. It was a way of operating when in the field looking to do battle with the enemy. It also kept you alive more often than not, especially with missions like the one they were on right now. This was enemy territory, a place the enemy knew well and they didn't.

Ten minutes went by when Pauli paused alongside one of the banyan-like trees. He wasn't sure why, but something inside him told him to pause what he was doing and take a knee. With more than twenty years of service, which included the entire First Zodark War, he had learned to trust his gut, to listen to that silent inner voice that got louder the longer you ignored it, until something terrible happened.

He eyed his Rangers to his front for a moment, smiling as he watched them move with a predator's grace, silent save for the periodic soft crunching noise of alien soil underfoot. The weight of their gear, the grip of their weapons, every detail was honed by the relentless forge of combat—the shock troops of the Republic, the commander's scalpel when stealth or precision and force of action were needed most.

He activated his helmet's built-in HUD or heads-up display, and the digital topographical map of the forest populated with the locations of his scout element, the three-man team that coordinated the movements of the five C100s advancing twenty meters ahead of his platoon. The sensor arrays built into the combat synthetics were actively scanning for heat signatures, radio transmissions, and anything that didn't look correct based on the expected patterns. With the demand for C100s and even C300s outstripping Walburg Industries' ability to supply them, he felt lucky to have been granted twelve C100s and four of the vaunted C300s for this mission. With their enhanced armor, tactics, and improved speed, agility, and reaction times, the C300s were the culmination of decades of trial and error during peacetime and war.

As he momentarily took in the scene of his scouts methodically advancing, he could feel the thickness of the atmosphere, the unspoken tension ratcheting up the closer they got to Skyfall. The Pharaonis fortress and its ion cannons were the only things standing between allied control of the high ground—the planet's orbit—and being stuck in their current position, slowly chipping away at the enemy forts until eventually they could wrest control of the high ground over time.

"Stay sharp, Brawlers," he said, his confident yet hardened tone clear in its meaning. Standing back up, he resumed his silent but steady stalk toward the Rangers in First Squad, the lead element just behind his scouts.

Suddenly, they heard a rustle, causing everyone to pause—to freeze in their tracks as their eyes and ears joined in their helmets' built-in sensors, desperately searching to identify the sound they'd heard. With every Ranger tensed, their instincts, honed by thousands of drills, snapped them to immediate readiness.

A message flashed across the bottom of their HUD—Staff Sergeant Hill, alerting them it was a false alarm. He shared a picture of some small creature that had darted in front of him. Staring at the furry grayish animal, Pauli exhaled a breath he hadn't realized he had been holding. Moments later, they resumed their march, a steady yet relentless advance towards Skyfall.

"Halt! Take a knee! Multiple tangos to my front!" alerted Staff Sergeant Hill over the comms. "Scout Three has a visual ID on Skyfall. Scouts Four and Five have visual ID on three defensive works—bunkers with three tangos each. Scouts One and Two have visual confirmation on three fortified positions near a gated entrance with multiple tangos. How copy?"

"Brawler Nine, Brawler Actual, good copy. Stand by. Break. Brawler One-Six, I want you to change formation to line abreast and advance cautiously until aligned with Brawler Nine. Break. Brawler Two-Six, Three-Six, Four-Six, Five-Six, formation line abreast. Advance cautiously, maintaining ten-meter intervals until you reach One-Six, then go to ground and halt. How copy?" Pauli ordered, quickly changing the direction of the company's firepower to their front.

Calls of acknowledgment came rapidly. Pauli's BlueForce tracker confirmed the formation shifts as the platoons reorganized themselves before advancing—closing the gap while bringing the company's firepower to bear.

****

Alpha Company, 24th Spartan Regiment

Major Tom Bacich wiped the sweat from his brow before placing his helmet back on. For hours, he'd been trekking through this godforsaken nightmarish forest with the soldiers of Alpha Company. He wanted to be as close to the fighting as possible so he could better direct his forces in support of the Rangers. *Why on earth did I think it would be a good idea for me to tag along with Alpha? I could have waited until the Luganos finished clearing a vehicle path…*, he thought before getting back on the move.

Hearing a rustling noise coming from behind him, he turned in time to see his XO, Captain Mathew Tapusoa, push through a tangled web of hanging vines. "Damn these stupid vines. Sir, you asked me to keep you apprised of what the Rangers were up to," he commented as he hastened his stride to walk next to him. "They stopped moving here, maybe a klick from the objective. Now it looks like they've spread themselves out in a line that stretches from this point to this point here." His index finger traced the map as he spoke.

They continued to walk, talking softly as they ducked beneath another cluster of vines that seemed to latch onto anything that came near them. Bacich grunted in acknowledgment, feeling every bit the forty-six years of age he was. "Matt, this infantry crap is a young man's game, and I, my friend, am no spring chicken anymore," he commented to his XO, who grinned at him.

Laughing, Tapusoa countered, "That's nonsense, sir. You're just as fit as those National Guardsmen who joined our regiment before leaving New Eden."

Now it was Bacich who laughed at his comparison. The soldiers from one of the Emerald City National Guard units, who helped to fill out their ranks following the previous campaign, weren't exactly adhering to the Republic Army's weight and physical requirements. It had taken Bacich's command three weeks to whip them into reasonable shape so they could pass the minimum standard on the physical fitness test.

Taking a ragged breath, he paused, standing against the side of a tree. "Um, I'm not sure if that's a compliment or a slight, Matt, but don't forget who has to sign your OPR next month."

"Ouch, sir, you know I would never disparage you. It was a compliment. It takes real skill and determination to allow oneself to meet or exceed the minimum physical fitness standard to join the Rangers. I'd say for a forty-six-year-old, you knocked that out of the park," Tapusoa smirked in response.

Technically, his XO was right. Bacich pushed the soldiers of his regiment hard. His no-nonsense demeanor and hard training had earned his regiment the nickname of "Spartans." Of course, having multiple

38

soldiers and teams from the regiment competing yearly in the Spartan races and even winning a few had helped to solidify the name.

Bacich was about to say something when his XO held a hand up and then placed it over the side of his helmet. Whatever message he was receiving, it had to be serious. The color seemed to drain from his face with whatever he was being told. Then, as if on cue, the rhythmic booms of friendly artillery pounding the enemy base changed—now it sounded like a freight train heading straight for them.

Someone nearby shouted, "Incoming!" causing everyone to drop to the ground and attempt to make themselves as small a target as possible.

BAM, BAM, BAM.

The shells landed long, overshooting their positions, but not by much. Whatever the caliber, the explosions and concussive blasts were enormous. Moments after the explosion, the sound of incoming shells screaming overhead—exploding further behind them.

"Sir, I've got a message from Brawler Actual, Captain Smith. He said they're receiving indirect fire, likely from another firebase. He said his Rangers are going to initiate their assault. They're going to breach the enemy lines and are demanding we hurry up and join 'em," shouted Captain Tapusoa.

"Ah, damn. This plan sure went to hell in a hurry," Bacich replied as another volley of shells overshot their position. Scrambling to his feet, he broadcast a message across the regiment. "ALCON, Spartan Actual. Enemy artillery is attempting to interdict our force before we can reach Skyfall. I need every unit to dig deep and haul ass as quickly as possible to link up with the Rangers. It's paramount we hug the enemy so their artillery can't hit us without hitting their own people. Now *go!*"

****

Echo Company "Brawlers," 2nd Regiment

"Echo Ten, hit the bunker! Take it out!" a Ranger shouted to one of the C100s.

Zip, zip, zip.

Pauli ducked for cover, the blaster bolts zipping through the air where he had just been moments earlier. Peering around the side of a tree, he saw the C100 they called Echo Ten lower his rifle as he repositioned it to his side. Using his free arm, he grabbed the MPL, or multipurpose launcher, slung behind him, bringing it to his shoulder, aiming for the bunker—then firing.

Pop...swoosh...BAM!

The missile rocketed out of the launcher and scored a direct hit. Flame and black smoke briefly engulfed the bunker, silencing the gunners inside.

"Bunker's down. Let's go!" shouted Master Sergeant Pope as he leaped to his feet and charged into the newly created gap in the enemy trench. Others soon followed, pushing through the gap while a few soldiers paused. Then they proceeded to clear the enemy trenches to either side of the still-smoldering bunker, further widening the gap in the enemy lines.

"Brawler Actual, Spartan Actual, how copy?" came the radio call just as Pauli was about to follow his Rangers into the breach.

Taking a knee behind a tree for cover, he responded, "Spartan Actual, Brawler Actual, send it."

Major Bacich responded quickly, letting him know that he was traveling with Alpha Company and that they were almost to his position. He gave him a quick update, letting him know the other companies would be arriving in roughly thirty-minute intervals.

Pauli responded, "Spartan Actual, Brawler Actual, good copy on the last transmission. Be advised that the first of two enemy lines has been breached. We're expanding along the sides of the breach— widening it further. Brawlers One, Two, and Three are nearly through the secondary trench. Break.

"Spartan, have your Alpha Company push through the first breach in the enemy lines," Pauli ordered. "Establish visual contact with Brawlers One, Two, or Three and assist in the final assault. How copy?"

A couple of seconds passed before Major Bacich confirmed the instructions, then distributed them across his regiment. They were nearly through the outer perimeter of the enemy fortress. It wouldn't be long now before they'd be in a position to damage or destroy those ion cannons, preventing the Fleet from moving its battleships into orbit and putting an end to the enemy's formal resistance.

****

Alpha Company, 24th Spartan Regiment

Major Bacich was breathing hard by the time Alpha Company had reached the first line of defense. The Rangers had already moved on and were pressing their way deeper into the fortress. Seeing the numbers of dead Pharaonis, a couple of C100s, and a dozen or more Rangers, he felt sick to his stomach at how long it had taken him and his men to reach this point—and they still had a little further to go before linking up with the Rangers.

These Rangers are dead because we were too slow…

"Geez, sir, look at those ugly bastards. They weren't joking when they said their faces looked like demonic ants," commented Captain Tapusoa as he took a seat next to him. The three other soldiers accompanying him as security seemed relieved at the momentary pause to catch their breath and wipe the sweat from their brows.

"They sure do, XO, but it took us entirely too long to get here. That forest was ridiculous, and it's going to stay that way until the engineers cut us a path through it. So let's try something different. Get on the horn to Colonel Bill Murray from the 11th CAR, the Iron Eagles, and let him know the Rangers have broken through the enemy's first defensive line and are pressing the second. Pass along the difficulty we're having in getting through that forest," Bacich explained, his hand pointing to the forest they had emerged from with the Fifth Platoon. "Matt, do what you can to see if Murray's Chickenhawks can fly us some reinforcements—we've got Echo and Fox Companies, who haven't started trekking into that forest yet. I want to see if his Chickenhawks can ferry 'em closer to the front. We can't help the Rangers breach their way into this fortress if it's going to take this long to get reinforcements to them."

"Roger that, sir. That forest is no joke. I'd like to wring the neck of the person who thought it was a good idea to have reinforcements trek damn near ten klicks through that hell," Tapusoa commented, then contacted their combat aviation regiment to try and get the ball rolling.
****

Echo Company "Brawlers," 2nd Regiment

"Captain, I think we've got a weak spot in the line right there. Lieutenant Sanders also wanted me to ask about those reinforcements we've been promised," Master Sergeant Pope said, pointing to the weak spot developing in the enemy line and the frustration they were all feeling at how long it was taking for their reinforcements to arrive. "Have you heard anything from the 24th?"

Pauli sighed at the question, then replied, "That spot does look weak, especially after you guys took out that pair of bunkers. As to the 24th—yes, I've heard from them. They ran into the same troubles we did getting here. But good news, Alpha Company has reached the first line of defense. They should be here shortly." Pauli then added, "Master Sergeant, we've only got four C100s left and two C300s. I'm going to assign them to assist your platoon. When those soldiers from the 24th arrive, I'll send them your way. Make sure to tell Lieutenant Sanders not to attack until at least one platoon of reinforcements has linked up with your platoon. If you guys succeed in breaking through their lines, I need to know you'll be able to hold the gap open so we can shift more forces your way."

"Roger that, sir. I'm sure Yogi will appreciate the Synths. We'll put 'em to good use and hopefully return a few once we're through the line," Pope replied, then left to head back to his platoon, the newly acquired combat Synths disengaging and moving to link up with Lieutenant Sanders and Second Platoon.

"Brawler Actual, Bulldog One, how copy?"

Pauli bunched his eyebrows as he tried to recall who had the call sign Bulldog. Then it hit him—*Bulldog, that's Squadron 223 from the* Wasp—*B99s, Raiders.* "Bulldog One, Brawler Actual, good copy. Go for traffic."

"Brawler Actual, I've got four Raiders five minutes from your position with a full load of ordnance. Do you have some targets for us, or should we contact another Ranger element?" came the cool, calm voice of the drone pilot aboard the *Wasp.*

Smiling at the unexpected gift, Pauli quickly replied, "Bulldog One, that's affirmative. We've got targets for you. I'll denote the ones that are danger-close to friendlies. By the way, do you think your guys might be able to try and knock out those ion cannons for us?"

"Brawler Actual, that last request depends on what kind of air defense we encounter on this first run. The command isn't too keen on us conducting suicide runs with replacement birds running low. We'll check it out and get back to you," the pilot replied as Pauli denoted targets on the digital map for the bombers to go after.

"That's a good copy, Bulldog. Target package sent, confirm? Over."

"That's affirmative, Brawler, targets received. ETA two mikes. Coming in hot. Will stand by for BDA, out," the pilot confirmed, Pauli now scrambling to make sure his platoon leaders and senior NCOs knew an airstrike was inbound.

Looking toward the fortress, Pauli saw a missile leap into the air as it accelerated rapidly in the direction of the inbound Raiders. A second and then third missile shot into the air before angling for its attack. Suddenly, the sound of jet engines and roaring aircraft filled the air.

"Missiles inbound! Everyone down!" Pauli shouted over the comms as missiles streaked overhead. Suddenly, out of nowhere, multiple guns opened fire on the incoming missiles.

Pauli watched as one of the missiles blew apart when it flew into a stream of projectiles. Another missile evaded the gunfire, trying to intercept it before plowing into a fortified gun emplacement that had been blocking his Rangers from breaking into the fortress directly. He watched as missile after missile streaked in, blowing apart enemy ground defenses and the gun systems shooting at the Raiders and their missiles. Pauli felt a strange sense of satisfaction as he watched the targets he had identified getting blown up, opening huge holes in the enemy defense.

"Brawler Actual, Spartan Actual. Alpha Company is advancing towards your position now. I have Echo and Fox Companies inbound to near your location, courtesy of the Iron Eagles. Their ETA is ten minutes. How copy?" the voice of Major Bacich announced, to Pauli's surprise.

"Spartan, Brawler, good copy on last transmission. Haul ass up here if you can. We're getting ready to breach the fortress and could use your assistance," Pauli responded, then shared his map of where he wanted the platoons of Alpha Company to reinforce his own.

"Brawler Actual, Bulldog. I can't guarantee anything, but we took out a few of those gun towers in that last run. I may take an ass-chewing for this, but I think we can take a shot at going after those ion cannons. Hell, they're the primary target anyway. Stand by, we're coming back around to make a run at them."

"Hey, if you guys can take 'em out, there's no reason for us to lose more men trying to. Just do what you can, Brawler out."

"Come on, Rangers! Let's *go*!" Lieutenant Sanders shouted, leaping to his feet, charging after the pair of C300s and the four C100s already blazing a path of death and destruction.

Pauli gripped his rifle tightly as he joined Second Platoon in their assault against the last line of defense before reaching the outer wall of the fortress known simply as Skyfall. Running at times in a crouched position, then jinking to his right, then to his left before ducking behind cover, he fired relentlessly at the Pharaonis soldiers—some shots finding their mark, others missing, but it kept the enemies' heads down while his Rangers bounded forward. This bounding overwatch was a textbook tactic, meticulously implemented with teams of two and four soldiers at a time laying down suppressive fire while another team charged forward, advancing a handful of meters at a time before the roles switched.

"Frag out!" shouted a soldier as a grenade sailed through the air, exploding overtop an enemy trench. Loud screeches and horrific wailing like fingernails being scraped down a chalkboard soon emanated from that part of the trench.

"Charlie Three-Two, right flank!" Pauli heard Master Sergeant Pope shout, warning the C300 a few meters to his right.

As Pauli turned to see the enemy threat, he barely caught sight of the C300 as it caught the Pharaonis grenade with one hand and tossed it back. It blew up a second later as it neared the soldier who had thrown it. *Wow, I can't believe I just saw that*, he marveled.

"Salinas, shift fire to the right! Keep your LMG focused on that sector! Charlie One-Six, One-Seven, execute bounding overwatch and clear that trench!" barked Lieutenant Yassin as Fourth and Second Platoons merged in this final push to break through the enemy position.

Aiming at a Pharaonis soldier wielding some sort of rapid-fire energy weapon, Pauli exhaled, then squeezed the trigger. He saw the ant-like head explode before his ears had time to process the firing of his rifle, before he even felt the recoil against his shoulder. Without skipping a beat, Pauli shifted positions slightly as he zeroed in on another target, firing once more. Another Pharaonis dropped, his weapon now silent as the Rangers continued their assault.

Suddenly, out of the periphery of his vision, Pauli saw the sky above them come alive with brilliant flashes of light as the Pharaonis

44

attempted to intercept whatever missiles or aircraft were heading toward Skyfall. Still looking to the sky, he saw what had to be multiple missiles heading straight for several of the guns firing at them. A couple of missiles were easily taken out, exploding before they got close enough to cause damage. Then, missile after missile slammed into the gun turrets of the remaining air-defense weapons along this side of the fortress.

Pauli felt his heart skip a beat moments later when he saw the four B-99 Raiders zip by with blinding speed as they flew meters above the walls of the fortress. The Raiders had flown so fast, his ears had barely heard the sonic booms before the Raiders were gone—replaced moments later with the image of multiple growing fireballs where the ion cannons had just been.

"Holy crap! They did it! Those Fleeters actually did it!" Yogi shouted excitedly over the company net. A raucous cheer then erupted from the soldiers as they watched the barrels of the giant ion cannons collapse to the ground.

I'll be damned, Pauli thought excitedly as he saw the flash of an incoming message. "Brawler Actual, Bulldog One. Requesting BDA. Bulldogs One through Four got zapped at the last minute—did we get the cannons?" asked the flight leader.

Smiling at the request, Pauli replied, "Bulldog, Brawler— confirmed, targets eliminated. I don't know how you did it, but those ion cannons are gone—all four of them. Hot damn, that was some fancy flying right there."

"Thanks, Brawler. Glad we were of service. Bulldogs out."

Pauli heard the sound of soldiers approaching from behind. As he turned his head to verify it wasn't hostile, he smiled at the sight of Major Bacich and at least a platoon's worth of soldiers approaching him. "Huh, I see how this works. The Spartans arrive just as the battle is ending so they can still be credited with being part of its victory, eh?" he joked with the major.

"Ah, come on—you Rangers could have left us some table scraps," Major Bacich replied with a grin. He then pointed in a few directions as the soldiers headed toward the Rangers, who looked to have finished the fighting, at least the portion of the fighting outside the walls of the fortress.

"No matter, Major, it's not your fault some knucklehead thought this forest would be an easy stroll while concealing our movement. These hanging vines are ridiculous," Pauli commented as he motioned for Bacich to take a seat next to him. They were out of the line of fire and could talk safely here. "So, with those cannons gone, it kind of negates the reason for us needing to break into this fortress. I propose we wait here and find out from headquarters what they want us to do next. If we're lucky, they'll call it a day and we won't have to lose any more soldiers trying to take this place—the Fleeters can pound it from orbit."

Bacich nodded in agreement. "I like the sound of that a lot more than I do trying to fight our way into that fortress. You guys did a hell of a job clearing a path to it, but I can only imagine what's waiting inside for us. Besides, hanging out and waiting gives the rest of my regiment some time to get here."

"Great, then we're in agreement. Now let's make sure the rest of our guys know to keep their heads down while we wait for orders on what to do next."

Chapter Four
Humtar Origin Story

Approaching Humtar
Edge of Andromeda Galaxy

Viceroy Miles Hunt had never been on a Humtar ship before. He tried to suppress his overwhelming curiosity and his constant desire to ask questions. Miles glanced over at the two aides who doubled as security personnel that had been tapped to come along with him—they were clearly geeking out on the inside but somehow managing not to voice the reactions that might have been akin to those of a superfan at a comic convention.

Everything on the outside of the Humtar ship had a strange texture to it—almost as if it were...alive. *They have to be using some type of organic material in their construction*, Miles surmised. He started to take mental notes of questions he had about Humtar technology. He had so many; he realized that he didn't know what he didn't know. This wasn't the time or the place for a rundown of all the advancements these humans from the other side of the stargate had made, but the day would come, and Miles would be ready.

Miles had traveled using wormhole technology before. Once they'd settled into their seats in an observation section of the bridge, he braced himself for that strange feeling that he was being stretched as flat as a piece of paper before being returned to his normal 3-D state, but it never came. One moment, they were in the Sol system, and the next, they weren't. Miles detected only the slightest shudder, and if he had blinked, he might have missed it.

The crew aboard went through their standard procedures, scanning for any possible threats that they might not have anticipated, but the corner of the Andromeda galaxy where they had emerged was empty, having been completely abandoned thousands of years after the Humtars had either died or left.

"Planet Humtar coming into visual range," announced one of the crew members. President Gudea stood, seemingly in reverence, and the other personnel followed. Miles, wanting to follow the cultural cue set before him, stood as well, signaling his aides to join them.

Miles had seen quite a few planets during his time as the Viceroy, but he was immediately struck by the majestic beauty of Humtar. The whole planet was a network of islands on the most azure-blue water he could imagine. At one time, the Humtars must have joined many of these isles together with bridges, because even thousands of years later, some of these structures or their remains were still visible from space.

"It's stunning," Miles said aloud.

"We came of the sea...," said President Gudea, his voice trailing off. He sounded like he was not quite in his body but having some sort of spiritual experience in another realm.

An awkward silence hung in the room as everyone simply soaked in the striking view before them. After a moment, Gudea shifted on his feet slightly, and then, now fully present, he turned to the ship's captain. "Let's find ourselves a beacon, shall we?" Gudea directed.

"Yes, sir," the captain replied.

The ship's officers went into action without any further direction, and within a moment, a young woman aboard the bridge announced, "We have one, sir."

****

The satellite that the Humtars had retrieved was no larger than the size of a birthday balloon, but Viceroy Miles Hunt marveled at how it had stood the test of time for all these years.

"We had a few backups on the surface," President Gudea explained, "but it is always easier to retrieve a beacon from orbit."

The device underwent a decontamination process, just like Miles and his aides had done when they'd entered this Humtar vessel. Thousands of years after an extremely deadly virus had ravaged their people, the Humtars remained germophobic at a level that could have been characterized as an obsession.

The data transfer itself took almost no time at all, but sorting through that mountain of data would have taken years if it weren't for neurolinks. President Gudea sat down at a terminal, searching through different files, using his eyes and commands from his mind to move pages around until he had a stack of relevant information for him to read. Time passed slowly as they all waited.

Is he…crying? Miles wondered. He wasn't sure, but the Humtar leader definitely seemed to be getting emotional.

"Are you all right?" Miles asked cautiously.

"I will be," Gudea replied. He paused, wiping a tear away from his cheek. "I just learned where the contagion that killed my people came from."

"What happened?" Miles pressed.

President Gudea sat back, running his fingers through his hair. He took a deep breath and let it out slowly. "Your people already know about how some of the Humtars had taken part in 'stripping' their consciousness from their physical bodies. Well, the opposition to this movement was so severe that those who were in favor of stripping exiled themselves to a planet in a galaxy nearby, which your people call the Triangulum galaxy. They set up all the servers and other equipment they would need there on Gan-Edin in order to continue transitioning Humtars into the essence of their consciousness.

"The movement continued to gain traction, although it was opposed by the vast majority of all residents here. Pressure simply drove people into hiding, and a sort of cultlike religious philosophy emerged, called Nungala, with underground meetings and unauthorized flights to Gan-Edin occurring on a regular basis. Soon, any tolerance of Nungala had been eroded, and when political solutions failed, our ancestors turned to warfare.

"The battle of Gan-Edin was surprisingly hard-fought. The followers of Nungala were skilled at insurgent warfare, and those who had already participated in the stripping were able to animate entire ships without any other crew aboard. Ultimately, though, the ancient Humtars dealt a critical blow, destroying all the servers that allowed those who had become only souls to maintain their immortality."

"President Gudea, I'm not sure I understand," Miles interjected.

"You see, as their situation became more desperate, the Nungala set into motion a plan that they believed would either force all Humtars to join them in stripping or eliminate them as a threat altogether. They engineered the Neurocyte-7 virus."

Miles felt sick to his stomach. A strange groan emerged from his throat.

"My sentiments exactly, Miles," Gudea said. "As you know, this virus had a long incubation period and a high level of contagiousness, so once it was released, it spread like wildfire. Only, before our ancestors knew the origin of the disease, the settlement on Gan-Edin was razed to the ground, destroying not just the servers and many of the Nungala warriors, both physical and soul, but also any knowledge of the exact mechanisms of the N-7 virus. We only learned of the origins of the virus at the very end of our existence here, by interrogating some of the few remaining Nungala who had gone into hiding on Humtar."

"This is such a tragic story," Miles remarked.

"So many died…," Gudea agreed. He rested his head on his hands, rubbing his temples with his index fingers. "There is some good news here, though."

"What is that, Gudea?" asked Miles.

"We now know that this virus was Humtar-engineered, essentially 3-D printed. Because of its very specific synthetic nature, it was incapable of mutation. This means that the cure your doctors uncovered on Himzurleppak would still be viable, even today. We don't have to suffer the same fate as a people ever again."

Miles put his hand on Gudea's shoulder. He wasn't sure if it would be the right gesture, but he felt he needed to do something to convey that he understood the gravity of the loss that had happened here, and also that he hoped all these people had not died in vain.

Gudea put his own hand on top of Miles's and smiled weakly. "Miles, there is a lot more to research from this beacon, but I have what I need now in order to travel to Alliance City. Why don't you tell me more about this Emperor of yours?"

Chapter Five
New Orders, New Mission

Future Republic Capital
Mountain Home, Idaho
Earth, Sol System

Admiral Fran McKee was still getting used to her new office when an alarm buzzed, the five-minute warning before the start of her next meeting. With most of the city of Jacksonville and Little Rock still lying in ruins, Space Command was still technically without a home.

While the Republic's new capital city was still being built, the Chancellor's Office and the Senate had temporarily relocated to one of the new megacities being erected in a wheel-and-spoke design. Emerald City was at the center and New Cambria at the end of one spoke, sixty-five kilometers northwest of Emerald City and seventy-three kilometers north of Alliance City. Fran understood why Admiral Bailey had temporarily relocated Space Command Headquarters to New Cambria. It allowed him to stay close to the Chancellor Pro Tempore, who had designated the city as the Republic's temporary capital until the city of Mountain Home was ready to assume that title—Capital of the Republic.

While Admiral Bailey managed the headquarters out of New Cambria, Fran continued to manage the daily tasks of Space Operations out of the small, overcrowded facilities of Naval Support Base–Mountain Home. Prior to the Zodarks' attack, the base had been home to Space Wing 6, the fighter and bomber squadrons deployed aboard the *Victory*-class battleships RNS *Cassiopeia* and *Hercules*—and now it housed Space Operations.

Knock...knock... "Excuse me, Admiral. Ripley is here for his nine o'clock. Should I go ahead and send him in?" asked her aide, Lieutenant Worthey.

Fran looked up from her desk. "Yes, send him back—oh, and before you leave, send a message to General Hackworth to see if he's still joining us for this mission."

Her aide nodded, then withdrew from the room to head back to his station.

A few moments later, Rear Admiral Ripley Willis Lee walked into her office, taking a seat while Lieutenant Worthey fixed everyone a coffee. While Fran did her best to make small talk with one of her rising stars, she felt oddly relieved when Lieutenant General William Hackworth, the relatively new Commander, Special Operations Command, walked into the room with a colonel she hadn't expected.

She gave him a sideways look at the unexpected guest.

"Morning, Fran, hope you don't mind—I brought Colonel Eliason with me. He's the commander for 3rd Special Forces Group. He'll be tagging along with 3rd Regiment for this mission," General Hackworth explained, everyone shaking hands before taking a seat and getting down to business.

Fran motioned for Worthey to bring up the orders she'd crafted just for this mission. Armed with the mission objectives, she turned to face Admiral Lee, explaining, "Ripley, I know you've been itching to get some payback for the loss of your ship, the *Shangri La*. And it probably feels like I'm punishing you by not reassigning you a ship or squadron of your own in support of Operation Orion's Hammer.

"So, here's the deal, Ripley. I did hold you back from being a part of Orion's Hammer. Admiral Dobbs and Admiral Rosentreter both pleaded with me on your behalf to assign you a ship or squadron under either of their commands—you've established quite the reputation as a sound tactician—"

"Pardon my interruption, Admiral. Why are you telling me that I've been passed over for command of a new ship or squadron of my own? I've been without a command, without a purpose for months," lamented Admiral Lee.

Fran shook her head dismissively. "Come on, Lee, don't be so hard on yourself. Trust that I've got other assignments for you—you just needed a short break before we threw you back to the wolves. You'll get your chance to get back into the fight."

Lee bit his lower lip, slowly nodding in agreement, then sighing. "All right, I suppose I probably could have used a short break after losing the *Shangri La*. It's been a few months now. I'm ready, Admiral, just give me a command and put me back into the fight."

"See? That's the kind of attitude I'm talking about," Fran replied, then she picked the tablet up off the table, activating it before handing it to him. "These are your new orders, Lee. I'm giving you command of the RNS *Cassiopeia*—it's a *Victory*-class battleship right out of the shipyard. I'm also placing you in command of Task Force 28.

The *Cassiopeia* will be your flagship, but you'll also have the *Hercules* and the *Mars*, two more *Victory*-class battleships, to go along with the squadron of warships I'll be assigning your command during the next few days. In the meantime, General Hackworth here has something he'd like to bring you on now that we have a commander for TF 28."

General Hackworth leaned forward, closing the distance between his face and Lee's. "Congrats, Lee, on being given command of TF 28. First things first. The reason why TF 28 is being formed up over the next couple of days comes down to the simple reality that I have a mission that needs to get done—and you're the instrument that's going to get it done.

"Once you've taken command of your ship, when you go into the captain's office, you'll see a pair of safes built into the wall behind the desk. One is for the captain, the ship's skipper. The other is a means of delivering secretive orders that can't necessarily be transmitted electronically. We're telling you this, Lee, because once you cross into the Primord system of Pfeinstgard, the safe will unlock. When that happens, we need you to retrieve the orders and prepare to implement them. Needless to say, they'll be classified Top Secret NOFORN—so don't go and share with anyone, especially nonhumans. You think you can handle that?" explained General Hackworth, then waited for Lee to respond.

"Yeah, I can handle that," Lee replied, his tone a little skeptical. "So I'm going to take a wild guess here and assume this is why Colonel Eliason and a regiment of Deltas are accompanying us on this 'patrol' of the neutral zone." Lee used air quotes around the word *patrol*.

This time it was Colonel Eliason who leaned closer to Lee, beating General Hackworth in responding to his question. "Admiral McKee says you're pretty sharp, a brilliant tactician, and you know how to fight a battleship better than anyone in the Fleet," Eliason complimented, then turned briefly to look at McKee and Hackworth. "Permission to at least provide the mission BLUF?"

Fran looked at the Army soldiers, shrugging her shoulders dismissively. "I don't see a problem giving him the mission BLUF."

"I'm all ears, as they say," replied Lee, eager to hear what the "bottom line up front" or BLUF was for this mysterious mission.

Hackworth gave Eliason a curt nod to proceed. Lee just smiled as he watched the interplay between the three of them. Now he was really curious about what was happening.

"Admiral, the real reason your squadron is being deployed to Pfeinstgard, a heavily militarized and defensive Primord system along the neutral zone, is this…"

As Lee read from the mission BLUF, he realized his eyes were widening before regaining control of his poker face. Seeing it in detail on the tablet the colonel held between them—it suddenly made sense. He was staring at a pair of Altairian-Human hybrid frigates—a variant called the *McRaven* class. It was a Special Forces version of the Gallentine *Vraxerian*-class stealth ship. His task force, his ships, it was all a ruse to run cover for the pair of Special Forces frigates and the regiment of Deltas accompanying them on their journey. The alliance was preparing for the next campaign—the invasion of the Zodark Empire.

"Admiral Lee, judging by the look on your face, I think it's safe for us to assume you understand the reason why you're being given a task force that's not traveling toward Pharaonis space but headed toward a system the Primords liken to a fortress," the colonel stated flatly.

Lee spontaneously chuckled to himself as it all fell into place. Him being in reserve until a new task force could be formed and his subsequent deployment to a Primord system in no danger of being overrun. *The moment my ships start arriving along the neutral zone, the Zodarks will have to pull forces from elsewhere, believing my ships may be the vanguard of the alliance's next offensive…*

Lee looked at the three of them. "Yes, Colonel—I understand—perfectly."

Chapter Six
Enemy Mind

Headquarters
Republic Third Expeditionary Army
Astrionis, Tau Sagittarii System

Lieutenant General Jayden Hopper sat at the briefing table, listening intently to the report his G2 intelligence directorate had finally finished creating for him. It had been a few months since the Orbots had surrendered, and they still knew very little about how this society of cyborgs operated. With the war over, he felt now was the time to begin peeling away the layers of the onion and figuring out what, if any, connections there might be between how the Orbots functioned and how Legion, the Collective's foot soldiers, operated. He was hoping to find something of value—something they might be able to leverage against Legion if they were lucky.

"I think this next part of the briefing will help to explain a lot of questions many of us have had over the years," explained Colonel Blake Townsend, the deputy G2. "Since our first encounter with the Orbots, we haven't had a good handle on how the hierarchy of the Orbots actually works. I'm proud to report, General, that during the past couple of months, we have finally made a breakthrough with the Orbot named A17—"

"Huh, isn't that the one who claimed to be the leader of their people since those above had been terminated?" General Hopper interrupted, leaning forward, his interest piqued.

Undeterred by the interruption, Colonel Townsend nodded. "He is. In fact, he's actually been incredibly helpful the past couple of months in detailing how their society functions. For instance, we've learned that they have a series of ranking systems that classify them into various functions. Take Alpha 17 as an example. He explained how every Orbot has a letter in front of their rank. A or Alpha means they're in leadership or a command position. The lower their number, the more important they are. Incidentally, should they be killed, when they're brought back, they don't usually assume their previous rank or number. Instead, they fill in vacancies based on need. My understanding is that there are twenty-five

Alpha leaders, and when ten are killed, the Orbots reshuffle the positions and another randomized twenty-five Alphas are chosen.

"What's unique about their jobs or positional assignments is how broad they are. Here's an example: if their assigned name begins with W, then that means they're classified as a 'worker' and given just about any kind of menial tasks from, say, construction worker to being assigned as a worker in their shipyards constructing warships. We know they function pretty similar to how Legion and the Collective have been explained to us. These 'workers' are able to access shared knowledge and experience in performing whatever tasks they have been assigned to.

"If their name begins with S, it means they're soldiers or fighters. These are the Orbots that our soldiers fought and the ones that operate their warships. However, it's always the Alphas who are in charge. They're the ones who ultimately issue the orders the other Orbots follow," explained Townsend, pausing a moment to see if Hopper had a question.

Blowing some air past his lips, Hopper asked, "OK, so if this is essentially how they function, how do they reanimate or come back from the dead if they're killed on, say, a warship or something along those lines?"

Nodding at the question, Townsend explained, "This goes back to those data centers with the obelisk-like structures we destroyed, which ultimately led to their surrender. We know their fleets operate with those Collector ships, and we know if they die, they transmit a subatomic microburst transmission that seems to contain all their experiences and memories up to the very moment of their death. When those Collector ships jump into a system that has one of those data centers, that's when they synch. As to coming back from the dead—it's as we suspected. They have these places they call biological labs. Basically, they're growing biological clones of Primords and humans. There are still some Altairians, but Alpha 17 explained they largely moved away from using Altairian clones as their bodies weren't as large-framed or as capable as Primord and human bodies."

"Good grief, that's barbaric. So this is how they create their 'new cyborg bodies' after they're killed," General Hopper said disgustedly.

"Yes, sir, that sums up how the process works."

Hopper shook his head. "OK, good job, Colonel. It sounds like we now have a pretty good dossier and library of who, what, and how the Orbots function as a society. The question I'd like to ask now is, what happens next with them? Do we attempt to integrate them into the alliance as an equal partner? Do we fold them into the Republic? We've got some tough questions to answer and not a lot of time before the next alliance council meeting."

"Sir, if I can suggest something—meet with Alpha 17 and ask it those questions directly," offered Townsend.

"You know what—that's a good idea. Set up a meeting for tomorrow. Bring it here, to my office. I'll question it here."
****

Following Day
Headquarters
Republic Third Expeditionary Army

Looking around the office Lieutenant General Jayden Hopper had taken over since he'd established his headquarters on the Planet Astrionis, he had to hand it to the cyborgs. They weren't exactly known for their opulence or creature comforts. Everything about them was utilitarian, a place and a purpose for everything.

If I'm going to stay here more than a month, then I'm going to speak to someone about sprucing this place up a bit, he thought to himself as he prepared his mind and emotions for the conversation he was about to have.

Knock, knock.

Jayden's head turned to the door, and he stood. "Sir, we have prisoner Alpha 17," announced Captain Tedros. A trio of guards accompanied him and the lone Orbot who had identified himself as their "leader."

"Thank you, Captain, please, come on in. Alpha 17, you can sit opposite me while we talk," Hopper directed, then motioned with his hand for where he wanted Captain Tedros and his guards to sit while he spoke with the Orbot.

As Hopper took his seat opposite Alpha 17, he stared silently at the Orbot, wondering what it was thinking, *if* it was thinking, or if it was even capable of independent thought. There were no pretenses of emotion in its demeanor—Alpha 17 was the epitome of Orbot efficiency and logic, devoid of free will and thought. Its upper half, constructed from a Primord body, had no more of a soul than its four mechanical legs.

Wasting no time on formalities, Hopper decided to begin. "Alpha 17, the war has ended, correct?"

The Orbot stared at him for a moment, unresponsive, then it canted its head to the side as it replied. "Yes. The war has ended. Why do you ask a question when you know the answer?"

"To make sure *you* know it's over," he countered.

"Yes, the war is over. The Orbots have surrendered. What is the purpose of this meeting?" the Orbot asked.

Staring at the cyborg, Hopper thought about that question. *What is the reason for this meeting…?*

"The reason for this meeting is we're in a place now where we need to look forward, to the future," said Hopper. "Which brings me to a question I seek an answer to. What do you see as the future for your people—the Orbots?"

Alpha 17 responded to the question in a tone that was precise and devoid of any emotion. "General Hopper, Alpha 01 had not extended our operational parameters beyond the renewed conflict with your alliance. Our 'future,' as you term it, is a variable that remains to be defined, as no further instructions had been given to any Alphas prior to the demise of our leader. In the absence of 01, I was notified that I was now the leader until a lower-ranked Alpha was found. Currently, as to our future, it must encompass the establishment of a functional status quo within the given parameters of our surrender and the peace between our societies."

Hopper grunted at the complexity of this response. He wasn't sure if this Orbot fully understood the situation his species now found themselves in. "Hmm, speaking plainly, what you're basically saying is you're navigating new territory without a map and are unsure what to do next?"

The Orbot stared at him for a moment. "Yes, I suppose that is a good analogy for the situation."

Hopper chuckled at his discomfort. "I'll bet this is the first time in centuries your kind has faced such unpredictability, isn't it?"

"Indeed, unpredictability is a novel parameter for us—we function on orders in a society that revolves around order. However, since the end of this war, we have found ourselves confronting a new layer of complexity we had not anticipated and do not know what to do. For example, why are we, the Orbots, still operational? That deviates from our preestablished contingency protocols."

Hopper bunched his eyebrows as he leaned in, his interest piqued by the unexpected turn in the conversation. "Contingency protocols—explain."

"In the event of our subjugation by an adversary, a protocol existed within the Collective for an emergency measure—a termination sequence transmitted from a Collector ship, ensuring the preservation of our collective consciousness, is activated and swiftly implemented. This measure was designed to prevent any form of compromise or exploitation of our society by external entities who may conquer or occupy our worlds. In the event that such an occurrence were to transpire, our consciousness would be safeguarded, transmitted across space, and eventually reintegrated within a secure location where we would start over again. Yet that did not happen. We are still here, still operational, still…alive."

Hopper sat back in his chair as he contemplated the Orbot's response for a moment, processing the information and recognizing the strategic implications. "You said there is a Collective protocol that would be activated in the event your people might become occupied. Why wasn't this protocol enacted? What stopped it, and do you think it could still be implemented?"

"I am unsure. This remains unknown to me," Alpha 17 admitted, its voice betraying no frustration, only a statement of fact. "It is possible that the absence of the protocol's activation could be the result of a deviation from our strategic imperatives. It could suggest either an external intervention—the signal sent to the Collective failed—or a significant internal recalibration of our directives moments before Alpha 01 was terminated."

Whoa, this could be big. Hopper realized this revelation could be monumental not just for its strategic ramifications, the Collective appearing in their galaxy, but also for the philosophical questions it raised about their autonomy, their survival, and the nature of their consciousness.

Ever the pragmatist, Hopper saw the immediate and tangible aspect of the mystery. "I'm going to call you Alpha 01 since, by rights and order, you're the lowest-ranking Alpha and therefore the leader. I want to come back to something you just said. Does this mean that the signal that was sent to the Collective was intercepted before it could be received?" he asked. "Or was it never sent in the first place? What would be expected if the directives were recalibrated?" He ran his fingers nervously through his hair. "These decisions, or indecisions...could redefine the balance of power in our galaxy."

Alpha 01 concurred. "As to *how* this happened, the most likely explanation is that during the height of the battle, at least ten of the Alphas were killed, leading to a new, randomized selection of twenty-five new decision-makers from all surviving Orbots. This selection process was happening at the same time as your forces were destroying the remainder of our fleet and conducting the orbital bombardment of our command and control facilities. My belief is that ten or more of the newly selected leaders were quickly killed during these battles, either before they knew they had been selected to assume new leadership roles or directly after assuming them. This chaotic process of rapidly losing decision-makers could easily have caused a cascading effect that led to whoever was assigned the role of Alpha 01 not having enough time to transmit anything to the Collective.

"As to your second point, yes, clearly the strategic implications are significant," Alpha 01 reiterated. "Our continued existence opens a multitude of potential pathways for future operations, alliances, and integration within the galactic framework if we are free of the Collective, free to choose our own path as Orbots, our own future."

Hopper steepled his fingers as he thought. He stood, his mind racing through the possibilities. The thought of having the Orbots as allies and the Collective showing up unexpectedly to claim the Orbots sent shivers down his spine. "Alpha 01, this was a good conversation. We will have more of these conversations as we discuss the future of your people. In the meantime, speak with them. See what the Orbots would like—what kind of future, what path would they like to chart? We need to know if the Collective returned or if another lower-ranking Alpha appeared and ordered your people to fight with what they have available, would they fight, or would they respect the terms of their surrender and remain neutral? We will speak again. In the meantime, find an answer to that question."

As the meeting concluded, the Orbot left. Hopper began to wonder what kind of Trojan horse he was dealing with. Sure, they had surrendered, for now. But would it last? Could the Orbots ever be trusted?

I guess we'll find out soon enough...

Chapter Seven
Not a Palace

Security Council Chamber
Tiberius Hall
Alliance City, New Eden
Rhea System

Emperor Tibus SuVee felt completely out of his element. He didn't leave Cobalt Prime unless it was very important, and although this was the official capital of the Republic until the new one was completed on Earth, it lacked a certain sense of majesty he had been raised to enjoy. The meeting hall was innovative, and while it had been designed by some of the best architects in the Republic, there weren't any gilding or gem-encrusted adornments. It was far from the royal trappings he had become accustomed to.

Very few things would have enticed Emperor Tibus to travel to Alliance City, but a meeting with the President of the Humtars, after all these years—that was worth the trip in his mind. He had been hearing stories about the mysterious Humtars since he was just a young boy being tucked in by his father. He was shocked that Miles's people had actually found survivors.

Emperor Tibus had mixed feelings about the meeting he was about to have. On the one hand, the possibility that they could have encountered another ally to help them in this war against the Dominion was very promising. However, the Humtars would have their own motivations as well, and Tibus was known to be shrewd and not always trusting. Besides, the Gallentines had been occupying the territory of the Humtars for thousands of years, using technology that was often derivative of this ancient people—that might not sit well with this President Gudea character.

Then there was another worry. *What if the Republic and these Humtars decide to reunite and create their own faction?* he wondered.

No, Miles is an honorable man. Tibus shook aside the fear. He felt confident that his current Viceroy had shown himself to be a reputable person who wouldn't suddenly double-cross him.

When Viceroy Miles Hunt opened the door and ushered in President Gudea, a strange sensation rose up within Tibus. He was intimidated. Gudea was like the perfect specimen of strength, health, and good looks. Tibus had no idea how old he was—he looked like a thirty-year-old Terran, but he knew that might not be the case.

Never in all his years had Emperor Tibus stood when meeting with another leader. People came to him; they kissed his ring. And yet, Tibus looked down and found that he was on his feet, involuntarily pulled there by some inner force.

For about ten minutes, Tibus had an out-of-body experience. He was aware of what was being said, and that he was in fact responding, but it was as if he were floating above the room, incapable of making decisions himself and merely watching the interaction take place.

President Gudea began to describe some of the technology that they had, which he was willing to make available to the Galactic Empire. It was daunting to realize how much more advanced the Humtars were than the Gallentines. He wasn't certain yet if he could trust President Gudea, but he certainly did not want him to become his enemy.

"One thing that will almost certainly increase your capabilities is using our power generation technology," Gudea explained. "Antimatter is both more powerful and more efficient than what you have available to you."

"Our scientists have experimented with antimatter reactions, but without proper storage, it's incredibly dangerous," said Miles.

"Exactly," Gudea agreed. "And that is the 'nut we have cracked.' I think I am using your expression correctly."

"The message is understood," Emperor Tibus heard himself say.

"And of course, once you have more power, then you will be able to employ our updated wormhole devices," President Gudea offered. "Our travel range is so much farther than what you currently have—imagine what that would do for your military strategy."

Something about this statement brought Emperor Tibus back into his body. He immediately began to calculate how being able to move faster than the Zodarks would impact this war against the Dominion, and potentially against the Collective as well. It really was a game-changer.

"Another advancement we've made is in the area of communications systems," said Gudea. "Emperor, your Gallentine people have begun to use a quantum beam system—it can cover vast distances with low detectability. We Humtars have something that utilizes the same principles, but it works even better. It would allow planet-to-planet communications in real time, with no lag. Doctors Kato and Johnson told me that they have been waiting weeks to send and receive messages. This would completely eliminate that wait time."

"Incredible," Tibus remarked.

"If I may," said Miles as he turned to Emperor Tibus with a slight bow, "I have a question for President Gudea about something I observed during my brief travels with him."

"I'll allow it," Tibus confirmed.

"Before I entered your ship, I noticed that the outer hull had a strange appearance. I wondered if…well, it sounds strange—but do you use organic materials in your construction?" Miles asked.

Emperor Tibus felt stunned. *Is this even possible?* he wondered.

"Yes…our people are always interested in ways to incorporate nature into technology," Gudea began. "Our botanists found a species of microorganism that is able to survive in the vacuum of space. That was a tremendous discovery in and of itself, but it turns out they absorb and dissipate energy-based weapons."

"So, this species acts as a shield against lasers?" asked Tibus incredulously.

"One could put it that way," Gudea responded.

Emperor Tibus felt a little threatened, knowing that the Humtar ships were so far superior to his own.

"I have a question for you, Miles," said President Gudea.

"Oh?"

"I noticed that your ships have magnetic railguns on them," he remarked. "Isn't that a bit of, well…an elementary weapon?"

Miles and the Emperor both smiled.

"I would understand why that would be your first inclination," said Miles. "It was the same opinion the Zodarks held. You see, their ships were more advanced than ours in many ways, but although they were well insulated against energy-based weapons, they were no match for kinetic weapons.

"Our strength has been our superior electronic warfare capabilities. Lasers are instant, but they only work if a ship can lock onto a target, and by jamming their signals, we essentially made them blind, forcing them to come in closer—and that allows us to use our magrails. They have actually been key in our battles against the Dominion."

"Very interesting…," said President Gudea, stroking his chin. "Emperor Tibus, Viceroy Miles, in terms of putting 'boots on the ground,' I'm not sure that we would be of much value to you as of yet. You see, while we may have more advanced technology in many areas and we do have practice at fighting over on the other side of our stargate, we are not accustomed to large-scale wars. My suggestion is that we provide observers to learn from your methods, to see what you are using and how your strategies work. Then, we can perhaps have a better insight as to what additional technologies may be helpful to you, and we can work on a training program that will allow some of our troops to integrate with yours."

A small part of Emperor Tibus worried that perhaps the Humtars were sending in spies. However, reflection on that point proved it to be illogical. They already had more advanced technology in almost every way, and they did not have any true obligation to the Galactic Empire other than a sense of loyalty to the Terrans and perhaps a sense of self-preservation against the ever-looming Collective.

Tibus walked over to President Gudea and stuck out his hand. "We will be very grateful for your assistance, and we look forward to a long and prosperous relationship."

It was the first time he had ever shaken anyone's hand.

Chapter Eight
Task Force 28

Task Force 28
RNS *Cassiopeia*
Pfeinstgard System

Rear Admiral Ripley Willis Lee stood at the expansive port holo window of his office aboard the RNS *Cassiopeia*, also known as *Cassi*. His gaze swept over the assembled might of Task Force 28, *his* task force. From the vantage point of the holo display, the ships of his task force stretched into the void like some monstrous titan—powerful and poised, ready to strike. Following a short stopover at the Republic naval facility they leased from the Primords, they'd taken on some final crewmen and last-minute supplies before continuing on to their present location—Pfeinstgard.

It had been a little over a year since he had been promoted, exchanging his captain's eagles for a singular rear admiral star. Following the savage attack against Earth, he had hoped he could be among the first officers and ships to bring justice against the enemies of the Republic. When Vice Admiral Fran McKee had pulled him aside, sharing with him the plan she had devised for him, he was a bit taken aback by what she had proposed. Instead of being part of the invasion of Orbot and later Pharaonis territory, she wanted him to command a new task force she was assembling. This task force would be unlike any previous ones the Republic had fielded. His task force would be formed with newly built or recently retrofitted warships, fresh from Altairian and Republic shipyards, and crews fresh from the academy.

Staring out the window of the assembled force, he observed a fleet of forty-five warships and a host of soldiers large enough to populate a small city. Lee's journey from green Navy ensign to rear admiral seemed almost mythical in its arc.

He glanced over his shoulder at a pair of safes built into the wall. One safe belonged to the captain of the ship, the other belonged to Space Command. If they had special orders for him once underway, this was where he would receive them. Admiral McKee had already given him a heads-up to expect a classified set of orders to unseal themselves once he had entered the star system Pfeinstgard. In fact, it was scheduled to unlock around this time, but thus far it had remained locked. Waiting patiently, he turned, and with a flick of his wrist over the port holo, the view outside shifted. The hologram cycled from the imposing silhouettes of *Victory*-class battleships to a single *Stonefish*-class flak cruiser.

"RNS *Gallant*," Lee said out loud. The name rolled off his tongue like a promise. Captain Quenten Walkup, a good friend from the academy days, commanded the *Gallant*. A smile tugged at Lee's lips as memories of their youthful exuberance at the Naval Academy flooded into his mind.

After he moved from the window, Lee settled into the chair behind his desk, a robust structure of reinforced steel and dark, polished wood. The office itself mirrored the balance of military functionality and personal sanctuary, its walls adorned with digital plaques of past campaigns and battles the ship had fought in. Sitting on the table beneath the plaques was a well-used coffeemaker along with a hefty bag of his favorite coffee brand—Death Wish, a highly caffeinated brew from the gods.

He tapped the desk's comm device. Its interface lit up with a series of icons. "Lieutenant Harrow, status report."

"Sir, all still quiet across the board in Pfeinstgard. No movements from Gravaxia gate, and recon drones show clear scans. We're holding steady along the neutral zone," the firm voice of Lieutenant Harrow said.

"Excellent, have we established comms with *Guardian Spire*, and if so, when was the last time they encountered a Zodark vessel?" Lee's finger paused over a glowing section of the holo map projected above his desk.

"Sir, we have established comms with *Guardian Spire*. They report there has been no activity from the stargate—not since the last skirmish some nine months ago."

Lee nodded. With his eyes, he traced the lines of the map that illustrated the vital nerve center of Zodark territory, Tueblets. A system just two stargate jumps away. What made Tueblets such a strategic system was the network of stargates connected to it—six of them, each connecting to a different part of the Zodark Empire. Control of it would isolate elements of the Empire and make it that much easier to dismantle.

Control Tueblets, and you control the gates to an empire, Lee thought.

With a heavy sigh reflecting his long, exhausting day, Lee stood and walked over to the coffeemaker. After another glance at the safe, he poured himself a dark brew. The rich aroma of roasted coffee filled the room. It carried hints of dark chocolate and a touch of smokiness, complemented by a subtle undertone of caramel sweetness. The scent offered a brief respite from the weight of command. As he sipped the hot coffee, he turned to view another segment of his fleet displaying on the port holo view. His eyes settled on a *Neptune*-class corvette. Stars shined all around it in the vast expanse.

The taste of the coffee turned bittersweet as his thoughts drifted to darker days. How many young faces had he sent into the void, never to return? How many letters had he penned to the grieving families of fallen heroes? These were the burdens of an admiral. The unseen scars carried by those who led.

Then Commander James Oldendorf's valiant death flashed before him. It was a memory that never dulled with time. Lee had been just a tactical action officer on the RNS *Kentucky* when tragedy had thrust command upon him for the first time. He'd watched Oldendorf die on the bridge, the gruesome scene giving him nightmares throughout the years. Oldendorf's last words were like a push for Lee, propelling him into a decorated career, enabling him to put his mark on many battles: "Save the ship. Save the crew. I order you to assume command now!"

The *Kentucky* had survived, but many had died that day. It was a harsh baptism by fire, and to this day, he chided himself for not saving more souls.

Now, many of those who had stood with him through that fiery trial were here on the *Cassi*, at his insistence. Chief Engineer Boyd MacGregor, who could coax life from the coldest engine; Lieutenant Lewis Reynolds, his navigator and astrogator, whose hands had steered them through star fields and military engagements alike; and Communications Officer Lucia Rodriguez, whose voice had been their lifeline to the deepest sectors in space.

Lee took another sip of coffee. His gaze once again moved to the holographic fleets. Each ship, each life aboard, was his responsibility—a mantle he bore with solemn pride. They were his to command and his to keep safe.

A soft beep sounded behind Lee. He twisted around toward the sturdy safe. This was no ordinary storage unit; if it unsealed, it did so because it contained a set of classified orders from Space Command, and it had finally opened.

As he approached the safe, he positioned his eye before the iris scanner. Once the retinal match confirmed Lee's identity, he placed his hand on the cool metallic palm reader. With a soft click, the safe's door swung open.

Inside lay a single data pad. Its blank surface was dormant until activated by its designated user. Lee retrieved the tablet.

As he turned and walked back to his desk, Lee caught a digital frame on the wall. It displayed a photograph of him shaking hands with his mentor, Captain James Oldendorf. They were on the observation deck of the command center, where Oldendorf had once said, "Courage, like fear, is contagious; make sure you're carrying the right disease." The memory brought a grin to Lee's face.

Once Lee sat at his desk, he powered on the tablet in the same way he had opened the safe. The screen blinked to life as he navigated through even more security protocols and applications. He opened a document labeled "Orders"—a detailed dossier from Vice Admiral Fran McKee, Head of Space Command Operations.

Lee read through the directives slowly. Before he'd left on this mission, he'd been placed in command of Task Force 28 and tasked with reinforcing the garrison at Pfeinstgard, a strategic position in the Primord system. It was adjacent to the volatile Zodark system. His fleet would serve as a bulwark against any Zodark aggression to ensure the unimpeded flow of supplies from the Republic and Altairian space to the allied military bases.

Before their departure from New Eden, Lieutenant General William "Wild Bill" Hackworth of Special Operations Command had hinted at the additional responsibilities that would fall to Lee upon his arrival at Pfeinstgard. The safe in his office and its contents were part of this greater plan. It revealed why a company of Delta operators was included in his task force. These Special Forces were essential for the covert operations intended within the neighboring Gravaxia system— Zodark territory.

As he continued reading, the document detailed that the Gravaxia system was crucial as it formed a conduit between the alliance's supply lines and the heart of the Zodark Empire. Lee's immediate mission was to fortify Pfeinstgard and prevent any Zodark buildup in Gravaxia that could threaten their position. His fleet would also support the deployment of Delta teams to various strategic locations across Gravaxia, scouting for Zodark installations and assessing their military capabilities.

Each section of the orders layered more weight onto Lee's shoulders. He was to oversee the coordination of ground and space operations and to make certain the Republic's Special Forces frigates were strategically positioned to deploy teams undetected.

As always, easier said than done. And, as always, Lee was up to the challenge.

While he digested the magnitude of his tasks, Lee leaned back in his chair. His mind raced through logistics, the potential conflicts, and the lives at stake. The coffee had grown cold beside him, forgotten in the unfolding plans.

With each scroll through the tablet, Lee visualized the coming movements: the silent arrival of his fleet in the shadowed space of the Gravaxia system, the quiet drop of Special Forces onto cold, distant moons, and the tense wait for reports that would either signal success or summon the horrific ghost of battle.

Over the next few hours, there would be a lot to think about and even more planning.

He tapped the comm and patched in to his XO, Noriko Sato. "Sato, come to my office. The new orders have come in."

Chapter Nine
New Orders

Task Force 28
RNS *Maddox*
Pfeinstgard System

The occasional muted directives issued through the comms pierced the quiet command center aboard the RNS *Maddox*. Amidst it all, a figure stood over her console. She scanned her holo display, which projected the operational status of the vast fleet. This was Captain Naomi Love, Commander of Flight Operations. She was known widely by her not-so-creative call sign, Love.

Around Love, the vessel's command center throbbed with the pulse of interstellar operations. Holographic displays streamed data from across the Pfeinstgard system, bathing the crew's faces in an ethereal glow. The terminals emitted a soft periodic chirp, in synch with the lights dotting the architecture of the room. Shadows moved across the reinforced alloy ceilings as officers navigated their stations. The sterile scent of filtered oxygen mixed with the faint warmth of running electronics filled the air. Tactical maps and live feeds relayed from sensors and drones lined the walls to provide a panoramic view of space operations. Each control hub was busy with activity, manned by crew members whose subdued orders and swift strokes across their holo interfaces kept the vessel at peak readiness.

Love squinted at the status indicators of the ships in her command—three squadrons of F-97Cs and B-99Cs, six squadrons of AS-90C Reapers, six AT-70C Ospreys, and three AHT-12 Scarabs. A few icons blinked yellow, signaling minor issues currently being addressed in the maintenance bay. She opened a secure channel to her master crew chief, Brian Ford.

"Ford, I need a report on the maintenance status of the units showing yellow on my board," Love said.

Ford's voice crackled through the comm, the sound of clanking tools faintly audible behind him. "Aye, Captain. We're just handling a couple of sensor recalibrations on the Reapers and a turbine tweak on an Osprey. It's no big deal. Should be green across the board by 1100 hours."

"Good work. Also, ensure those recalibrations are double-checked. I need those birds fully operational. We can't afford sensor ghosts or turbine issues if Zodarks come our way."

"Absolutely, and as always, I'm your man. We're running diagnostics twice over and maybe a third time for the charm. The new firmware updates should also enhance the sensor suites, so you'll have them performing better than before."

"Excellent, Ford. Keep it on schedule. I'll need a full report first thing after you've cleared them. Also, update the duty logs with the specifics of the firmware updates for future reference."

"Will do, Captain. You'll have the updates by 1200 at the latest. We're on it."

"Thank you, Chief. Love out." She cut the communication and turned her attention back to her other duties.

As she proceeded with her work, Love allowed herself a brief glance at an old, faded photograph of her husband, Lieutenant Jack Love. It was propped against her console.

Love withheld a tear. No matter how long it had been, getting over Jack took everything she had and more. Still, the love for him never drifted from her heart. Jack had died years ago from a small precise laser wound while they were helping evacuate a civilian transport under fire. She'd held him as the life ebbed away, his blood staining her uniform. His final breath was a whisper of his nickname for her: *darlin'*.

She traced the outline of Jack's face with her finger. Then she placed her hand over her heart and felt the ache as fresh as it was when the tragedy had occurred.

Once she returned to her holo, she sighed while reviewing the flight schedules to make sure crew rotations met the optimal balance for readiness and rest. She took her job seriously, knowing each decision she made could affect hundreds of lives aboard the *Maddox*.

Just as she was about to approve the final rotation, her console beeped with an incoming priority message. She tapped the display and scanned the encrypted text. It was an update from the intelligence division. They required her to adjust patrol routes based on new data about possible Zodark activity near their sector. As Love inputted the final adjustments, the system accepted her commands with a confirming beep.

A second later, a stern voice came over her console's comm. "Captain Love, report to Captain Firth's office immediately."

That's odd, Love thought as she furrowed her brow. It wasn't typical for Captain Firth to summon her directly. Usually, he allowed her a considerable degree of autonomy in her operations.

"I'll be there right away," Love said before she toggled off the communication.

After exiting the command center, Captain Love entered one of *Maddox*'s many corridors. Efficiency LED strips lining the walls cast a soft light on the metallic surfaces. Digital readouts and emergency equipment secured behind glass also found their spots on the walls. Access panels and ventilation shafts occasionally interrupted the smooth steel ceiling. Beneath her boots, the grated flooring vibrated with the subtle resonance of the ship's engines.

Once Love navigated through the corridor, she approached a lift and stepped inside. She pressed the control panel and selected the deck for the captain's quarters—a location she didn't often visit but knew well enough. The lift whirred to life and ascended with a gentle acceleration.

Moments later, the doors slid open with a soft hiss. Love stepped out into another corridor, this one leading directly to Captain Firth's office. She walked with purpose, her mind full of possibilities about the nature of this unexpected meeting. She stopped at the heavy door marked with the ship's crest and Captain Firth's name. She knocked firmly.

"Enter," a voice said from within.

The door slid aside and revealed the interior of Captain Firth's office. It was an impressive contrast to the blunt corridors outside. One wall was entirely composed of holoport windows, offering a dynamic view of the star-studded expanse.

Captain Kofi Firth sat behind a substantial desk made of dark synthetic wood. He held his posture upright as he sorted through a digital dossier on his screen. He wore a crisp uniform, decorated with shoulder insignia marking his rank as captain and a chest array of ribbons and medals, some earned from combat, others bespeaking a career filled with personal sacrifice and achievements. Looking up as she entered, he smiled, diffusing the anxiety of being summoned to speak with the captain. He then gestured to the chair across from him.

"Naomi, please, take a seat. Something has come up that I need to speak with you about. How do you take your coffee?" he asked as he got up to refill his mug.

"Dark and bitter, like my late husband," she replied, attempting a bit of humor.

He laughed as he grabbed another mug and began filling it. While he tended to their drinks, she looked around the room, noting how neatly organized it was. It was a reflection of Firth's meticulous nature. She smiled when she caught a glimpse of his family as the holographic frame cycled through some images of his kids. It added a personal touch to the otherwise formal space.

As he sat, he handed her a cup of coffee and got down to brass tacks. "I'm sure you're wondering why I asked you here."

"Did something change in our orders?" Love asked with a raised eyebrow.

"Kind of, yeah, or at least for you it has," Firth stumbled, catching her by surprise. "Shortly after entering the system, the admiral received a FRAGO from Special Operations Command. Apparently, that contingent of Delta operators we took on in New Eden has a special set of orders we're to assist them in accomplishing. Unfortunately, to make sure their mission isn't interrupted, I'm going to have to transfer you temporarily to the RNS *Donovan*, effective immediately."

Naomi paused, trying her best to make her expression unreadable. In truth, this was a major surprise to her. "Sir, the *Donovan*? Isn't that one of those stealth frigates?"

Firth nodded. "It is. It carries a few of the Army SLX Shadow Lynx troop transports. It's a modified Chickenhawk, which is why you're being transferred to the *Donovan*—you're the Fleet pilot we have who has experience flying one of them."

"Wait, what happened to their pilot? They should have more than one if they're carrying a couple of birds in the bay with them," Naomi asked.

"They do and they don't. When we stopped over at Kita, the pilot got a Red Cross message that he needed to return home. Some kind of family emergency. They figured they would be all right with the copilot filling in while he was gone, but once they got this new set of orders, the copilot, a rookie at that, informed the admiral he didn't think he had the kind of skills and experience necessary to pull off the mission.

He said he'd give it a try if the Fleet didn't have another qualified pilot. That's when I seemed to recall that you'd done a stint with Joint Special Operations Command a while back and were even rated on flying the Chickenhawk—earned a Distinguished Flying Cross if I'm not mistaken," Firth said, his gaze fixed on her. "I know it's not a hundred percent the same thing as a Lynx, but if anyone could figure it out, it'd be you. The admiral also put in an emergency request for another pilot just in case, but it'll take weeks for someone to show up."

Naomi nodded, and a memory flickered in her mind—the feel of the controls of a similar aircraft, the Chickenhawk, which she had flown a fair bit during her stint in a Joint Special Operations aviation unit. She'd heard about the Shadow Lynx. It was a newer beast, with stealth capabilities and all. "I'm a bit rusty on flying a Chickenhawk, sir. It's been years—and this Lynx, it's quite different from what I've flown."

Firth cracked a small smile, one trying to fight through his exhaustion. "Captain, you're the best and most experienced pilot we have on this ship, maybe even in the entire Task Force 28. I have every confidence in your abilities."

Naomi nodded with a firm set to her jaw. "I understand, sir. I'll figure it out."

"Good. I'll arrange a shuttle for you while you pack a bag. Once you're aboard the *Donovan*, you'll be briefed in full on the mission." Firth handed her a small data pad. "This contains your transfer orders and the details on the Lynx. Everything you need is right here."

Naomi took the data pad, her fingers automatically curling around the slim device. "Thank you, Captain. I'll review it and be prepared for the briefing."

As Firth nodded, Love stood to leave, but she hesitated. "Sir, can I make a request?"

"Go ahead."

"I need Master Chief Ford with me on the *Donovan*, and on that Shadow Lynx I'll be piloting. We've been through countless operations together. He's the finest mechanic and troubleshooter I've known, vital for any transport and vessel operations."

Their partnership had lasted over a decade, during which time they'd fine-tuned their collaboration to near perfection. Ford's ability to diagnose and fix issues on the fly was unparalleled, making him indispensable, especially in operations involving the intricacies of a ship like the Shadow Lynx.

Captain Firth paused, his expression contemplative. He exhaled quietly, his breath barely audible. He cupped his hands together in his lap as he considered her request. After a few seconds, he nodded. "Very well."

He pressed the comm button from his desk. The device lit up at his touch. "Lieutenant Garner, I need you to prepare Master Chief Brian Ford for transfer. He's to accompany Captain Naomi Love on Shuttle 001 to the RNS *Donovan*. Get his transfer data tablet ready and all necessary clearance. Make it quick; this is priority one."

The lieutenant acknowledged the order with a sharp "Aye, Captain."

Firth turned back to Naomi. "Once this operation is over, I want you back on the *Maddox*."

"Aye, sir," she said.

"All right, you can go now." As she turned to leave, Firth called out, "Naomi?"

She stopped and faced him. "Yes, Captain?"

Firth trained an intense gaze on her. "Be careful out there. Lives will depend on you—I have the utmost confidence you'll handle it well. You have one of the steadiest heads under pressure I've seen. And, most importantly, we need you back here, and safe. That's an order."

"I will, sir," she said.

"Good. Now that will be all."

As she exited Firth's office, a smile spread across her lips. The thrill of returning to the pilot's seat was palpable, stirring within her the deep-seated passion for flight that had defined her career. Flying wasn't just a job for Naomi; it was a calling—one demanding courage, precision, and a calm demeanor amidst the hell of war zones. It was about being the lifeline for troops who depended on her skills to return safely to their ships. And it had been too long since she had been in command of a cockpit.

Her steps quickened as she headed toward the lift that would take her to the shuttle bay, but not before she grabbed the most important thing to her in the entire galaxy: Jack's pendant and dog tag.

Chapter Ten
Back to Basics

RNS *Donovan*
Pfeinstgard System

In the cavernous hangar of the RNS *Donovan*, the clang and echo of metal reverberated through the space. The distant sound of machinery pierced the air, which was thick with the odors of oil and fuel cells—a scent Captain Naomi Love had come to recognize as the unmistakable harbinger of mission readiness.

Outside, and a few steps away from the shuttle that had delivered her here, Love and Master Chief Brian Ford held their data pads. The digital screens were lit with details of their unexpected assignment. In front of them sat a Shadow Lynx, a troop transport as advanced as it was beautiful. Its dark hull was a major contrast against the brightly illuminated hangar. Its presence was imposing, a silent behemoth of stealth.

Ford turned to Love, his face set in a serious line as he glanced back at the transfer orders on his pad. "Did you get a heads-up about this specific op?"

Love shook her head, her eyes never leaving the Lynx. "Negative. I read the same thing you did on the flight over. Looks like we're in for quite the operation."

Ford raised his brows. "I haven't seen you this excited in a long time."

"I know. It's been ages since I've flown, but never in a Shadow Lynx. Gonna be…" She grinned. "Interesting."

Ford narrowed his eyes, giving him a momentary crease in his forehead. "Covert ops aren't our usual fare anymore."

"We're not strangers to it, though, so dropping Delta teams behind enemy lines"—she smiled again—"well, it's where we started."

The Lynx was much smaller than the Ospreys they typically flew with the Fleet. It carried a lot less armor and weapons, relying more on its maneuverability, speed, and stealth than brute force like the Scarab or the Osprey. It was armed, just like its predecessor, the Chickenhawk. It had a chin-mounted twin-barrel blaster and could be fitted with missile pods or additional guns on the pylons beneath the wings. In the troop compartment, it had enough room for a flight engineer or crew chief, and twenty occupants.

As Love walked around the Lynx, she spotted a few additional bulges along the sides of the fuselage—electronic warfare pods. When she ran her hand across the exterior, it felt different—almost soft, or rubber-like, rather than the tough armored exterior she was familiar with.

"I noticed it too," Chief Ford commented, obviously seeing the puzzled look on her face. "The outer coating—it's supposed to help absorb the radio frequencies used by Zodark search and targeting radars. According to an EWO I spoke with, it's supposed to make us appear like a ghost on a radar scope."

"Huh, is that so, Chief? I think I might need a little verification before I take the word of some electronic warfare officer who isn't riding along with us," Love commented as she ran a hand along the cool metal of the Lynx's landing gear. "We have less than a day to familiarize ourselves with this ghost before the *Donovan* jumps through the stargate. It's not a lot of time."

In the din of the hangar, a metallic clang reverberated as a wrench slipped from a mechanic's grasp. It clattered across the steel floor. Farther off, the voice of an NCO cut through the noise. He barked orders at a team securing cargo. Amidst the bedlam, the sergeant turned, his eyes locking on Love and Ford as he began striding toward them.

"Looks like we got a welcoming party coming our way," Ford said.

Love had expected someone to meet them upon landing, but it seemed things were too hectic for any immediate greetings. "Good. The sooner we can begin drills with this craft, the better."

As the sergeant made his way to them, Ford rounded the ship's stern. He leaned back, staring at the Lynx's rear-mounted blaster turret. "It's just as defensive as it is offensive. You see this turret here? I bet you this also has a full ECM/ECCM suite. This ship's equipped with twin .50-cal magrail guns too, along with that chin-mounted blaster. It's nice."

"This ship is as ready as we are to get into the thick of things," she commented.

Truthfully, Love thought, *how ready am I?* She pushed her hand into the pocket of her flight suit, touching the heart-shaped pendant her now deceased husband had given her and his dog tag. "Be with me,

Jack," she whispered. She called them her lucky charms—carried them with her in every bird she flew.

As the NCO approached, she saw his rank, recognizing the master sergeant chevrons and rockers as he halted next to her. He was dressed in the coveralls of a crew chief. Patches displayed his rank and role as they were stitched neatly across his chest and shoulders. His face was marked with the day's labor; grit and grime shadowed his cheeks. His brown eyes sparkled with an indefatigable spirit, and his black crew cut stood perfectly trimmed. He introduced himself with a firm voice. "Captain Love, Master Chief Ford, I'm Master Sergeant Kasim Adeku— the crew chief for this bird, at your service."

Adeku's gaze briefly swept over the Lynx with a mixture of pride and readiness. He then shifted back to the new arrivals. Behind him, the hangar buzzed with activity. Mechanics and technicians swarmed around and worked on an assortment of spacecraft—a second Lynx, an Osprey, and a standard shuttlecraft.

Love nodded to Adeku. "It's nice to meet you, Master Sergeant. Is the captain on his way or did he leave instructions for us to meet him somewhere?"

Adeku tightened his lips as he stood a little taller. "The captain is currently tied up, ma'am. You have me, and from what I've gathered, you're here to get acquainted with this Lynx—and time's not on our side. So, I'll do what I can to help get you acquainted with it quickly."

Ford stepped closer. "Sounds good, Master Sergeant. When do we start?"

"There's no better time than now, sir." Adeku turned and gestured toward the Lynx. He reached up and tapped a control on the side of the ship. The back ramp whirred and slowly descended with a heavy thud against the hangar floor. "Welcome to the RA *Ghost One*."

The trio entered the *Ghost*. Their boots resounded as they entered the troop bay. In its present configuration, it featured harnesses and seating for twelve soldiers. Each station was equipped to allow them to quickly exit with all their gear. Above, storage compartments were arranged to optimize the space. It was markedly different from the Ospreys that Love traditionally piloted. Here, the design was more streamlined; the walkways were narrower, the equipment more integrated into the ship's architecture, which reduced clutter. The troop deployment areas were optimized for rapid exits, just like the Osprey.

Adeku motioned toward the front of the craft. "Let's head to the cockpit. You can start your flight familiarization immediately."

"Sounds good. Oh, and where will we be able to conduct a few practice runs?" Love asked.

"There's a small moon about twenty-six thousand kilometers from the RNS *Donovan* right now," Adeku said. "The place has been checked out with our sensors and scans, and it's safe. It's got a thick atmosphere, perfect for your drills once the ship settles in orbit."

As they walked to the cockpit, Love outlined the session ahead. "Good. We'll execute atmospheric entries and exits, and practice maneuver sequences for deploying and recovering troops. Of course, no troops for this run, just the bare maneuvers."

Inside the cockpit, the controls were almost minimalist. Holodisplays and tactile interfaces promised precision handling and response. This was a pilot's haven, equipped for the kind of rigorous flying covert operations demanded.

Two seats, the pilot's and copilot's, faced a sweeping dashboard. The controls blended traditional manual inputs and advanced technology, including a weapons array showing the Lynx's formidable capabilities.

Adeku pointed out the features. "This craft is equipped with the latest in tactical displays, integrated directly into the flight control systems. You'll find the weapons are managed here"—he indicated a console to the right—"and here"—he pointed to another panel—"you have the ECM and navigation suites. The ECM and ECCM are incredibly powerful. They're almost like one of those Nighthawk EW birds. You'll be ghosts in this thing."

Love took the pilot's seat, running her hands over the controls to familiarize herself. Ford examined the navigation systems and scanned each display with skilled scrutiny.

As they settled in, Adeku stood by the doorway. "I'll leave you to get a feel for her. If you need anything, I'm just outside. I'll let you know once the *Donny* has entered orbit. Should be less than thirty minutes."

Ford and Love exchanged glances. Each registered a hint of surprise in the other's expression without a word.

Love raised an eyebrow. "We're launching right away?"

Adeku dipped his head. "You mentioned over the comms during your transit you wanted to maximize drill time with the Shadow Lynx, given the criticality of our pending mission. The captain went ahead and set course for the moon the moment you came aboard and said to expedite your launch schedule to accommodate your requirement."

"Huh. Thank you, Master Sergeant," Love replied.

Adeku's lips slightly curled upward. "Happy to assist, ma'am."

Ford thumbed over his shoulder. "As long as my station in the crew chief's cabin is set up, I'm ready to launch now."

Love tapped the copilot's seat beside her. "Negative, you're here."

"Outstanding." Ford took his seat beside her.

Love turned to Adeku. "Flight suits?"

"Right here." Adeku pressed his palm against a section of the cockpit wall. A door, perfectly blended into the surroundings, swung open to reveal two pilot-rated pressure suits and helmets designed for atmospheric entry operations. "These are tailored to your specifications."

Ford glanced at the weapons racks beside the suits and smirked. "Looks like we're dressed to impress with all this firepower."

"We've needed those before. It's reassuring to have a full arsenal at our disposal—wait, are those M1-Minis?" Love asked, sharing a glance with Ford, who had a wicked smile on his face.

"They sure are. We used to carry those older M-87s. Swapped 'em out for the Minis once they started fielding them. Do you know how to work 'em?" Adeku asked.

Love waved him off. "Oh yeah, we're good."

"Very well. Comm me if you need anything. I'll be outside until your departure." Adeku exited the cockpit and walked down the ramp. Shortly after, the hiss of the ramp closing and sealing vibrated through the Shadow Lynx.

Ford exhaled. "Ever think about where we'd be if we weren't flying through the stars, dropping into hot zones?"

Love chuckled. "Probably bored out of our minds on some peaceful planet, farming or something tranquil."

"We're kind of doing that now with our current positions—bored out of our minds."

"Sounds about right. Let's get our suits on and take this thing for a spin."

"Aye, Captain."

After securing their flight suits—which sealed magnetically along the seams for a tight, atmosphere-resistant fit—Love and Ford snapped their helmets into place.

The moment Love's helmet locked, her visor lit up with an incredibly detailed heads-up display that put her old helmet to shame. The HUD populated with critical flight data—altitude, speed, bearing, and a tactical overview of the airspace around the RNS *Donovan*, even though they hadn't turned the engine on yet. It also highlighted the various system checks in green—all systems go. Symbols for communication status, life support levels, and weapon systems readiness moved before her eyes. All were layered over a real-time feed of the external environment. It was absolutely incredible and beyond anything she had seen before.

"Captain Love," came the voice of Master Sergeant Adeku. "The captain wanted me to let you know the *Donny* has entered orbit. If you want to take her for a spin—you're clear."

Love gave Ford a smile as they strapped into their seats, then initiated the start-up sequence. Her fingers glided over touch-sensitive panels, lighting them up with soft blues and whites. Each interface chirped affirmatively as she confirmed their statuses. Engines, navigation, and communications were all operational.

Love glanced at the clock. It was go time. "*Donovan*, Flight Control—*Ghost One* requesting clearance for launch."

A brief crackle came over the comm. "*Ghost One*, you are cleared for launch. Safe travels, Captain."

Acknowledging the clearance, Love engaged the Lynx's hover engines. The ship lifted off the hangar deck and she glided it past the launch bay. She moved the craft slowly, passing other docked ships—a Lynx, an Osprey and a shuttle—some undergoing repairs. Mechanics and tech teams maneuvered around, avoiding forklifts hauling equipment and large toolboxes. Near the bay doors, Adeku gave a firm, respectful salute.

As the bay doors retracted, they could see the black vacuum of space shining with stars unveiled before them—thick clouds sat in the upper atmosphere below them. As Love increased the throttle, the Lynx slid out of the shielded bay into the moon's orbit.

Spread before them like a canvas was grayish cloud cover, obscuring the moon's surface below. It was time to get acquainted with the *Ghost* and see what it could do.

"Are you set, Ford?"

"It's been a while, Captain, but there's no place I'd rather be. I'm ready."

"We've got a tight schedule to keep to, and after today's drills, we need to ensure at least five hours of crew rest before tomorrow's operations. We need to be swift and efficient out here."

"Under your command, Captain, our performance will go above and beyond."

Out of her character, Love winked. "You bet your butt they will." She pushed forward on the throttle control. The craft responded instantly with a surge of acceleration.

****

Verdant Ridge loomed large in the viewport—the distance between them and the *Donovan* growing. Somewhere inside those dark clouds a red aura signaled volatile atmospheric conditions and potential storms or even volcanic activity below. Its thick, swirling atmosphere concealed secrets beneath a canopy whispering of an ancient and untamed wilderness. As Captain Naomi Love guided the Lynx down into the moon known as Verdant Ridge, the view from her HUD painted an eerie and majestic landscape.

Verdant Ridge, roughly the size of Earth's moon, was cloaked in a dense atmosphere, giving it an almost mystical appearance. The moon's surface was lush with green vegetation, deep craters, occasional volcanic eruptions and towering mountains. All were veiled in a perpetual mist that spoke of its wild nature.

Master Chief Brian Ford peered over the readings on his display. His brow crinkled under the weight of concentration. "The atmosphere's thicker than I expected."

Love scanned the data streaming across her screen. "It's going to make maneuvering a challenge." She adjusted the *Ghost*'s descent trajectory slightly. "The thick carbon dioxide and sulfur hexafluoride add resistance. It's like flying through soup."

Ford clicked his tongue. "The atmo's not breathable, either. Not even close. We'll need to keep our suits sealed."

That goes without saying, Love thought.

Ford read an interface on the dashboard. "Clear skies at latitude thirty-four degrees north, longitude one-one-eight degrees west. No environmental threats or storm activity detected in that sector."

"Copy that. Heading there now," Love replied.

The *Ghost*, fortified with reinforced plating designed for such conditions, began to vibrate as it entered the upper layers of Verdant Ridge's atmosphere. The ship's hull groaned under the pressure and dense air but held strong. For a few moments, the ship shuddered, then it smoothed out.

The descent accelerated as Love pushed the Shadow Lynx in the direction of what appeared to be a good landing zone in one of the moon's tropical regions. Below them, the canopy of dark green foliage stretched far and wide. The jungle was rich with colors both familiar and otherworldly. The trees bore broad, glossy leaves reflecting the light of the moon's twin suns to cast gleaming shadows on the forest floor.

Love gritted her teeth. Flying was like riding a bicycle; the rust seemed to fall away from her fingers—and mostly her brain—with each passing second. She inhaled deeply, the thrill of landing in challenging locales making her feel right at home again.

Ford grinned. "You're loving this, aren't you?"

"More than you know, Master Chief."

With precision, Love maneuvered the *Ghost* through the thick air. Each adjustment was a struggle against the atmospheric drag. She steered the troop transport toward the landing zone—a flat clearing enveloped by the jungle's towering vegetation where thick vines and wide-leaved plants intertwined.

Love descended the ship. The landing gears deployed with a solid thump and secured the Lynx to the soft, fertile soil. The green landscape stretched into the horizon. The jungle's canopy hid most of the twin suns' light.

Ford grabbed a rifle from the rack and moved toward the ramp as he acted out his part in the drill. He checked the ramp doors that would assist troops in a rapid deploy.

Love activated the chin blaster and magrails, the weapons array scanning the jungle for the invisible enemies of their simulated practice round. The sensors picked up faint, quick movement.

"Contact, two-four-zero degrees, left flank, rapid movement," she said. "Stay sharp."

Ford played along with the scenario. "Roger that. Troops would need extraction under fire."

She needed to intensify the drill. "Weapons system's off-line, I'm out of ammo." She raced out of her pilot's seat and to the rack, slinging her own rifle, then rushed through the transport's cabin and stepped down the ramp into the dense underbrush.

The humidity hit her like a wall, even through the suit. The air was thick and wet and clung to everything with a palpable weight. Her HUD flashed with environmental data. Thermal readings highlighted the shapes of the forest's small animals as she and Ford maneuvered through the dense undergrowth around the Lynx.

Love raised her rifle and aligned the sight with a shadowy fake figure flitting across her HUD. "Simulated fire," she said into her comms. She squeezed the trigger. The rifle emitted a series of controlled, silent pulses. It mimicked the recoil and report of live ammunition. Ford followed suit as he targeted another area of movement to their right.

"Covering fire at three-three-zero degrees," Ford called out. He mirrored the motion of launching a grenade, counting off the seconds for imaginary shrapnel dispersal. "Frag out," he shouted like he'd tossed a real grenade.

They moved in a synchronized pattern, communicating their actions as they would in a live fire situation. This drill reinforced their teamwork, although they had been working well together for years and years, since before their promotions. To Love, this felt good.

She withheld another grin.

"Move, move, move!" Love yelled as they doubled back toward the *Ghost*. After they entered the ship, the ramp sealed behind them.

They didn't waste a moment and sprinted to the cockpit. Love threw herself into the pilot's seat, her hands flying over the controls. She pulled the Shadow Lynx up, the ship shaking as it fought against the gravitational pull and the dense atmosphere.

Once she broke through the cloud cover, the *Ghost* cleared the lower atmosphere. Resistance fell away as they returned to the vacuum of space. Love let out a breath she hadn't realized she'd been holding. The stars before them were bright and clear—a contrast to the blackness of the *Donovan* they were to link up with.

"Not bad for us rusty old-timers." Ford clapped his hands.

Love glared at the moon, the red aura almost all-consuming. "We did good. We're getting our muscle memory back."

"Back? I never lost it."

"From what you did back there, I believe you."

"Same to you, Captain."

She inhaled, gathering her breath. "You ready for round two?"

"Born that way, ma'am."

For the next six hours, Love piloted the *Ghost* through a grueling series of military drills. Each drill tested their precision under pressure. They practiced troop exfiltration, where Love maneuvered the craft into hostile simulation zones. There, they swiftly loaded virtual troops under fake enemy fire before making a rapid withdrawal. Love executed landings in a variety of terrains. She coordinated closely with feigned ground forces to ensure quick, safe embarkation. For troop insertions, Love and Ford navigated to predetermined zones. They handled the *Ghost*'s approach and hover phases to deploy the troops faster, then lifted off immediately to minimize the spacecraft's exposure to potential threats.

In orbit above the moon, Love glanced at the fuel reserves showing digitally on her dashboard. "We're running low on juice." Sweat dripped from her temples. "I could use a shower about now." She imagined Ford was in a similar tired and sweaty state.

"Aye, Captain."

Even though they were both worn and well drilled, their procedural memory was finely tuned.

"Let's knock out one more, then it's back to the barn," Love said.

Ford tilted his head. "Looking forward to some chow too. You think the food's any good on *Donovan*?"

"We'll find out soon enough after this last run."

Love began their descent into another part of Verdant Ridge's atmosphere. This area was fraught with patchy storm clouds. Lightning crackled around the *Ghost*. Thunder boomed so loud it felt like nuclear explosions rocking the ship.

Love steered through the tempest. Despite the turbulence, she remained steady. Below, a valley opened up, inviting them with a peculiar beauty. They landed on a flat, rocky spot beside a stream flowing like a ribbon of silver through the landscape. The surrounding flowers were unlike any terrestrial flora; their petals spiraled outwards in geometric patterns. Every single petal was vibrant and luminescent under the moon's multiple suns.

The ship touched down and the landing gears locked into place with a heavy clunk. "Troops overrun! Immediate exfiltration, immediate covering fire! Go, Go!" Love shouted, the drill scenario peaking in intensity the moment they landed.

Love and Ford burst from the *Ghost*, rifles at the ready. Both scanned the terrain as they sprinted to a cluster of boulders dotting the landscape. They took cover, the rough, jagged surfaces of the rocks providing a scant barrier between them and the virtual assailants. Their HUDs brightened with the shadowy figures of enemy soldiers materializing across the field, advancing with simulated gunfire.

"Contact, eleven o'clock," Ford said. He squeezed off rounds. The HUD's simulation responded right away, with return fire zipping past them.

Love ducked. "Suppressing fire on my mark." She popped up from her position and aimed at the brightest blips on her HUD. Her shots were timed to pin the enemy down.

"Moving!" Ford darted from one boulder to another while he laid down a heavy line of fire to cover his movement. The simulated enemy retaliated and forced him to crouch low.

As the scenario escalated, the sound of their rifles echoed across Love's helmet's auditory speakers. "Keep them busy!" She glanced at the ship as the first of their virtual Delta soldiers sprinted up the ramp.

"Go, go, go!" Ford barked to the imaginary soldiers, covering their retreat with controlled bursts.

"Cover me, I'm falling back to pilot!"

Ford took a kneeling position behind a larger rock. "Roger that! All elements, retreat!"

Love hustled back to the Lynx, her boots kicking up grass as she ran. She clambered up the ramp, not wasting a second before she was in the cockpit. The sound of Ford's rifle continued to boom in her helmet as he still held the line.

Love sat on the pilot's seat and flipped the switches and gauges, her eyes moving between the controls and the rear camera feed showing

Ford making a strategic retreat in the *Ghost*'s direction. "Engines are hot, Ford, time to bug out!"

Ford gave one last sweep with his rifle. With a final burst of cover fire, he dashed toward the transport. His figure bounded in the camera feed as he headed Love's way, nearly fifty meters from the ramp.

Through the rear cam feed, an unexpected movement caught Love off guard. A creature, resembling a cross between a Terran bear and a scorpion, erupted from the ground. In half a second, its claws sliced through Ford's suit.

Love rose from her seat and dashed out of the ship. *So much for this moon being safe!*

The beast thrust another claw at Ford.

"Contact!" Ford said as he backpedaled. As he stumbled, the creature's pincers closed around him.

While she approached closer, Love could hear through her helmet comm the air from Ford's suit hissing out. The gash had no doubt exposed the poisonous atmosphere to his lungs.

Love fired two rounds into the creature's face. Green blood splattered. The animal recoiled and released the master sergeant. But Ford was down, wheezing, struggling to draw breath in the thinning air of his compromised suit.

"Approaching your position!" Love pumped her legs as fast as she could.

Green liquid dripped from the beast's nose and forehead as it reared on its back legs and lurched at Ford. Love blasted three rounds into the creature's skull, and it dropped to the ground before it could land another injury to Ford.

When Love reached him, his face was turning gray and he held his hands around his neck. It was the international sign for not being able to breathe. She grasped his hands and dragged him toward the Lynx.

The creature lolled its head and raised its pincers before it jumped to its feet. The half-bear, half-scorpion rushed in their direction, each step closing the distance. Its massive claw swiped near Love's head. She ducked, returning fire into its abdomen. It screamed, and even through Love's helmet, she could hear the penetrating sound.

With only a few more meters to the ramp, a second beast punctured through the soil. Rocks flung and dirt flew skyward. Love's heart pounded as she let go of Ford and fired at the new threat. The rounds seemed to barely faze it as the creature was twice the size of the first animal.

The wild demon rushed closer. With a desperate heave, Love pulled Ford up the ramp. The creature jumped at them, smashing into the closing ramp with a thunderous bang, shaking the Lynx. The sound of the creature's frustrated roars was muffled by the heavy metal door sealing itself shut.

Panting, Love secured Ford on a bench lining the cabin wall. Her hands shook as she looked at his wound. There was a gaping hole in his thigh, the blood pooling and running down the side of his inner leg. "Hang in there, Ford."

Love's first priority was ensuring the life support and oxygen levels inside the *Ghost* were sufficient to sustain her friend. She looked to her HUD, where the readouts glowed reassuringly—oxygen at ninety-eight percent, air quality at one hundred percent. All systems green.

Ford's breath was shallow and labored. She stripped the damaged suit from his body, revealing the extent of his injuries—along with his thigh wound, deep lacerations ran across his chest. Blood soaked through his undergarments.

Her mind raced with the possibility of alien toxins in his bloodstream. She darted to the medical station, fixed against the wall of the cockpit. It was labeled clearly under emergency lighting: "MEDICAL SUPPLY—AUTHORIZED PERSONNEL ONLY."

She snatched the first aid kit and a set of nanoinjections, tools that promoted rapid cellular repair and prevented infection.

When she returned to Ford, she knelt beside him. She applied pressure to the wounds to stem the bleeding, then cleaned the gashes. "Ford, can you hear me?"

Ford shivered; his teeth clenched. Without responding to her, his legs twitched repeatedly, and he grasped her arm.

"You're going to be OK." She didn't believe her own words but said them anyway. She loaded the nanoinjection device, its small vial filled with a silvery liquid. Pressing the device against Ford's skin, she triggered the injection. Ford winced at the sensation.

Good! he responded.

"Come on, Ford," Love said under her breath. She wrapped bandages tightly around his torso and then his leg. "Stay with me."

His eyes fluttered and panic tightened its grip around Love's heart. She leaned closer, her voice stern, laced with a desperate fear she couldn't hide. "Don't you be like my husband! Stay with me, Master Chief! That's an order!"

Ford's eyes closed, his face ashen and still.

"No!" Love positioned herself over him, hands poised over his chest, and began the rhythmic compressions of CPR.

Chapter Eleven
Don't Feed the Animals

Task Force 28
Pfeinstgard System
RNS *Donovan*

Moments felt like eternities as Love pressed down on Ford's chest, delivering each compression with hope beyond hope. "Come on, hang in there!" Love shouted when suddenly Ford gasped for air, his mouth wide, his eyes wider.

He jolted and lurched upright abruptly. "What the hell was that?" he blurted. I swear I saw some kind of wild demon in a dream or something."

"You're alive! Oh, thank God!" Love rocked backward, not expecting him to have recovered so quickly from the nanoinjector.

Ford had a confused look on his face as his eyes began to take in his surroundings. "Wait, that wasn't a dream? Oh, God—blood. I got hit—that demon was real?"

Love stared, confused at first by his gibberish, then helped him lie back down, asking, "Whoa, Master Chief. What exactly do you remember?"

He looked at her with confusion. "A nightmare—wait, how long have I been asleep?"

She snorted at his question. "Asleep—Ford...you were dead just a second ago."

He stared at her—or rather through her, the words either not computing or the realization of what just happened finally hitting him. Then his face contorted in pain. "Ahh—God, why does my leg hurt so badly?"

He tried to sit up again, then cringed. "Oh...my chest," he moaned.

"Whoa, there, Master Chief. You're still coming out of the fog. Just sit back a moment and let the nanites do their thing, all right?"

He lifted his head, glaring down for the first time at the bandages on his chest and leg. Then he looked up at her, his eyes finally alert with recognition. "Holy...wow—that was real?! There really was a monster or demon—something actually attacked me, didn't it?"

Love stared at him for a moment. She gave a soft nod. "Yeah—it's still out there. Can you stand now?"

No sooner had she finished speaking than a loud bang rattled the craft—startling them back to the reality that they were still in danger.

Staring at Ford, Love saw him freeze for an instant. "Jesus. It's still out there?"

"Yeah, sure is. We need to get the hell out of this place," she replied, turning to face the ramp as another bang thudded against it, the vibration rattling the craft. "Screw this—we're getting in the air and I'm gonna smoke that thing!"

Ford looked at her as she stood, attempting to follow suit until a shooting pain caused him to reconsider.

Love put her palms up. "Hey, I told you to sit still."

"Oh, damn. Feels like I've been run over by a forklift—just help me up, will ya?"

Bunching her eyebrows, she asked, "Are you sure?"

Bang, bang, bang—the walls reverberated as whatever the hell that thing outside was pounded against the side of the craft.

"You hear that? Now help me up. You're getting us the hell out of here," Ford countered through gritted teeth. "And hit me with another nanite injection or a painkiller—this freaking hurts!"

Love grunted at his bravado. She grabbed his hand and pulled him to his feet. "OK, tough guy. I'll strap you in and get us out of here."

Ford just grinned as she swung his arm over her shoulder, a wave of pain washing over his face as the lacerations across his chest stretched against the nanites still working to close the wound and stop the bleeding.

As he rode out the pain with a clenched jaw, she helped him into his seat and then reached for the med kit. *Painkiller or more nanites…?* She knew once they boarded the *Donovan*, he'd be fine. The docs would have him patched up in no time. *Painkiller it is…*

"I'm sending you to la-la land, Master Chief. I'll let the docs hit you with a second round of nanites," she explained as the autoinjector pressed against his neck and spat the drug into his bloodstream.

"Oh wow—that's good stuff, Naomi," he stammered as his eyes went glossy, the drugs hitting his neuroreceptors.

With Ford taken care of, Love slid into her seat—strapping herself in as her fingers danced across the controls, firing up the engines.

Lights began activating, the familiar sequence of buttons and switches turning on as the engines powered up—ready for takeoff.

"Here we go," Love announced as she lifted the craft into the air.

As they ascended, Love toggled the rear cam view and pointed at the screen to Ford.

With the adrenaline fading and her breathing evening out, she got a better look at their assailants—almost wishing she hadn't. The creatures on the monitor looked like something out of a horror holo.

A scorpion mated with a bear? she thought.

The creatures bore thick, dark, matted fur covering powerful limbs that ended in sharp claws. When one of them lifted its head, she saw its eyes, small and beady and yellow.

The bulky torso of whatever this beast was called led to a bearlike head that didn't seem natural or possible, yet it stared at her, opening its snout, revealing rows of jagged teeth and jaws she'd bet could crush metal.

"Look at that thing's tail." Ford pointed, drawing her eyes toward a long, menacing tail curled over its back with a bony tip that looked like it could kill. It was a miracle Ford had survived, let alone remained in one piece.

Ford turned to face her, his eyes a bit glossy from the painkiller. "Didn't they say this moon was supposed to be safe?"

She laughed. "Clear as day from the master sergeant. But, truthfully, that was some dumb John Wick stuff we were doing. What were we thinking, landing like that, then jumping out of the bird like we're pretending to be some augmented supersoldiers? We're freaking pilots, Master Chief. We're supposed to be smarter than grunts, not emulate them."

"Whoa, Captain, I've met plenty of grunts who are a whole lot smarter than some of your pilots—point taken about the John Wick stuff, trust me. I get it," Ford shot back, the meds clearly talking.

She sighed. He was right. She was wrong. Flying might require some added book smarts and reflexes, but grunts, on the other hand— they were tough as nails and brave as hell to battle against the Zodarks, the Pharaonis, and those cyborgs, the Orbots. Letting his comment slide, she gave the engines more power and headed for home—back to the *Donny* and a medbay. *I can see the paperwork now…*

"Damn you, Ford. Why did you have to get hurt? I'm going to get my ass chewed for this—and I deserve every bit of it."

Grunting at her comment, Ford said, "Paperwork, shaker work. I'll be right as rain for the op after I see the doc. It'll be fine."

"Yeah, well, you better be ready for the op." She flashed a grin. "After this, I'm adding a new rule: no getting mauled by local wildlife."
****

28 Hours Later

Love stirred from her brief nap. The fabric of the bunk's cushion left an impression on her cheek. With a grunt of annoyance, she wiped the slobber from her lips and swung her legs over the side of the bed. Her quarters were small, a necessity on a starship like the *Donovan*. It was well appointed enough for a captain, though. A compact desk bolted to one side of the chamber, strewn with digital pads and mission briefs. On the opposite wall, a narrow locker stood open and revealed neatly arranged uniforms and a small arsenal of personal sidearms. Jack's photo graced the bulkhead—a face she tried not to forget.

After she rose, she moved to the tiny sink nestled in a corner of the room. The mirror above it reflected a face marked by years of service and recent stress. Premature wrinkles creased the skin around her mouth and eyes, and it was all too deepened by the shipboard lighting.

"Damn," she said as she traced the lines with a finger. "Gonna need some of those age restoration sessions next time I go on leave."

Love splashed cold water on her face. The chill jolted her awake. She dried off with a rough towel hanging from a nearby hook.

Hours after they'd returned from the drills on Verdant Ridge, *Donovan*'s captain had given Ford and Love an ass-chewing for nearly getting themselves killed and endangering the ghost ship before the mission even started. Once he'd finished his obligatory reprimand of their actions, he'd gotten down to business with a thorough briefing of the moons and planets they were to drop the Deltas on before handing them off to the ship's N2, or intelligence officer, to provide the latest summary of the intel on the system and to answer any questions they still had.

As the briefing ended, she had to admit, the plan was solid. Task Force 28 was to execute covert drops on several moons and planets. Her and Ford's specific mission focused on the moon Lunakor, orbiting planet Torvulkis. RNS *Donovan* and RNS *Valiant* would go through the stargate first, hopefully undetected. Intel on the other side was limited. They didn't have precise details on the size of the forces stationed on or near the various celestial bodies and planetary systems. The success of their insertion depended on navigating the stargate into the Gravaxia system undetected, a feat demanding all the stealth capabilities they had.

Love had been impressed by the captain during the briefing. It was her first time meeting him. The man's command of the details and his crew was nothing short of professional. And Ford had looked remarkably better, the nanoinjections she'd administered having proved their worth. Without them, Ford would likely be dead or confined to the medbay.

Glancing at her gear in the locker, Love suited up. The flight suit brought a surge of readiness. She hefted her helmet under her arm, its visor catching the light as she stepped out into the corridor.

The ship was a hive of activity. Crew members hustled past in their premission tasks. Love kept an eye on the clock mounted above the corridor's intersection—thirty-two minutes to stargate entry. As she navigated the bustling passageway, a young ensign bumped into her.

"Sorry, Captain!" the ensign said.

"No worries, Ensign. Keep moving."

When she reached the launch bay, Master Sergeant Kasim Adeku greeted her. He crossed his arms. "Heard about your scrape back on Verdant Ridge."

"Just part of the perks of naval life, Sergeant. You take the good with the bad."

"Well, that's a failing on our end, ma'am. The place should have been scanned for potentially dangerous wildlife."

She patted his shoulder. "Things happen, Adeku, but I tell you what. Ford couldn't agree with you more," she said as she eyed the troop transport. "Speaking of wildlife—how's *Ghost One* holding up?"

"Good. With Master Chief Ford's help, we patched her up faster than I thought we could. In a way, we got lucky. Whatever that beast was, it put a hell of a dent in the ramp, but thankfully, it didn't beat up any critical sensor arrays along the sides of the craft or the lower quarter panels near the ramp. In fact, your master chief taught us a few tricks about pulling dents out of the paneling and reattaching it to the armor—

something he learned from working on your Ospreys," Adeku explained, then turned to look back at the Lynx. "Oh, before I forget, ma'am. The transfer from the *Maddox* is complete. Our VIPs finalized their gear and are waiting aboard the *Ghost* as we speak."

Love crunched her eyebrows, "VIPs—you mean the Deltas? And they're loaded and ready to go?"

Adeku nodded. "Yes, ma'am. They came aboard a few hours ago with their kits and gear for the extended mission on the surface. They loaded the *Ghost* while you and Ford were still being briefed."

"Huh. Thank you, Adeku, that'll be all," Love commented as she dismissed him.

Seeing Master Chief Ford finishing his premission checks of *Ghost One*, she felt at ease about the mission, knowing he was part of it. He was meticulous when it came to inspecting the transports before a mission and he was cool as a cucumber under pressure.

As she approached, he flashed a thumbs-up. His limp was still present, his body still healing.

"Master Chief—how are you holding up?" she called out to him as she approached.

"Eh, still ticking, Captain. All systems green—for the ship and me if that's what you're asking."

She laughed. "Good to know. Let's go ahead and board. We've got a schedule to keep."

Walking together into the Shadow Lynx, they strode up the ramp into the troop compartment as the SF soldiers moved out, checking and rechecking their gear. As they squeezed past the soldiers, some donned their helmets while others enjoyed the reprieve of not having to wear them yet. These soldiers were the elite of the elite, kitted out in state-of-the-art Dragon Skin battle gear. Their helmets and visors presented a formidable sight. The Deltas, being augmented supersoldiers, were by nature larger than the average human soldier— standing a few inches taller in their gear. Their presence alone was both impressive and intimidating—these operators were killers, harbingers of death, destroyers of the enemies of the Republic.

As Love walked through the troop compartment to the flight deck, she realized it had been a long time since she had directly worked with Deltas—not since her promotion to lieutenant commander and the required midcareer joint assignment all officers had to fulfill. Jack had spoken about how thrilling an assignment to JSOC would be. In his absence, she'd felt obliged to volunteer for the high-risk assignment, knowing it was what Jack would have done. Seeing their appearance now was a stark reminder of the gravity of their mission.

As Love and Ford crossed onto the flight deck, a Delta captain caught her attention. "Morning, ma'am, Master Chief," he said, his voice modulated through his helmet's speaker. "ODA 3235 is prepped and ready to deploy."

Love gave a slight nod. "Thank you, Captain, for the update. The *Donovan* should be crossing the stargate shortly. I'll apprise you once it happens and hopefully have an ETA for you on when we'll be able to disembark the *Donovan* to get you dirtside."

With the formalities observed, she nodded to Ford. The two of them performed their final system checks as they got the shuttle ready. Once they exited the stargate, they would be in enemy territory—alone and on their own.

"Hey, once we're through the gate, we'll need to do a full systems check again—you know how it seems to have a way of resetting things like navigation?"

Ford snickered at the comment. "Acknowledged. Maybe one of these days, they'll figure out why the stargate seems to jack with the flight navigation systems." It was a common problem with the Ospreys and Scarabs, but the larger warships seemed immune to it.

The countdown displayed on the HUD continued to tick closer to zero—the moment the gate would hurl them across dozens of lightyears in fractions of a second. For now, the digital timer read ten minutes, thirty-one seconds.

"Ready to make history?" Love asked.

"Ah, duh, of course I'm ready to make history. I can't believe, of all people, that you asked me that."

"Hey, people change," she quipped. "Just making sure you've kept that warrior spirit burning from our glory days."

"You mean our younger days—yeah, that part of me will never change no matter how many new gray hairs I find."

Love pulled Jack's picture from her pocket. She then unwrapped a piece of chewing gum and popped it into her mouth. As soon as the gum was sticky enough, she pressed it against an empty spot on her dashboard, using it to secure his photo. She blew a kiss to the image of her deceased husband. It was an old ritual from the days when she used to fly transports in the first war against the Zodarks, the menacing orc-like foes responsible for his death.

Ford glanced over. "You gonna christen this ship the RNS *Jack*, like the first Osprey we flew?"

She shook her head, her gaze steady on the console. "No. We're sticking with *Ghost One*."

"Are you sure?" Ford pressed. "Jack's always been our lucky charm."

She exhaled a short breath as her eyes dropped to the dashboard before meeting Ford's again. "I know, but it's time to let Jack go, at least little by little. I've been holding on too long. And I know this is just a small step, not naming this ship *Jack*, but it gets me closer, you know?"

Ford nodded sympathetically.

Love straightened in her seat. "And we've always made our own luck, through preparation and skill. That's what's kept us alive, not charms or names or good luck images like my Jack. Good old-fashioned hard work and in service to those we protect."

"I agree, Captain. I think, however, you gotta leave some room for grace. Skill is widespread, but sometimes a bit of luck can take you places talent and preparation can't."

"True, but that's not helping me get over Jack right now." She winked.

He chuckled. "Still, that was quite the lecture on luck you just served up. How long have you been holding on to that?"

He knows me better than anyone. "About a day if you must know. Did you notice I forgot to place Jack's picture on the dash when we drilled at Verdant Ridge?"

"You noticed I almost got torn apart by a mutant bear, right?"

Love patted the photo. "All right, Jack. Given that Ford nearly met his end at the claws of a creature scarier than any horror movie I've seen, you get to stay."

"Good." Ford smiled. "I feel much better now."

Love glanced at the countdown. "Five minutes. You ready?"

He gave a sideways grin. "How many times do I have to tell you?"

"As your captain, as many times as I ask."

He nodded. "True. And sometimes, annoyingly true."

"We've got a lot of combat drops ahead of us. It's going to be a long day." She cracked her knuckles. "Four minutes until go time."

Chapter Twelve
Behind Enemy Lines

RNS *Maddox*
Pfeinstgard System

Captain Tim Haas drummed his fingers on the table as he sat with the other company commanders in the SCIF or sensitive compartmented information facility, waiting for the briefing to begin. For six weeks, the *Maddox* and its expeditionary force had traveled across much of Primord space until they reached the Kita system—the headquarters of the Primord Navy. The Fleet stopped for a week, allowing the soldiers a chance to get off the ship and explore another world, another planet where the local populace wasn't trying to kill you.

After the short stayover, the Fleet resumed its journey, a bit larger, having collected a couple dozen troop transports and warships from the Primords, with the combined fleet underway. Tim was counting the days until they would eventually reach Pfeinstgard, a Primord star system and major logistical hub along the periphery of the Zodark Empire. No one had been read in on what the mission was or where it would take place. The only thing they had been told was to focus their training on deep reconnaissance—typically behind enemy lines, alone and on your own for long periods. In Tim's mind, this likely meant they'd be inserting onto a Zodark-controlled planet or moon.

I wonder if we're finally going to invade Tueblets—the hub of the Zodark Empire…

The door to the SCIF opened and Captain Toni Gosinski walked in. She pulled the door closed behind her before walking to her seat.

Ugh, why is it always the ship captain who's late? Tim thought to himself as he tried to keep the look on his face benign.

"Afternoon, Colonel Eliason, Captains. I apologize for my tardiness. We just entered the Pfeinstgard system before I came here. Call me old-fashioned, but I like to make sure the system my ship jumps into is, in fact, friendly before leaving the bridge," explained Captain Gosinski, the clock on the wall showing seventeen minutes past the time she had told them to meet her in the SCIF.

Colonel Eliason waved a hand at the apology. "Water under the bridge, Captain. From the request to meet in the SCIF, I assume it's time to share what our mission is," the colonel said, giving voice to what all his captains suspected.

Tim watched her smile, nodding in agreement. "That would be an astute assessment, Colonel. I would have shared sooner if it had been my call," she commented, then tapped a few times on her Qpad. "Each of you should receive a nondisclosure agreement you'll need to sign. It's the cover sheet for your orders. I'll give everyone a few minutes to skim them over before seeing if anyone has some questions. I've got some additional information to pass along before we end."

Tim opened his Qpad, signing the NDA after just a cursory glance. He found the NDAs a bit redundant. They were Deltas. Everything they did was classified, and every Delta held a Top Secret–Counterintelligence Level IV clearance. There was little they weren't cleared to know.

Searching for the summary, he found the BLUF statement, reading it once, then a second time before moving to the body of the text. *Damn, this is going to be tough...*

The more he read, the more he understood why the briefing was being held in one of the ship's four dedicated SCIFs. These were special rooms and workspaces built with enhanced electronic shielding and protection from eavesdropping both from within and outside the ship.

"Colonel, tell me this isn't a one-way mission?" Captain Jenna Tulip or JT from Delta Company asked.

When he didn't hear a response, Tim looked up, seeing the other captains had done the same as they collectively looked at Colonel Eliason, who still hadn't responded to the question.

"Sir—"

"I heard you the first time, JT—no, this isn't a one-way mission," Eliason interrupted hotly. "Look, no one said this was going to be an easy mission. If it's being given to Delta, it's because we're the only ones who can do it. Captain Gosinski, you said you had some additional information to share with us. I think now would be a good time."

Gosinski nodded, her facial expression serious. "As Colonel Eliason pointed out, this is not meant to be a one-way mission. The Gravaxia system is next door to Tueblets. If the alliance is going to invade Tueblets, it needs to secure the Gravaxia system. Now, the Fleet isn't going to expect you to just use the stargates and waltz right into a Zodark core world.

"For those of you who don't know what ships are traveling with our task force, we have an Altairian *Digimon* supercarrier with us. When the time is right, the Altairians will open a bridge connecting the Primord system Pfeinstgard with Gravaxia. Once the bridge is open, you'll cross in this." An image of a Republic frigate began floating in the center of the conference table and the room fell silent, everyone staring at the ship before them.

"What you're looking at is the SOCOM Type-001.1 frigate RNS *Donovan*. The *Donovan* is as close to a stealth or ghost ship as we can get. While it's no *Vraxerian*-class stealth corvette, it's pretty damn close to that Gallentine ship, as close as we can build," Gosinski explained as Tim and his fellow captains looked on with excitement.

"The plan calls for the *Donovan* to cross into the Gravaxia system and then continue until it reaches the planet Torvulkis." As she spoke, an image of the planet replaced the *Donovan* on the center of the briefing table. A sidebar menu displayed some details of the planet, denoting it as a lush Earth-like world with sprawling mountain ranges and deep blue oceans. It was noted that the planet hosted a variety of bioluminescent forests, which were supposed to be home to several sentient species, according to Altairian intelligence.

"Torvulkis also has a habitable moon, Lunakor. According to Altairian intelligence, the moon has a thin atmosphere and gravity close to Earth's. It's known for its rich mineral deposits and peculiar magnetic anomalies. Nearby is the next planet, Zenthara—a semi-arid planet dotted with massive canyons and deep lakes. Intelligence reports it has some kind of flora and fauna that thrive in its unique climate, but the Zodarks themselves do not. As such, they have developed a series of habitable domed cities within its canyons—creating economic zones for commerce and scientific research per Altairian intelligence, blah, blah, blah," Captain Gosinski chuckled as she read aloud.

She then leaned forward, her face serious again. "Look, all kidding aside, this mission is important. The Fleet must succeed in capturing Tueblets. This would effectively split the Zodark Empire into five separate segments as Tueblets is a critical stargate hub. But before we can move on to Tueblets, we have to capture the Gravaxia system. With Gravaxia secured, our supply depots will be connected with the

Primord system Pfeinstgard, all the way to Tueblets. With this pathway secured, we'll be able to support our invasion of Tueblets and across the rest of their empire.

"This is an important mission; we have to capture the Gravaxia system, and before we can do that, it has to be scouted," Gosinski explained, then held a tablet up. "What little information we have on this system is thanks to our Altairian friends. While I'm not one to look a gift horse in the mouth, the intelligence is, how shall we say…lacking in depth and detail. What we do know is this. We have to destroy the Zodark communication relay facility on the moon Lunakor and the military bases on the planets Torvulkis and Zenthara. On each of these planets are three fighter bases from which the Zodarks can launch starfighters and bombers to attack our supply convoys en route to Tueblets.

"This means we need to deal with this threat. To do that, we need a more detailed reconnaissance of these locations. That's where you guys come in and why the *Donovan* has been chopped to us for this mission. Now, once the *Donovan* has crossed into the Gravaxia system, the ship will head to the moon and the two planets, dropping your units off to conduct your missions. Once on the surface, you'll have six days to complete your reconnaissance and mission objectives before returning to a set of coordinates to await evac back to the *Donovan*—"

"Sorry to interrupt, Captain, but about that evac? How exactly is that going to be done, considering we're going to HALO to the surface from the *Donovan* itself?" JT interrupted. Tim smiled and nodded approvingly.

Gosinski tapped at the keys in front of her. The holographic image of the *Donovan* changed to a new image, and there were a few gasps of surprise.

"The *Donovan* will get you into orbit—the SLX Shadow Lynx will return you from the surface to the *Donovan*," she explained as Tim and his fellow captains looked on in amazement at this newest shuttle.

"Wow, that is slick as hell," one of the captains commented.

As Tim stared at the Lynx, a thought popped into his mind. "Hold up a second. That kind of looks like a Chickenhawk—"

"No way. Tell me that's not a reconfigured Chickenhawk," JT interrupted, bemused.

Captain Gosinski quickly cut in. "As I was saying, the Lynx is the vehicle that's going to get you off the surface and back to the

Donovan. Once all units have been recovered, the ship will return to the jump point and wait for the bridge to reopen.

"Now, back to this question about the Chickenhawk—yeah, it's basically a heavily modified Chickenhawk. It does the job, and that's what matters. Colonel Eliason, this concludes the Fleet's portion of your brief. I'll leave the rest of it up to you and how you want to assign your ODAs. In eight hours, the *Donovan* will dock with us. You'll have four hours to get your gear and people aboard before it shoves off to link up with the Altairians for the bridge. Good luck, Colonel—to victory!" Gosinski finished, standing as she saluted, then exited the SCIF, leaving him to his officers.

Chapter Thirteen
Tomb of the Warriors of Taldrek

High Council Building
Private Study of the Zon
Drokanis, Zinconia
Zodark Home World

Zon Otro sat in his private study, a room that reflected both his storied past and the burdens of his current responsibilities. The walls were adorned with relics from countless campaigns: the shattered remnants of an enemy's standard, a collection of meticulously polished weapons, and the preserved heads of the most formidable adversaries he had vanquished. These trophies, glinting in the dim light, served as constant reminders of the battles fought and the empires built on the bones of the defeated.

The latest intelligence report from the Groff lay open on his desk, its contents heavy with the grim reality of their situation. The Galactic Empire, having dismantled the Orbots—the Zodarks' once-mighty patrons—were now setting their sights on territory belonging to the Pharaonis, the last significant power within the Dominion Alliance. With the Orbots' fall, the Zodarks had assumed leadership of the fractured alliance, but their newfound authority came with the impossible task of holding the line against an unstoppable force.

Otro's eyes scanned the report, his mind racing to find a strategy that could save the Empire. The holographic display flickered, showing troop movements, enemy ship deployments, and the grim prognosis of their analysts. The enemy was methodical, relentless, and it always seemed a step ahead.

"Damn it," Otro muttered, slamming his fist on the desk. The vibrations caused a small, intricately carved statuette—a gift from a conquered chieftain—to topple over. He barely noticed. His mind was elsewhere, grappling with the grim calculations of war. "How the froth do we stop them?"

The door to his study slid open silently, and NOS Vorun Talvex entered, his expression one of urgency. A childhood friend and trusted advisor, Vorun had always served with honor, and his loyalty was beyond question.

"Zon," Vorun began, his voice steady but tinged with concern. "NOS Zarun is requesting a private audience. He says it's a matter of grave importance."

Otro's eyes narrowed. Zarun was not one to overstate issues. If he deemed something grave, it likely was. "Did he give any indication of what it was about?"

Vorun shook his head. "No, only that it couldn't wait."

Otro sighed, pushing the report aside. The weight of leadership was a heavy mantle, one that seemed to grow heavier with each passing day. "Very well. But no one can see him visit the High Council Building or know that we met."

"Do you want me to ask him where and when the two of you should meet, or do you have a place in mind?" Vorun asked.

Otro paused as his mind raced through potential locations where they could meet while obfuscating their true purpose for visiting the same place should either of them be spotted. "No, I have an idea. Tell Zarun to meet at the Tomb of the Warriors of Taldrek at Taldrek Park tonight—the three a.m. changing of the guard, when most are asleep. Ensure the security detail is aware of my movements and takes every precaution to remain unseen. I don't want anyone to know about this in advance."

Vorun nodded. "Good choice for a meeting location. Taldrek Park, that's in the Zenarix Grove District, correct?"

"It is. It's along one of the routes my security detail drives me through on my way here from my estate. Stopping to pay homage to the Tomb would not be seen as going out of my way. It's perfect cover," Otro explained.

Vorun seemed impressed. "Very clever, Zon. I will make the arrangements immediately."

The door closed behind Vorun, and Otro leaned back in his chair, contemplating the evening ahead. Taldrek Park was a secluded area, far enough from the main thoroughfares to avoid prying eyes but close enough to the Council building for a swift retreat if necessary.

He glanced at the clock on the wall. There were still several hours before their planned clandestine meeting. Until then, he needed to prepare himself mentally for whatever revelations Zarun would bring.

The weight of his responsibilities pressed down on him like never before. He rose and began to pace the room, his eyes falling again on the various trophies of his past victories. Each item told a story of triumph and resilience, of battles won against formidable foes. But this new battle, one fought in the shadows of politics and deceit, felt different—more insidious.

As the hours passed, Otro continued to pore over the intelligence reports, cross-referencing troop movements and supply lines, trying to find any angle, any opportunity to exploit. The Galactic Empire's advance was relentless, and with the internal threat now looming, the stakes were higher than ever.

Finally, the time came. Otro donned his jacket, then let his security detail know he was ready to head home and asked to bring the vehicle around. When he saw his head of security, he shared the details of his appointment at Taldrek Park, making sure they were ready to handle it.

As they reached Taldrek Park, the vehicle came to a halt. When Otro stepped out into the stillness of the night, the only noise he could hear was the rustling of leaves and the distant hum of the city. Otro moved to a secluded bench under the cover of large, ancient trees, waiting for Zarun to arrive.
****

Taldrek Park, Zenarix Grove District
Drokanis, Zinconia
Zodark Home World

Zarun moved silently through the shadows, his senses alert. Years of being a master spy and assassin within the Groff had honed his instincts. He had just returned from a multiyear operation, uncovering a massive corruption scheme. When he'd started working at the Groff's main office, he had begun to notice troubling activity. Digging deeper, he'd found corruption reaching the highest echelons of power.

As he approached the meeting spot, he saw Zon Otro standing by a secluded bench. This 3:00 a.m. changing of the guard was rarely well attended, but it would not have been uncommon for Zodarks of their rank to give honor in this way. Zarun remembered that Zon Otro's security detail regularly traveled a route that took them past this park. Since becoming Zon, Otro had developed a routine of stopping to pay homage to several of the war memorials along the different routes his security detail routinely traveled. To Zarun, it made sense that Otro would choose a meeting location that wouldn't deviate from his normal routine. That would make it easier to conduct secretive meetings like the one they were about to have. Taking a deep breath as he confirmed no one else beyond the Zon, his security detail, and the guards were present, Zarun felt it was safe to step into the clearing, his footsteps soft against the grass as he silently acknowledged the guards, their nods letting him know it was safe to approach.

"Zarun," Otro greeted him, his voice low. "You said this was urgent. What do you have?"

"Yes, Zon, this matter is urgent and troubling," Zarun began, keeping his voice ominous and steady as he began to explain. "As you know, Zon Utulf recalled me from an operation he had tasked me with many years ago, in his final acts as Zon and before transferring his title and authorities to you. He gave me one final task, a final mission to protect what the two of you had achieved for the Empire during this transition period from those who might seek to take advantage of it—"

"Yes, Utulf warned me of this period," Otro interrupted, his patience running short. "Cut to the chase, Zarun. You found something— what is it?"

Zarun smiled at Otro's perceptiveness. "A few weeks ago, I began to observe some unusual activity from Director Vak'Atioth's office. Two of his more loyal henchmen were quietly transferred to Sector Quaqua[1] along with several large tranches of money. Suspecting something wasn't right, I continued to monitor the activities of these individuals until it became clear what they were doing. As I am sure you are aware, during the past few moona,[2] there has been growing distrust in your leadership since you became Zon, and now I know why," explained Zarun as he motioned for Otro to let him finish. "Sector Quaqua appears to be the source of this whisper campaign to call into question your fitness to hold the title of Zon. Rumor has it that, in fact, you colluded with Zon Utulf to purchase not just your seat on the Council but your position as Zon. There is even a rumor that Councilman Tanhilff is not leaving because his final term is ending—he is leaving because you have either blackmailed him into it or offered him money to leave

---

[1] Qua is the Zodark word for the number four. Quaqua is 44.
[2] Moona is the Zodark word for month.

early—creating a vacancy on the Council that you plan to sell to the highest bidder or to fill with a loyalist to further your ambitions and secure future votes."

Zarun saw Otro's eyes flash with anger as he spoke—the eternal flame burning near the Tomb illuminating them in the dark. "Tell me, Zarun," he growled, "what is the purpose of this scheme?"

"To undermine your authority, your legitimacy—to create civil unrest and chaos," replied Zarun. "They even say Councilman Gorax Nivtur of the Niftar tribe, a member of the Clan Tash-Murkon—of Murkon shipyards and TM Industries—was given his seat to ensure more of the Malvari's future warships are produced through Murkon shipyards and not the shipyards of other clans. There is a claim that for every warship they produce, both of you are given kickbacks, a percentage of a prearranged cost overrun for each ship."

Otro's expression continued to darken the more Zarun shared. "Zarun, you are certain that this whisper campaign—this tarnishing of my honor—is happening at the direction of Director Vak'Atioth?"

Zarun hesitated at the gravity of what these actions would ultimately lead to if they were not stopped and countered. "Yes, Zon. I believe Director Vak'Atioth is directing the spreading of these rumors through Sector Quaqua for the purposes of destroying your reputation, your honor, and public trust in you. It almost feels like this whisper campaign of lies and deceit is intended to prepare the public for more brazen accusations and eventual public support for investigating the High Council, and you in particular—"

"To what end, Zarun? What is Vak'Atioth hoping to achieve?"

"Isn't it clear, Zon? Vak'Atioth and the Groff can't move against the High Council without broad, sweeping support from the people likely demanding such actions. The Groff is going to need the will of the people to move against the Council. It's a coup, Zon, and it's against you."

Otro's eyes narrowed. "So Vak'Atioth thinks he can pull off a coup...do you think Heltet is involved?"

Zarun shook his head quickly. "No, there's no evidence of that. In fact, Vak and Heltet's relationship has spiraled badly since the disaster in Sol. Since it was discovered that Dakkuri, Heltet's spymaster, was the betrayer, the reason the Malvari was defeated in Sol, the two seldom talk, let alone trust each other."

Otro grunted at the assessment, then paced for a moment, deep in thought. "Maybe Heltet could help us. Keep us apprised of whatever activities you guys think are worth monitoring."

Zarun nodded. It wasn't a bad idea. He was the Lakish, after all, and that role gave him broad powers he could use when the time was right. "I hadn't considered approaching Heltet. After further consideration, though, it's not a bad idea. Having the Lakish on our side when it comes time to put an end to this, to present our case to the court and remove Vak'Atioth from power…"

Otro stopped pacing and turned to him, his eyes burning with resolve. "You have done a great service to the Empire, Zarun. Utulf was wise to have you watch our backs during the transition period. Moving against the Groff will not be easy. We will need to document everything because when the time comes, we will have to act swiftly. The Empire stands on the verge of being invaded. We cannot be a divided people, not at this moment, not if the Empire is to survive."

With that, they parted ways, each knowing their tasks, lost in thought as they contemplated the turbulent days ahead and the battles they would face to protect the Empire.

Chapter Fourteen
Hot Drop

Task Force 28
RNS *Donovan*
Gravaxia System

Captain Naomi Love glanced at the onboard clock, noting it had been thirty-seven hours since RNS *Donovan* and *Valiant* had successfully slipped through the stargate undetected by the Zodarks. They had inserted Delta teams on the surface of five planets and moons without being detected. Now, with the fifth mission complete, *Ghost One* was returning to the barn to reset and prep for the sixth.

Love kept her eyes hidden beneath her visor, a constant display of data and other essential information constantly updating. The chill of space did little to dampen the intensity of her latest mission, a covert operation taking her and Master Chief Brian Ford across Lunakor. Previously, they'd performed several insertions on another Gravaxia system moon. It'd been a long day.

They were in Zodark territory. *Ghost One*'s electromagnetic stealth capabilities were among the most advanced in the fleet, rendering the ship virtually invisible to enemy sensors. Engineered with a sophisticated skin made to absorb and diffuse energy waves, the Lynx faded into the background noise of space. When Love had asked how it worked, she'd been told the hull had been coated in a sort of composite material that diffused its thermal signature. The Lynx also had the benefit of operating with a near-nonexistent electromagnetic output. This made it impossible for Zodark sensors to detect them. If there was an advantage the Republic held over its adversaries and allies alike, it was in the field of electronic warfare.

Even the engine emissions were modified to emit a frequency closely resembling the background noise of cosmic microwave radiation. As its moniker suggested, *Ghost One* was a digital ghost ship—evading enemy sensors near and far.

"Hey, Ford, you feeling tired yet?" Love asked.

Ford chuckled. His voice crackled through her helmet with a familiar sarcasm. "Tired? Me? Come on. I'm just getting started?" He adjusted his seat, turning to face her with a grin. "That landing back on

Lunakor was something else, though. It had to be one of your slickest maneuvers yet. You know, skirting right through that canyon with barely a meter to spare to either side."

Love nodded as she glided the Shadow Lynx into *Donovan*'s docking bay. "Couldn't have done it without your helpful commentary. 'Port side, three degrees... starboard, now!' It's like dancing to your tune, Master Chief."

As they touched down, Ford unbuckled and hurried through the cabin to the ramp. He hit the ground running, inspecting the undercarriage and engines. His voice buzzed through the comm as he listed off a few minor tweaks needed before their next run. "Thrusters are showing slight wear, nothing a quick tune-up won't fix. Fuel lines are all clear, though—good for another round, but we need fuel cells charged in the auxiliary bay. That last maneuver drew more power than usual."

Meanwhile, Love stepped out of the cockpit, her boots thumping softly against the metal deck as she walked through the cabin. She paused to check the nav-com interface to make sure their route data for the upcoming mission had been successfully uploaded. The cabin soon bustled with the arrival of the next ODA team, prepped for their own deployment.

She glanced at the name patch on one of the operators' battle suits. "Sergeant Goodwin, everything's set for the quick drop?"

"Affirmative, Captain. We're ready to ghost in, gather intel on the Zodarks, and ghost out. Minimal fuss, maximum impact," he responded.

"Good. Let's keep it smooth and tight. I want everyone back here for the jump home when it's time. No heroes," Love said.

A massive soldier approached Love with a firm stride, his Dragon Skin armor gleaming under *Ghost One*'s lights. "Heard a lot of good things about you, Captain Love. They say you're the best flier in town."

Love glanced at the patch on the man's suit. It read "Capt. Tim Haas." She corrected him with a wry grin. "No. Not *flier*, Captain. It's pilot. And not just the best in town. I'm the best across the entire galaxy. Get it right."

Haas laughed as he took a seat, inspecting his rifle. "Got it." He locked the weapon's action into place. "Glad we've got you on board, that's all I'm saying. I heard there used to be a wall plate or something soldiers would tap before boarding your Osprey back in the day?"

She nodded. "You know me well, Captain. I'm glad to see you've done your homework. Indeed, right after the ramp—I had it engraved with 'Vivere Pugnare Alium Diem.' It means 'Live to Fight Another Day.' I expect you and the rest of your team to take that to heart."

He dipped his head. "Yes, ma'am. Gladly."

Love surveyed the gathering. The elite soldiers looked like titans in their gear. If superheroes were real, these were them—the bravest of the brave, ready to follow their brothers and sisters into the fray of any battle.

Ford reentered the ship, clapping his hands as if brushing off dust. "All set, Captain. Let's not keep the moon waiting."

They returned to the cockpit, initiating preflight checks with a series of holographic taps, bringing the ship's systems to life. Love's fingers paused over the photograph glued by chewing gum to the dashboard. She kissed her fingers and pressed them against the image of a smiling man in uniform. "For luck, Jack."

Love flipped the final switches. *Ghost One* hummed with power. Its systems lit up green across the board.

"Strap in. We're about to make our exit," she announced over the comm system. Next to her, Ford secured his harness, his eyes on the forward viewport.

Love engaged the thrusters. The Shadow Lynx vibrated underfoot as it detached from *Donovan*'s docking clamps. The ship's hull receded from view as they maneuvered out of the hangar bay.

The bay doors ahead opened slowly. A sliver of darkness grew with each passing second. Outside the viewport, the stars shined against the infinite black. Love adjusted the thrusters. *Ghost One* moved smoothly, its engines emitting a low, powerful thrum as they approached the bay exit.

As they crossed the threshold, the light from the nearby asteroid belt caught the edges of the Lynx. It cast shadows against the craft's angular body. The belt's rocky bodies tumbled silently in their age-old dance.

"*Ghost One* is clear of the *Donovan*, proceeding to Lunakor," Love said over the comm. She steadied the controls as she steered the

Lynx into a calculated trajectory around the other side of the *Donovan*, taking them away from the asteroids. She found the pattern of the asteroids odd, almost like they were part of the planet's rings, yet a stream of the giant rocks looked to have carved its own path across part of the rings before extending back into deeper space. As they rounded the *Donovan*, the view was breathtaking. They could see Torvulkis, with its dense rings of ice crystals, cosmic dust, giant chunks of rocks, and other material.

"There, that's it." Ford pointed down at a seventy-degree angle.

Love's eyes followed his finger until she saw it—Lunakor. Its unique orbit around Torvulkis had thankfully kept it traveling at an angle that avoided the planet's rings and the dangers within that would all but doom it. Instead, its path acted like a protective shroud, obscuring it at first glance from prying eyes. That was likely why intelligence believed this moon was certain to have a large Zodark presence. It made sense to utilize a habitable moon with such natural defenses and proximity to the stargate that led into the Primord system Pfeinstgard.

Ford sighed audibly, commenting, "I'm glad we're on the final mission—the last team. I'm beat and ready to get back to my book."

"Haha, that's funny. You said book," she replied, poking fun at him.

"Whatever, ma'am. You've got your thing, and I've got mine."

As the *Donovan* continued to slip further away, Love kept the *Ghost* on a steady speed and trajectory toward Lunakor. In contrast to many of the planets and moons they had dropped troops on, Lunakor was the prettiest of them. It was filled with a lush landscape—veiled with verdant forests creeping over gentle hills and deep valleys. It was even dotted with sparkling lakes that gave the moon's atmosphere a green glow around the small celestial sphere.

Somewhere down there, there were supposed to be hidden Zodark bases and covert operations beneath its canopy. Nearby, Torvulkis's vibrant swirl of blues and greens lit up space with an azure aura. Its vast oceans and sprawling mountain ranges stretched across the horizon, a scene so reminiscent of Earth.

Ford peered into the dimly lit radar screen. "Unknown vessel detected at bearing zero-four-eight, range fifty-one thousand kilometers, trajectory holding steady in the asteroid belt aft of our current vector."

Love stayed on course. "Visual on target. Confirm our stealth systems are active?"

"Aye, Captain. All stealth measures are active and holding. We're ghosts out here. No detection or targeting by enemy sensors."

"Keep a sharp eye; we're moving down in the atmosphere," Love said, double-checking her trajectory. All was good as they began their descent.

She patched into the intercom. "Listen up, Deltas. We're dipping into the atmospheric entry. Prepare for turbulence."

As *Ghost One* breached the upper atmosphere, the craft began to shudder violently, a little too violently for her taste.

Suddenly, Love's interface started flashing red—alarms blaring that something was wrong. "What did we just hit?"

As *Ghost One* bucked and shuddered, Ford had a hunch he wanted to check. Activating the onboard Doppler weather radar, he throttled the radar's power output to just twenty percent—if he went any higher, he'd risk detection.

He watched as the radar swept the area a couple of times to build a picture of what was happening around them. "Whoa, look at that—I've never seen a weather disturbance like this. The computer is saying it's something called a gravitic cyclone?"

Love looked perplexed. "Wait, explain that to me again?" No sooner had the words left her lips than the Lynx dropped more than a thousand meters in the span of seconds.

"Hang on!" she shouted, pulling back hard on the flight control as she fought to pull them out of whatever downward vortex they had somehow fallen into. As she regained control, she leveled the Lynx into a hover.

Everything in front of them was covered in fog. "Holy hell, Ford. That was insane."

"Yeah, let's not do that again," Ford stammered. "And what is this now? It's like we're flying through a white blanket all of a sudden."

"Who knows—but that anomaly or whatever it is on the Doppler looks like trouble," Love responded. Their eyes were now fixed on the onboard weather program as it fed them a real-time update of their current weather situation. "I don't like this, Ford. That weather pattern looks fast-moving, and it's directly in our path."

She veered to the right as she readjusted their course and headed to get them back on track. "Damn, this storm is crazy. It's a fight to keep on course—you got more data on this thing yet?" Whatever loomed outside, it covered everything in white for as far as the eye could see.

"I'm waiting for it to come up and…" Ford's lips moved as he read silently, wrinkles creasing his brow. "Uh, yeah… it's some type of volatile mix of gravitational fluctuations and charged particles. It's creating severe, unpredictable turbulence, is what the computer said."

"Well, yeah! It's off the charts, Ford! I'm keeping her steady, but hang on to something!" Love shouted over the roar of the struggling engines. The ship banked seemingly on its own and dove. Numbers on the instrument panels ticked wildly as they passed through the dense, swirling currents of the storm they had flown into.

Bang, bang, bang came a pounding noise against the cabin door behind them.

Love motioned toward the cabin. "Check on the Deltas—find out what's going on," she said through gritted teeth as the ship continued to lurch about.

"On it." Ford unstrapped, grabbing the back of his chair as Love continued to fight the storm. Reaching the door, he pushed it open, walking into the bay. Seconds after he entered, his strained voice carried through into Love's helmet. "I made it to the bay—it's a mess back here. Something happened with the straps. They must have come loose— we've got supplies, gear, ammo, and explosives strewn about in here. Hell, I can barely stay on my feet right now."

"Copy that. Nothing we can do about it until we're out of this mess. Do what you can to help, but get it fixed and get up here!"

"Roger."

Love continued to wrestle with the controls, her every move countered by another violent jolt from the Lynx. *I wouldn't be surprised if those Deltas are turning green about now. So much for me being the best pilot in the galaxy.*

The Shadow Lynx's engines whined loudly, a clear sign of distress from the gravitational strains. Ford reported from the back, his voice tense: "Captain, that loud whining noise from the engines—it's coming from the power conduits. They're misaligning from the stress of these storm vortexes that keep tossing us about. I'm going to try manually rerouting the power flow to stabilize them again!"

The cockpit shook hard as the dashboard blinked off—the engines were dead. "Whoa, what the hell, Ford! Get the power back online *now*!" Without power to the engines, the vessel dipped and angled downward. It was in free fall until the engines could restart.

"I'm working on it!" Ford yelled.

At worst, they'd crash and die—but maybe not the Deltas. They could jump if they had to once they got closer to the ground. If no last-ditch efforts worked, both Love and Ford would strap on a chute and leap out of the falling Shadow Lynx as well.

Not on my watch, Love thought. She'd only lost one ship in her whole career, and she refused to bring that count up to two.

Love pulled back on the controls. They still didn't respond. "Come on, Ford!"

For a second, the power turned on. But the engines were a no-go.

She flicked the small window on one of her dashboard interfaces and switched to a cabin view. The Deltas sat, seemingly unfazed. One of them glanced at his watch. Another pointed to the cabin door, a way out via a jump.

Her heart thumped as the altimeter ticked down. In three minutes, *Ghost One* would plummet to a fiery death if they didn't get the engines fixed ASAP. Then the power flicked off a second time.

"Status, Ford!"

"Captain, I'm rerouting auxiliary power to the main drive. I've got to reset and align the magnetic coils and recalibrate the cell charge to the thrusters. Hang tight. I'm almost there." The sound of tools clanked in the background as he worked in the small engine compartment. "Just about..." Ford's voice trailed off for a moment. "Now!"

The ship's power grid hummed back to life. Then the engines kicked on, ramping up to full power as she sought to regain control of their descent.

From the cockpit, Love gripped the controls. *Ghost One* renewed its strength beneath her. With a skilled pull, Love leveled out the craft and steadied it against the lingering buffets of the storm. As if in response to their regained power, the white mist enveloping them dissipated. The hectic chaos of the storm cleared, and they emerged into calmer skies. Below them lay a lush expanse bordered by massive, spindly trees. Their canopies formed a dense green roof over a forest floor.

Hot damn, all that and we're still on course to the DZ. "All right, we're approaching the drop zone on this ridge. Looks like we're clear of enemy activity," Love said over the intercom.

The engines thrummed with power as Love guided the craft downward. *Ghost One* hovered momentarily over an opening in the forest canopy. Its downward thrusters displaced leaves and small branches in a flurry. Slowly, Love lowered the craft through the gap. The underbelly sensors calculated the distance to the forest floor with meticulous accuracy.

As the Shadow Lynx descended, the landing gear deployed with a solid clunk. The craft made gentle contact with the hard topsoil and thick foliage below. A slight bounce indicated the dampening systems adjusting to the uneven terrain.

Inside the cockpit, Ford kept his eyes glued to the sensor readouts, scanning for any signs of possible enemy movements they might have missed. He pursed his lips. "Area's clear of hostiles," he said over the comm. "We're not detecting any Zodark soldiers near our position."

Love lowered the ramp as the craft settled on the ground. "Delta team, you are green to go." Love relayed the information through her headset to the operators in the cargo bay. "Exit is clear. Good luck down there. I'll be back for extraction. Stay sharp."

One by one, the Deltas activated their gear. The sound of clasps being secured and the hum of personal armor activating filled the air. They disembarked fast, their boots thudding against the soil as they formed up in a tight perimeter outside the Shadow Lynx.

Haas signaled with a hand gesture, and the group moved out. They disappeared into the underbrush with weapons at the ready. As the last of the Deltas vanished into the dense foliage, Love and Ford turned their attention back to the systems monitor inside the cockpit. The display flashed a critical alert: the landing gear couldn't retract as programmed. Diagnostic codes scrolled across the holographic interface. They pointed to a malfunction within the hydraulic system—most assuredly a casualty of their recent tumult amidst the gravitic cyclone.

Ford patched into the diagnostic subsystem, overlaying the schematics of the landing gear on the main screen. "Looks like we've got a breach in the hydraulic fluid lines. Probably debris impact from that storm. The pressure's not holding in the retract actuators."

Love pushed her bottom lip out. "We gotta go manual on this fix."

"The usual." Ford shrugged.

They opened the Lynx's maintenance hatch and stepped into the cramped outer service bay. The external maintenance monitor lit up as Love keyed in her access codes.

Ford, with a portable tool kit strapped to his side, began disassembling the gear's protective casing. "I'm venting the remaining hydraulic fluid now to clear the line. Watch for any spillage."

"Got it," Love confirmed. I see the crack. It looks like a direct hit from a smaller fragment. The patch kit's ready." She looked around, making sure no person or creature lurked.

Ford applied a high-density sealant to the damaged lines, a temporary fix until they could perform a full replacement on the RNS *Donovan*. He repressurized the system from a compact handheld device as he watched the readouts carefully. "Pressure's stable... and... we have full retraction capability. Gear will be tucking in clean now."

"Good work," Love said. "Let's button up and get back to the cockpit. The day's not getting any shorter."

When they sat back in the cockpit, Ford exhaled. "Well, again, good piloting back there."

As Love looked up into the sky through her front viewport, the dense white storm began to crowd overhead. "You think that was good piloting? Wait until you see me bust through it from the ground."

"I'd rather fly around it."

"Well, all right. You didn't need to twist my arm for me to agree with you on that one. Strap in; it's time we return to *Donovan*."

Love revved the engines and lifted them into the air. She checked the course settings and blasted toward the moon's upper atmosphere. It'd been a long day, but in military time, the day had just begun.

Chapter Fifteen
Package Delivered

Five Days Later
ODA 3236
Surface of the Moon Lunakor
Orbit of Planet Torvulkis

"Tag, you're it. It's my turn to eat and sack out," jested Staff Sergeant Robert Goodwin as he crawled into the shared hide tent the three-man team was using.

Captain Tim Haas yawned as he stretched his limbs. Sitting up, he nodded. "I'm up. Anything happen that I need to know about?"

"No, nothing really. Same stuff, different day," Goodwin replied as he grabbed for an MRE pouch. "Ah, come on. Was it you or KM who swiped my lasagna?"

Pulling the straps to his boots tight, Haas looked at Goodwin. "I'm going to pretend you didn't just compare Menu Number 8 with real lasagna—and, no, I didn't take that tube of orangish red paste, and judging by what's left, neither did KM."

"Oh, well, it's only the three of us, so it has to be you or KM," responded Goodwin, annoyed that his favorite Meal Ready to Eat had been swiped.

"Here, look at—that's TJ's calling card." Haas pointed to the MRE tube labeled Menu Number 19—chicken à la king.

"Mother—"

"Language," Haas cut in before Goodwin could finish.

"Right, I forgot we're in grade school," replied Goodwin, referring to the new team rule—no cursing.

Haas shrugged, then grabbed the offending MRE tube, stuffing it in his pocket. "Call me crazy, I actually like the chicken à la king. But here." Haas tossed an MRE he'd retrieved from his patrol pack before placing it on his shoulders. "Like I said earlier. Don't pretend that's lasagna."

Goodwin's grin widened as he clutched the MRE tube, his frustration about the lasagna momentarily forgotten. "Whoa, you're giving me yours? You are a lifesaver, sir. I don't think I could stomach more chicken à la thing."

Haas chuckled, shaking his head as he grabbed his rifle. "Just remember, Goodwin, out here, it's the little things that keep us going. A familiar taste, reading a letter from home, or even a bad joke at the right time can make all the difference between those who survive this insane war and those who don't. Out here"—he waved his arm—"we're all we got."

"You're right, sir—but I'm still gonna mess with TJ after we get back," Goodwin said, his eyes twinkling with mischief. "He knows the code and the consequences if it's broken."

Haas, already halfway out of the hide, paused and looked back, intrigued. "The code—consequences?"

"Yeah, the code that says you don't mess with a man's food as he's about to leave on a mission," Goodwin explained. "The consequence for such an action is quite severe…Menu Number 17—a whole week!"

Haas laughed and cringed at the idea of one of his operators being down for a week. No one could be around a person who ate more than one chili mac in a row—let alone ate nothing else for seven days. "Oh man, I may need to intervene before a war crime is committed. Sentencing a man to seven days of chili mac constitutes cruel and inhumane punishment, Staff Sergeant. For the sake of good order and discipline, I may need to grant clemency in this matter."

Goodwin audibly sighed, replying with a mock salute. "Clemency, Captain? OK, but just this once."

As Haas exited, he glanced back at Goodwin, already sucking on the tube of lasagna paste. "Goodnight, Goodwin. See you in a few hours."

"Will do, Cap. Give KM my regards," replied Goodwin with a wave.

Haas turned away and started navigating the twenty or so meters to where he knew Master Sergeant Kevin Moorhead was set up. Checking the time, he saw they had two hours till dawn, the start of a new day and maybe new activity at the spaceport. Crawling slowly, methodically across and overtop the dense foliage and trees that covered the surface of this alien moon, he couldn't help but notice how different it was from New Eden—and even New Eden had stark differences from Earth and the different environments his Delta training had taken place in.

When his twelve-man team had landed on Lunakor two days ago, Haas had split them up into four three-man teams to cover the expanse of this Zodark spaceport properly. He didn't like the idea of splitting up like this, especially on a hostile planet. Unfortunately, since they couldn't use the kinds of surveillance drones they normally would when it didn't matter if the Zodarks knew they were in the area, he wasn't left with a lot of options for how to surveil the size of the target they had been given—the Tumikhala Spaceport. The facility was huge and sprawling, with two distinct halves to it. One was commercial in nature, mostly focusing on the export of whatever mineral or resource the Zodarks were mining. Thus far, they had only seen a couple of what looked to be commercial transports, likely ferrying nonmilitary Zodarks between the moon and other spaceports and cities.

On the other side of the facility, the larger side, sat what they had quickly determined was the military half of the spaceport. They saw rows of starfighters and other vehicles that could pose a threat to allied forces, particularly supply convoys. Earlier the day before, Goodwin had counted forty-three Zeeks, which meant a strong chance there were three squadrons based at the facility assuming a squadron consisting of sixteen fighters. It was likely the missing five Zeeks were in some of the hangars or undergoing repairs or maintenance out of sight. But Zeeks weren't the only things they found. They had counted seventy-three Vultures and sixty-eight Glaives—starfighters and bombers parked in neat rows in front of giant hangars and repair facilities.

While identifying the squadrons was certainly a big deal, their discovery of the vessels docked at the spaceport's main terminals for larger vessels had immediately caught the attention of Haas and his three teams. Docked at these larger terminals were eight of the Zodarks' newest vessels—the Torvex Qyiln. These were the Zodarks' newest corvettes or torpedo boats. The Zodarks had introduced them in the final year of the First Zodark War as a counter to the Republic's growing fleet of Type-001 frigates and the venerable Type-002 heavy cruisers. What made the Torvex Qyiln so dangerous was their speed and increased agility, especially when working together with other corvettes. This was also the first vessel into which the Zodarks had incorporated an increased use of antiship missile and torpedo batteries—enabling the Zodarks to launch coordinated missile and torpedo swarm attacks effectively for the first time.

Haas, is that you making all that racket behind me? If I can hear you struggling through those damn vines and thorn bushes—so can the Zodarks, challenged Master Sergeant Kevin Moorhead over their neurolink.

Haas could feel his cheeks flush—he knew his senior noncommissioned officer was right. He was failing to maintain the noise discipline necessary to avoid detection.

He confirmed his reply using the neurolink: *Affirmative, KM. I'm adjusting my approach and noise discipline. I'll be there shortly.* He readjusted his crawl to KM's position. *Stop letting your mind wander…it's going to get you and/or your team killed,* he chided himself privately.

He wasn't the only one who found it a struggle at times, getting distracted by the strange sights and sounds of this place, this alien moon in orbit of a beautiful planet. Looking up as he neared Moorhead's position, he could still see the planet Torvulkis, lush in greens, blues, and browns as they orbited the planet.

When he reached the rear of Moorhead's position, he announced his presence via their neurolink. *It's Haas—I'm approaching from your six.*

Copy, you're clear on this end. Oh, by the way, did Goodwin remind you to bring an MRE for me? Moorhead replied.

Ah crap, Haas thought, then remembered he'd placed the chicken à la thing in his cargo pocket. *As it turns out, KM, you're in luck. I happen to have an MRE tube in my pocket. I'll see you in a minute.*

Crawling next to Moorhead, he asked, "Anything to report?"

"Yeah, actually, there is something I think you might want to know. About twenty minutes ago, we had some ships come in—I got no idea if they came down from orbit or flew in from another base. But here, zooming in, you can see it," explained KM as he pointed to several darkened silhouettes docked next to the corvettes. "If you look at the silhouette of that one—compared to the Torvex Qyiln—it's got to be those Plarix Drexols—those destroyers they told us to watch out for," KM reported, showing some images he had taken with the telephoto lens.

Haas scooted closer to KM, stared intently at the images displayed on the monitor. *Damn, it does look like one of those Plarix Drexols.*

"How many did you say arrived?"

"Six. This is the closest one. The others look to have parked farthest down. I tried to see if I could find a better spot, but this is about as good as we're going to get," he replied.

"What about the other teams? Any of them got a better view?"

"Um, you know, I don't think I contacted them yet. I'm still a little hesitant about the Q-Link and not being detected. If those Zodarks so much as catch a whiff of us out here…it's not like we've got some help available should we need it. It's just us, sir," explained KM.

Haas shook his head, frustrated at KM's lack of trust in their newest piece of kit. The Q-Link stood for quantum link. It was, technically, a Special Forces version of a Quantum Nexus Communicator and used a breakthrough in the principle of quantum entanglement communications. This was where two particles remained interconnected regardless of the distance separating them, allowing for instant communication. The system could transmit voice, video, and data without using traditional signal transmission methods, making it virtually undetectable and immune to jamming or interception. It was the holy grail for SOF who routinely operated behind enemy lines or in positions where it wasn't advisable to use a comms system that would be triangulated by the enemy.

Rolling onto his side, Haas looked at KM. "I understand the reluctance, Master Sergeant. I can assure you, though, this isn't something the Zodarks are able to detect. Tell you what." Haas reached into his cargo pocket, retrieving the MRE he'd stuffed in his pocket and handing it to KM. "This might not be the MRE you wanted, but it's the one I have and it's yours. In fact, why don't you go ahead and head back to camp? Goodwin will join me in three and a half hours. I've got plenty of stuff to do that'll keep me awake. You, on the other hand, are practically falling asleep on me."

KM gave a reluctant smile but nodded in silent agreement. Grabbing his patrol pack and rifle, he scooted out of the blind they had set up and began his slow, silent crawl to their campsite.

Haas waited around for twenty minutes after KM had left before reaching into his patrol pack to retrieve one of the small containers he'd brought with him. Holding the small canister in his hand, he thought back to the printed instructions for how to activate the device's contents—the Zeta Respiratory Inhibitor.

Depressing the small button on the top of the cap, he turned the cap to the left, as if unscrewing it. Listening intently, he heard and felt three distinct clicks. Pressing the same small button again, he turned the cap to the left, one click, then two, then the final click. At this point, the small button blinked a yellow light. *Ah, now it's activating the gnats after injecting them.* He recalled the note explaining how the device worked and what it was doing at each stage. Once the blinking yellow turned a steady green, he finished unscrewing the top, opening it to the environment around him.

Unsure if he was doing this right, Haas made sure to empty the contents of the container just in front and a few feet to the right of the blind. With the first canister empty, he placed it back into his patrol pack. They had three more nights and four days left on this moon. He still had two canisters to disperse. *Plenty of time, no need to rush this...I just hope it'll work. I'm not exactly dumping this on a Zodark or in its immediate vicinity. I'll just have to trust my uncle and them to know what they were doing when creating this virus and choosing gnats as the transmission vector.*

Taking a deep breath, Haas returned his attention to the tablet connected to the Q-Link and began typing a message to his other teams. It was time to ask for a SITREP and figure out what was left on the surveillance checklist before they ran out of time to finish it.

Chapter Sixteen
Dropping Like Flies

Zidara, Gurista Prime

David and the other Kites had been brainstorming methods of eliminating one of their targets without arousing suspicion, but this particular individual was a tough nut to crack.

"Etana is just…I mean, he's kind of boring," Jess lamented, flipping her blond ponytail in frustration.

"No girlfriends who might be feeling jaded," Catalina confirmed. "And he isn't spending time with seedy company that can't be trusted."

"No penchant for gambling," said Amir, crossing his arms.

Somchai joined in: "And his job doesn't involve heavy use of technology that could become faulty."

David felt stumped as well. Etana was in excellent shape and had a clean bill of health; he had a marriage that appeared stable from the outside and eleven children that kept him very busy when he wasn't at work or involved in political activities. Every stretch of his day was filled with responsibilities. If he wasn't such a staunch supporter of the Zodarks, he'd be a solid guy. However, as the executive director of security for Enlil Labs, the manufacturer of the P2 devices, he was a linchpin in the system that needed to make way. Otherwise, it was going to be incredibly difficult to move sympathetic people into positions of power.

"Let's run through his routine again," David suggested.

Jess took it from the top, citing everything from what time he woke up to when and where he worked out, and including all the details of his daily lunch plans. He always brought his own food unless he was required to meet with someone for his job, but that was usually communicated to him no more than forty-eight hours in advance, making it difficult to slip something into his meal.

Suddenly Somchai perked up. "I think I've got it," he announced.

"Do tell," said Jess with a smile.

"Etana is not a flashy guy—even though he has eleven kids, he doesn't live in a mansion. He drives around the same vehicle he's used for almost twenty years…and *that's* our in," Somchai explained.

"I don't follow," David responded.

"See, he's avoided any trouble with the law, but he does run perpetually behind on getting his routine vehicle maintenance. Those pesky sensors…after a while, they don't calibrate the same way they used to," said Somchai, smirking.

"Now I get it," Jess replied, "but what are the details? How are we going to make this happen?"

Somchai always became a little giddy whenever anything involving technology came up, so David and the rest of the group indulged him a bit as he went into the nitty gritty of what would need to happen. Hacking into the vehicle's systems wasn't actually that hard given some of the equipment they had been given access to by Dakkuri and Ashurina, but Somchai had thought about more than just the logistics of changing the code in the vehicle's distance gauges.

"The way I see it, we will have to make adjustments at least four times over the course of a few weeks. If we do it all at once, Etana is likely to panic and manually override. However, if we get him progressively used to having less and less space in between his vehicle and those around him, when we make the final adjustment, he won't have enough reaction time left even if he were to try and take control back from the autopilot."

****

The Next Evening

For the first access into Etana's vehicle system, the Kites would actually have to put a physical device underneath the motor area—it was programmed to release sometime during the first drive, making it virtually untraceable, but it was absolutely vital to hacking the sensors. This would be the most difficult part of their mission. As a security director, Etana had cameras pointed all over every angle of his home, including his driveway. At work, the parking structure was well monitored as well. That left the two times a week that he went to watch his children practice or play for the local sports league.

Since they had been tracking Etana for a couple of weeks now, they were already very familiar with the venue. There were generally quite a few parents and children at these events, which had some benefit in that their presence wouldn't immediately be suspicious, but it also meant a lot of eyes to see what they were doing.

Jess dressed for the occasion as the Gurista equivalent of a soccer mom that was just a little too sexy to be completely kid-appropriate. The men at the event experienced whiplash at alarming rates, and the wives quickly responded with the appropriate glares.

Jess carried a large bag with food inside it, as if she were the designated snack provider for the week, and balanced a chair on her left hip. When one of the men swooped in to save her from her excessive load, Amir suddenly showed up with a large duffel bag of sports equipment, which he threw down on the ground in full temper tantrum style.

"Why are you hitting on my wife?" he yelled accusingly. "You think you can just snatch her away from me?"

The Gurista in question threw up his hands in surrender, stammering and generally unable to respond in a coherent fashion. Like a moth to the light, a crowd circled around, waiting to see what would happen. Fistfights were generally relegated to middle school on Gurista Prime, but when one did break out among the adults, everyone wanted to watch like it was a professional pay-per-view martial arts competition.

We have their attention, Somchai and Catalina, David announced over the neurolinks.

Copy that, they both replied.

Somchai approached Etana's vehicle, reading distractedly from his P2 as if he'd gotten a really important message from work and he was going to have to go back to the office to handle it. Catalina left her vehicle with her arms loaded up with gear, walking with her view partially obstructed, until she bumped right into Somchai.

He yelped as his P2 leapt from his hands and flew directly under Etana's van. He dashed over, on his hands and knees, swiftly placed the quarter-sized device in the appropriate location, and then emerged holding his P2. Somchai looked around—no one seemed to notice him. The crowd around the possible fight had grown.

Done, said Somchai.

At this point, David figured Amir had had enough fun with his acting lessons and pushed his way into the circle, where he pulled Amir back and then "talked some sense into him." Without an actual brawl, the crowd quickly dispersed, and everyone seemed to go about their business pretty quickly.

****

A Few Weeks Later

Somchai pointed to his P2 excitedly. "We did it," he announced.

"All right, go ahead," said Jess teasingly. "We know you want to read all about it so you can take the credit."

"Well, yes," Somchai replied. "You all have your strengths, and I have mine. Gather round for story time," he teased back.

Everyone humored him and took a seat, giving him their undivided attention.

"From the *Gurista Daily*. 'Tragic vehicle accident claims the life of the chief security director at Enlil Labs. Yesterday at approximately 5:23 p.m., a freight truck hit the driver's side of the vehicle belonging to Etana of the clan Kish. First responders found that Etana died on impact, and no lifesaving efforts were successful. Accident investigators found that maintenance on Etana's vehicle was overdue and that the sensors had malfunctioned, causing his vehicle to calculate that it had enough space to cross the intersection before the freight truck arrived. The driver of the truck has been fully exonerated as no foul play is suspected and he did attempt to manually override before impact.

"'Etana leaves behind a wife and eleven children. He was very active in the community and held a key role in his position at Enlil Labs, securing the P2 devices. His tragic loss is a reminder to all to stay on top of vehicle maintenance schedules. A public memorial will be held at Zidara Botanical Gardens in three days at 6 p.m. May Etana rest in peace.'"

David walked over and gave Somchai a congratulatory slap on the shoulder. "Yup, you did it. This one was all you," he declared.

"Well, not just me," Somchai admitted. "Jess and Amir deserve an Emmy for their acting, I would say." He laughed. "And thanks for tripping me, Catalina."

They all chuckled. Even in cases like this, it was always a team effort.

Chapter Seventeen
Freedom Isn't Free

Free Gurista Training Camp
Gurista Prime

Drew Kanter sat alone in the operation tent, the morning sun burning away the remnants of the morning dew. He sipped on his coffee as he placed the Kite report on the table, satisfied with the results of another successful operation. It was a grim part of the shaping operation to prepare the way for the Gurista people to eventually walk away from their Zodark benefactors and join with the Republic and the rest of humanity. Part of the shaping of the environment was the removal of problematic figures who might oppose this effort once it got underway. Drew wasn't particularly fond of this part of the operation. In the end, though, he knew if they were to have a chance of successfully pulling this off, key figures and leaders from different areas of Gurista society would need to be carefully eliminated and, ideally, replaced with like-minded people who would be open to the idea of rebelling against the Zodarks and joining with the Republic in their war to eliminate the Zodark Empire's continual threat to humanity.

Still, deep inside, Drew disliked the idea of assassinating people based on the belief that if given a choice, they would side with the Zodarks and not the Republic—their fellow humans. Of course, the names largely came from Ashurina's father, Tammuz Zidan. While he wanted to believe Tammuz had honest intentions, he still had an uneasy feeling from time to time with each list of new names. But having never lived in a society where humans and Zodarks worked together as one, he had to rely on Tammuz's judgment and trust that he knew what he was doing.

Drew sighed audibly to himself as he reached for his coffee. He stared again at the report he had finished reading earlier. He found it ironic that this particular guy, a man named Uruk, had found himself on the list of individuals Tammuz Zidan had identified as Zodark loyalists. Tammuz had explained how Uruk had worked his way up through the ranks of the capital's largest labor union, Lugal. Lugal was responsible for managing much of the public transportation that moved the goods and people about the capital. Tammuz had made a compelling case for

131

the necessity of ensuring whoever held this position would be on the side of the people when the time came.

"You look troubled," commented First Soldier Kyvorin Drayce as he sat down at the table opposite Drew. "Your operatives—the Kites—handled the Lugal mission with incredible skill and precision. You should be proud of them."

Drew gave a half-hearted smile. "Thanks. I am very proud of their professionalism and skill. I just question if what we're doing is just," he responded glumly.

The Gallentine soldier stared at him for a moment. "Perhaps this is a human trait, and I still have yet to understand it. You have a clear mission to achieve. Yet, in order to achieve it, you must first remove the obstacles to success from your path. You should count yourself fortunate to have a reliable local source who is able to help you identify the obstacles before you. What is there to be dour about?" the Gallentine questioned.

"I suppose you're right, Kyvorin. Sometimes it feels more like we're eliminating potential challengers or threats to Tammuz's new position as the Primarch. His elevation to the position came as a result of our arranging for those ahead of him to have 'convenient' and 'untimely' demises," Drew responded, using air quotes.

Kyvorin slapped Drew on the shoulder. "You worry too much, my friend. Come, let's review the success of labor," he explained as he stood, motioning for Drew to follow him outside the tent and toward the sounds of training happening nearby.

Making their way to a nearby clearing, they stopped at the edge of the trees, watching a trio of Delta operators demonstrating some fire and maneuver tactics to a couple of dozen recently recruited Free Guristas soldiers. Months after the Kites had launched their campaign of leaked videos of what the Zodarks had done to Sumer and its people, the Gurista-born people were questioning their blind loyalty to the Zodarks. They'd heard some of these claims before from those taken in tribute. But the adult tributes had, after all, been taken from their families, from all they had known, so it was easy to dismiss their outlandish claims. The videos, however, had shed an irrefutable light on just how brutal and evil the Zodarks truly were.

It was in the wake of this knowledge and with a little nudge from Dakkuri's operation that a new movement was born—Free

Guristas. At first it started with protests, street demonstrations calling for transparency in their partnership with the Zodarks. This had quickly morphed into people calling into question the Zodarks' true aim and purpose for them. Why would they act as benevolent gods with them, while treating the people of Sumer like subjugated slaves? Drew had to hand it to Dakkuri. Once this protest movement had started, he had quickly fanned its flames, spreading it to other Gurista worlds and cities. But when someone had asked why the Zodarks had begun helping them to create a spacefaring navy and a ground force that this navy would ferry to other worlds, it wasn't long until people began to grasp a more sinister reasoning behind the Zodarks' moves. They planned to use them in future wars of conquest.

It was in the aftermath of this realization that the idea of a free Gurista society—one free of their Zodark overlords—took shape and soon, it called for more than just peaceful protest. Dakkuri's operation was identifying and even recruiting civilians to join what quickly became known as the Free Gurista movement. As recruits joined the movement, they were eventually smuggled into the countryside, to a covert training facility eventually operated by not one ODA team but an entire company of six operation teams and their headquarters element.

"This right here, Drew"—Kyvorin waved his hand across, indicating the recruits listening intently to the instructions of the Delta operators—"is why those 'accidents' and 'untimely' deaths are necessary. If key positions to make this plan work are held by those who remain steadfast in their loyalty to the Zodarks, the plan will fail, as Dakkuri has pointed out. If the Director of Finance for the Zidara Treasury was not a member of the Free Guristas, we would not be able to maintain the anonymity of our recruits and their P2 devices. Without administrative access to the backend operating software of the P2 devices, Seraphel could not make the necessary changes to maintain everyone's cover and finance this operation."

First Officer Seraphel Tavon may be the only reason we haven't been discovered, Drew thought to himself—that was how indispensable the Gallentine pilot had become.

Drew sighed softly, then turned to face Kyvorin. "You're right, of course. I suppose I needed a reminder of why we have to do what we do. Cleaving the Guristas from the clutches of these bastards isn't just important for the Republic. It's important for the future of mankind and may determine whether humanity will remain a free people or become one that's subjugated to serve those with greater power. How much longer until you believe we'll be ready to start this insurgency?"

Kyvorin smiled, his demeanor brighter. "Ah, now that's the Drew I'm used to seeing. Now to your question—when should the insurgency begin?" The Gallentine soldier motioned with his head for Drew to follow him toward the still-hidden Gallentine stealth ship. "Knowing when to start an insurgency, Drew, is a complicated question. If the timing is off, the insurgency could end before it has a chance to get started.

"If I am not mistaken, Dakkuri is supposed to attend the next meeting in person. I believe the answer to the question you asked is best answered by him. His ghost operation within the Mukhabarat gives him a greater insight into what is happening behind the scenes than what we can see. In the meantime, let us discuss what kind of opening acts this insurgency should start with," offered the Gallentine soldier as they continued their walk toward the hidden stealth ship.
****

Three Days Later
Free Gurista Training Camp
Gurista Prime

Drew stared at David and his band of Kites, then turned to face the pair of Gallentine advisors before settling his gaze on Dakkuri and Ashurina. It wasn't very often that he called meetings like this. Gatherings where the entire leadership of this mission, of this insurgency, met together in one location. It was dangerous. A timely and coordinated raid could capture or kill them all—still, this meeting was important, so he'd made the call that they would meet.

Drew called the meeting to order, the conversations pausing as he began to address them. "Thank you, to everyone, for attending this gathering. I know it's risky for us to meet like this, but what we're about to discuss requires everyone's participation and input. Most of us have been on this planet for a year or more as we prepare it for what comes next. I believe we're now at that point when it's going to become necessary for us to initiate our coup against the government or start the insurgency that will inevitably lead to its downfall. Our activities can only go unnoticed for so long.

"With a little help from Dakkuri, we have successfully helped Ashurina's father, Tammuz Zidan, become the next Primarch—leader of the Guristas. In this new, expanded role he now holds, he has gone on to identify members throughout the government who he believes would remain more loyal to the Zodarks than to their own people. He has helped us identify the key players in various sectors of the government and local economy that could either help or hinder our cause. For those who haven't noticed, a string of these important people have experienced some unique and strange accidents leading to their untimely deaths. Their deaths create a hole in private and public entities that we just so happen to have a candidate ready to fill in and take their place," explained Drew as he brought everyone up to speed.

Then Drew turned to Dakkuri. "How are things going on your end? Are there any signs they might be on to you yet?"

Dakkuri acknowledged the question but stayed silent a moment more before he responded. "I do not have definitive evidence that the Mukhabarat or the Groff are on to me yet. That said, it really is just a matter of time until they eventually figure out my operation was never sanctioned. For all I know, I could show up to work tomorrow only to be greeted by a security team ready to take me in. Speaking to your question, Drew, I believe we still need more time before we initiate the coup and take control of the government. Our targeted assassinations have been working. However, the people we've moved into position need more time in their new roles to get things set in place. Additionally, should the coup fail and we have to turn this effort into an insurgency to go after the Zodarks and the Mukhabarat, we would definitely need more time.

"In an insurgency scenario, we would need a lot more weapons and explosives then we currently have. We still do not have cells established on the other colony worlds, and we've barely even begun recruiting new people on those colonies to join our cause. I'd prefer we wait to launch this operation until we are capable of executing the coup and also an insurgency. We need to be prepared in case Plan B becomes necessary."

"Dakkuri's right," David said speaking for the Kites. "I second that motion. We still have a few more targets to eliminate before we have all our people in place. Once we have our assets in position across the critical elements of the government, we can begin identifying targets we'll need the Deltas to neutralize for us during the opening hours of the coup."

The Gallentine soldier, Kyvorin Drayce, went on to add, "Should it be necessary to go after more targets, you would be wise to have small teams within many of the cities to conduct targeted attacks against Mukhabarat stations and any security force installations. Hitting them fast and hard before they have a chance to figure out what is happening or organize a defense should be among your top priorities."

First Officer Seraphel Tavon, the Gallentine naval officer and ship commander for their stealth ship, offered, "No matter which path is ultimately chosen, I can use the ship's equipment to jam communications and make sure nothing is transmitted off-world to alert the Zodarks to what's happening or request additional support in putting down the uprising."

Drew nodded along in agreement to the proposals being offered. Inwardly, he felt relieved. They were being cautious, but not to the point of jeopardizing the plan. They just needed a bit more time. Standing, he said, "OK, then it's agreed. We have some additional milestones to meet before we can implement Free Gurista."

Turning to face David, he instructed, "Move ahead with finishing your missions. I'm traveling back to New Eden to give an account of our situation and a status report of when we will likely be ready to initiate this coup. While I am at Fleet HQ, I will be requesting an alliance fleet to help us defeat the few Zodark warships in orbit and ensure we can secure the gate and prevent the Zodarks from dispatching reinforcements. For now, identify the targets that need to be neutralized once the coup is initiated. Continue to recruit, train, and prepare our recruits for their missions, and wait until I return with word from the Viceroy on when we can expect them to be ready to assist us."

As the meeting broke up, Drew hoped their plan would work. Deposing a foreign government wasn't a task he had a lot of experience with. He just hoped the unknown unknowns wouldn't come back to bite him in the ass once things got underway.

Chapter Eighteen
You Want a Quarantine?

High Council Chambers
Drokanis, Zinconia
Zodark Home World

The High Council room, with its imposing stone pillars and intricate carvings depicting the Zodarks' storied history, felt colder than usual. The Circle of Truth, a hallowed space in the center, cast long shadows under the harsh lights. NOS Tarvox Nilkar stood at attention, his eyes scanning the faces of the Council members, who scrutinized him from their elevated seats. The gravity of the situation weighed heavily on his shoulders.

Zon Otro's voice cut through the tense silence. "NOS Tarvox, explain the Malvari's request to quarantine the Gravaxia system."

Tarvox took a deep breath, steadying himself. "Councillors, as you already know, we have experienced escalating border skirmishes with Republic forces crossing into Gravaxia from neighboring Pfeinstgard, a Primord system. While these incursions could serve as a pretext for the quarantine, they are not the primary reason."

Murmurs rippled through the chamber. Councillor Gorax leaned forward, his expression severe. "Then what is the real reason, Tarvox?"

"There have been reports of a strange illness spreading quickly among soldiers across our military facilities in the Gravaxia system," Tarvox replied, his voice unwavering. "This illness is unlike anything we have previously encountered. It spreads rapidly. We have not yet detected it in other systems, but to prevent further spread, we have implemented a temporary travel restriction."

The room fell silent again, the gravity of Tarvox's words sinking in. Councillor Gorax spoke next, his tone skeptical. "What kind of illness are we talking about? Symptoms? Origin?"

Tarvox shook his head. "We are still investigating. Symptoms include high fever, delirium, and severe fatigue. It spreads through vectors, and our medics are working around the clock to understand its origin. Until our medical experts know more about the disease, we believe the system should be quarantined to help us contain it. The protocol we have in place is that any ship or soldier that enters the Gravaxia system and docks at any facilities in the system or comes into contact with anyone already present in the system must remain in the system."

Zon Otro exchanged a glance with Councillor Zulon. "This is a serious measure, Tarvox. You're suggesting we *cut off* an entire system. Is this the advice of our medical experts? What further evidence do you have that a quarantine is necessary?"

Tarvox's jaw tightened. "Our medical officials within Gravaxia first reported the odd symptoms a few months ago when a few dozen cases appeared on two military bases on the moon Lunakor, in orbit of Torvulkis. A few days later, the cases jumped to several hundred, but now they were also being reported on the planet Zenthara, its moon Selenarax, and several of our mining facilities. As of last week, the number of known cases has now increased to more than thirty thousand and the disease is present in every facility in the system. I'm afraid we have also experienced our first fatality from whatever this is."

Councillor Gorax looked concerned. "Has anyone outside of the system been told about this strange illness yet?"

"No, Councillor," Tarvox replied. "We have kept this information contained for the moment under the guise of increased cross-border raids. For now, the skirmishes provide a convenient cover for the quarantine—but that won't last, and we need an official order from the Council."

Councillor Zulon nodded slowly. "Do you believe this could be the entry point from which the Republic and their alliance might invade our territory?"

Tarvox hesitated for a moment, choosing his words carefully. "It's a possibility. The Republic's increased activity in Pfeinstgard could be a precursor. They are certainly testing our defenses and reaction times."

The Council members exchanged worried glances, the implications of Tarvox's report weighing heavily on their minds. Zon Otro finally spoke, his voice resolute. "You have made us aware of a grave risk to the Empire. We cannot afford to take unnecessary risks, especially with all the civil unrest among our people. No, we must keep this quiet as long as possible. Pursuant to the Emergency Powers Act, the Malvari's request to quarantine the Gravaxia system is approved by me. Ensure all measures are taken to contain this illness and prevent any potential breach by the Republic or their alliance."

Tarvox bowed his head slightly in acknowledgment. "Thank you, Councillors. I will ensure the quarantine is implemented immediately."

As he stepped back from the Circle of Truth, the weight of the Council's decision settled on him. The room buzzed with quiet conversations as the Council members discussed the ramifications. Tarvox's mind raced with plans to fortify Gravaxia and protect the Empire from this unseen threat.

The meeting adjourned, and the Council members filed out, their expressions a mix of concern and determination. Tarvox lingered for a moment, his thoughts heavy with the responsibilities that lay ahead. He exited the chamber, the cold corridors echoing with his footsteps as he contemplated the challenges the Empire faced.

The threat of the illness was real, but the specter of the Galactic Empire's invasion loomed larger. He needed to prepare for both—to ensure the Zodark Empire remained strong and unyielding in the face of adversity. The battle for Gravaxia had just begun, and he would be at the forefront, ready to defend his people against all odds.

Chapter Nineteen
Really, Krzysztof—Superman?

Ring Two, Gates 1–16
Terminal One, Paradise Station
New Eden, Rhea System

As Drew stepped through the hidden door into the back office of the duty-free store, he felt a wave of relief wash over him. Krzysztof's assurances had been correct; the room was empty. He glanced at his watch, noting the recent arrival of a transport from Intus. Leaving the office, he walked down the hallway, pausing just inside the shadows to observe the passengers filing through the store toward the customs agents.

A boisterous group of Republic soldiers entered, making a beeline for the Premium Interstellar Wines and Alcohol section. Drew recognized the behavior—typical of soldiers and spacers embarking on leave. Seizing the opportunity, he stepped out of the shadows and into the nearest aisle, blending in with the other shoppers. He meandered through a couple of aisles, feigning interest in various items before casually making his way towards the exit, merging seamlessly with the newly arrived passengers.

As more soldiers approached the customs agents, Drew made his move, joining the queue of humans and Primords. He strategically chose a line several stations away from the rowdy soldiers, positioning himself behind a Primord family. The presence of large army and naval bases on Intus and Kita meant that a significant number of Republic citizens frequently traveled to and from Primord space. Drew had heard about the Republic's redesigned entry process, but this was his first direct experience with it. The reforms implemented following the Zodark and Orbot invasions were a welcome sight, and the centralization of entry ports into a single station seemed like a stroke of genius to him.

"Next," the customs agent called out, prompting the Primord family ahead of Drew to step forward.

Drew watched as they presented their passports and submitted their biometrics. The agent ran their information through a database and, satisfied with the results, returned their IDs. Turning to Drew, he said, "Next."

Approaching the counter, Drew handed over his ID and waited. The agent studied the document before scanning it, then held it at eye level as he compared it to him. "Huh, Mr. Clark Kent, is it? Are you returning from business or pleasure—a ComicCon or something?"

Drew had to suppress a laugh when he heard the pseudonym the IMS had given him for this trip. *Superman? Really, Krzysztof?*

"A bit of both, I suppose—and, yeah, I get the reference. My dad was obviously a fan." Drew hastily spun the question into a joke at his own expense. "Right now, I'm just eager to get back to my own bed and some recognizable food that doesn't require me to know where the closest bathroom is."

The agent chuckled as he handed his ID back. "Yeah, strange how parents pick our names and from then on we're stuck with it." He shrugged, motioning for him to leave. "You're good. Welcome back to the Republic, Mr. Kent. Next!"

Drew collected his documents and made his way through the promenade, marveling at the design of Paradise Station. Each visit to the Rhea system showcased the incredible progress being made. The station's unique layout—a central two-kilometer-wide, four-kilometer-tall circular cylinder connected to four cylindrical rings by a series of spokes—was a testament to its efficient design.

As he approached the escalators leading to Ring One, Drew hesitated momentarily, taking in the sight of the glass tubing encasing the moving staircase. A woman in a United Travels flight uniform noticed his apprehension and reassured him, "It's safe. The escalator is enclosed in a transparent material."

"Well, I don't see anyone getting sucked into space," Drew quipped, following her onto the escalator.

As they ascended into the darkness, Drew found himself gripping the sides, awestruck by the surreal experience of traveling through space in this manner. He glanced around, noticing other travelers similarly stunned and frozen in place as they moved closer to the next level.

Reaching the end of the escalator, Drew eagerly stepped off, scanning the promenade for his destination—Hazel's Southern Home Cooking. He entered the restaurant, his eyes searching for the old-fashioned John Deere ball cap that had become increasingly popular in recent times. Suddenly, he sensed a presence behind him. Calmly, he began to turn, only to be greeted by a familiar voice.

"Welcome home, Drew. I trust your journey was uneventful?" Deputy Director Krzysztof Waclawek extended his hand in greeting.

Drew grasped his hand firmly, shaking it with a smile. "Hey, good to see you, Krzysztof—oh, and what the hell, man—Superman? Really?"

Krzysztof broke out in laughter, nearly doubling over as his face turned beet red. "Ah, come on, Drew. You have to admit, that was funny—truth be told, it was Pierre's idea. Clark Kent and all."

Drew stuck his tongue out, making a sour face. "I'm just glad it didn't cause a delay or get me pulled into secondary screening. That was a long trip, for sure. Come on, Krzysztof, let's grab a beer and some food. After the stuff I've been eating, I'm craving some good old-fashioned home cooking."

Krzysztof nodded, gesturing toward an empty table near the back of the restaurant. "I can only imagine. We have much to discuss, but first, let's get you something to eat. I hear the fried chicken here is particularly good."

As they made their way to the table, Drew couldn't help but feel a sense of unease. Despite the continued progress of his mission, he knew the real work was still ongoing, and success had not been assured. Prying the Gurista society away from the Zodarks was not going to be easy.

Settling into their seats, Krzysztof leaned back, a warm smile on his face. "So, Drew, how's your son's baseball team shaping up for the new season? I hear they've got some promising new talent."

Drew met Krzysztof's gaze, understanding the true meaning behind the innocuous question. He took a moment to gather his thoughts before responding, "The team's looking good, Krzysztof. We've been putting in a lot of work over the past fifteen months. I think it's starting to pay off. It's rewarding to see how the new players are starting to gel with the rest of the team."

Krzysztof nodded, his expression remaining casual despite the gravity of the conversation. "That's excellent news. I know you've been dedicating a lot of time and effort to get them ready for the coming season. How do you think the team's strategy is coming along?"

Drew leaned forward, lowering his voice slightly. "We've been focusing on building strong relationships with key players, both on and off the field, within the community, and with the players' parents. It hasn't been easy, but I think we're beginning to make some real progress. Some of the newer members are beginning to see the value in aligning with *our* approach to the game."

"That's crucial," Krzysztof agreed, his tone serious. "We need them to understand that *our* way of playing is the best path forward for everyone involved. Have you identified any potential leaders who could help sway the rest of the team?"

"Yeah, there are a few individuals who show promise," Drew confirmed, his mind flashing to the several Gurista government officials with whom he had been carefully cultivating relationships. "They have influence within the team and seem open to *our* ideas. If we can get them fully on board, I believe they could be instrumental in bringing about the change we're hoping for."

Krzysztof smiled, a glimmer of satisfaction in his eyes. "Excellent work, Drew. I knew you were the right man for this job. Keep fostering those relationships and building trust. We're counting on you to bring this team around to *our* way of thinking."

Drew nodded, feeling the constant weight of responsibility on his shoulders. "I understand. It won't be easy, but I'm committed to seeing this through. Their future depends on it."

"And the future of the league as a whole," Krzysztof added, his words heavy with subtle implications. "A successful season for your son's team could have far-reaching consequences. It could inspire other teams to follow suit and change the face of the game as we know it."

Drew leaned back in his chair, his mind racing with the possibilities. He knew that the success of his mission on Gurista Prime could be the key to turning the tide in the ongoing struggle against the Zodarks. If he could convince the Gurista government to align with the Republic, it would be a major blow to the Zodarks' future plans to use them as a janissary force. It would take away the blue four-armed giants' proxy that happened to have a high birth rate, eliminating the Zodarks' ability to absorb huge casualties without decimating their own population.

"I know the stakes. Don't forget I have a small cadre of Gallentines with me," Drew said, his voice filled with determination. "They're a wealth of information and a resource I didn't know I needed until I did."

Krzysztof smiled as he reached across the table, clasping Drew's shoulder in a gesture of support. "I'm jealous of you, Drew, and extremely proud to call you friend. Now, let's enjoy this meal and talk about something a little less heavy. I hear the peach cobbler here is not to be missed."

As they turned their attention to the menu, they ordered a pair of Stella Artois to get things started. Then Drew ordered the Bourbon Street Chicken and Shrimp, while Krzysztof went for the Asiago Chicken. Once their beers arrived, Krzysztof leaned in closer, his voice low and serious as he casually placed the small device on the table next to his Qpad—the HushBaby device activating. Unless you were seated with them, the HB device would make it impossible to listen in on their conversation. "Drew, I don't mean to be all business and whatnot. But while we're waiting for our food, I need you to be honest with me," he said as his eyes looked down at the antisurveillance device between them. "Last I checked, you've got that pair of Gallentine Special Forces and two ODA teams. You know the situation on the ground and what you're up against. Do you think you'll need more Special Forces support from the Republic or the Gallentines to pull this coup off if that's what it comes to? Director Gehlen has authorized me to provide you with whatever kind of support you think the IMS can provide—analyst, tactical teams, case officers, whatever we can provide, consider it yours. We just need to be sure we don't overplay our hand."

Drew took a couple of sips of his beer as he considered the question, his brow furrowed in thought, his eyes distant. "Right now, I don't think I need the kind of support Gehlen can provide. Dakkuri has been working tirelessly to build a parallel Mukhabarat network to spy on their colleagues so our organization can continue to stay a few steps ahead of them. We have managed to infiltrate the leadership echelons of the Gurista government and their military. What I could use if this plan goes to hell is another three or four ODA teams and a lot more explosives."

Krzysztof grunted, but his expression remained grave. "OK, that makes sense. What about weapons? If things go to hell, the coup fails, do you have the resources to switch tactics to an insurgency? To arm and sustain a guerrilla force to make life miserable for the Zodarks and their collaborators?"

144

Drew felt his jaw tightening at the thought. "If the coup fails, Krzysztof—hell, even if it works—the Guristas will need support from the Fleet to remove any Zodark ships in either of the systems the Guristas call home. Fortunately, the Gallentines detected no more than three Zodark warships in either system at a given time. Still, unless they are dealt with, our little coup d'état won't last more than a few weeks at best. The moment a Zodark contingency force arrives, they'll brush aside the fledgling Gurista Navy, and then it'll just be a matter of time as their warships pick off our units from orbit and their ground forces mop up what's left."

"Huh, yeah, that's a question you'll need to speak with the Viceroy or Admiral Bailey about. If they're able to provide some sort of expeditionary force or task force of ships, it would at least give you a chance of succeeding in fully evicting the blue devils from their territory and keeping them out," Krzysztof elaborated, his gaze intense.

Drew sighed, running a hand through his hair. "One problem at a time, Krzysztof. I've got a meeting tomorrow at ten with the Viceroy. This is an action item I had planned to bring up during the meeting. I'm sure they'll figure something out."

Krzysztof sat back in his chair, his expression a mix of concern and approval. He was about to say more when the automated server arrived with their food, still steaming fresh from the grill. "Well, I guess we can discuss things further another time. You've earned this dinner, and I'm not going to spoil it with talk of business."

"I appreciate that, Krzysztof," Drew said, his voice heavy with responsibility. "We've got time to catch up. Let's eat, and you can tell me what's up with that girlfriend you'd been seeing before I left."

"Oh man, don't get me started with that chick—the moment I mentioned taking our relationship to the next level, all she talked about was how many babies she wanted. As if I didn't have enough kids and child support from my last two failed marriages."

Drew tried not to laugh as he dug into his food.

****

Following Day
Security Council Chamber, Tiberius Hall
Alliance City, New Eden
Rhea System

As Drew stepped out of the transport, he found himself marveling at the progress Alliance City had made in his fifteen-month absence. The towering apartment buildings and condominiums, housing the myriad of races that made up the alliance's workforce, seemed to have sprouted from the ground like metallic trees reaching for the heavens. Altairians, Primords, Tully, and Ry'lians, all working in harmony to support the intricate tapestry of the alliance's military, political, and economic functions.

He approached Tiberius Hall, a monolithic structure that exuded both power and elegance. The building's exterior was adorned with intricate designs, a testament to the craftsmanship and attention to detail that had gone into its construction. The landscaping surrounding the edifice was equally impressive, with manicured gardens and sculptural elements that seemed to pay homage to the importance of the work carried out within its walls.

Drew's thoughts drifted to the various councils housed within Tiberius Hall, each responsible for a different aspect of the alliance's governance. The Council of Military Affairs, the Council of Industrial, Trade, and Economics, the Council of Foreign Affairs, the Council of Law and Justice, and the Council of Education, History, Research, and Development—all overseen by the paramount Governing Council. A wry smile played on his lips as he silently thanked the universe for steering him away from the labyrinthine world of politics, a path his brother Micah had chosen to embrace.

In his absence, Drew had allowed his brother to stay in his palatial, overly fancy, and way-too-expensive condominium penthouse. He had sunk his life savings into purchasing it a number of years ago. He had a feeling it was one of those rare opportunities where the value of the property was likely to increase many times beyond what he had purchased it for. There weren't a lot of opportunities for soldiers and operatives to increase their net worth. Owning a house, a condo, or a property was still the best way to increase a person's net worth or retirement account. His condo sat atop one of the few one-hundred-and-thirty-two-story-tall buildings adjacent to the Office of the Viceroy, Drew's office when he wasn't on assignment, and a block away from Tiberius Hall, where Micah worked.

As Drew neared the main entrance, he found himself craning his neck to take in the sheer scale of the intricately carved wooden doors. The double doors, standing an impressive thirty feet tall, were flanked by a more modest pair of sixteen-foot doors, which appeared to be the primary point of entry for employees and visitors alike.

He joined the line of individuals waiting to pass through security, noting the presence of heavily armed Republic Security Guards. The guards, outfitted in state-of-the-art Dragon Skin armor and wielding M-111 Slayer rifles, exuded an air of unwavering vigilance. Drew raised an eyebrow at the level of security, silently questioning the necessity of such firepower within the heart of the alliance's capital.

As he reached the front of the line, Drew was surprised when the guard, a captain judging by the bars on his armor, waved off his attempt to present identification. The captain informed him that he had been preauthorized to proceed directly to the Council of Military Affairs' conference room, where Viceroy Hunt and Admiral Bailey were expecting him.

Intrigued by this development, Drew entered the cavernous lobby of Tiberius Hall. Within moments, a holographic guide materialized before him, introducing itself as Dexter. As he followed the shimmering figure through the halls, Drew found himself absorbing the wealth of information Dexter provided about the building's namesake and the emperors who had preceded him.

The anticipation grew as they approached the conference room, the holographic guide vanishing as suddenly as it had appeared. Viceroy Hunt stood before him, a warm smile on his face as he extended his hand in greeting. The two men exchanged pleasantries, the Viceroy expressing his satisfaction at seeing Drew in person after months of holo communications.

As they entered the conference room, Drew's mind raced as he took his seat at the table, the eyes of allied partners focusing on the obvious outsider seated before them.

****

Security Council Chamber

Viceroy Miles Hunt stood at the head of the conference table, his presence commanding the attention of the alliance members gathered before him. The room hummed with anticipation and tension as he prepared to address them. When Miles cleared his throat, the conversations stopped, and all ears focused on what he said next.

"Good morning, everyone," Miles began, his voice resonating with authority as he took charge of the room. "Before we start the meeting, I'd like to take a moment to address the obvious—why our military commanders from the Lyrius system have been recalled from the front lines to join us. If you bear with me a moment, everything will be revealed, and the reason why this meeting was called will be explained.

"It's been said that some decisions have generational impacts and ripples felt for eternity. The decision we are about to make today, I believe, is one of these. Let me start by explaining why I believe that and also introduce you to a key person in this struggle against the Zodark Empire and this Dominion Alliance." He gestured to the seat beside him, where Drew Kanter sat, his expression a mask of calm determination. "Joining us today is Drew Kanter, a key figure in the success of the project we're about to discuss and how its outcome will impact generations to come."

Admiral Wiyrkomi, Miles's trusted friend and advisor, nodded in recognition. He had been deeply involved in Drew's work, privy to the sensitive information shared between Miles and his inner circle. "I second what the Viceroy has said about Drew's contributions to our cause and the mission he is presently leading. He has become an invaluable leader and operator for the Republic and the alliance writ large," Wiyrkomi affirmed, his voice carrying a note of respect.

Miles continued, "As many of you are aware, the Zodark spy web, run by their human proxy, the Guristas, had infiltrated the Republic and, through them, the alliance. It was through the collaborative efforts of our intelligence agencies that we eventually uncovered their espionage ring. I wish I could report that this allowed us to prevent future attacks against the Republic and our alliance. But we were too late to dismantle it before they could provide our enemies with the necessary information to make an invasion possible. Earth, my home world, the capital of the Republic, paid for that failure."

The room grew somber as the facts were laid bare before them, the weight of them hanging heavy in the air. Admiral Bailey, still filling the temporary role as Chancellor of the Republic, leaned forward, his brow furrowed. "I suspect this has something to do with our ongoing interrogations of captured Gurgorra and what we have been uncovering about the Zodarks' experimental creations?"

Miles looked grim as he nodded before turning to Zudolly, the Altairian representative from their intelligence agency.

"I am Zudolly, from the Schendolly—Altairian Intelligence. Our agency has been collecting intelligence against the Zodark Empire for centuries. At times, our knowledge of their affairs is broad and deep. We have our successes. We have our failures. What we have not succeeded in understanding is to what extent the Zodarks have dabbled in genetics and biological weapons. Our knowledge of the Gurgorra program—what it was, what they had created—was limited at best. We had known the Zodarks were running experiments, but what kind of experiments and the extent of their progress were unclear. However, the humans on the planet Sumer—their tribute system—and this parallel society the Zodarks call the Gurista were something on which we had collected extensive information. This allowed Republic Intelligence to vet and validate the information being provided to them, leading to the formulation of a daring plan, a stratagem that would alter the course of this war and the future of humanity should it succeed."

At this point, Drew took the lead as he addressed the council. "When we turned the Mukhabarat deep-cover operatives Ashurina and Dakkuri, we gained a wealth of information about the Gurista society, the locations of their star systems and planets, and how they operate. In the lead-up before the Zodark attack on Earth, the Mukhabarat Karaff, the spymaster and head of their operation, Dakkuri, had apparently been contemplating switching sides—the facade of who he was working for had steadily eroded until it fell away completely. It was his surrender, his cooperation, and his desire to rid his people of their blind allegiance to the Zodarks that led us to believe that maybe—with their help—we could attempt to sway the public from their Zodark hero worship—freeing the Guristas from their grasp and turning them into an ally against them."

The more Drew spoke, the more excitement and energy filled the room, which buzzed with a mix of surprise at what was being said and cautious optimism that it might work.

Lieutenant General Hopper, commander of the Republic Third Expeditionary Army, was the first to speak. "Wait, are you saying there is a real, legitimate opportunity to infiltrate Gurista Prime and potentially sway their loyalty away from the Zodarks?"

Drew smiled, his eyes glinting with determination. "We already have. In fact—"

"Wait, what do you mean we already have?" interrupted General Hopper.

"In the days following the Zodarks' attack on Earth, we began working on a plan with Ashurina and Dakkuri to figure out how best to unmask the Zodarks and expose them and their plan for the Gurista people if they don't break from their allegiance with them. Once we had developed a plan, the Gallentines offered to help us infiltrate the star system and planet," Drew replied.

Admiral Helixar signaled that he wanted to speak. "General Hopper, when we saw the opportunity to weaken the Zodark Empire, we offered the Viceroy the services of one of our *Vraxerian*-class stealth corvettes and some intelligence support during their operations on the planet," Admiral Helixar explained, pausing a moment to collect his thoughts. "This was and is a risky endeavor, General. The potential rewards should we succeed outweigh the cost should we fail, however. If we can turn the Guristas to our side, it could be a turning point in the war."

Miles nodded as the Gallentine surmised the situation, his gaze sweeping over the assembled leaders, his eyes sharp as he searched for questions or doubts in their expressions. "Indeed, Admiral Helixar. It has been more than a year since we first launched this operation. We knew from the beginning that the plan was fraught with danger, but we had a unique opportunity to strike a blow against the Zodarks and liberate a fellow human society. Right now, we're at a crossroads, and a decision must be made, our next move decided—here, today. The seeds of doubt sown this past year are yielding their fruit. The pieces to initiate this coup, this overthrow of the Zodark-controlled government, are in place. If we are to pull this off, it means forces will have to be drawn from both of your commands," Miles explained as he looked at General Hooper and Admiral Rosentreter. "We cannot launch a coup and expect it to succeed if we're not able to intercept Zodark warships and reinforcements. Fortunately, the location of the Gurista planets is on the far side of Zodark territory—a long way from reinforcements beyond what's in the nearby garrison two systems away."

Admiral Rosentreter laughed, his hand smacking the table in excitement. "Hell yeah, Viceroy, this decision is a no-brainer. My command just received replacement ships and personnel along with an additional squadron of warships. I can detail off Admiral Dobbs to command a reinforced squadron of ships. If Hopper can spare an SOF regiment in case a ground contingent is needed, I think we can easily handle supporting this mission—we just need a bridge for us to cross and we're good."

"Excellent—a bridge won't be a problem. Our Gallentine allies have that covered," Miles replied, then turned to face Drew. "I think we have our answer. Let's go ahead and move forward with Operation Free Gurista."

Drew nodded solemnly, a determined look on his face, a fire burning in his eyes as he saw victory not far off.

Task Force 28
RNS *Cassiopeia*
Gravaxia System

"Jump complete. We are now in the Gravaxia system," the helmsman informed them the moment they were through the gate.

"Antenna array extended, initiating PELS," announced Lieutenant Harris, the ship's electronic warfare officer, who controlled the ship's pulsar echolocation system or PELS. Within seconds of transmitting its rapid pulse signal, it populated the TAMs table near the TAO station. "Admiral, initial scans show no sign of enemy warships, surveillance drones, or warning beacons near the gate—OSTSA is beginning a system-wide scan now. That should get us a better view of what we're facing within the Gravaxia system. ETA on the full scan should be around ninety minutes."

Admiral Lee was taking the information in as fast as the scanners were providing it. The most vulnerable time for any ship was the first thirty seconds to three minutes after exiting the stargate—the time it took a ship's sensors to recalibrate following the jump.

"Very well, thank you, Lieutenant Harris. Let us know immediately if the long-range sensors detect any military or civilian craft in the system," Admiral Lee directed. He then turned to face his comms officer. "Lieutenant Rodriguez, get a status report from the ships that crossed with us. Then establish comms with the *Donovan* and *Valiant*—we need an update on their present situation and their coordinates," he ordered calmly, setting the tone for the bridge staff.

"Yes, Admiral—Quantum Beamlink has been established with the squadron. We should have comms with the *Valiant* and *Donovan* shortly," responded Rodriguez, his fingers dancing across his control panel.

"Outstanding, Rodriguez. I'm digging this new comms system. I only wish we had more of our warships equipped with it," praised Lee.

The Quantum Beamlink, or QB, was among the most valued promising technologies Doctors Johnson and Sakura had discovered during their ongoing exploits of Lab Site X amid the buried Humtar technology they were exploring. It was the beginning of a revolutionary technology in the field of interstellar communications. The QB system employed a combination of quantum entanglement for encryption and a secure narrow-beam laser communications system. It would provide the ships equipped with it a secure method of data transmission in near real time and with nearly unlimited range. It was also a newly fielded comms system, which meant only new warships from the shipyards or those retrofitted at the newly created IMB Quantum Naval Shipyard were in possession of it. Lee had lucked out in that the ships comprising his task force were all equipped with this latest communication system.

"I couldn't agree more, Admiral. This new QB system is going to allow us to coordinate actions in real time instead of fighting against the lag time we had with our older system," surmised Lieutenant Rodriguez. As the comms officer, he had become an unabashed advocate of the QB system.

Lee grimaced when he looked at the clock on the far right of the bridge monitor—six hours. That was how long it had been since they had received an urgent communiqué from the pair of Republic stealth frigates that had been operating in the neighboring Zodark-controlled space of the Gravaxia system for nearly two days. This was their second trip into the system; the first trip was to drop off the Delta teams across Gravaxia. A few days later, they went back, this time to collect the Deltas and the intel they'd gathered.

When an emergency beacon had exited the Pfeinstgard stargate, it had broadcast an urgent contact report from the skipper of the *Valiant*. When Lee read it, his stomach tightened, and he felt his pulse quickening. It was a call for help, a plea for Admiral Lee to intervene before it was too late. The message read, "*Valiant* and *Donovan* likely detected. Enemy force entrapping us in asteroid belt. Requesting immediate assistance—critical intelligence aboard—must be saved."

Lee's orders were specific. His task force was meant to protect the Pfeinstgard system and prevent any Zodark warships from entering the Gravaxia stargate. His secondary orders from SOCOM and Republic Intelligence were for his task force to support and protect the pair of stealth frigates being assigned to his task force. It was because of this last set of orders and the message from the *Valiant* that he felt compelled to intervene—despite having orders forbidding him from conducting raiding strikes in the Gravaxia system. *Damn it to hell—this better be some good intel I'm disobeying orders to retrieve*, Lee thought to himself as he took in the sight of the warships he'd brought with him. It was by no means the entire task force, but he felt it sufficient to rescue the frigates and the intelligence aboard them.

While the minutes ticked by, the crew worked feverishly as they readied the *Cassiopeia* for whatever might lie ahead. *Things are happening too fast*, he kept thinking. *We aren't ready for this.*

"Bingo! We found them," declared Lieutenant Harris. "I have the coordinates for the *Donovan* and the *Valiant*. The OSA[3] scanners place the ships near the Alpha Quadrant mining facility."

"Excellent job, Lieutenant, keep us apprised of any warships operating in the area. Helmsman, set a course placing us near the coordinates I'm sending to your station," responded Admiral Lee. It was time to go rescue their comrades.

****

IVO Alpha Quadrant Mining Facility

Admiral Lee's gaze fixed on the forward screen, but his mind dwelled on the asteroid belt mining facilities the RNS *Donovan* and *Valiant* had somehow been herded closer to. He turned to his XO, Commander Noriko Sato, her eyes sifting through the data streaming on her console. "Sato, any updates on those mining facilities or what seems to have forced our friends closer to them?"

Commander Sato glanced up from her console, her eyebrows bunched together. "Negative, Admiral. We're not detecting anything unusual from those facilities, or anything that could have herded the *Valiant* and *Donovan* further into the asteroid field." She smiled. "On a good note, sir, they've recovered fifteen out of eighteen of the deployed teams. Unfortunately, given their current situation, they're way out of position to recover those three remaining teams. Perhaps once we figure out what's going on, they can make a beeline to the pickup points and recover them before the whole system goes to crap on us."

Lee nodded in agreement. "Thanks, Sato, you're right. Once we figure out what's happening here, they can double back and pick up those teams." He turned to his tactical action officer. "In the meantime—TAO,

---

[3] Omni-Spectral Array

let's go ahead and get our weapons spun up and ready. And, Lieutenant Harris, send a message to the squadron—all ships go to condition two. I don't want everyone sitting at battle stations potentially for hours—just the weapons and our space wings in the tube, ready for launch."

As the flurry of activity commenced on the bridge, Lee turned his attention to one of the monitors that showed the Delta icons and where they had been deployed. If a team had been recovered, it was highlighted in green. If a team was highlighted in amber, it was still awaiting pickup. Thankfully, most of the units were aboard one of the two frigates.

For ten minutes, Admiral Lee monitored the data cascading across his chair's holo display or the main monitor on the bridge. What he found astonishing was the level of detail and precision within the intelligence reports the teams were now transmitting to his ship. Much of their reporting included detailed photos and videos of likely targets should the facilities need to be attacked directly or numbers of starfighters and bombers stationed at the facilities. It was incredible, and they had managed to do it all without being detected or losing a single soldier.

The intel was invaluable; that wasn't the thing bugging him. What was bugging him was the apparent lack of security and the absence of any sort of resistance at and around the stargate. In the past, even if the Zodarks weren't going to lock down the gate, they left some sort of surveillance drones and antiship mines.

Is it possible their reputation is a sufficient deterrent—or is something more going on? he thought. Then to his surprise, he recalled a personal encounter—a time when he had faced an unexpected confrontation in a Mexican alley, outnumbered and outgunned. His survival had hinged solely on his quick reflexes and sharpshooting prowess—skills that had earned him multiple Olympic medals years later. It was a story he planned to include when he wrote a book someday. Ironically, the scenario was eerily similar to their current situation. As he connected more dots, the emerging picture pointed to the unpleasant possibility that they had been lured into the system, into a carefully laid trap in the Velos Belt.

This potential strategy resonated with his past experience: an enemy, hidden within the shadows, waiting for the perfect moment to strike. In space, just as in that alley, the element of surprise was a

155

formidable weapon—oftentimes a deadly one. As he strategized their next move, still searching for what had spooked the *Valiant* and *Donovan* to call for help, Lee remained aware of the potential for a sudden, devastating engagement from somewhere within the deceptive calm of the belt. A vast forest of giant floating rocks and ice, an ideal location from which to initiate an ambush.

Lieutenant Harris turned from his sensor panel. "Admiral, I think we got something. We're picking up a significant anomaly. It's positioned directly above the Alpha Quadrant mining facility—could be an enemy fleet waiting to spring their trap."

"Hmm…that's possible. How many recon drones do we have near that sector?" Lee asked.

"We have eighteen drones deployed. Nine of them are near that area, and the other nine are scouting a different area. Actually, let me tap into one of the drone camera feeds and get us a live video," Harris explained as he took control of a drone. "Here, I'm projecting the live feed to the monitor while I maneuver for a better visual of the facility."

The video feed displayed on the bridge monitor revealed a sprawling mining facility attached to the side of an enormous rock. As Harris zoomed in closer, they spotted eight ships, each with a conveyor belt feeding smaller chunks of unrefined minerals into their hulls.

Zodark ore haulers…are they truly unaware of our presence? How could they not have detected us by now?

These bulky, slow-moving ships might have been perfect for moving massive quantities of ore. However, in a fight, they wouldn't last long with weapons meant for self-defense against rogue pirates. They'd get squashed in seconds in a battle against warships.

"This doesn't make sense—ore haulers?" Lee said aloud, then turned to his comms officer. "Harris, continue the visual sweeps, and let's rule out the possibility of some hidden warships or bombers on the dark side of those asteroids. A few of them look big enough to be planetoids. Something isn't adding up here."

"I agree, Admiral—something isn't right. I've had the PELS system drop a couple of pings every few minutes to see if it's detecting anything, but nothing. Since we're still technically at EMCON, it's limiting our ability to utilize the full capabilities of our spectral tactical sensors. That would give us a better, more complete picture of what's happening in the system. It would also allow us to detect any chatter or mentions of our presence or request for reinforcements," Harris explained. "On the other hand, the pulse echolocation system has consistently reported on the presence of weapon signatures akin to those found aboard a Zodark cruiser or battleship. But we've yet to identify where these weapons are or locate a warship capable of this kind of weapon."

No sooner had Harris finished speaking than a sudden flash of blinding light temporarily whited out the bridge monitor. As the video feed returned, the image was hazy for a moment until the drone refocused.

"What the hell?" Lee stammered.

"Admiral, there was an unknown energy discharge. I'm still trying to locate where it came from," Harris calmly explained. "Oh damn—it zapped one of our drones."

Lee practically jumped out of his chair the moment Harris confirmed one of their drones had been zapped. Looking for his comms officer, he ordered, "Rodriguez, get me a secure channel to all ships now!"

Rodriguez complied instantly, her fingers a blur. "Aye, Admiral. I've got the ships waiting on channel two for you."

Lee gave her a curt nod as he bit his lower lip before responding. "Attention all ships, this is Admiral Lee. Set condition one, battle stations. A hostile engagement just occurred in the Velos Belt, near the mining camp. One of our reconnaissance drones was destroyed by an unidentified energy weapon. I want all ships ready to counter whatever this threat is. Stay sharp and be prepared for whatever happens next. *Cassiopeia* out."

The second he finished speaking to the other ship captains, his tactical officer's tone rose in excitement. "Admiral, we have visual confirmation of additional Zodark haulers, this time at the Velos Belt's Delta Quadrant facility. However, we're still not detecting any signs of enemy ships, let alone the presence of a fleet."

Lee turned to Commander Connor Rhom at the tactical action station. "Rhom, is it possible we're seeing malfunctions in our drone feeds—that maybe that's why they aren't detecting any Zodark warships?"

Rhom looked terrified before responding. "Ah, let me reboot the system. Then I'll run another diagnostic and see if we have any gremlins in the system."

Harris's voice boomed. "Bloody hell, we've just lost signals from two additional drones."

Lee clenched his fist in frustration at not knowing what was shooting at them. "Do we have a point of origin for where these shots are coming from?"

Harris checked the readings again. "No, not yet. What I can confirm is that we've detected energy surges consistent with high-energy weapons—"

"Excuse me, Admiral," Rhom interrupted. "We found it! It's a laser cannon turret affixed to the asteroid above the mining facility. I'm transferring the video feed to the main bridge monitor now."

On the bridge's main display, a pair of icons highlighted two of the turret positions that fired on their drones. Seconds after broadcasting the feed to the bridge monitor, another drone was zapped, then another before the feed on the monitor cut out. They had gone from nine drones to five. The enemy was clearly engaging their drones. It wouldn't be long now before they targeted one of Admiral Lee's ships.

"Have there been any attempted communications from the mining facilities or calls for help?" Lee asked, his brow furrowed.

"Negative, Admiral," Rodriguez responded, her eyes never leaving her station's console. "We haven't detected any attempts on their end. Lieutenant Harris is still scrambling their radios. He's got them thoroughly jammed—nothing in or out."

Lee nodded, acknowledging her report, then switched his comms channel to the flight deck. "Commander Cooper—this is the admiral. Are your squadrons ready to launch?"

Commander Blake Cooper, call sign Coop, had been monitoring the situation, ensuring both he and his pilots knew what was happening before the admiral even called. Responding from the cockpit of his F-11 Gripens, he said, "Yes, Admiral, all pilots are aboard their respective Gripen fighters and Valkyrie bombers. I've got both squadrons of Gripens loaded in the launch tubes. We're ready to move on your command."

"Excellent, Coop. The TAO is assigning a target package for your squadrons to hit and another location where we suspect more laser turrets are likely hidden. Good luck, Coop, and happy hunting," Lee ordered. He then waved his hand, catching Rodriguez's attention. "Get me a secure channel to all ships!"

Within moments, Lee's channel buzzed to life. "This is Admiral Lee to all ships. Deploy your squadrons to the designated strike coordinates being sent to you. I know our orders weren't supposed to involve raiding Gravaxia. Obviously, the situation has changed, and we must adapt. Launch your squadrons and prepare your ships for battle—we're going in."

Lee then activated his communications link to the pair of *Stonefish*-class flak cruisers he had brought with him—the RNS *Trident* and *Harbinger*. "*Trident*, *Harbinger*, you are to reposition forward of our positions and stand by to engage any fighters, missiles, or torpedoes targeting our ships. Be advised Gripens and Valkyries will provide combat support. Ensure no Zodark vessels break from the asteroid field—kill them all."

Chapter Twenty-One
Fox Three

Task Force 28
RNS *Cassiopeia*
Gravaxia System

In RNS *Cassiopeia*'s cavernous launch bay, Commander of Flight Operations Blake "Coop" Cooper surveyed his domain as he hurried toward his starfighter. All around him were F-11 Gripen fighters and B-11 Valkyrie bombers being readied for launch as ground crews and pilots ran through final system checks.

Coop settled into the cockpit of his sleek Gripen fighter. He spun up the engines and activated the onboard systems. The holographic displays and control panels illuminated the cockpit in a soft blue glow. His hands moved instinctively over the controls, his fingers tapping across the holo buttons as he initiated the preflight sequence.

Around him, the hangar bay buzzed with activity as his squadrons prepared for the mission. It was a full-court press; one hundred and twenty-eight pilots under his command were about to lay a hurt on the Zodarks that they wouldn't soon forget. They were ready to follow him into battle—to the gates of hell if so ordered.

The objective was clear and daunting as it was dangerous—destroy the Zodarks' ability to mine resources and freely operate in the Gravaxia system. Coop was to lead four squadrons to destroy the Alpha Quadrant mining facilities, while Commander Mason would lead the other four squadrons to smash and destroy the Delta Quadrant facilities. By leaving nothing intact, they were going to deny the enemy the use of these platforms as listening posts or staging areas for future attacks.

On Coop's console, pilot icons blinked with life. Each represented one of the expert pilots under his command. He knew some well, but others were fresh from flight school. He worried about the new pilots—had he been tough enough on them in training so they would have the skills to survive real combat? He hoped he had; after today, he'd know for sure.

The one thing he knew he could count on was their hatred of this enemy. A fight against the Zodarks was an all-or-nothing affair. The Zodarks wanted one thing—complete subjugation of the human race, of humanity wherever they were found. They were not an adversary one could negotiate with. They had to be defeated so they could never pose a threat to the Republic or anyone else. *We will triumph against this darkness...of that I am sure of...*

With his Gripen ready for launch, the ground crew signaled launch control, and the automated system assumed control, guiding him into the launch tube. With a starboard and port launch system, the *Victory*-class battleships could launch an entire squadron per side—thirty-two fighters and bombers in one go.

Among his lead pilots was Commander Anaya Singh, a good friend. She commanded Gold Squadron, a Valkyrie bomber squadron, her call sign—Rogue.

"Rogue, how's Gold Squadron?"

"Good as gold, sir. My pilots are ready to kill some Zodarks!" she replied jovially.

"Outstanding, Rogue. I'll see you after we get back. Coop out."

Feeling better after checking on his friend, Coop opened a channel to the rest of his pilots to address them all at once. "Attention all squadrons! This is Blue Leader. Once we deploy from the ship, I want all Gripens to form up on your designated squadrons. We don't know for certain if the Zodarks have any fighters out here. If they do, it's your job to keep 'em off the backs of our bombers so they can accomplish their mission. Stay tight to your wingman, and let's blow some things up. Blue Leader out."

With a final check of his systems, Coop signaled to Flight Ops that he was ready. A moment later, the launch doors slid open, revealing the vast expanse of space beyond. Coop's grip tightened on the control stick. "Flight Ops—launch all units!"

The second he finished speaking, his fighter was hurled down the launch tube, the light around him a blur, his body being pressed into the back of his chair. The moment he left the *Cassi*, the blur of lights was gone, the pressure lifting as he took control, his engines propelling him forward. It was a strange feeling those first few moments after launching. One moment, you were in gravity. The next, you were weightless in space.

In a flurry of blue and amber thrusters streaking against the black to his left and right, the rest of the Gripens and Valkyries began forming into their squadrons. While they waited for all the squadrons to launch and form up, Coop used the time to check on his squadron leaders and go over the plan a final time. When the last of the fighters and bombers formed into tight formations, they started to speed toward their targets, Coop leading the charge.

As they weaved through the asteroid belt, Coop's eyes narrowed. Large asteroids, some the size of small planetoids, moved across Coop's vista and enlarged as he and his squadrons closed in on the mining facilities. On his monitor's camera feed, over one hundred and twenty-eight Gripens and Valkyries flew in perfect formation, their hulls dull against the blackness. Thruster trails blazed like ethereal contrails in their wake.

Minutes ticked by like seconds as they approached their destination. Coop's eyes never wavered from his viewscreen. His fingertips moved across the controls, and on his helmet's HUD, he flipped between camera feeds and sensor readings. His interface lit up with green—oddly, no enemy had detected their advance. "Goonz, we're still in the clear," said Coop, using the nickname his space wing went by. "Let's strike 'em hard and don't give them a chance to blink."

"Aye, Commander," came the responses from his squadron leaders.

Rogue's squadron flew to the right of his wing as they veered around a massive floating rock when the mining camp came into full view. Unfolding before them, the Alpha Quadrant mining facility was anchored to a colossal asteroid the size of a small moon. Coop zoomed in on his monitor's feed. He could see the complex structures that melded into the rugged landscape. Carved into a massive crater, the mining camp was a hive of activity. Its enormous machines—some as tall as buildings—were still active as Coop and his teams closed in. They looked to be digging deep into the asteroid's crust, extracting valuable ore. They had been told this mine contained a material called luminescent Utonium, a mineral you could spot by its cobalt-blue color, illuminated amongst the gray of raw asteroid rock.

Coop zoomed in further for better intel on the target. This mining behemoth sprawled across several kilometers, its numerous sectors interconnected by a network of elevated metal walkways and conveyor belts. Gigantic cranes towered overhead. Their long arms swung with rhythmic precision as they transported raw ore to processing centers, none of which appeared to be wise to the strike that was about to hit them.

Why are we not spotting any defenses? Where are the damn turrets? He continued to scan until he spotted something. *There it is!*

On Coop's screens, the facility's defenses started to populate. His scanner showed an outline of eighteen laser turrets positioned around the perimeter of the mining operations. These turrets, cylindrical and robust, search the horizon for targets.

He checked the data he had received from the *Cassi*. It indicated the turrets were active and on high alert. He knew this was the calm before the storm. The moment those guns detected them, they'd unleash hell on his strike force. As targeting data from the *Cassi* continued to flow into his computer, his screens began to display each turret's estimated field of vision. With this advantage, Coop could anticipate what lanes of attack might have fewer defenses guarding them than others and direct his squadrons accordingly.

Floating above the mining facility, small craft loaded the much larger Zodark mining haulers. The haulers resembled oversized rectangular train cars. They were slow and could be handled last but no one could be left alive to report what happened. If the admiral wanted them to remain ghosts to the Zodarks, they would need to make sure they left nothing that could report back on what had happened in the Velos Belt.

Zooming in further on the haulers, he could see they were painted in green with bold streaks of warning yellow along their sides. Each of the haulers was equipped with powerful thrusters and small laser cannons to clear away debris and smaller rocks that might clutter their path. Their bulky forms slid across the screen, slow-moving targets against the frantic view of mining activity below. The detailed feeds provided him with a multiangled view of the operation.

"All right, listen up," Coop said. "Gold Squadron, your primary target is those laser turrets. Take them out like we talked about in the briefing. Blues, we're providing cover and engaging any enemy fighters that try to interfere if they're around. If no fighters show up, we'll support the bombers in taking out any turrets left before strafing the mining facility."

"Affirmative, sir!" the pilots replied almost in unison.

"Visual on target, Coop. Looks like minimal resistance. But...wait." Rogue's voice crackled.

Coop watched his interface as he zoomed in on the menacing turrets, their barrels now glowing as they charged to fire.

Crap, they found us. A sense of momentary panic raced through his mind as Gold Squadron started its attack run.

"Enemy guns hot! Activate ECM and stand by to deploy countermeasures," Coop ordered his pilots.

Moments before the turrets unleashed their fury, a volley of Sandies launched—the high-speed missiles packed with a sand-water mixture detonated one hundred and fifty kilometers to their front. The explosion of sand mixed with water that instantly froze created a momentary buffer between the Valkyries and the laser turrets about to fire on them. If the laser shot hit the misty buffer, it would scatter and defray the intensity of the laser shot—reducing its impact should it go on to hit its target.

"Blue Squadron," shouted Coop. "Hit those cannons I highlighted with your missiles. Then, I want you to go to max power, following me as I approach from vector zero-nine-zero relative. Minus fifteen degrees. After our missiles hit and those guns are down, we're going to strafe whatever we're in range of as we circle around for another pass."

"Good copy, Blue Leader," came a reply from Blue Two, Coop's XO. Moments later, the radio chatter picked up with shouts of "Fox Three, missile away," as his pilots began firing their joint advanced tactical missiles or JATMs, active radar-guided missiles, at the designated laser turrets.

As Coop placed the targeting reticle over the turret, his targeting computer deconflicted with his squadron's fighters. He depressed the firing stud, and the missile ejected from its internal weapons bay moments before its engine came to life. He turned his head to the side, closing his eyes just in time as the missile shot through the darkness of space.

With their missiles now streaking toward the laser turrets, Coop led his squadron through a series of maneuvers that, coupled with their active electronic countermeasures, made it that much harder for the enemy to gain a lock on them as his fighters continued to close the gap between them and the rest of the mining facility.

Coop switched over to his wing commander's view just in time to catch Rogue's Gold Squadron executing their bombing run. He watched Rogue's Valkyrie bomber dip its nose first, evading laser fire as it sliced through the darkness, the rest of her bombers following closely behind. Seconds later, he watched as a pair of plasma torpedoes fell from the bomber's internal weapons bay—its engines coming to life fractions of a second later as it rocketed toward its target.

As Rogue pulled her bomber up and away from the rapidly approaching surface, the space around her Valkyrie lit up like a Christmas tree, with red flashes piercing the darkness around her. Then, more enemy gun towers joined the mix, filling the darkness around them with red flashes of light—zipping around the Valkyries as one after the other released their plasma torpedoes, their engines rapidly accelerating them to maximum power. When the torpedoes got within five hundred meters of their target, they transformed from self-guiding bringers of death into molten comets of plasma—unguideable deadly bolts that would crash into their targets, obliterating whatever they hit.

"Target neutralized!" Rogue shouted excitedly, her first torpedo having scored a hit. It could have been minutes, but it felt like seconds. The laser turrets atop the ridgeline exploded in a series of what looked like controlled detonations as turret after turret went up in a fleeting eruption of multicolored flames before the vacuum of space snuffed them out.

Coop turned from the ridge as he surveyed his monitors. One was tracking Copper Squadron—another bomber squadron. The other was his Blue Squadron. Connecting to Copper Squadron, he transmitted, "Pronto, Coop. Good hits on those primary targets. Move to secondary targets, and let's finish this."

"Affirmative, Coop. We're lighting them up out here—it's a turkey shoot," replied Commander Tate Silvers, call sign Pronto.

Coop laughed at the turkey shoot reference. Shifting focus to his Blue Squadron, he called out, "Blues, form a line on me. I've tagged a target we're going to strafe with our guns—it's that grouping of what looks to be habitat zones. Everyone is to maintain our approach, two-seven-zero degrees—descend to minus ten. Break. Blue Thirteen, Blue Fourteen, go to maximum speed. Target the western defense grid. I've highlighted the four gun towers you need to take out. Hit 'em with your

JATMs—I want those guns silenced before they have a chance to shoot us up."

"Free Bird, Blue Leader—affirmative. Nomad, form up on me. Let's do this thing!" replied Lieutenant Jace Hawley, call sign Free Bird.

"Good copy, Free Bird. I'm coming up on your six—moving to your slot position now," Nomad confirmed as the pair of Gripens zoomed ahead of Coop and the rest of his fighters.

Coop heard Nomad's voice over the comms. "Free Bird, I'm in position. Let's light 'em up and rain fire on these Zodarks."

Coop smiled as he listened to the banter between Free Bird and Nomad, their resident four-time ace—outside of Coop and Rogue. Nomad had the most experience in the cockpit and the second-highest kill ratio next to Coop. He was a killer in the cockpit and a hell of a pilot.

With the battle over the Alpha Quadrant mining facility in full swing, Coop was receiving status reports from his bomber and fighter squadrons of priority targets hit and those still left. What surprised him most about this backwater mining facility was the number of laser defense turrets that seemed to keep popping up out of nowhere. Each time they eliminated a set of guns, a new set would appear.

When this happened, Coop would identify the closest fighter or bomber and assign the target to them. His biggest concern right now was the sudden appearance of Vultures—the Zodarks' equivalent to the Republic's Gripens.

"Blue Leader, Rogue. Requesting assistance. I've got multiple gun turrets appearing out of nowhere. I'm tagging the location for you now," came the urgent call for help from Commander Anaya Singh.

"Hang on, Rogue—I see them. I'm on my way to you now."

Damn, that's a lot of groundfire, Coop thought as he angled his Gripen toward the worst of it. As he drew closer to the target, the laser fire grew in intensity, crisscrossing wildly as it attempted to target the more maneuverable Valkyries.

As Coop accelerated toward the pair of gun turrets, he activated two more of his JATMs, assigning each missile to a different gun turret. He checked his threat board—his ECM pod was still working, jamming any remaining tracking radars still operational. When he heard the tonal signal that his missiles had acquired their targets and were ready to fire, he smashed the firing stud with his thumb. The first missile dropped from the weapons bay, and the engine activating it streaked through the darkness toward the assigned gun turret. He hit the firing stud once more, and his second missile dropped from the internal bay, its engine kicking in and sending it zipping through the blackness toward its target.

Blast after blast continued to rock the mining facility, some of them causing chain reactions—one section led to another.

"Turrets are down. Repeat, turrets are down," Rogue exclaimed.

As Coop banked hard, his heads-up display highlighted another laser turret that seemed to pop right out of the ground. He barely had time to switch to his guns as the crosshairs lined up squarely on the target. He squeezed the trigger, and a volley of blaster shots and magrail slugs plowed into the structure, causing it to explode in a brilliant flash before the cold of space snuffed it out.

Continuing to pull his Gripen up and away from the remaining enemy defenses, he saw another pair of laser turrets pop up and began firing on him. Spotting one of his Gripens nearby, Coop called out, "Deuce, two turrets, my six o'clock. Take 'em out!"

"I'm on it, Coop!" replied Deuce as he banked his Gripen into a turning dive and reoriented for his attack. Suddenly the guns changed targets, no longer firing at Coop. They shifted their fire in the direction Deuce was flying toward. When Coop craned his neck around to try and see how he was doing, he saw streaks of red light zip all around his Gripen until a single shot ripped his left wing off, sending the Gripen into an uncontrollable spin. Then, two more shots hit the Gripen. It exploded in a brief flash before the void snuffed it out, the blackness enveloping the debris.

"Ah, damn it! We lost Deuce!" Coop said over the comms.

He immediately felt the loss, a sharp sting in his chest. *Stay focused, we can mourn the dead later…*, he reminded himself, then told his pilots to do the same.

On Coop's command HUD and dashboard holos, the displays showed his squadrons' ongoing assault. He locked onto the status update: a fuel depot and two lasers were all that was still operational. Tapping into his interface, he pinpointed the lasers. One hid within a rock formation on the asteroid's surface, the other near the fuel depot.

"Blue Six, initiate another strafe run on grid sector 4-Charlie. Target coordinates are Alpha-9 at three-two degrees approach angle.

Target is embedded in the rock formation; bring the hammer and hit it hard," Coop directed.

As Gold and Blue Squadrons repositioned, Coop ordered them in. "Gold One, Gold Three, and Gold Four, you're green-lit for a bombing run on that southern grid—the fuel depot. Target coordinates Delta-5 and Delta-6, approach at two-seven degrees. Make it count and let's finish this."

As they dove, a sudden burst of laser fire from the mining facility targeted Rogue's bomber. While Coop maneuvered his craft away from the asteroid, a laser strike impacted her ship. Since she was one of his lead pilots, this triggered a new window to open on the upper-right portion of Coop's heads-up display, showcasing the live video feed from her ship's forward cameras. Moments later, another laser blast struck, causing momentary static to disrupt Rogue's video feed before it stabilized once again. Rogue veered her craft for a brief second. Warnings sent from her ship's computer to Coop's dash console flashed on his interface in an instant—minor damage to her craft's aft stabilizer, critical for maneuverability but not flight capability. A red warning icon blinked next to Rogue's ship status.

"Rogue, abort your run and regroup," Coop commanded. He veered his fighter toward the mining camp after her.

"Negative, Commander, I'm right on the target."

"Rogue, that's a direct order!" Coop's fist clenched as he tried to catch up to them.

Coop saw her torpedoes release—then his HUD zoomed in, catching the torpedoes as they plowed into the adjacent turret. The explosion was massive, ripping through the metal structures of nearby walkways. Secondary explosions blossomed, causing further havoc on the facility.

Rogue's strained voice came over the comm just before her bomber was caught in the blast radius. "My controls are jammed. I can't pull up!"

"Eject, Rogue, eject!" Coop shouted as he held his breath, hoping she ejected.

A small blip showed on his HUD, a data tag next to it confirming it was Rogue—she'd made it. Her cockpit had ejected in time. Coop was about to call the *Cassi* for a rescue tug to come pick her up when her signal blinked erratically before it stopped, and she disappeared.

"No, no, no, this can't be happening," Coop said to himself as he quickly pinpointed the closest pilot to where her signal had stopped.

"Pronto, move to where Rogue was last seen immediately. I'm sending you the grid I had. Try and get eyes on her, protect her if you can while we get a rescue boat to collect her."

"I'm on it, Coop. I got this!" Pronto quickly replied.

Coop felt his stomach knot with the fear of losing another one of his pilots. As he watched the monitors for any sign of Rogue, another update caught his attention.

"Blue Leader, those Zodark haulers are breaking off from the asteroid belt at high speed," Free Bird said.

Looking in the direction of the haulers, Coop saw it too. The haulers, typically slow-moving ships, were now accelerating away at a higher speed than this kind of ship was known to be capable of. He cursed to himself before connecting to his pilots. "Listen up, Blues! Do not let those haulers escape! Burn your engines and reactors out if you have to—but take them out now before they can radio for help!"

As Coop's squadron surged after the fleeing haulers, he reangled his Gripen and took off after Pronto. Looking at the distance between them, he saw they were almost five hundred kilometers apart. Coop shouted angrily in his cockpit, deactivating the reactor safety switch. He increased the reactor output to 105 percent, rapidly accelerating his fighter after Pronto.

A moment later, his radio crackled with static. A new source of jamming had just blanketed the area. Then Coop heard it. Piercing the jamming but sounding subdued. Pronto's voice barely cut through the jamming as he said, "My God, Coop. You have to see this. It's—"

Then, nothing—the voice went silent. The transmission ended. The blue icon representing Pronto's Gripen flashed yellow twice, then disappeared from the screen—just like Rogue.

Chapter Twenty-Two
Pitfall

Task Force 28
IVO Alpha Quadrant Mining Facility
Gravaxia System

Coop watched the reactor inch closer to 110 percent, the engines propelling the Gripen faster than it was rated to fly. The distance between him and Pronto's last known location was diminishing quickly. Doing a quick inventor, he saw he still had two of his six JATMs and sixty-four percent of his ammo for the pair of rotary magrail guns, and his four laser blasters were fully charged and ready. In addition, he still had half his decoy flares and two loads of chaff decoys. With his weapons ready, he confirmed his defensive suite of ECM and ECCM electronic wizardry—electronic countermeasures and electronic counter-countermeasures—was fully operational. He smiled when he saw his defensive suite hadn't deployed any of his four antimissile drone interceptors. *At least I'm not out of defensive options yet*, Coop told himself as he rapidly closed the distance to Pronto and Rogue.

Without warning, a flurry of movement caught Coop's attention, his eyes widening in shock at the sight. On the far side of the mining facility—the area Gold Squadron was supposed to attack next—he saw something unimaginable—something he had never encountered in all his fights against the Zodarks. Several of what appeared to be storage containers near a pair of cranes connecting to some habitat domes began the process of transforming themselves into something new—something deadly.

Warning—Targeting Radar Detected—Warning—Targeting Radar Detected.

"Oh crap!" he said aloud as he pressed the blue ECM button, then the red—activating full-spectrum jamming.

Warning—Missile Launch Detected—Warning—Missile Launch Detected.

Coop's heart practically jumped out of his throat as he watched missiles fire from what they had thought were storage containers.

Two missiles—five missiles—nine missiles—fifteen missile launches detected.

A red warning alarm started flashing across his HUD. One or more of those missiles had been fired at him. The rest, he assumed, were headed for his Gripens and the Valkyries of Gold Squadron lining up for the next attack. Shaking away the daze he'd momentarily fallen into, he banked his Gripen hard to the left, pulling away from the vector that would have taken him to Pronto and Rogue.

"Evasive maneuvers!" Coop's voice cut through the chaos, his command clear and decisive.

His squadron scattered, reacting instantly to the threat. Coop's pilots were desperately trying to shake off the incoming missiles—trajectories for each marking his pilots.

Warning—Ten Seconds to Impact—Warning—Nine Seconds to Impact...

Beads of sweat ran down the sides of Coop's face as he yanked his control stick harder to the left and down, sending his Gripen into a spiral toward the asteroid's surface. The g-forces pressed him back into his seat as he struggled to outmaneuver the missile or missiles still bearing down on him.

"Gold Squadron, form up on me," Coop heard the familiar French-accented voice of Rogue's XO, Lone Wolf. "The Blues are in trouble—I want all Valkyries to start targeting those missiles going after our Gripens," ordered Lone Wolf.

Coop suddenly remembered he had signed an AMA in sickbay just the other day so she could fly. She had recently broken her left wrist. The doctors wanted her off flight status for a week. Rogue and Wolf had petitioned for him as their commanding officer to sign a waiver so she could get airborne. Now he was happy as hell he had as he watched the Valkyries heading straight for the incoming missiles, guns blazing as missile after missile exploded.

Warning—Impact Imminent—Warning—Impact Imminent.

Coop felt his Gripen ejecting flares and a chaff canister as he jinked the Gripen hard to the right while pulling up. *Firing drone interceptor*, the automated voice of the Gripen's onboard computer declared.

Flash! Coop saw the flash wash harmlessly over his Gripen as the computer announced, *Missile Destroyed—Missile Destroyed.*

Coop hollered with excitement, having cheated death for a moment more. As he turned his head to the right, red flashes zipped around Gripens and Valkyries alike as their pilots deftly maneuvered their instruments of death like the cast of a choreographed musical.

Then he saw multiple laser turrets change targets, focusing solely on Free Bird—his Gripen jinking wildly. Coop's heart raced again at the sight of another friend in trouble. The comms crackled noticeably as Free Bird's voice cut through the jamming. "I'm maneuvering as best I can—could use a little help right now!"

Free Bird banked hard to the left, pulling his Gripen into a tight spiral. The missile chasing him was unable to match the sudden change, sailing past him. He'd dodged the first one, but two more were hot on his trail—locked onto the Gripen's heat signature, zeroing in for the kill.

"I can't shake 'em. There's two still on my tail!" shouted Free Bird, his voice strained, warnings and alarms blaring in the background.

"Hold on, Free Bird—I'm on my way," Coop responded. He scanned the battlefield for a way to assist him. Then a thought came to mind. "Free Bird, listen to me. Turn into the asteroid field—see if you can't confuse their tracking system until I'm in range to shoot at those missiles."

Free Bird acknowledged, pushing his Gripen to its limits as he raced for the dense field of spinning rocks. The missiles changed course, continuing their pursuit of him. As Free Bird neared the asteroids, he slowed considerably, relying more on the Gripen's maneuvering thrusters as he tried to navigate a treacherous field of spinning rocks of varying sizes.

The first missile failed to adjust its trajectory before slamming into an asteroid. The missile got a little further into the asteroid field before it collided and blew up. Then Free Bird emerged from the asteroid field, his Gripen intact and ready to fight.

"Hot damn, Free Bird! Nice flying!" Coop praised him as he worked to get a handle on how the battle was going.

The comm crackled with the voices of pilots as they whittled down the swarm of missiles until Deuce's desperate cry pierced through the chatter. His words were laced with fear as ground lasers tried to bracket him and missiles gave chase. "I can't shake them! They're all over me!"

Coop heard the man's plea. "I see you, Deuce," he said. "I need you to bank hard right and deploy flares. Nomad, get in there and draw some of the heat off him—see if you can't hit one or more of those missiles still chasing him."

"On it, Coop," Nomad confirmed. His Gripen raced toward the embattled craft. "Deuce, I'm coming up on your six. Get ready to break left on my mark."

Deuce's ship veered to the right. Flares burst from its hull, scattering in its wake—one of the missiles went for the flare, detonating on impact. The blast threw shrapnel into the Gripen's right wing, shredding metal and components alike. The damaged wing sparked a few times from shredded wiring and the gaping hole in its wing. But Deuce was alive, and that was all that mattered.

Then Nomad's ship closed the distance, lasers primed as he fired on the missiles that were still chasing Deuce.

Coop gritted his teeth and wrestled with the controls to stabilize his fighter as he kept the speed on. He'd knocked out three of the missiles, yet for each one he destroyed, another three took their place. "Focus on Deuce. We need to get him out of there," Coop said aloud to no one in particular.

Deuce's ship limped through space, its hull scorched, his Gripen becoming less maneuverable by the minute. "Coop, I've taken some damage. Maneuverability is cut in half."

Coop clenched his jaw. He refused to lose another pilot. "Hold on, Deuce. We're almost there." He turned toward him, engines at maximum speed, lasers primed and targeting the missiles headed toward him.

A few of his Blues used their lasers, cutting swaths into the void, searing through the incoming missiles. Explosions lit up space as missiles detonated.

An asteroid the size of a house tumbled into the fray, its jagged surface reflecting the flares' light. The incoming missiles were momentarily confused by the shadows and heat signatures of the flares and the floating rock.

"Nomad, asteroid at your two o'clock," Coop warned.

"I see it, Coop." Nomad's ship swerved, narrowly avoiding a collision with the asteroid. "Deuce, break left now!"

Deuce's ship jinked to the left as the missile struggled to reacquire its target. Then Nomad swooped in, lasers firing away into the blackness of space as he rapidly nailed several of the missiles in brilliant flashes of light. The attack happened so fast that Coop barely had time to react to an errant missile he failed to realize had circled back around them to reacquire him.

He jinked hard to the left as he pushed his engine hard to accelerate away from the missile bearing down on him. With warning alarms and flashing lights filling the cockpit, he didn't realize the Gripen's automated self-defensive system had taken the initiative to fire one of his drone interceptors at the missile still rapidly closing on his tail.

While there was no audible bang of the missile exploding behind him, a blinding flash of light illuminating the space around him had confirmed a successful hit. What Coop had no problem hearing, however, was the shards of shrapnel that blasted the rear portion of his Gripen. As Coop tried to shrug off the near-death experience, he realized his starfighter was in a slow downward spin, new sets of alarms blaring more urgently, if possible, than before.

Trying to regain control of his fighter, his thoughts racing through scenarios of what to do next, Nomad shouted over the noise of alarms. "Coop, you've been hit! How bad is it?"

Coop heard the question. But before he responded, he gritted his teeth and wrestled with the controls, trying to stabilize his ship. "Nomad, I'm a bit busy right now. Focus on Deuce—we need to get him out of here before a missile hits or the guns take another crack at him."

Looking around his fighter for Deuce, he spotted him not that far from his own Gripen. When Deuce announced he was going to restart his thrusters, Coop watched for the Gripen's tailpipes, hoping to see a continuous soft azure glow light that would indicate sustained power. Instead, the tailpipes briefly lit up, only to sputter and fade before blinking out entirely.

As Coop was about to say something to Deuce, he suddenly realized a giant freaking asteroid was tumbling through space—heading right for him. Somehow his mind had tuned out the blaring warning alerting him to the asteroid barreling at him. Hitting his thrusters, he rapidly darted out of the way, and just in time as he watched the giant rock float right past him. Continuing to give the engines more power, he could feel how sluggishly the Gripen was handling. Warning lights continued to blink, and some turned a steady red—system no longer working.

Ah, damn it. I'm not going to last long out here if this bird starts falling apart on me...

Coop returned his gaze to what was left of the giant mining complex. This facility was huge—far larger than he had first thought. Seeing the rest of his Blues darting toward the mining complex, he smiled as he heard the familiar voice of Lone Wolf: "If you have missiles, fire them at those missile launchers. If you don't, then strafe 'em with your guns, but take 'em out—now!"

The few large mine haulers that still remained in the area attempted to escape, only to fall prey as easy targets for his Blues. They were going to make sure no Zodark ships or soldiers escaped this asteroid belt.

"I'm losing power," Deuce said over the comms. His fighter somersaulted toward the asteroid like they were magnets.

That kid's going to die and there's not a damn thing I can do about it, Coop thought.

As Coop and Nomad fought to protect Deuce's crippled ship from incoming missiles, a new voice crackled over the comm. "Valkyrie One to Deuce. I have a visual on your position. Hang tight. I'm coming in hot."

Coop's eyes widened as he recognized the voice of Jax, the squadron's lead bomber pilot.

"Heard you boys needed a hand," Jax added. "I've got a few tricks up my sleeve."

Deuce's ship drifted, the damaged wing sparking. The asteroid tumbled closer.

"Deuce, I'm going to fire a magnetic tether," Jax explained, his bomber closing in. "It'll clamp onto your hull and pull you clear of the asteroid."

Deuce's voice strained over the comm. "Roger that, Jax. I'm ready."

Coop watched as Jax's Valkyrie swooped in, its thrusters flaring. The magnetic tether launcher swiveled, locking onto Deuce's ship. With a burst of compressed gas, the tether shot its metal cable in the starlight.

The tether's magnetic clamp snapped onto Deuce's hull with a resounding clang. Jax's bomber engines brightened as he pulled away, the cable snapping taut.

"Hang tight, Deuce," Jax said.

Deuce's ship lurched, pulled by the tether.

The asteroid filled Coop's viewscreen, its surface a few hundred meters away. Coop's breath caught in his throat.

Jax's bomber strained, its engines pushed to their limits. Slowly, Deuce's ship began to move, the tether pulling it away from the asteroid's path.

"Hold on, Deuce!" Coop shouted, his heart pounding.

The asteroid tumbled past, missing Deuce's ship by a hair's breadth. The shockwave buffeted the craft, sending it spinning on the end of the tether.

Jax's voice filled the comm, triumphant. "Got him! Deuce, you're clear."

Deuce let out a shaky laugh, relief flooding his voice. "Thanks, Jax. I owe you a drink."

Coop grinned. "Nice work, Jax."

The bomber pulled Deuce's ship away from the battlefield, the fighter trailing behind like a fish on a line. Coop and Nomad formed up around them, their ships battered but victorious.

"All remaining units, concentrate fire on their defenses," Coop commanded. "We need to cut off the source of these missiles."

The comm filled with acknowledgments as the squadron focused their efforts on the mining facility. Laser fire and plasma torpedoes lit up the void, slamming into containers and setting off devastating chain reactions.

"That's it, keep it up!" Coop encouraged. "We're hitting them where it hurts."

The shapes of what had once appeared as shadows against the asteroid's surface sharpened into discernible forms. Flashes of light erupted past the lip of the crater. Beams of energy raced across the void. Coop's sensors showed five ground-to-space laser turrets powerful enough to tear a hole in a frigate.

"Evasive action, now!" Coop clamped his hand on the stick. "All units, focus fire on those new lasers," he ordered. *Where'd they come from? We might've flown into a trap.* "Gripens, break formation and engage countermeasures. Valkyries, maintain distance and prepare for long-range support."

The remaining ships of the squadron rallied around Coop, their weapons primed and ready. They dove toward the mining facility, weaving through the asteroid field and dodging the incoming fire.

As they closed in, Coop targeted the nearest storage container, his finger hovering over the trigger. He waited for the perfect moment, his breath caught in his throat. Then, with a roar of engines and a blaze of laser fire, he let loose a barrage of missiles.

The missiles streaked through space, their blue rocket fire illuminating the asteroid's craggy surface. They struck the container with devastating force, setting off a cascading effect that ripped through the mining facility's superstructure.

Explosions blossomed like fiery flowers, debris careening off into space.

As the last of the missile containers exploded in a brilliant display of fire and debris, a new warning blaring across his HUD shattered Coop's momentary sense of relief. "Commander, I'm picking up multiple contacts emerging from the asteroid field," Nomad reported, his voice tense. "They're Zodark fighters, and there's a hell of a lot of them."

Coop's eyes narrowed as enemy ships materialized on his display. "All units, be advised," he said, broadcasting over the squadron channel. "We've got incoming Zodark reinforcements. Looks like they're bringing the party to us."

Chapter Twenty-Three
Reconnaissance in Force

Ripley's Raiders
RNS *Cassiopeia*
Velos Belt, Gravaxia System

Rear Admiral Ripley Willis Lee stood next to the holo table displaying the TAMs, which showed the disposition and deployment of his raiding party. A sudden flash of déjà vu hit him—a memory from long ago surfacing at this critical moment. It was a conversation with his mentor a week before his death, a conversation that had shaped Lee's entire career.

Closing his eyes for a moment, Lee recalled Commander James Oldendorf's piercing gaze and the wisdom in his words. "Ripley, leadership and command are about more than just giving orders," Oldendorf had said, pointing to his heart. "They're about establishing standards and principles you and your command will uphold. Instill a sense of pride and duty, and honor the oath we take as officers. Hold yourself accountable to the same standards you set for your subordinates."

Oldendorf had leaned closer, his voice intense. "True leaders are revered not out of fear but out of respect. When you inspire such loyalty, your men will follow you even into certain death, executing orders with a resolve that could be the difference between victory and defeat. Do you understand, Ripley?"

Lee had taken those words to heart. Throughout the relentless war with the Zodark Empire, he had striven to live up to Oldendorf's legacy. Even now, as he reviewed the strategic deployment plans, he felt the weight of those principles guiding his actions.

Opening his eyes, Lee refocused on the present. The TAMs glowed with the positions of his fleet. The Zodarks were closing in on the stargate that led to the Rhea System and New Eden. Lee's resolve hardened. He would lead his men with the honor and accountability his mentor had instilled in him, hoping to bring an end to this war and make Oldendorf proud.

It had been two days since operations had commenced in the Gravaxia system, and so far, they had succeeded in obliterating what looked to be a major Zodark mining operation and potentially something more.

When Lee, together with his executive officer, Noriko Sato, had analyzed all the reports and scouting missions they had conducted in the Gravaxia system, they'd concluded that, for whatever reason, the Gravaxia system was not just vulnerable. It was weakly defended. It was possible this was a result of the devastating warship losses the Zodarks had sustained during the invasion of Sol and the battle for Earth. It was also possible the Zodarks had not anticipated an incursion into their territory from Pfeinstgard. In any case, this presented an opportunity Lee felt he couldn't pass up—even if his orders were to protect Pfeinstgard while the alliance began the arduous process of stockpiling resources and munitions in preparation for the eventual invasion of the Zodark Empire.

"Admiral, long-range scanners are detecting enemy fighters emerging from the vicinity of the mining camp. They're not in range of our strike force just yet, but they're closing to engage," Lieutenant Harris exclaimed.

Commander Sato turned to face him. "Sir, I recommend we recall the fighters and bombers now, so we can get them rearmed and back in the fight."

"Rodriguez, connect me to Commander Cooper, ASAP!" Lee directed, taking in the information as fast as it was coming. A moment later, Rodriguez gestured with two fingers—he had Cooper on channel two for him.

"Commander Cooper, Admiral Lee. I'm sure you're probably tracking Zodark Vultures vectoring to your location. Long-range scanners on our end show at least four squadrons' worth of Vultures inbound. How copy?" asked Lee.

"Good copy on all, Admiral. Right now, our scanners are showing a single squadron. I was about to direct my wing to engage until you mentioned three additional squadrons we hadn't detected yet. What are your orders, Admiral?" Cooper asked.

"Coop, I want you to RTB to the *Cassi* ASAP—rearm your Gripens and prepare to launch again and engage those Vultures. We don't know yet if there are any Glaives following behind them or within their formations, but the way they let you guys expend most of your munitions on the mining facility before they suddenly showed themselves leads me to believe this may be part of a more elaborate plot to lure us in," Lee responded, relaying what info they knew up to this point.

"Good copy. If that was their plan, it would help to explain the sudden appearance of missile launchers spamming us toward the end of our attack. What little ordnance we had left, we expended neutralizing them. I just sent the RTB signal. We'll be home soon, Admiral—out." The call terminated—the RTB sent.

Commander Rhom from the tactical station asked, "Admiral, do you think there's going to be enough time to recover Coop's squadrons before those Zodark fighters begin arriving?"

Lee stared at Rhom for a moment. "I'm not certain. I guess it'll depend on if they have any damaged fighters and if they don't crash during landing," he finally responded.

****

Task Force 28
RNS *Cassiopeia*
Gravaxia System

Lieutenant Harris's voice broke the tense silence on the bridge. "Vultures and Glaives coming into view, Admiral." The bridge monitor began to display multiple squadrons of Zodark fighters and bombers heading towards his ships.

"Admiral, this is Commander Cooper. That was the last Valkyrie—all craft aboard. We're rearming and repairing the Gripens for launch again—ETA twenty minutes. It's the best I can do, Admiral," Lee's Commander, Flight Operations, exclaimed, the noise of the flight bay and clanging of tools in the background.

"Thanks, Coop. We're repositioning our escorts to deal with the threat until we can get your birds back in the fight. Bridge out," Lee replied. *That pilot should have ejected—we lost precious time clearing the flight deck after he crashed.* Lee shook his head in frustration. The Valkyrie had been damaged during the attack against the refinery. The pilot had managed to limp it back to the *Cassi*, then insisted on landing it despite their encouragement to ditch it. When the bomber had crossed the magnetic containment field into the flight bay, it had crashed immediately as the laws of gravity returned and the true extent of the damage to the Valkyrie made itself known.

The crash wouldn't have been so bad if its forward momentum hadn't slid the wreckage into a nearby shuttle, taking on fuel. The ensuing fireball had shut down the flight deck for nearly twenty minutes—time they didn't have if they were going to refit and launch before the Zodarks showed up. Now, Lee would have to rely on his escort ships to protect them from the Zodark Glaives and their deadly torpedoes.

Lee stood to his feet, turning to face Lieutenant Rodriguez, when Lieutenant Harris excitedly announced, "Admiral! New contacts—Zodark warships bearing one-seven-two degrees to our current five o'clock position. They're emerging from the southern end of the Velos Belt, not far from the Delta Quadrant mining facility!"

"Wait, what? How did we not see this and how many contacts are we talking about?" shouted Commander Noriko Sato, running to the holo table as it populated the new contacts into the TAM of the battlespace.

"I don't know what happened—the Omni-Spectral Array wasn't detecting anything hiding in the belt or moving through it. It was the PELS, the pulsar echo sensors, that detected the ships," Lieutenant Harris replied defensively.

"Forget about it, Harris. We can resolve what happened later. How many ships are we looking at, and what types?" Admiral Lee cut into their conversation.

"Sir, PELS is reporting two battleships, five cruisers, and thirteen frigates—plus we have thirty-six Vultures and twenty-four Glaives still bearing down on us," Harris responded, a look of grave concern on his face.

It's a trap—and we foolishly walked right into it, Lee realized as the information sank in. Lifting the comms mic close to his lips, he pressed the talk button with his thumb, connecting him to the fleet. "All ships, this is Admiral Lee. Prepare for contact. We have two enemy forces bearing down on our position. Artemis, launch your fighters to engage those incoming Glaives and Vultures. Orion, your fighters are to provide cover and engage Zodark torpedoes before they convert to plasma. Your Valkyries are to focus on the Zodark frigates and cruisers. Your main weapons are to remain focused on the battleships approaching from our rear. The *Oregon*, *Nebraska*, and *Virginia* are to concentrate on the enemy cruisers. The remainder of you I haven't called out are to focus on keeping those Zodark frigates and Glaives away from our battleships. *Cassiopeia* out," finished Lee, directing his warships as the battle began to take shape and the galaxy held its breath.

Everything around Lee felt like it was moving in slow motion. He heard Commander Sato directing Lieutenant Reynolds to bring the *Cassi*'s engines to ahead one-third—changing their course to 306 degrees starboard and readjusting the ship's angle to fire its pair of giant ion cannons.

The ships of Ripley's Raiders moved into position as the battle lines between the two sides began to form. Despite the awesome firepower at Lee's disposal, he now regretted not bringing the entire task force with him. He certainly could have used those extra battleships right about now.

As the first wave of Zodark fast-attack ships raced ahead of the slower, heavier battleships forming an impressive line of naval power, Lee's voice blared through the comm to the fleet. "All ships, weapons free. Engage enemy warships. Burn them out of the stars!" he roared.

As Ripley's Raiders unleashed their power, Lee could feel the *Cassiopeia* shudder from the recoil of the six dual-barreled thirty-six-inch magrails as they fired. For the briefest of moments, he could just barely make out the projectiles being hurled at blinding speeds toward the enemy ships closing in. Then a bright flash erupted from the bow. The ion cannons fired. A pair of giant plumes of fire erupted from one of the Zodark battleships—an instant hit.

Cheers of excitement rippled across the bridge. They had scored first blood. They had landed the first blow. Then the *Cassi* shook violently. Lee furrowed his brow, the skin between his eyes creasing. These didn't feel like ordinary tremors from his vessel's weapons.

Another sudden jolt thundered through the *Cassiopeia*, warning lights flashing on the damage control boards to either side of the bridge.

"What the hell is going on?" Lee shouted in confusion. *Are these hits from those battleships…?*

"Sir, we've been hit by a pair of plasma torpedoes," Commander Sato yelled over the alarms blaring on the bridge. "We have damage reports coming in from decks one, two, and four in Section J—rear quadrant."

"Brace for impact! Torpedo bearing one-seven-four degrees aft!" exclaimed Commander Rhom seconds before impact.

BAM!

The bridge's lights flickered off and on a second later. Alarms continue to sound for attention. Silhouetted parts of the ship were now flashing yellow—some flashing red, indicating serious damage.

"New contacts!" Lieutenant Harris shouted.

"Where—" Lee's words cut off as he turned to the tactical display. A contingent of forty-one new contacts advanced rapidly from astern, coming in from a rear angle—one that pointed toward the Tueblets stargate. The new contacts were jumping right on top of his force.

"Helm, come to course zero-nine-one degrees port! All ahead flank!" Lee commanded. The crew rushed to carry out his orders.

"Aye, sir! Coming to course zero-nine-one degrees port, all ahead flank!" Reynolds repeated.

Lee was watching a nightmare materialize before his eyes. *How did our sensors miss this other enemy fleet?*

"More torpedoes incoming, bearing two-two-three degrees starboard!" reported the tactical officer. The scene around the *Cassi* came to life as the ship's point-defense weapons fired at the incoming threats at prodigious rates of fire.

"Evasive maneuvers, now! Launch all countermeasures!" Lee ordered. "Helm, maintain course zero-nine-one degrees port."

"Maintaining course zero-nine-one degrees port, aye!" Reynolds reiterated.

A strained voice came through the comm. "Admiral, this is the *Pike*. We're taking heavy damage, sustaining casualties!"

Lee pulled up the schematics of the *Pike*, a frigate. The display was a grim show of devastation: critical breaches in the hull, fires in the engine section, and life support systems failing in several decks. "*Pike*, pull back to the rally point—get out of here. I'll redirect additional firepower to cover your retreat."

Lee turned to the tactical officer, Commander Connor Rhom. "Rhom, get the weapons closest to that lead ship bearing two-two-three degrees starboard and start hammering them. We gotta start thinning out these corvettes and frigates hammering us with torpedoes!"

Rhom nodded, a grim look on his face as he complied, targeting a Zodark battleship at the center of this new attack force to their rear. *Cassi*'s magrails whirred to life, the projectiles launching at blinding

183

speeds. Each tungsten round struck the enemy ship at a distance of twenty-three hundred kilometers, plowing into the propulsion module to the rear of the ship. The critical blow flashed on Lee's screen, a devilish smile of satisfaction spreading across his face.

"Good shot, Rhom! See if you can't target that exposed area with another shot. If we're lucky—you might hit the reactor," Lee encouraged excitedly.

"Targeting it now—firing!" Rhom shouted over the noise of alarms still sounding.

Lee watched the shot, practically following the projectile into the gash of the ship's armor. Then, a flash nearly whited out their screen as an explosion erupted somewhere deep within the ship. He pumped his fist in excitement—hooting and hollering excitedly with others at the sight of what they knew to be a decisive blow.

When the rounds from the rear turret hit perfectly, the explosion buckled the rear section of the ship. A second later, a giant explosion erupted—severing the rear half of the ship from the rest of it—the two parts now drifting apart. Another volley of magrail slugs crashed into the front half of the battleship. Moments later, the projectiles tore into the forward section of the ship. When they exploded, the blast was so massive it disintegrated the enemy vessel in a flash. Soon, they saw pieces spiraling off into space, illuminated by sparks and remnants of atmosphere burning off.

The *Cassi* shuddered as a direct hit rocked its stern. On the main holo display, two Zodark heavy cruisers maneuvered into a flanking position behind them, one at thirty-eight hundred kilometers and the other forty-three hundred kilometers from the *Cassi*. Their menacing forms cut through the darkness of space like sharks in deep water.

"Enemy cruisers moving to our aft quarter, bearing one-eight-four degrees stern!" Sato reported as she stared at the TAO position.

"We're on it. Aft guns preparing to fire—firing!" Rhom declared excitedly.

A pair of projectiles zipped right over the top of one of the heavy cruisers as it executed a punishing twisting turn to avoid the shot they anticipated coming their way. The other gun on the starboard side drilled the heavy cruiser companion—thirty-six-inch projectiles tore through the ship's armor and bored into the guts of the Zodark vessel. A fraction of a second later, a geyser of flame a hundred meters long ejected from the tears in the armor—lighting the void around the vessel for the briefest of moments before secondary explosions began ripping the cruiser apart.

"Hot damn, Rhom! Pass my compliments to your gunners!" Lee said, congratulating him on an incredible hit. The feeling of excitement was short-lived. The *Cassiopeia* shook from another hit. The heavy cruiser was still behind them, the one that had barely outmaneuvered the pair of slugs they'd fired at it.

Another blast from one of the cruisers to their rear seared through *Cassiopeia*'s aft port side. The cruiser didn't have the same hitting power as one of their battleships, but you wouldn't want to let it sit there and continue to shoot at you either.

"He's firing again—brace for impact!" announced Rhom.

The ship vibrated from the hit. Wall panels and stations clattered on the bridge.

The more Admiral Lee watched what was happening around them, the more he came to the conclusion they were in trouble. "We're being surrounded—they're bracketing us into a kill box," Lee said as he surveyed the tactical situation unfurling around him—around *his* ship. Then he spotted something—four new contacts. A battleship and three heavy cruisers. They were preparing to fire. Lee shouted, "All hands, brace for impact! Prepare to counter on my mark."

The crew responded in unison. A chorus of determined voices reverberated through the command deck. "Aye-aye, sir!"

"Lieutenant Harris, deploy countermeasures—now! I want that battleship jammed," Lee commanded, then added, "Deploy flares and chaffs now, and someone better deploy that damn decoy, or they're going to answer to me when this is over!"

Commander Rhom had responded to Lee with a quick nod. "Flares and chaff decoys have been launched. I've redirected our ECM to focus on the battleship closest to us."

"Commander Rhom, that Zodark ship is turning—he's positioning for a broadside," Lee said as they watched the giant Zodark warship finish its turn and bring the bulk of its firepower to bear on the *Cassi*.

"I see, Admiral—our port side guns are coming online now. Preparing to fire…firing now!"

The ship shuddered beneath his feet as the eight thirty-six-inch twin-barreled magnetic railguns pummeled the Zodark battleship. Then came the volley from the four triple-barreled antiship turbo laser turrets. The sheer volume of firepower and destruction being hurled at the Zodark warship reminded Lee of ancient holo vids he had seen of warships from the fifteenth through eighteenth centuries as they lined up against each other—firing broadsides at near point-blank.

"Brace for impact!" Lee heard someone shout moments before the Zodarks fired.

The *Cassiopeia* shook violently from the broadside. Alarms were going off, and new damage reports were coming in. The two ships continued to fire. Laser beams cut deep gashes into the side of Lee's flagship. Magrail slugs continued to punch holes through the sides of the Zodark battleship, exploding within the ship. Within a minute of the two battleships going toe-to-toe, the Zodark vessel lost power, its exterior lights flashing twice before blinking out entirely, the ship now adrift as the *Cassiopeia* fired once more into the crippled warship. The battleship exploded in a giant flash.

Flares, chaff canisters, and red tracer rounds filled the space around the *Cassiopeia*. Missiles and torpedoes exploded as interceptors were launched, and point-defense weapons kept enemy missiles and torpedoes from pummeling the *Cassi* more than they already had.

"Rhom," Admiral Lee said, "see if you can't hammer that remaining cruiser behind with our Havoc-IIs. We can't allow that guy to sit back there and systematically destroy gun turrets. He's already managed to take out a pair of them. No more, Rhom!"

"Aye, Admiral. We're on it,"

Lee watched the rear-facing camera as Havoc antiship missiles began firing, their trajectory lines arcing across the holo screen. Moments later, the display lit up with the bright flashes of contact. The cruiser reeled from the impact. The missiles struck true.

Plumes of escaping gas and debris marked where the missiles breached the cruiser's hull. Electrical fires sparked visibly even from the distance, outlining the cruiser in a hellish glow.

"It's taken a hit, Admiral, but it's still combat-capable," Rhom said as he read the readouts streaming with the latest damage assessments. "Propulsion is damaged, but not off-line. They're slowing but still in the fight."

Lee absorbed the update with a grimace. "Keep pressure on that target, Rhom. Ready another volley and take out their propulsion completely."

The two more enemy cruisers on their stern returned fire with a vengeful barrage. A volley of plasma torpedoes pierced the expanse and struck the *Cassiopeia* amidships. Alarms blared as systems temporarily faltered under the sudden electrical strain. The main holo displayed superficial damage, with a few external sensors fried and minor hull abrasions.

Lee set his jaw. "Helm, turn us to starboard six-five degrees, maintain speed. Rhom, as the ship turns, ready the main railguns. Target those cruisers' propulsion systems. I want them adrift in space and that lead cruiser out of the fight for good."

The *Cassiopeia* turned, the bridge crew grabbing for just about anything to hold while it completed its maneuver.

"Admiral, we're lining the shot up now," Commander Rhom replied. He was in constant communication with the gun batteries— getting status reports on ammo, casualties, and ability to stay in the fight. "Stand by. Weapons charging to fire—weapons firing."

This time, the *Cassiopeia*'s main guns unleashed a devastating onslaught. The rounds hit with precision, and the results were catastrophic. The targeted cruiser's propulsion tanks ruptured, igniting a violent explosion that tore through the vessel. It sent large fragments of the cruiser's hull spiraling uncontrollably into space.

One sizable chunk of debris collided with another enemy cruiser nearby. The collision didn't destroy the second cruiser, but the impact caused significant structural damage. A gaping hole formed where the debris struck and caused a hull breach. The vacuum of space snuffed out any flames, but escaping gases and the brief ignition of volatile materials became visible as a quick flash before dissipating into the void.

The other cruiser they had fired on was hit with nearly a dozen rounds. Explosions rippled across the ship—jets of flame shot out through the gaping holes in the armor. Moments later the entire ship exploded, the *Cassiopeia* having scored another ship kill in a battle that should have never happened.

"Good hit, Rhom! My congratulations to the gun crews! It looks like keeping their formation behind us like that worked in our favor," Lee complimented. "Keep up the assault. Let's finish them off."

While they had been battling the Zodark vessels within their midst, two enemy battleships along the outer line of the battle sniped from range at the *Cassi*, their hits doing minor damage. As the battle carried on, the *Cassiopeia* fired one salvo after another.

Lee turned his attention to the ships of his fleet. As damage reports flooded in through the fleet's central hub, the screens flickered with updates from the respective ships: the RNS *Oregon* and *Poseidon* showed critical breaches and propulsion failures; *Nebraska* reported a catastrophic failure in its main engine room, with uncontrollable fires spreading through vital compartments.

While his focus had been fighting the *Cassi*, his raiding force was in bad shape.

Lee felt a cold pit form in his stomach as he watched the frigate *Halifax* explode, life pods scattered about the wreckage. *My overconfidence and arrogance got the better of me*, he thought.

The bitter taste of a strategic miscalculation was unfamiliar and harsh to him. He had only known victory to this point, and it stung to admit this was not turning into one.

As the enemy fleet seemed to swarm them, another ship of his raiding force, the frigate *Halcyon*, suffered a devastating hit. He saw it on the holo display, a fiery wreck before the frigate exploded—one blast following another until the ship broke apart. Its dying embers streaked across space.

Lee's chest contracted. He felt a tightness he hadn't known before as he witnessed the devastation in real time.

"Admiral, we just lost the *Virginia*," Sato announced in shock. "Admiral, we have three additional enemy cruisers closing in on us, bearing three-one-six degrees off the port bow!"

Amidst the chaos, Lee's voice rose once more, commanding and clear. "All ships, focus fire on the lead battleship. Target coordinates are Alpha-three-nine Tango. Helm, come about to bearing two-four-five degrees, ahead full!"

"Aye, sir, coming about to two-four-five degrees, full ahead," Reynolds confirmed as he maneuvered the *Cassiopeia*. They had maneuvered themselves closer to the asteroid field, the floating rocks providing cover at times and an obstacle when maneuvering.

With the battle intensifying, Lee opened the channel to the combat information center. "CIC, Bridge. This is the admiral. What are your thoughts on launching the Gripens to help thin these Glaives and Vultures out?"

The CIC officer, Commander Haley Tig, responded, "Sir, that's a tough one. The fights are too close, and we're just as liable to shoot our own people—at the same time, if they could thin out those bombers for us…"

"Yeah, Tig, I hear you—damn it, go ahead and scramble the fighters. Tell Coop to do what he can. Out." He ended the conversation not happy at all about sending his fighters into the maelstrom but also not sure what else he could do.

Outside in the darkness of space, there was the deadly movement of Glaives as they darted toward the *Cassi*, unleashing torpedo after torpedo on it.

"Status, people. Talk to me," Lee said.

Lieutenant Rodriguez responded first from the comms station. "Glaives squadrons increasing, Admiral. They're hitting our ships hard on all sectors. Right now, we're detecting multiple incoming bombers, bearing zero-eight-three degrees off the starboard quarter."

Commander Sato then added, "We somehow ended up maneuvering ourselves into the edge of this asteroid field. They're seriously limiting our evasion options. It's a tight squeeze everywhere we turn, sir," she explained. "Helm, recommend course correction, come right to bearing one-two-four to avoid collision."

Lee nodded in agreement. They had to get out of this. "Reynolds, do as she says. Get us out of here."

"Copy that," Reynolds replied. "Coming right to bearing one-two-four, aye."

Tig's right—we gotta get out of here… They were rapidly becoming outmatched and outnumbered. Lee turned to Rodriguez, asking her to open a fleet-wide channel. After she complied, Lee said, "This is the Admiral. I'm ordering all ships to execute a tactical withdrawal to the rally point immediately. Set course for the Pfeinstgard stargate and stand by to jump—Admiral Lee out." When Lee finished issuing the order to retreat, he saw the look of concern on the faces of his bridge crew. He felt as if he had somehow let them down. Turning to face Lieutenant Reynolds, he ordered, "Helm, plot an escape vector and prepare to engage at full sublight thrust. We'll wait until the others have left, then we'll leave."

"Aye, Admiral," Reynolds acknowledged, his voice tense. "Plotting a course that might give us some breathing room, but it's going to be close with these asteroids."

"Admiral," said Chief Engineer MacGregor gruffly, coming on the line, "our propulsion systems are at max stress dodging these rock piles! And those Vultures and Glaives hitting us with missiles and torpedoes aren't tickling in a good way either. We push any harder, I can't promise she'll hold together!"

Lee clenched his jaw. "Keep her together, Chief. Divert power from nonessential systems if you have to."

"Aye, pushing her to the limits, but don't say I didn't warn you!" MacGregor replied.

With a nod to his tactical officer, Lee commanded, "Fire magrails at the lead battleship, now! Let's end her. Full salvo, all batteries."

The *Cassiopeia* shuddered as the magnetic railguns charged and fired, sending projectiles hurtling through space. On the holo display, the targeted Zodark battleship was struck squarely. The impact was visible from two thousand kilometers away.

As the enemy vessel reeled from the hits, more of his ships sent all they had at the battleship. Sparks sprayed from its damaged exterior as some smaller shells ricocheted off; others tore right through the armor, detonating inside its guts. "Rhom, keep the pressure on. Redirect batteries Alpha through Echo, target their engines and weapon systems."

Amid the relentless barrage, another of Admiral Lee's ships, the RNS *Phuket*, another frigate, faltered under a heavy assault. On the bridge of the *Cassiopeia*, Lee witnessed the *Phuket* enveloped in an Armageddon-like display off *Cassi*'s port side, seven hundred klicks away. The vessel was beyond saving. It buckled, and in a cataclysmic blast, it was gone. Admiral Lee felt a pang in his chest; he knew Captain Jensen of the *Phuket* well—a friend and a seasoned officer. Silently, he vowed he'd write to Jensen's family himself.

No sooner had the *Vanguard* met its end than klaxons blared anew. "Contact, starboard side! We're being surrounded again. Zodark cruiser, bearing eight-eight, closing fast!"

Lee's head snapped to the display just in time to see a Zodark cruiser closing in at eighteen hundred kilometers in the cramped asteroid belt, the ship's lasers already spitting deadly energy.

Captain Gordon of the RNS *Oregon* broke through the comm chatter. "Admiral, the *Oregon* is engaging the hostiles on your starboard flank. We're redirecting all firepower to assist."

"Copy that, Gordon. We align to your fire," Lee responded. "Rhom, target their engines. Reynolds, come about to bearing two-seven-zero, align us for a broadside—let's punch a hole."

The *Cassiopeia*'s crew coordinated their response.

"Missiles and magrails aligned, firing on your mark," Rhom said.

"Now!" Lee squinted, willing a successful retreat with everything he had left in him.

With precise synchronization, the *Cassiopeia* and the *Oregon* unleashed their fury. Missiles and magnetic rail projectiles converged on the Zodark craft. Within moments, the enemy ship's hull ruptured. Fire blossomed along its frame as it was torn apart.

"There's a gap!" Lee pointed to the opening. "Reynolds, take us through—come right eight-eight degrees, ahead full thrust."

"Aye, sir, coming eight-eight degrees, ahead full."

The *Cassiopeia* lurched as it maneuvered through the newly created opening in the enemy line.

As they moved, another blip vanished from the tactical display—the frigate RNS *Halifax*. Now just metal floating in space. The sight was a brutal reminder of the cost of this trap they'd blundered into. For a fleeting second, guilt surged through Lee. *Foolish. I walked right into their hands.*

Firmly pushing aside the self-reproach, Admiral Lee focused on the tactical display and prepared for the next phase of this desperate fight for survival.

Chapter Twenty-Four
Gangsters & Robo Taxis

Zidara, Gurista Prime

Catalina, who was usually rather optimistic, surprised David and the rest of the Kites when she announced, "Frankly, I'm surprised no one else has taken out this Adad character already. He sounds like a real piece of work."

David nodded. Adad of the Clan Nippur was notorious for being a miserable hellraiser. His five wives and twenty-three children all had the look of someone who was forced to smile for the benefit of the dictator they were subjugated to—and he was known to be a philanderer, using women for his pleasure and then throwing them out like trash when they no longer served his needs.

"Honestly, they're probably too afraid of the consequences," Amir replied. A likely narcissist, Adad knew how to flatter those in power and ingratiate himself with them. He'd leveraged his extreme loyalty to the Zodarks to rule those around him with an iron fist. More than one of his enemies had ended up dead under suspicious circumstances.

"Well, it's his turn to face the music," said Jess. "How are we going to go about it this time?"

"He has one obvious weakness with his pacemaker," David responded, "but the trick is how to cause it to malfunction without any obvious signs of foul play."

"We'd need a power surge of some kind," said Somchai. "In our case, it would be best if this occurred with something he usually interacts with in his environment."

"It might be a bit too difficult to fry his work terminal," Amir suggested. "The security at LugalDrive is tight."

Somchai nodded. "He's right. Apparently, *lugal* means something like king or ruler—Adad runs his business empire the same way he does the rest of his life, with an extreme amount of authority and control."

"Well, he can't run this automated taxi service across not just Zidara but all of Gurista Prime and even in the nearby planet of Moraga without having garnered some enemies," David insisted.

"I'm sure that the manager he has set up in Moraga won't mind when his boss is dead, but if you were hoping someone would be willing to do the deed for us, you are barking up the wrong tree," Amir explained. "He's got the Zodarks so wrapped around his finger that no bribe would be sufficient."

"All right, so let's go back to the drawing board on this power surge idea. What about some of the IoT devices in his home, like his refrigerator?" asked David.

Somchai looked up some of the specs of the food coolers on Gurista Prime, then shook his head. "We aren't going to be able to get a big enough surge that way," he explained.

"I'd say go after him at his girlfriend's house, but he's got more than one, plus the five wives," said Catalina, a bit exasperated. "It's hard to know where this guy is even going to spend the night."

"He sure does get around a lot for an older crusty guy with a pacemaker," joked Amir.

Jess twisted her face at the thought. "If it weren't for all the medical nanites and advanced Sumerian technology, he wouldn't be able to have a harem like that."

"All right, so we don't know where he sleeps, but we do know where he works," said David. "Where else do we definitely know that he goes?"

"Well, he's got his favorite bars, but that schedule is unpredictable as well," offered Amir. "There's the council meetings, but it seems rather risky to try something there. Other than the drinking, the women, and the power-grabbing, he doesn't really have any hobbies."

"No...but we *do* know where he parks his car," said Catalina, smirking.

"OK, what are you thinking?" asked David.

"Every morning, Adad walks along the same route from the garage to his office, and he just so happens to pass by several rows of streetlights. There's construction going on about a block away—is there some way we could manipulate that to cause a power surge in the vicinity?"

David thought she was onto something there, but there seemed to be a few missing links. "I'm not sure that we could just sneak our way into a construction site. I mean, we could download the skills to run an excavator, but it actually takes some pull to get into construction here on Gurista Prime."

"That's the thing, we don't need to be on the crew," Catalina explained. "Since the workers follow preplanned instructions on when and how to dig, we just need to hack into their *blueprints*. So, what do you think, Somchai? Can we make it look like a clerical error?"

Somchai scrunched his eyebrows. Without responding, he started clicking away on his P2, grunting and mumbling to himself as he did. After a few minutes, he turned to the group, a wry smile forming across his lips. "Catalina, I think I've found our backdoor. Although, after this mission, we probably should let Dakkuri and Ashurina know about it. We wouldn't want the same weakness to be exploited by the Zodarks later."

****

Two Days Later
Penthouse Suite at Lagash Towers

Adad's alarm went off at 5:30 a.m. as usual. He threw his blanket off and sat up straight as a board. He was an early riser, always making sure to keep all aspects of his empire running as smoothly as possible.

His current most-favored girlfriend, Lila, groaned and rolled over, the satin sheets barely covering her lingerie.

No matter, he thought. He didn't really care what she did during the day as long as she was available to him at night.

Adad sent Lila a message through his P2, informing her that a package would be delivered to the suite around noon and that he looked forward to seeing her that night around 8 p.m. A little jewelry and a little flattery went a long way with a woman like Lila. She was beautiful, high-maintenance, and not that bright—exactly the way Adad liked his women.

He took a shower, then donned his expensive designer clothing, carefully designed to convey his wealth and authority. His tailored suit had the LugalDrive emblem emblazoned on it, reminding everyone of his utter dominance of the transportation industry on Gurista Prime.

As Adad drank his morning cup of taqaffa, the warm liquid started his brain buzzing, and he set to work responding to the many messages he'd received while he was sleeping. First and foremost on his mind was a note from one of his Zodark contacts—they wanted him to collect some intelligence for them again. It was one of the many ways he kept them on his side.

With that handled, Adad grabbed a second cup of taqaffa to go and left his penthouse. The head of the front desk saw him as he exited the elevator and rushed over.

"We have everything arranged with your special package, sir," the man said, following him like an eager puppy as he spoke. "Is there anything else I can do for you this morning?" he asked.

"Nothing more today, thank you." Adad threw him a tip and left him at the door to the parking garage. As such a frequent flier at the Lagash Towers penthouse suite, he was afforded a certain level of notoriety whenever he walked into the lobby.

Adad's luxury vehicle beeped as he approached, and when he got close enough, a camera scanned his retina and the door automatically opened. With his route set, the fancy car took off.

Using the onboard hands-free system, Adad had several reports read to him on his way in to the office, tracking every aspect of his business dominance. He also listened to dossiers on his competitors in Moraga, which he had not fully taken over just yet. A plan formed in his mind as to how to peel control away from each one.

When Adad arrived at the parking garage near his office, he straightened his suit and grabbed his P2, making some notes as he walked along his usual route. It was still dark out; he loved to get a jump on things before the rest of the world got to work.

Suddenly, the streetlights began to pulsate. As they did, a sharp pain radiated from his chest through his left arm. Adad fell to the ground, clutching the area where his heart was. His P2 had fallen out of his reach, but he knew something had gone wrong with his pacemaker.

Adad moaned in pain, but the streets were still empty. By the time help arrived, he would be clinically dead.
****

The Next Day

David handed Catalina her morning cup of coffee and gave her a kiss on the cheek. "Congratulations, babe. Your plan worked exactly as you envisioned."

"Ah, did you already read the news?" she asked.

"Yep, right here in the *Gurista Daily*. 'Freak Accident Causes Major Power Surge: Transportation Magnate Adad of LugalDrive Dead.'"

She grabbed her own P2 and scoured the article for herself. It detailed how faulty records had led to an excavator disturbing a supercapacitor, which had caused a significant power surge and the untimely death of their target. The rest of the article went into depth about Adad's five wives and many children and speculated as to the manner in which his personal and business assets were to be distributed.

Catalina walked over to David and gave him a hug. "You know, sometimes this 'job' can be a bit heavy, but Gurista Prime is definitely a better place without that scumbag."

David nodded. "I think you're right."

Chapter Twenty-Five
The Gates of Hell

Ripley's Raiders
RNS *Cassiopeia*
Gravaxia System

Commander Cooper sprinted across the hangar bay. His boots thudded against the deck plates as he ran. He reached his Gripen starfighter, its smooth lines and deadly armaments a welcome sight.

"She's all repaired, sir. Good as new and fully armed," his crew chief affirmed.

"Thanks, Chief. I know I brought her in with a few holes in her. Thanks for getting her fixed up in a jiffy for me," Coop said, thanking the man who kept his bird ready at a moment's notice.

"Just try and bring her back in one piece, sir, and we'll take care of the rest," the chief petty officer jested with him.

Coop smiled, giving him a thumbs-up as he climbed into the cockpit, settling into the ejection seat and strapping himself in. He donned his helmet, activating the communications system as he rapidly went through his preflight checklist while getting himself and his squadron leaders up on comms.

"Goonz, this is Coop. Sound off and report status. We're going back—they want us to thin out those Glaives as much as possible to keep those torpedoes off the *Cassi*."

One by one, his pilots checked in. Seventy voices, each filled with determination.

"Red Squadron, standing by," Raptor reported.

"Orange Squadron, all systems green," Nomad chimed in.

Coop scanned the tactical screen on his heads-up display. The battle raged beyond the confines of the hangar bay in a swirling maelstrom of ships and weapons fire. They were being launched into the gates of hell.

Admiral Ripley Lee's voice crackled over the comm. "Commander Cooper—Coop, I wanted to call you personally. I know I'm sending you into a nightmare. I wouldn't do this if it wasn't important. I need you to engage the enemy, thin out those bombers for us and provide support for our capital ships. Good luck out there, Coop, and happy hunting."

"Acknowledged, Admiral. We won't let you down."

"You better not, Commander. I'm not giving you that option. Out."

Coop took a deep breath. This was the big one—the one fight every pilot was unsure if they'd return from. Shaking the negative thoughts from his mind, he said, "Goonz, once we've launched, I want everyone to form up on me. We're going to start a diamond formation. We're going in hot moments after we enter free space."

"Aye, Commander!"

The fighters were loaded into the launch tubes. The scene outside the ship was like a chapter from Dante's Inferno—chaos. Moving his thruster levers forward, Coop heard his engines roar to life, and then the brakes holding him tight released, hurling him down the launch tube before ejecting him into the black expanse.

No sooner had they cleared *Cassi*'s launch bay than an enemy starfighter, a Vulture, barreled toward them. Coop reacted instinctively, rolling the Gripen sideways as a missile jetted past where he'd been mere moments before. He deployed countermeasures, a stream of metallic chaff and flares erupting behind him to confuse the Vulture's tracking systems.

"Locking on," Lone Wolf said over the comm. "Arming a Fox Three."

"Wolf, negative on the missiles. Save 'em for the cruisers or a Glaive—use the magrails on the Vultures," Coop said. His eyes flicked between his instruments and the enemy as he activated his primary guns.

As the Vulture looped for another pass, Coop squeezed the trigger. The Gripen's rotary magrail guns spun up, hurling hypervelocity rounds chewing through the space between them and the Vulture.

A direct hit sent the enemy starfighter spiraling into a fiery demise. Coop narrowly flew through the debris, the bits and chunks of metal pelting the armor of his fighter like hail.

"Squadron leaders, listen up. Take your squadrons and engage targets of opportunity—focus on the Glaives if possible. The cruisers secondarily. Don't let your wingmen stray, and watch your sixes. Orange Squadron, you're with me and Blue Squadron."

"Aye, sir!" came a chorus of voices.

The Gripens peeled away and streaked toward the enemy bombers swarming around the Republic fleet. Eight of his best, those of Orange Squadron, followed Coop and his Blues. Beyond the dogfighting starfighters, the larger battle unfolded before them. Republic battleships, cruisers, and frigates engaged their Zodark counterparts in a struggle for survival.

About six hundred kilometers out from Coop, a Republic battleship's magrail cannons unleashed a barrage of tungsten rounds. The projectiles streaked through the void, leaving trails of ionized particles behind. They slammed into the hull of a Zodark cruiser, puncturing its armor and sending geysers of molten metal spewing into space.

Close by, a Republic frigate—its hull scarred and battered— maneuvered to avoid a salvo of torpedoes. The deadly projectiles detonated in blinding flashes of light. The frigate emerged unscathed; its point-defense lasers had intercepted the incoming ordnance before it converted to plasma.

The frigate returned fire, and though its magrails were smaller in comparison to the larger cruiser or battleships, their hypersonic rounds still tore into the Zodark battleship's flank. They blasted through deck after deck, leaving gaping wounds in the ship's structure.

Coop veered and locked onto a Zodark Vulture firing on one of his fighters. His targeting reticle turned red, his guns certain to hit.

He squeezed the trigger, sending a stream of bullets toward the enemy craft. The projectiles burst through the Vulture's armor and the enemy fighter spun away in a cloud of debris.

"Coop to Orange Squadron, report." Coop regained formation control as his display lit up with updates.

"Nomad here, splash one Vulture," came the first reply over the channel.

"Deuce, tally one!" another voice chimed in.

"Copy that. Good hunting," Coop said. "Form up, echelon right. We're making a run on that Zodark cruiser, bearing two-one-one degrees, twenty-four hundred kilometers out. Follow my lead. Weapons hot, aim for their boosters. Let's give them something to think about."

As Orange Squadron adjusted their formation, the frantic skirmish of starfighters and capital ships continued to unfold around them. Coop's hands were steady on the controls, his mind racing ahead to the next move in this game of cosmic chess. They approached the Zodark cruiser, a behemoth bristling with armaments.

Coop banked his Gripen fighter hard as he led Orange Squadron in a tight arc toward the cruiser's stern. The massive vessel's engines flared with bluish plasma, propelling it through the void.

"Orange Squadron, form up in attack position delta," Coop ordered. "Arm missiles and synchronize targeting solutions."

Sixteen acknowledgment lights winked on his heads-up display as the pilots complied. The Gripens fell into a staggered formation, their noses pointed directly at the cruiser's vulnerable propulsion systems.

Coop's eyes flicked over his instrument panels. Tactical data streamed across the screens. The cruiser's armor still held but was almost crippled under the sustained bombardment from the Republic fleet. Structural integrity readings showed mounting stress along its aft quarter.

"Fire on my mark." Coop gripped his controls. His finger hovered over the trigger. The targeting reticle in his HUD pulsed red as it locked onto the cruiser's primary thruster array. "Mark!"

A volley of missiles and laser fire streaked across the dark expanse. They slammed into the cruiser's stern with devastating force. Explosions blossomed along its hull as the warheads detonated, ripping through armor plating into vital systems.

On Coop's display, a cascade of red warning indicators flared to life across the Zodark vessel's schematic. Its aft armor nearly collapsed under the onslaught. Secondary blasts rippled through its engines as feedback surges overloaded power conduits.

Coop watched the data flow while analyzing the damage inflicted. The cruiser's acceleration dropped by a significant margin. Its main thrusters blinked erratically.

"Confirmed hits on primary propulsion," Coop reported, his voice steady. "Target's velocity decreasing. Orange Squadron, break the attack and regroup."

As they broke off from the beleaguered Zodark ship, laser fire and magrail rounds from the RNS *Poseidon* lashed the enemy's hull.

"I'm taking fire," Free Bird called out. "Releasing countermeasures."

"Deploying countermeasures as well," Dag responded. A cloud of chaff and flares bloomed around Free Bird's Gripen, confusing the cruiser's weapons systems.

"Watch it! That battleship is launching more Vultures!" Outlaw said over the channel.

A swarm of the nimble Zodark starfighters poured from the battleship's hangar bays, heading toward the Gripens with lasers blazing. Coop jinked hard to starboard as energy flashes zipped in front of his canopy.

Coop gritted his teeth, perspiration dotting his forehead. "Orange Squadron, initiate Lufbery maneuvers!" Coop had drilled this World War I dogfighting tactic into every pilot on the *Cassi* from their earliest training.

Coop banked his Gripen hard to port. The inertial compensators strained against the brutal maneuver, fighting to keep the intense g-forces from rendering him unconscious. Even in space, violent changes in velocity and direction could overwhelm the fighter's systems and wreak havoc on a pilot's body. While inertial dampeners negated the effects of steady acceleration, the abrupt twisting and turning of a starfighter dogfight produced incredible momentum shifts. The human body simply wasn't designed to withstand such extreme forces unaided.

His squadron mirrored the tight turn. Their fighters left brilliant azure trails in the void as their engines flared.

They flew in a rapidly tightening spiral. The distance between each ship shrank with every revolution. Coop's threat receiver shrilled as the Vultures followed them.

"Hold it steady," Coop grunted. His muscles tensed against the punishing g-forces. In the void, inertia was their only ally. With no air to provide lift or drag, their momentum was all that kept them from drifting apart.

The Vultures loomed large in Coop's canopy. Their cockpits gave the alien fighters an almost hornet-like appearance. Their wings were studded with laser cannons, fanning out from their fuselages as they pushed their drives to the limit while they tried to maintain pursuit.

Coop fought against the strain from his steep turn. "Nomad... Free Bird... mark!"

The two Gripens opened up with their magrail cannons in a blinding stutter of fire. Streams of hypersonic slugs tore into the Vulture and shredded its armored hide. The stricken fighter tumbled away in a cloud of broken alloys and frozen atmosphere.

"Good kill!" Dag's voice crackled over the comm.

Another Vulture drifted into Coop's sights. His reticle moved across the lead Vulture as Coop's computer tracked the enemy fighter's erratic movements. He triggered his own guns. The recoil hammered through Coop's fighter. Return laser fire burned across his Gripen's nose, but his armor held.

"I'm hit, but still flying! And, yeah, I still nailed that guy good!" Coop excitedly reported.

The crippled Vulture broke off its attack. Atmosphere and flames trailed it as it fled. Coop's threat receiver fell silent.

"Scratch one Vulture!" Raptor said.

"Outstanding," Coop replied. "Reform on me, we're not done yet."

Nomad's voice barked through the channel. "Got two more."

The Gripens pulled back into their arrowhead as more Vultures swarmed in. Coop rolled as target lock warnings blinked on his HUD. The g-forces slammed him back in the cockpit. A missile scorched past, far too close for comfort.

"I can't shake this one!" Free Bird's voice rang with panic.

"I'm on it," Nomad responded.

Coop watched his display as Nomad's Gripen slipped in behind the Vulture with his cannons blazing. The alien fighter's icon disappeared off Coop's screen.

"Thanks for the assist," Free Bird said.

Narrowing his eyes, Coop radioed to his pilots. "Let's put this cruiser out of commission. Another run on its thrusters."

Coop's cockpit dimmed red as alarms on his dash's holo warned of another missile locked onto his ship's signature. "Nomad, Dag, I've got a missile inbound!"

Without a moment's hesitation, both Gripens, along with Coop, unleashed a blistering barrage of countermeasures. The projectile's rocket flared as it tried to reacquire its target. The warhead swung wildly through the decoy fields. Coop held his breath, hands tightening around the control stick as the weapon snaked back and forth.

Dag's voice burst into Coop's helmet. "It's no good, the countermeasures fooled it. It can't get a lock."

Sure enough, the missile lost its tracking ability. The motor burned out as it tumbled past the Gripens.

Coop grinned. "Good work, now let's finish this cruiser off."

They came around in a tight formation. The hulking Zodark cruiser's stern loomed before them. Weapon locks chimed in their cockpits as targeting systems acquired the engine cluster.

Coop tightened, ready for the attack run. "Orange Squadron, switch arms hot. Cobra One, Mad Dog, launch missiles on my order."

The two pilots acknowledged. The squadron was eight hundred kilometers out from the target. Just a bit closer, and the rounds and projectiles could dig into the enemy vessel that much better.

"Free Bird, Outlaw, stand by with magrails. Nomad, stay glued to my wing. We'll hammer them with our railguns once that thruster housing is exposed." The magrail cannons were brutal at close range, their tungsten darts capable of blasting through the toughest alloys.

Coop's warning displays pulsed as the cruiser's point-defense turrets swiveled to track the incoming strike package. "Here it comes, people. Mark!"

Twin missiles streaked away from Mad Dog and Cobra One's Gripens, yellow-white trails scorching space. Coop and the rest of his squad opened fire with their magrail guns.

The missiles slammed home and tungsten rounds hit their spots with success. They detonated against the Zodarks' armored flank. A gaping rent appeared in the thruster housing as the explosive force sheared through bulkheads and decks.

"Scratch one thruster cluster," Nomad said. "She's crippled, and badly!"

"Let's finish this," Coop growled. "Magrails hot."

Now five hundred kilometers in front of them, the cruiser bled gas and debris. It tilted slightly toward starboard.

The heavy magrail cannons spat lethal streams into the cruiser's compromised engine spaces. Bulkheads buckled and shattered as critical systems were scythed apart by the hypersonic metal storm.

"Nice flying there, Orange Squadron," Coop said. "OK, we—"

His comm crackled with a burst of static as the Zodark cruiser's cannons found their mark. Coop's displays trembled and died as his fighter's systems were disabled before him.

"I've lost control inputs!" Coop said, fighting the dead stick as his Gripen began to tumble through the void. "Orange Squadron, I'm hit! I need—"

An explosion rocked his cockpit as a Vulture's lasers raked across his crippled starfighter. Warning lights flashed as the ship began to crack under the onslaught. Coop's world shattered into a color of fire and darkness.

Coop squeezed his fingers around the bright-yellow-and-black striped handle between his legs. With a firm pull, mechanisms fired, and explosive bolts severed the canopy latches. In a rush of escaping atmosphere, the canopy blasted away into the black expanse.

An automatic sequence initiated, and the ejection seat's rockets ignited. Coop launched clear of his stricken fighter in an arc. For an endless moment, he hung suspended against a background of stars as the battle raged around him. In the next instant, a Zodark Vulture headed right for him.

****

RNS *Cassiopeia*
IVO Velos Belt
Gravaxia System

Admiral Lee watched how the tactical action map continually updated the chaotic battle unfolding around them. In contrast to most maps, the TAM was a holographical three-dimensional rendering of the battlespace around them. It provided a more surreal, complete picture of how a battle was unfolding and, more importantly, how and where to utilize his warships to greater effect. Seeing a Zodark battleship had moved into a position that temporarily blocked his own escape toward the stargate leading to the Primord system next door, Lee spoke loud and confidently. "All batteries, focus fire on sector Delta-4. Target that battleship." He pointed his laser pen at it. "I want that battleship dead before we leave the system."

They'd exited the Velos Belt eleven minutes prior, their course now set for the stargate. Lee knew once they were through the gate, the Zodarks wouldn't follow. He was betting they had accomplished their mission—ambush Republic forces and send them back across the border.

He was also betting they had no real idea what kind of force might be lying in wait should they opt to follow him into the Primord system.

After his fleet's successful counterattack on the Zodark ambush—destroying multiple enemy warships—Lee believed the Zodarks might want to regroup before following his force through the stargate. It was what he would do if the roles were reversed.

With the Zodark battleship now just eleven hundred klicks away, Lee's fleet responded with a coordinated barrage, sending a hailstorm of torpedoes, missiles, and magrail slugs into the section of the battleship where they knew the ship's power reactors were located. With each salvo, with each Havoc-II missile boring into the ship's outer armored shell before detonating, they were that much closer to destroying yet another enemy battleship.

As he observed the conflagration on the main screen, the battleship's armor began to buckle under the relentless assault. Every hit depleted its defenses, bit by bit, until a final decisive strike ignited its core. A brilliant explosion ripped through the hull—a shockwave blasted across the void. In that instant, the ship went dark, its life extinguished— life pods emerged, sporadic at first, then a deluge of the tiny escape pods before the fires extinguished themselves, their oxygen spent.

"Target destroyed!" exclaimed Commander Rhom excitedly, the bridge crew erupting in cheers and a few high fives.

Still swirling about them, squadrons of Gripens continued their relentless attacks against the remaining Zodark ships. They darted about the battlefield, engaging both the Zodark starfighters and bombers and the nearest cruisers and frigates. Lee's attention shifted from the main screen to the TAMs, where an awe-inspiring scene unfolded before him. The expansive maelstrom of dogfights created breathtaking eruptions that punctuated the starlit darkness. It demonstrated the pilots' unwavering determination as they skillfully maneuvered their craft in a relentless battle, pushing themselves and their machines to the limits of their endurance and skill.

In the swirling melee, *Cassiopeia*'s starfighters clashed fiercely with the enemy. Their lasers cut through space, magrails sending blue tracer lines toward their targets until impact. The cost of this fight, of this battle, was too high for even his pilots to bear. Every burst of static on the comm was a grim reminder of another pilot who was lost. The holographic viewport marked each fallen starfighter with a fading light.

A sudden surge of energy shook *Cassi*'s bridge as an enemy salvo hit. Sparks flew from overhead panels as Lee grabbed his armrests, knuckles white. The restraining belt held him tight to his seat. He patched into damage control, demanding, "I need fire teams to the bridge! Electrical and medical teams are urgently needed on the bridge, *now*!"

"Aye, Admiral, teams en route. ETA two minutes," an officer replied from below decks.

As the teams hustled, Lee watched the tactical display. His mind raced with calculations and contingencies. The *Cassi* held her own as Ripley's Raiders continued to battle against the Zodarks harder than expected. The loss of so many ships—three frigates, two heavy cruisers, and a single battleship—these losses would hurt. It also made it even more important to get his raiding force out of the system and back to friendly space.

Lieutenant Harris called out, "Admiral, the Omni-Spectral Array has detected a new presence of enemy warships entering the system from the direction of sector Gamma-3, the Tueblets stargate. OSA is estimating the number of reinforcements to be around thirty-five additional warships. We have no further analysis yet on the type and composition of this new enemy force."

Lee heard a few groans and audible gasps at the news. It wasn't the kind of news they were hoping for. Unfortunately, this raid into the Gravaxia system had really kicked up a hornet's nest.

Clearing his throat, Lee confidently ordered, "Issue a recall to all fighters—they are to return to the nest ASAP. I want the ship ready to FTL in ten minutes or less to the stargate. Divert auxiliary power to the engines if necessary. We are going to conduct a tactical withdrawal from the system."

Lee then turned to face Lieutenant Rodriguez, signaling he wanted to address the raiding party. When Rodriguez gave him the signal, he began, "Attention all ships—this is the admiral. Our mission is complete. We've destroyed a mining colony and fuel and munition depots and eliminated a possible staging area for enemy forces to conduct raiding missions of their own into Primord space. We're now going to conduct a tactical withdrawal from the battlespace back to Pfeinstgard. Once all fighter squadrons have returned to their ships, the *Cassiopeia* will lead the way to the Pfeinstgard stargate—ensure all ships are prepared for FTL travel to the gate. Admiral Lee out."

A flurry of acknowledgments filled the comm lines as the starfighters peeled away from their strafing runs and dogfights to return home. One by one, the vessels of Ripley's Raiders awaited the final order to begin FTL transit to the stargate.

"Admiral, we just received the final word. All fighters have been recovered. All life pods and boats have been recovered—ships are ready to jump," said his XO, Commander Sato.

Lee nodded in acknowledgment, then gave the signal to jump—it was time to go home.

The ship jumped, squeezed between the fabric of space and time as they crossed the entire system in mere minutes. The moment they came out of FTL, the massive stargate loomed large on the horizon—just thirty-five hundred kilometers from the jump point.

One by one, the ships of his raiding force blinked existence once more, surrounding the *Cassi* and filling the void around them. Ahead, the massive ringed structure of the stargate pulsed with barely contained energy. As they approached it, the gate activated—a shimmering blue iris filled the circular aperture, beckoning them through the artificial wormhole.

As the *Cassi* surged forward, they began to enter the shimmering blue iris until it pulled the *Cassi* in, the ship suddenly passing through the artificial wormhole and, moments later, ejecting them from the opposite end.

Once the *Cassi* was free of the stargate and back under their own power, Lee ordered his comms officer to contact his Primord counterpart, Admiral Vargr Asgardsson. He was the military commander for the system, operating from the orbital outpost that roughly translated to Ice Fire One, in orbit of Valholl, the capital planet of the system.

"Admiral, we're receiving a message from IF1. It's Admiral Asgardsson. Would you like me to put him through to your headset?" asked Lieutenant Harrison.

"Yes, Lieutenant, go ahead," he responded, activating the headset.

"Welcome back, Admiral Lee. I trust all went well on your raiding expedition. Anything of significance that needs to be reported?" the generally friendly Primord admiral asked.

"Thank you, Admiral, for welcoming us back to your system. I am proud to report we successfully destroyed the Zodark mining facility in the Velos Belt, along with multiple other outposts and facilities that could have been used to support an invasion or incursion into Pfeinstgard. We did encounter a Zodark force lying in ambush for us on the far side of the Velos Belt near an ice field; we lost a couple of our ships, while others sustained heavy damage. With your permission, Admiral, I would like to order my ships to dock at IF1 and begin repair operations immediately. If you will grant me one day, my staff will prepare a detailed report of our actions. I will personally brief you and answer any questions you may have," Lee explained before he went through some of the protocol procedures he had learned during the short time they had been assigned to this sector.

The Primord admiral gave Lee a curt nod. "This sounds like a reasonable request," he replied. "A day's time is granted. I look forward to listening to and studying your exploits. During the time in which you have been gone, my office received a message from your Admiral Fran McKee, the Director of Space Operations. She has asked me to relay a request for you to return to New Eden for consultations and new orders."

Admiral Asgardsson must have sensed Lee's trepidation, because he quickly added, "I can see you look concerned by this request. While I do not know specifically what she intends to discuss with you, I wouldn't be too worried about it. Our Fleet Commander, Admiral Stavanger, visited our station a few days ago. He informed me that your Admiral Bailey is planning to begin a large build-up of warships in the system. I am to prepare our facilities to support these operations and the relocation of Ionis Fleet—the King's Fleet. I would suspect her conversation will probably have something to do with this."

Lee bunched his eyebrows forward upon hearing the news of the Ionis Fleet relocating to Gravaxia. It made him wonder why Admiral McKee would want to speak with him in person, as opposed to using their comms system. Something about the phrase "consultations and new orders," had caused Lee's heart to skip a beat.

Lee set aside his misgivings and summoned a smile. "Thank you, Admiral Asgardsson. That was most kind of you to pass along Admiral McKee's message. Unless she stated I must leave immediately for New Eden, I shall have the *Cassiopeia* dock so we may begin some urgent repairs before setting course for New Eden. I will have my staff prepare a detailed account of our actions in Gravaxia so it can be added to your own records of Zodark activities in the system. It may be a few days before we are ready to get underway to New Eden. In the meantime, I look forward to speaking with you tomorrow. Admiral Lee out."

He cut the connection and then turned to his XO. "What do you think, Sato? I'm being recalled to New Eden—new orders…? You don't think I'm being replaced or reassigned , do you?"

Commander Sato smiled sheepishly as she shrugged her shoulders. "I can't say, Admiral. It does seem a bit premature to replace you already. You've only been in command for what, nine, ten months tops?"

"Yeah, something like that." Lee struggled to stay positive in that moment.

Sato reached her hand out, touching the side of his left arm as she whispered so only they could hear. "I wouldn't read too much into it, Ripley. We just scored a major victory out here—even if we did lose some ships. This was a resounding victory, Rip. Heck, Fleet HQ hasn't even heard about it yet. Wait until they read our report on how we kicked some serious Zodark ass. Think about it, Rip. We just destroyed four battleships, seven cruisers, and seven frigates—on top of seventy-two Glaives and sixty-six Vultures," Sato reassured him excitedly. This was their third time serving together. If there was one officer Lee felt most comfortable around, it was her.

Lee smiled tepidly, then bit his lower lip. "You're right, Noriko. I have done nothing wrong. We didn't stray from our orders or lose territory because of a bad decision. After Admiral McKee hears about the success of our raid, it'll be promotions and medals for everyone."

Now Sato smiled, jokingly punching his arm. "Ah, there you go, Rip. See, it's not so bad. Now let's get the *Cassi* docked and start making these repairs. Maybe we can ask Fleet Ops if they'll let you report in a shuttle. I can stay behind with the crew and keep the repairs on the *Cassi* going while you're gone. This way, we'll be ready for action the moment you return."

"Sounds good to me," Lee offered, then turned to face the bridge crew. "Listen up, everyone. I just want to say how proud I am of what our team accomplished these past few weeks. This wasn't easy. We lost some friends and comrades we served with and that's always tough. We also hit the Zodarks hard. Each victory we score against them places us that much closer to defeating these bastards. Don't ever forget that.

"Once we have docked at IF1 and engineering has turned over repairs to IF1, an all-hands will be called where I will briefly address the crew and announce a seventy-two hour pass for all non-essential personnel," Lee explained. "I'll also announce that anyone who sees me at the Stargate Lounge—the first round of drinks is on me."

Chapter Twenty-Six
Those Tanks Won't Move Themselves

11th Spartacus Armor Regiment
Serenea, Tau Sagittarii System

Yetis were imposing machines. Their thick armor plating and large single cannon gave them an almost bestial appearance. As Colonel Steve Thomas's ground crew secured the first Yeti tank to the interior decking of the T-92 Starlifter transport, he could feel the deep thrum of its powerful engines as it idled.

He watched the pilots double-check the locks holding the tanks in place for their journey to orbit. Once the Starlifter was full, they would head to the *Callisto* waiting in orbit for them to finish loading his regiment for the trip to the next planet, the next hellhole the brass determined they needed to control.

Shielding his eyes as he looked into the sky, he watched in wonderment as two of the giant Starlifter transports descended to land near the parking ramp where the rest of his tanks sat, waiting to be loaded. If he strained his eyes and looked a little closer into the sky, he could just about see the outline of RNS *Callisto*—a *Jupiter*-class interstellar troop transport. The *Jupiters* were massive engineering works of art. Lord knew he'd spent more than a few years aboard them as the Navy ferried the Army from one battle or campaign to another. At 3,642 meters long, 340 meters wide, and with a height of 288 meters, the ships were essentially a mobile Army base—transporting the 15,600 soldiers of the 11th Infantry Division.

What he loved about the *Jupiters* over the transports of the past was their sheer size. It afforded the soldiers plenty of room to stretch out—from running tracks to climbing walls, to rifle ranges to massive multicompany-size virtual reality training simulators. Gone were the days when a division's skills could soften during a multimonth transport to a new region of space. The only thing that concerned him was the possibility of their ship falling prey to an enemy warship. Sure, the *Jupiters* had some weapons, but they lacked the depth and strength of armor found in the Republic's primary combat vessels.

Hearing the sound of boots approaching from behind, Thomas turned to see a pair of stars on the collar of the man approaching him. Rendering a salute, he said, "Good morning, General Varinius."

"At ease with that saluting stuff, Colonel, you're liable to get me shot by a sniper," Major General Spartacus Varinius jested as he waved off his salute. "It's just the two of us, Steve. Let's forget the salutes and sirs—give me a no-BS assessment. How's the move going and what's the morale of your troops like?"

"The move—it's nearly done," he replied, nodding his head toward a Yeti being guided into the belly of a Starlifter. "At least the loadmaster is letting us load 'em six at a time instead of the four they used to limit us to. Our remaining gear in that hangar is all that's left besides the troops. As to morale...eh, the flogging will continue until morale improves."

General Varinius stifled a laugh, commenting, "In all seriousness, Steve, it was kind of funny once I got over the embarrassment of pooping myself."

Thomas snorted. "I still don't know what to say other than I am so sorry that happened. My rear end is still recovering from the scolding General Hopper gave me. The bite marks are still fresh—I think I even saw some blood."

The general laughed, this time a deep belly laugh as he almost doubled over at the memory of events from over the weekend.

After a regimental awards ceremony last Friday, Colonel Thomas had organized a celebratory meal that evening to honor those receiving valor awards and to remember those who had passed away. He'd even managed to acquire some bootleg homebrew beer to make the BBQ more lively. However, an hour before the event, something unexpected had happened. When the news reached General Varinius's headquarters about what Colonel Thomas had arranged for his regiment, a surprise visit and tasting were ordered to ensure the quality of the food before the subordinates were allowed to partake.

Imagine a scenario where certain regulations, especially those pertaining to the consumption of exotic meats in the midst of a battle on an unfamiliar planet, actually hold merit and should be strictly adhered to. Within a mere ten minutes of feasting on this lavish spread of meats and illicitly brewed beverages, the general and his five senior officers were suddenly thrust into a completely novel and singular experience—

one that would be etched into their memories forever. This encounter necessitated multiple uniform changes over the ensuing forty-eight hours. For anyone familiar with the joyous mess that a newborn can create, the aftermath of partaking in this local meat delicacy could be likened to a rather euphemistic "blowout." Unsurprisingly, Colonel Thomas promptly called off the BBQ to spare others from enduring the same fate as the general and his staff.

After several hours, it wasn't General Varinius who had called him for a private meeting aboard the warships in orbit. Instead, it was Lieutenant General Jayden Hopper himself, the former Delta officer now in charge of the entire Third Army. The next seven minutes and forty-three seconds felt like an onslaught of criticism, threats, intimidation, and humiliation from a superior, unlike anything he had experienced before. As General Hopper paused to take a sip of water, Thomas couldn't help but wonder if he was on the verge of losing his command and possibly even his rank for blatantly disregarding Army regulations and the revered General Order Number One—no alcohol consumption in a combat zone.

To his shock and slight relief, the general gestured towards a chair positioned across from his desk and proceeded to pour a generous amount of an unfamiliar Scotch whiskey. They engaged in casual conversation for another ten or so minutes as they savored their drinks. Finally, the general addressed him. "All right, Colonel, I've kept you here long enough. I believe we've put on quite a performance. Let's consider this a temporary lapse in military conduct that will never recur."

Thomas agreed quickly to what was happening. He assured him this was a momentary lapse in judgment that would most certainly never happen again. By the time he returned to his regiment, his own staff had thought he was a goner, never to be heard from again. To their surprise and chagrin, he shared what happened. They had a good laugh at his expense and moved on.

"Don't worry about General Hopper, Steve. When he asked me if he should demote and fire you, I told him if he did, he'd have to do it over my stars because the last thing I can afford on the eve of the next campaign is to lose my top regiment commander. He laughed, said he'd read you the riot act, put a show on, and send you back—look, that was stupid what you did. Whoever was the source of that meat or whatever that alcoholic brew was—I just hope you shot him for me," the general deadpanned, then laughed and said he was joking, or was he?

"I appreciate you going to bat for me, sir. If you don't mind me asking, what have they told you about where they're sending us?" Thomas asked, looking to move on.

Varinius stoically stared off into the distance, the silence stretching until he said, "They call it Eurysa. It's supposed to be the Pharaonis home planet. All I know is this—we're moving up in the rotation. We'll be hitting dirtside among the first wave after the ODTs have secured us an LZ. You know what that means—"

"Yeah, it's going to be a hot landing—those Starlifters are sitting ducks. They gotta know that, right?" commented Thomas, knowing all too well what happened to a Starlifter if it landed too close to the action.

Varinius shrugged. "I'm sure they do. I'm also sure they don't care. I haven't been made privy to everything that's going on, and that kind of bugs me. What I do know is this. General Royce and his SF task force, along with a handful of ships from the Fleet, look to have been retasked somewhere else."

"Huh. Well, what is it they used to say back in the day—Semper Gumby or something like that?" Thomas offered.

Varinius grunted. "Yeah, something like that. See, that's why I couldn't let Jayden fire you. Who would remind me of these bygone military catchphrases?"

The two laughed before the general received a call. His attention was needed elsewhere, so he started walking back to his vehicle, the driver waiting to ferry him to where he was needed.

Thomas turned his gaze back to the flight line, a final pair of Yetis and a trio of Linebackers all that was left to load up. Checking the time, he decided to start walking toward the hangar where he knew his tankers would eventually start showing up, especially as it got closer to noon—closer to their departure time to the *Callisto* waiting in orbit.
****

One Hour Later

Another Yeti was loaded onto the final transports that would ferry them to the RNS *Callisto*, the *Jupiter*-class ship waiting for them in orbit.

A frosty mist puffed from Thomas's mouth as he exhaled. The chill of this rocky, sparsely vegetated area on this moon bit through his insulated uniform. The few scraggly trees dotting the landscape offered little in the way of shelter from the elements outside of the temporary hangars and structures around the flight line. The few trees and their gnarled branches reached toward the slate-gray sky like skeletal fingers.

"Hustle up!" Colonel Thomas yelled, his gruff voice carrying across the makeshift staging area. "Those Yetis aren't gonna load themselves!"

The crew snapped to attention and their movements became more urgent as they began prepping the next tank for loading. Thomas smiled inwardly. He might be rough around the edges, but his troops respected his no-nonsense approach. In fact, because of it, they were some of the best in the business. He ran a tight group and demanded nothing less than complete dedication from those under his command.

As another Yeti rumbled into position, its treads crunched against the frozen ground. Just behind, Thomas strode across the parking ramp. "All right, listen up!" he said. "Epsilon, mount up! The rest of you, double-time it with that last Yeti."

A group of soldiers grabbed their gear and made for the nearest transport. Thomas sent a nod of approval their way. Satisfied, he turned and headed for the same transport, his long strides eating up the distance.

When he neared the open rear ramp, the hulking forms of two Yetis secured within came into view. Beyond, his soldiers were already buckled into their crash seats and running final system checks on their armor and equipment.

Thomas stepped through the entranceway into the cabin and moved down the central aisle. Once he reached the front, he rapped his knuckles against the bulkhead separating them from the flight deck.

The door slid open with a hiss of hydraulics and revealed the flight engineer and the pilots. "We're locked and loaded back here. That was the last of our equipment and personnel. We're ready to go, Lieutenant."

The pilot, Lieutenant Ithica, met his stare. "You got it, Colonel. Once my loadmaster reports everyone's strapped in, we'll begin cycling engines to get us airborne and on our—oh, that was him. We're good to go."

The subtle vibration through the deck plating went through Thomas's boots as he felt the transport's powerful engines spooling up with an increasing whine. He slapped the wall and thumbed over his shoulder. "Hey, now." He winked. "Wait for me to strap in."

Ithica grinned. "Of course, sir."

After Thomas settled in his seat, he strapped into his restraining belt as the transport began its ascent. The whine reached a crescendo, and then the entire ship lurched as it hurried toward the upper atmosphere. Thomas popped his ears a few times with purposeful yawns.

With a straight face, he looked at Lieutenant Roger Charlton sitting next to him. "You can never beat the rush of that takeoff."

"Very true, sir." The blond young man kept his eyes forward. Streaks of grime accentuated Charlton's chiseled jawline.

Thomas's eyes settled on three parallel scratches running diagonally across Charlton's left cheek. "Souvenirs from the recent firefight?"

"Affirmative, sir."

"Well, Lieutenant, you did one hell of a job out there. In fact, I saw the after-action reports myself."

Charlton looked away for a brief second. "Thank you, sir. I was just doing my duty."

"Horse manure, son." Thomas gripped his pants' fabric as the ship continued to head toward the stars. Although he did his best to hide it, flying off-planet always made him nervous. "You pulled half your squad out of that death trap against overwhelming odds. Mark my words, I'll make sure the general knows about your guts and leadership."

The lieutenant gave a hesitant smile. "I appreciate that, Colonel. But I couldn't have done it without my men's courage and skills."

This kid's shy. I'll get him out of it one way or another. "Damn right. Taking that firebase almost singlehandedly… that was one for the record books."

"I had a lot of motivation, sir. Couldn't bear the thought of leaving anyone behind."

Good kid. Real good. "And that's what separates the great ones from the rest. You're a credit to the Army, Charlton. Now, don't let my words get to your head, because if you do, an enemy laser will hit. Stay humble and make sure to lead your brothers and sisters well, all right? They come first, always."

"Yes, sir."

"At the same time, Lieutenant, don't get soft on me either. This ride we're all on is just getting started, and I'm not talking about this transport ship."

Charlton nodded. "Roger, sir. My body's ready thanks to you whipping us into shape. My mind's ready after watching you in action. I—"

Thomas cut him off. "I don't like kiss-asses, son."

"My apologies, sir. I wasn't trying to—"

"I know. Just keep that in mind. Eventually you'll spot it with others."

"Yes, Colonel."

Leaning back, Thomas eyed the front viewports as the gray atmosphere started to drop away.

All around their transport, other transports were leaving the moon likewise and joining up into a loose formation. They angled their trajectories to breach the atmosphere and headed toward the waiting RNS *Callisto*, a massive troop carrier.

Thomas exhaled softly. Five months.

They'd been slugging it out that long on the lush, forest-pocked surface of the moon Serenea against one Pharaonis fort after another. Five brutal months of bloody skirmishes and hard-fought battles amidst the abundant lunar foliage and marshlands. His gut churned as he recalled one particularly harrowing engagement.

The stench of expended ordnance hung thick and mingled with the ever-present taste of the moon's dry oxygen inside the cramped confines of Thomas's M11 Yeti main battle tank. The colonel peered intently at the holographic tactical display and assessed the dire situation unfolding before the 11th Spartacus Armor Regiment.

"Cyclone Six, this is Cyclone Actual," Thomas said into the comm. "Enemy has broken through the northern perimeter. I need suppressing fire on grid niner-three-seven to cover Third Platoon's retreat."

"Roger that, Colonel," came the reply.

Through the narrow vision slits of his Yeti, Thomas watched bright energy beams searing back and forth amidst billowing clouds.

Dust kicked up by impacting shells. The harsh rays of the unfiltered sun glinted off the smashed and blackened husks of tanks and tactical vehicles littering the cratered battlefield.

"Cyclone Actual, be advised—" A burst of static blared through Thomas's comm piece. "—enth Armored has been completely neutralized. I repeat, Tenth Armored is gone. We're cut off and surrounded!"

The grim news hit Thomas like a physical blow. The implications sank in like a cold fist clenching his gut. With the Tenth wiped out, his regiment was left without crucial support.

Thomas cursed under his breath, his mind racing. "Sitrep, over," he demanded into the communications unit.

"Sir, it's Corporal Jenkins," the soldier replied, his breathing rapid. "We were ambushed by enemy forces. Outnumbered. They hit us hard. Didn't give us a chance to regroup." Jenkins paused, catching his breath. "The Tenth is gone, sir. All of 'em. We're all that's left."

Thomas grimaced. The Tenth Armored was supposed to be the regiment's backup, their reinforcements. Now, the 11th Spartacus Armor was isolated and vulnerable.

As he scanned the rugged terrain through his tank's optics, the jagged peaks and rocky outcrops nearby offered little cover. They were sitting ducks out here. With the Tenth gone, his regiment needed to pull back and regroup.

"Jenkins, what's your position? Over."

"Grid coordinates Alpha-Niner-Seven-Five, sir. We're holed up in a small canyon, but we can't hold out for long."

Cross-referencing the coordinates on his tactical map, Thomas saw that Jenkins's squad was less than two klicks away. Yet the path was treacherous and exposed.

Jenkins needed help, and the 11th Spartacus Armor needed to move now. It lined up well. "Hang tight, Corporal. We're coming to you. Cyclone Actual out." Thomas turned to his tank's gunner, Staff Sergeant Joe Wilson. "Wilson, get ready to provide covering fire. We're moving out to support Jenkins."

"Yes, sir!" Wilson replied, already zeroing in his sights.

The tanks of the 11th rumbled into motion. Their massive treads churned up the rocky soil as they navigated the rugged terrain. The sound of distant gunfire guided them towards Jenkins's position, and it grew louder as they approached the narrow canyon. The staccato bursts of automatic weapons fire pierced the air.

As the tanks reached the canyon rim, Thomas signaled for them to take up firing positions behind the large rocky outcroppings. While he peered through his optics, he saw Jenkins's squad pinned down at the base of the canyon, their backs against the towering walls of stone.

Enemy forces swarmed toward Jenkins and his team—towering ant-like bipeds with armored carapaces and razor-sharp mandibles. These insectoid beings, the Pharaonis, were a terrifying sight. With their compound eyes devoid of emotion, he imagined their clicking mandibles were eager for the taste of human flesh. They closed in on Jenkins's position with swift and coordinated precision, firing bursts of energy from their rifles.

Below, desolate canyon walls towered and sent shadows creeping across the rocky area while the scorching sun began to fall toward the horizon. The Pharaonis advanced, their exoskeletons glistening in the fading light. Countless multifaceted eyes scanned the rugged landscape. They sought their human prey.

Jenkyn's group of soldiers huddled behind makeshift barricades. The once-pristine desert camouflage fatigues were stained with sweat and blood. Around them, several armored vehicles stood mangled from the intense firefight and were scattered across the canyon floor. Motionless forms clad in tattered uniforms lay strewn about.

The Pharaonis opened fire. Jenkins's team ducked for shelter. Some of the enemy rounds found their mark, downing several of Jenkins's soldiers. Others sailed past and blasted rock debris from the canyon walls in a shower of shrapnel.

With a brisk signal, Thomas ordered the tanks to open fire on the advancing horde of alien insectoids.

"Fire!" Wilson called out.

The Yeti's main gun roared to life. It sent a high-explosive shell screaming toward the Pharaonis. The round impacted with devastating force, engulfing a cluster of the insectoid warriors in a fiery blast. Acidic ichor splattered the canyon walls as their armored bodies were torn apart.

The other tanks of the 11th Spartacus Armor followed suit. Their combined firepower rained down upon the enemy. The canyon erupted in deafening explosions and the shrieks of dying Pharaonis.

Under the onslaught, the ant-like creatures reeled. Their ranks were thrown into disarray. The reek of alien blood filled the air.

"Jenkins, get your people out of there!" Thomas shouted into his comm.

Jenkins seized the opportunity. His battered squad scrambled toward the narrow canyon exit, desperate to escape the kill zone. The tanks of the 11th Spartacus Armor continued to lay down suppressing fire, buying precious time for the infantry to reach safety.

A sudden violent shudder jarred Thomas back to the present as the troop transport began its final atmospheric break. Through the viewports, the eternal gray gave way to the brilliant curve of the moon's edge. The golden light of the star system's sun pecked against the horizon.

Up ahead, the lights blinked from the RNS *Callisto*. After they docked, Thomas told himself there would be a much-needed period of rest and resupply for his soldiers as they integrated with the main fleet. His troops had earned a respite after their grueling tour on Serenea. A chance to catch their breath and prepare for whatever fresh hell awaited them next.

The large bulk of the *Callisto* grew on the screen. The *Jupiter*-class ship was a behemoth. Thomas's transport maneuvered its approach toward the vessel's sprawling hangar bays.

The *Callisto* measured an imposing 3,642 meters in length, with a width of 340 meters and height of 288 meters. Yet the raw numbers failed to truly convey the overwhelming sense of scale.

He had committed the full specs to memory long ago. It was a quirk born from his innate fascination with the machines and hardware of war. If memory served right, the *Callisto* could transport a staggering thirty thousand TEUs—standard twenty-foot shipping containers—when loaded for full troop capacity with seventeen thousand soldiers and their accompanying equipment. Strip away the soldiers, and it became a dedicated cargo hauler capable of ferrying up to one hundred and sixty thousand of the boxy metal crates.

As a bulk cargo and troop transport, the *Callisto* could schlep an almost unfathomable 4.6 million tons in a single massive hold. Just picturing the sheer tonnage made Thomas smile. Barely anyone appreciated ships like he did.

His gaze moved to the holographic port display as he studied *Callisto* further. Usually, thirteen full logistical squadrons called *Callisto*'s hangar bay home: one Osprey squadron of twenty assault transports, four Scarab squadrons with sixty-four heavy lift transports, and eight Starlifter squadrons comprising ninety-six heavy cargo haulers.

A tighter grin creased Thomas's weathered features as the *Callisto*'s hangars yawned open. The armored doors slid apart to reveal the brightly lit interior. To the casual observer, these might seem like simple mundane details, but to him, understanding the minutiae of their tools and assets was key to outthinking and outmaneuvering their enemies. It was why he had committed the details of all enemy ships he could study to memory as well.

Thomas's ship shuddered as it made contact with *Callisto*'s arrival deck. The craft's landing gears absorbed the impact with a gentle thump. Colonel Thomas was already on his feet and unstrapping before the ramp began lowering with a hiss.

He turned to face his troops, his expression hard as granite. "No standing around with your thumbs up your you-know-whats." His gaze swept over them. "As soon as that ramp's down, stay aboard and get those Yetis prepped for offload. Understand?"

A chorus of crisp "Yes, sirs!" answered him.

The ramp clanged into place with a heavy bang. Not wasting a second, Thomas repeated, "You heard me, people! I want those Yetis ready to roll by the time they call for offload!"

Chapter Twenty-Seven
Rest & Refit

11th Spartacus Armor Regiment
RNS *Callisto*

The ravages of war left an indelible mark on a soldier. It was an undeniable truth. A battle-hardened veteran understood combat-inflicted wounds, both visible and invisible, and more profoundly than any other experience imaginable.

Colonel Thomas grunted as he applied the nanomedical lotion to the gash on his side. The wound still throbbed. It was a souvenir from the last engagement with the Pharaonis on the moon Serenea. He stood in front of the small mirror above the sink in his cramped quarters aboard the RNS *Callisto* and studied his reflection.

His face was caked with soot from the seven-month-long battle. He looked like hell, and he knew it. He ran a hand over his stubbled jaw and let out a sigh. It'd been an hour since he had boarded *Callisto*, and he needed a shower badly.

The events of the past few months played through his mind as he peeled off his sweat-stained fatigues. The images of a lieutenant's tank exploding before his eyes, those under his leadership gone in seconds, the onslaught of the Pharaonis disabling the Republic Army's Zeta Battalion a week into battle like they were nothing more than paper, the desperate fight to extract survivors, and on and on the memories went. It all blurred together, and strangely, the seven months had passed in a blink.

Thomas stepped toward the tiny shower stall. His muscles ached with fatigue. He reached in and turned the knob. A rush of anticipation hit him as the water sputtered to life. Steam began to fill the small space and fogged up the mirror.

Just as he was about to step under the inviting spray, a shrill beep cut through the room. Thomas froze. The beep sounded again, insistent.

With a muttered curse, he turned off the shower and stalked over to the comm unit on the wall. He jabbed the answer button with more force than necessary.

"Colonel Thomas here," he said.

The voice of Major General Spartacus Varinius rumbled through the speaker. "Colonel Thomas, your presence is requested in Conference Room Alpha-6 immediately."

Thomas closed his eyes briefly. *Of course it has to be now.* He glanced longingly at the shower, the steam still swirling with invitation. Duty called, as it always did. "Understood, sir. I'll be there ASAP."

He cut the connection and stood there for a moment. With a resigned sigh, he reached for his discarded fatigues, still dirty and reeking of battle. He pulled them on, the fabric rough against his skin.

In minutes, Thomas strode out into the ship's corridor. His boots thumped heavily on the metal deck. A young ensign snapped to attention and saluted as he passed, but Thomas ignored it, his mind focused on the summons from General Varinius.

He stepped into the lift and pressed the indicator for the upper deck. The lift whirred as it ascended. In a way, Thomas was glad for the meeting. When they'd pulled his division and several others from Serenea, it had come unexpectedly. Not that anything was expected in war other than death.

What could be so urgent that the general had pulled the entire division, though?

The elevator doors slid open. Thomas made his way down the hall and to the conference room. As he entered, he took in the gathered officers seated around the table—Peter Kennedy, the grizzled tank commander from the 11th Spartacus Armor Regiment, and Michael Martin, the Alpha Company commander who led a tank platoon under Kennedy.

Across from them sat Chris Dausch and Jackie Walkup from the 23rd Texas Mechanized Infantry Regiment. Dausch, a master sergeant, commanded Second Platoon in Bravo Company, while Walkup was a corporal under his command.

At the head of the table sat Rick Ahlstrom, the major in charge of the 24th Spartan Infantry Regiment, along with Captain Mathew Tapusoa, the commander of the regiment's Charlie Company.

They all wore the standard desert combat uniform, consisting of lightweight tan pants bloused over dusty boots and a long-sleeved shirt in a mottled desert camouflage pattern. Like Thomas's relatively dirty appearance, their clothes were sweat-stained and caked with reddish-brown dirt. They probably hadn't had time for a proper shower or change either.

There, standing at the front of the room, was Major General Spartacus Varinius himself. The man was a legend, a soldier's soldier who had fought in every major campaign since the Republic's discovery of the Zodarks. He was a big man with a commanding presence. Although sometimes Thomas and Varinius didn't see eye to eye, he still respected the major general and would easily give his life for the man.

Varinius gestured toward an empty chair. "Colonel Thomas, please take a seat."

Thomas sat down, his eyes never leaving the general's face. Varinius activated a holographic display in the center of the table, and a star system materialized in the air before them.

"Gentlemen, the reason I've called you here is because we've been tasked with a new operation," Varinius began, his voice deep and resonant. "The orbital assault divisions are preparing to secure a foothold on Eurysa, the Pharaonis home world and capital planet in the Zanthea system."

The hologram zoomed in on a planet, its surface a mottled green and brown. Thomas leaned forward, studying the display.

"Our division will be providing support for this operation," Varinius continued. "We'll be hitting the Pharaonis hard and fast, giving the assault divisions the opening they need to establish a beachhead."

The officers around the table nodded. Their faces were set with determination. Thomas figured like him, they all knew the stakes, the importance of this mission. If they could take Eurysa, it would change the war against the Pharaonis in every way.

The general's eyes swept the room, and his gaze locked with each officer in turn. "The main star of the Zanthea system is a G-type star, similar to Earth's sun." He motioned to the glowing orb at the center of the hologram. "This offers a stable environment for life on the planet Eurysa, making it suitable for humans."

The display zoomed in on the lush planet Eurysa, its surface dotted with vast oceans and archipelagos. Thomas rested on his elbows, straining to study the topography.

"Eurysa is rich in rare earth minerals, vital for advanced technology," Varinius continued. "These resources, along with others, make it a prime target for the Republic. In other words, we need this for many reasons outside of crippling the Pharaonis."

Master Sergeant Chris Dausch raised his hand. "Sir, what kind of resistance can we expect from the Pharaonis on Eurysa?"

Varinius nodded. "Intelligence suggests that the Pharaonis have heavily fortified the planet. They've had lifetimes to dig in and prepare their defenses. We can expect heavy resistance, both on the ground and in the air. It'll be a hot mess, one we'll win."

Captain Tapusoa spoke up next. "What about the terrain, sir? How will that affect our operations?"

"We'll be sending you a full report on that soon. But I'll answer your question to the best of my ability, as intel is still coming in. The archipelagos and dense vegetation will provide much cover for the enemy," Varinius replied. "With the amount of islands alone, we can bet on a long engagement." He hesitated and stood straighter. "Gentlemen, envision a vast armored formation, a steel leviathan comprised of tanks, infantry fighting vehicles, and mechanized forces. Now, picture that formation shattering, fragmenting into thousands upon thousands of dispersed elements. Those armored splinters scatter across the battlefield, stretching out for kilometers in every direction with a vast sea between each one. Our mission is to engage and eliminate those threats methodically, one by one, preventing them from massing their forces against our spearhead. We will advance with deliberate patience, striking with precision to degrade their defenses piece by piece. This will be a grueling campaign of attrition, but our training and discipline will ensure victory, no matter how long the engagement. Also, we'll need to be prepared for close-quarters combat and ambushes. The Pharaonis know the terrain intimately, and they'll use that to their advantage."

Thomas cleared his throat, drawing the attention of the room. "General, what's our timeline for this operation?"

Varinius met Thomas's gaze. "We'll be en route to the Zanthea system for the next two weeks. During that time, the division will stand down, allowing the soldiers to rest and decompress. After the R&R period, we'll restart training and preparations to support the assault on Eurysa."

Thomas nodded, his shoulders relaxing. Two weeks of rest sounded like a luxury, and it was. The real work would begin once they reached Eurysa, but until then, he'd give his men and women space to breathe and to enjoy their time outside of combat. Not only did they deserve it, they needed it for better battle awareness while on the ground.

"In the meantime," Varinius said, "I want all of you to study the intelligence we have on Eurysa, and as I mentioned, the reports will be coming your way soon. Familiarize yourselves with the terrain, the climate, and the Pharaonis' ever-evolving tactics. As always, we need to be prepared for anything."

Varinius surveyed the room, his gaze lingering on each officer in turn. "This is a crucial operation. The fate of the war may very well depend on our success on Eurysa. I know I can count on each and every one of you to give your all and to lead your men and women to victory."

Thomas knew the men and women under his command were the best of the best because he'd made them that way. Because of this, they'd stop at nothing to secure success for the Republic.

"Are there any other questions?" Varinius asked.

"Yeah," said Corporal Jackie Walkup, "do these bug-eyed freaks have a preference for barbecue or teriyaki sauce?"

Master Sergeant Dausch grinned. "You know, I'd just love to take those pests in my hand and squash them. Can't tell you how many times I've thought of doing that."

"But keep their antennae. I heard they make great antennae receivers for our old holo devices," Captain Tapusoa chimed in, drawing laughter from the others.

Thomas shook his head. "Look, y'all, on a serious note, while their appearance may seem unnerving, we must approach this situation with strategic objectivity and not allow ourselves to be blinded by prejudice. We need to see them as the enemy, not as a joke."

General Varinius dipped his head at Thomas. "Well said. Now, if there's nothing else, you're all dismissed."

Chapter Twenty-Eight
Facing the Music

Task Force 28
RNS *Maddox*
En Route to New Eden

Out the viewport, Captain Naomi Love watched the colorful FTL display as RNS *Maddox* tore through the cosmos toward New Eden. She recalled the final day she'd spent with her late husband, Jack, reminiscing about the vibrant array of colors during a civilian transport jump. It had been one of the happiest days of her life, until, inevitably, Jack had met his end at the hands of a Zodark with a laser.

She shook her head much like a dog shaking off water, trying to dispel the memory from her mind. In response, her mind flooded with thoughts of her family.

Back on Earth, her parents probably wondered if she still lived. Months had passed since her last transmission had filtered through the comm buoys to that pale blue world. She pictured them huddled around the old receiver right now, waiting, hoping for news—any word their daughter still breathed.

A pang of guilt stabbed her gut. Once they reached New Eden, she vowed to send a message to reassure them she'd survived the latest clash with the Zodark scum. She'd call her sister too and catch up with her niece and nephew. She smiled at the thought of hearing the simple joys of life back home.

In the harshness of deep space, those familial bonds were a lifeline to sanity. The reminder that something precious still existed beyond the merciless war and endless combat ops. Something to fight for, alongside the brothers and sisters who stood with her, fighting against the darkness.

Love sat on the edge of her bed, her hands clasped between her knees. Another successful run, dropping and retrieving Deltas at several of the moons and planets in the Gravaxia system. Simple and by the book. Until Admiral Ripley Lee had decided to take the fleet and enter the Velos Belt.

As she exhaled deeply, she pushed away thoughts of those lost. Love knew better than to judge a superior office's decisions without the full scope. Still, the casualties weighed heavily on her heart, and she felt pain for those she knew who were now gone. The torments of war, she supposed. Over time, she thought those feelings would fade. Yet, she realized she'd been with the Republic Navy for over a decade, and the hardship of losing friends still lingered. For all she figured, it never went away.

A firm rap at her door pulled her from her reverie. She turned toward the door. "Come."

The door slid open and Master Chief Brian Ford stepped inside. A crooked smile formed on his weathered face. "You up for company, Captain?"

Love straightened. "With you? Of course, Master Chief. Make yourself at home." She gestured to the chair beside her desk.

Ford dropped into the seat with a grunt. "Hell of a day, wouldn't you say?"

"That's one way to put it." She arched a brow. "I'd like to hear your take."

He leaned back, rubbing his jaw. "Can't fault the admiral for being aggressive. We had 'em on the ropes until that ambush sprung. You know, he entered the Gravaxia system to stave off a small convoy heading toward the mining facility. With one Delta team still in operation on one of the moons, he couldn't let the convoy notify their command." A somber look passed over his features. "Lost too many good people, though. Too many."

"That we did." Love exhaled slowly. "Still, we follow orders. The analysts will figure out what went wrong after the fact." She rested her elbows on her knees, a slight frown creasing her brow. "Lee bailed just before those Zodark reinforcements showed up, cutting it dang close. Gotta hand it to the admiral, his gut instincts are usually on point. But this time? Walked us straight into an ambush, plain and simple. Whole thing stinks like a busted plasma conduit."

Ford pushed his lower lip outward. "Doesn't change the fact he played it smart once the shots started flying. The admiral made their kill ratio look pitiful."

"Four to one," Love said. "I'll give him that much. Still, at what cost?"

Ford folded his hands in his lap. "I can't get over the fact we lost good people."

A heavy silence fell between them.

Love stared off at a blank point on her white wall. "The man's a legend. That's all there's to say about what he's accomplished. Just a good mission turned bad." She paused. "But, you know, our clandestine operations gathered a lot of intel. We came in and got what we wanted."

"Yes, ma'am. You're right." Ford dug into his pocket. "Almost forgot. I found something of yours, something you let slip your mind." He pulled out a battered photograph and handed it to her.

Love's breath caught as she studied the faded image. "How could I almost forget about Jack?"

"You'll never forget Jack, ma'am." Ford's voice lowered. "Not a day goes by, right?"

She set the photo beside her. "A little too right." Love cleared her throat. "Any word on the fleet-wide casualties?"

"It's... not good." Ford tapped his fingers on the desk and stood. "Anyway, just wanted to return that photo, Captain. I was due for a long nap like days ago." He yawned. "Gonna get that sleep."

"You and me both, Master Chief." She managed a tight smile as the door opened, showing the dim corridor beyond.

Pausing in the doorway, Ford glanced back. "When we make port back on Eden, drinks are on me, all right? Can't say no to a couple rounds of Blue Trout Willamette Ale."

Love's smile widened a fraction. "You know that's my favorite."

"Course I do, ma'am." Ford stepped into the passageway. "Some downtime will do us all some good."

****

Task Force 28
RNS *Cassiopeia*
En Route to New Eden

The scanner above Coop cast an amber light across his face as the med tech finished her examination.

Her voice was calm. "Well, Commander, you're one lucky pilot." The med tech stepped back. "That ejection seat saved your life."

Coop shifted on the hospital table, his back on the soft mattress. "Thanks for the confidence in my abilities, Doc."

The med tech arched a brow. "It's not your abilities I'm questioning. It's the fact you managed to survive an ordeal like that. Pilots don't usually walk away from ejecting in the middle of a fireball or in the heat of combat."

"Yeah. Can't argue your point." Coop lifted up, resting on his elbows. He winced from the pain going down his spine. He didn't know why he felt an ache there but lay back down to find relief.

The med tech shook her head. "Stay put and try not to move much. The injections and therapy will start to kick in and ease your pain, all right? That ejection took one hell of a toll on your body. I'll be right back, OK? Gotta poke you with another needle soon."

"Oh, joy." Coop nodded as she left the small room, his mind drifting back to the harrowing moments mere hours ago.

The alarms blared, warning of the incoming Zodark laser. He banked his Gripen hard. Thrusters flared as he adjusted his starfighter to avoid the energy weapon. For a split second, he'd thought he was in the clear, until a laser pierced his starboard engine.

The fighter spiraled out of control. With no other choice, Coop had punched the ejection. The explosive bolts blasted the canopy clear as the seat rocketed away.

His teeth rattled from the brutal acceleration as the seat's rockets burned for home—RNS *Cassiopeia*. The twin nozzles kicked out gouts of scorching plasma, slamming into his flight suit's thermal shielding. He was rapidly overtaking his own fighter, the tumbling wreck of his Gripen flashing past in a blur of debris.

As the seat's maneuvering thrusters took over, adjusting his course for the retrieval vector, Coop blinked against the strange silence. His breath came in ragged gasps within the confines of his helmet. The Zodark cruiser loomed larger by the second, its massive bulk blotting out the stars as its laser batteries continued to blaze away at the Republic fighters swarming around it like angry wasps.

The creak of the medbay door pulled Coop from his memory. He glanced up to see his squad member, Nomad, standing in the doorway. "Commander."

"Nomad. Come."

Nomad walked in, his arms behind his back. "How are you holding up, Commander?"

"Just call me Coop." Coop dipped his head. "And thank you. Without you, I'd be a floating corpse."

Nomad shrugged. "Least I could do, sir. Couldn't let you drift out there in the void."

"I'm in debt to you."

"No, sir."

"Again, call me Coop."

After the ejection, Nomad had scoured the area until he'd finally located Coop's beacon. He'd then hailed a shuttle from the *Cassiopeia* to retrieve the stranded pilot. Without this man's quick thinking, Coop would have been just another casualty of war, his life snuffed out amid the freeze of space.

Coop grimaced, shifting his weight. "Did the rest of my squadrons make it? The medic didn't know when I asked her."

"Most, but barely." A somber expression crossed his features. "It was a narrow escape during the full retreat."

"What about Pronto or Rogue? You know if they survived?" He knew one of them had died, but which one? But then maybe the intel he'd received was wrong, and both had lived.

Nomad's expression softened. "At the mining facility, Pronto didn't make it. Died on impact." He exhaled slowly. "Rogue's being patched up next door, actually. In surgery down the hall, but she'll live."

"Good." Remorse twisted his gut over Pronto's fate. "I'll make sure to inform Pronto's family." He wondered how many more families he'd need to write to after he looked at the full casualty report—a duty he always dreaded.

"I didn't know him well," Nomad said, "but everyone spoke highly of Pronto."

Coop nodded, his throat tightening. "He was one of a kind. Not enough good things to say about the man."

"Well, Coop, I wanted to say that you led us well out there today," Nomad said. "Your orders, the way you flew… it was damn impressive."

Coop managed a grin, despite the exhaustion weighing on him. Praise from a pilot of Nomad's caliber was no small thing. "Thanks, Nomad. That means a lot coming from you. Truly, I'm in debt to you. No if… ands… or buts, all right?"

"Understood, sir."

"When are you going to call me Coop?"

"Sorry… Coop." Nomad clapped Coop on the shoulder, his grip firm and reassuring. "You've trained your squadrons well. I'm proud to be a part of them. And I know that with you leading us, we'll give those Zodark a run for their money."

Coop nodded, his grin fading as the weight of his responsibilities settled back onto his chest. "We've got a long fight ahead of us, Nomad. But you're right. We've got a damn fine group of pilots here. And we'll do whatever it takes to keep the Republic safe, mark my words. We do this for humanity."

"Yes, sir." Nomad's expression turned serious. "No matter what people say about you, you can count on us. We've got your back. You're a good man."

What does that mean? Coop shifted uncomfortably. "What are people saying?"

Nomad lifted his chin. "Nothing, sir. I misspoke."

Coop was too tired to question him more, but there was something unspoken. "I see. Let everyone know I do my best and I won't let any of them down. Any of you."

Nomad grinned, the tension of the moment broken. "Damn right you won't. Now, what do you say we hit the mess hall? I'm starving."

Coop chuckled. "I don't know if you can tell, but I'm a little bedridden at the moment."

"Right, Coop. How about I get you some of that good chow?"

"I'll take you up on that."

The door slid open as the medical technician returned to the room. "Sir, I need you to leave for now. I've got to administer therapy to the commander."

"Of course, ma'am. I was just leaving." Nomad straightened. "Sir." He offered Coop a dip of his head before exiting.

The technician approached Coop's bedside, her expression all business. "Sit up, Commander. It's time for your nanoregenerative spinal therapy."

Coop frowned. "Is there something wrong with my spine?"

"Just the nerves. Now, turn to the side."

"I thought you told me I couldn't move much?"

"Well, I'm telling you to move now, unless you want to be in pain for the rest of your life."

Clenching his teeth, Coop pushed himself upright. A sharp stabbing sensation shot down his back to his glutes and throbbed down his left leg. "That didn't help, Doc."

The technician retrieved a slender injector, pressing it against the small of Coop's back. A sharp stinging sensation washed through him.

Coop jerked slightly. "I thought you said I didn't want to be in pain?"

"It'll help," she said, setting the injector aside. "The nanomachines will begin repairing the damaged nerves immediately."

Coop exhaled, the pain already subsiding. "When Rogue is out of surgery, let me know. I'd like to see her, even if I have to be in a wheelchair."

The technician arched a brow. "Rogue?"

"Captain Anaya Singh," Coop clarified. "Rogue is her call sign."

"Ah, yes. I'll inform you." The technician made a note on her data pad.

"Actually, one more thing," Coop said. "In my quarters, there's a journal I need retrieved. Ask Commander Mason about it. He'll know which one I'm referring to."

"I'll have someone fetch it right away."

As the technician departed, Coop's thoughts drifted to the worn leather-bound journal—his great-great-grandfather's diary from World War II. Mason would direct them to the keepsake, carefully preserved after all these years. It always kept Coop good company. Right now, he couldn't think of anything better to ease his mind.

Chapter Twenty-Nine
By Your Command

December 2113
Office of the Viceroy
Alliance City, New Eden
Rhea System

Miles Hunt sat across from Admiral Fran McKee in the solemn tranquility of his private office, a sanctuary from the busyness of Tiberius Hall, the recently completed alliance headquarters within the hustle and bustle of Alliance City. He stared intently at the holographic display between them as it flickered with updates showing the status reports of warships undergoing repairs, statuses of new hulls being constructed in the shipyards of the Republic, the Altairians, and even the Interstellar Irish Republic—it was a lot of information to take in. Of all the ships in this report, only one in particular caused him to question its status.

"Fran, the *Freedom*—I'd like to get her back in the action sooner than later. What are these repair figures not telling me, and how are things coming along?" quizzed Miles, masking his concern with a steady tone. His eyes fixed on the hologram displaying the flagship's repair progress.

Fran sighed as he asked, a look of tiredness in her eyes. "Slow, Viceroy; the progress is slow, difficult, and cumbersome. As you know, the Orbot invasion did more than just scar its hull—it's testing our capability to repair and rebuild it with the shipyard capabilities we presently have. Our engineers and shipbuilders are improvising, sending parts, if you can believe it, back to Gallentine space to handle the repairs we can't or that are technologically beyond us. I'm the first to admit this isn't ideal, but we have accepted it, and it's moving us forward."

Miles nodded as he took in the information. His thoughts drifted to the *Freedom*. The ship was more than just the flagship of the Republic. It had become a symbol of their rising power and resilience—a gift from the Emperor himself. Now, it sat in dire need of care they struggled to provide. "Call me Miles, Fran. Thank you for elaborating on the challenges the engineers are facing. The situation is what it is, so let's move on. How are things progressing with our arrangement and the

Altairian shipyards?" he pivoted, looking for a glimmer of progress where he could.

"It's a lot better on that front. We're at seventy percent delivery on the *Victory*-class battleships, the *Constellation* star carriers, and the *Kraken* heavy cruisers. The challenge now is crewing them," Fran explained as the display showed a list of ships alongside their training schedules and when they should be ready to join the Fleet. "We've known this would become an issue, and you know me, ever the planner and overthinker. My staff and I developed a comprehensive strategy and plan I can share with you, or we can move on if you like?"

"How about you give me the nickel tour? We have other things to talk about, but you've piqued my interest," Miles responded as he sat back in the chair, grabbing his coffee.

Fran smiled. "Sure, happy to. The way we're approaching this problem is that as the recruit completes basic training, they move on to a three-to-nine-month highly intensive training program in their assigned field. Upon completion of the training, they receive their ship class assignments and then undergo another four-to-nine-week condensed training program for the kinds of duties and responsibilities they will have aboard the class of ship they're assigned to. As they complete training, their name and job duty are listed as available for assignment in that ship class. Usually at this point, it's a matter of filling the most urgent needs of the Fleet. Sometimes, it's an assignment to a crew forming to take command of a new ship. Other times, it's backfilling combat losses from the active campaigns."

Miles nodded along as she finished and then complimented, "I don't say this enough, Fran—you are doing an exceptional job helping me and Chester rebuild the Navy to defeat these Zodarks and this insidious alliance."

Fran's cheeks flushed at the compliment. "Thank you, Miles. Abi left some big shoes to fill. I'm just trying to keep my head above water and not let you and the Republic down."

Miles leaned forward, reaching across the holo display as he took her hand in his. "Fran, I have the utmost confidence in you and your ability. Don't try to be Abi—I need you to be you, just the way you are. So put aside any doubts you have and just keep solving problems and finding solutions."

"No one can replace Abi," Fran replied as Miles sat back in his chair. The holo display restarted, displaying its stream of data.

"Changing topics, how are things progressing with the Pharaonis campaign?" Miles ventured, his voice a low rumble.

"It's progressing, albeit slower than Admiral Rosentreter had initially thought. It appears the Pharaonis had been preparing their defense of Serenea for some time. These forts and entrenched defensive positions have proven quite formidable. His last communiqué said that General Hopper had deployed most of the Third Expeditionary Army to the surface to finish the last of the holdouts. He seems confident their heavy artillery and tanks will make short work of their forts," replied Fran confidently. "I'll say this, Miles: the support we are receiving from the Altairian shipyards has been impressive—their shipbuilding capacity is enormous. It will take decades, if not half a century or more, for us to come close to matching them. Whatever the Emperor said to King Grigdolly, it sure got his attention and seemed to refocus their efforts. It's given us a real fighting chance. I think we're going to do this, defeat the Dominion."

Miles stood, pacing to the window overlooking the city. "I'm not privy to what the Emperor said to him. I suspect it was similar to the conversation he had with me. The important thing is we are growing in strength and numbers. Let's continue to prepare our people to ensure their hearts and minds are ready for the battles and campaigns ahead. The Republic has weathered storms before. We'll weather this one, too."

Suddenly, the door to his office burst open, and Admiral Wiyrkomi rushed in. "They are here, Viceroy!" the Gallentine shouted, a look of concern on his face.

"Whoa, hang on, Wiyrkomi. Who's here? What's going on?" stammered Miles as he tried to figure out what had spooked his longtime friend.

"Legion!" Wiyrkomi spat the word out. "We do not have many details yet on exactly what happened or if Legion is still present. We received a priority communiqué from an Altairian *Berkimon* battleship about a battle underway in the Elyxion star system. The communiqué said it had encountered an Orbot Collector ship—"

"What! A Collector ship! How is that possible?" interrupted Miles in a near rage.

"There is more I need to say before I can answer that question," Wiyrkomi replied, Miles motioning for him to continue. "The Altairian ship received a report from a Republic frigate in the neighboring system that it detected the Orbot Collector ship and a trio of vessels they had never encountered before. Then, they started receiving a series of strange calls for help from nearby planets and moons, saying that something was happening to the Orbots—they just collapsed.

"The Altairian system commander began rallying his ships near the stargate connecting to Tau Sagittarii, the star system where our expeditionary force is headquartered. When the Collector and unknown ships entered the Elyxion system, the Orbots seemed to have just been turned off—wait, let me play the video file attached with the message," Wiyrkomi explained as he walked towards the holo device displaying the status updates of various warships.

Once Wiyrkomi started the video, the holo display transformed into a three-dimensional video representation of what the Altairian ship's sensors were detecting. Miles watched with rapt attention as three of the most unique and strange-looking vessels he had ever seen approached the alliance battle line, blocking their access through the stargate. The Altairian battleship was flanked by two Altairian frigates, a heavy cruiser, a Republic battle cruiser, a flak cruiser, and two more heavy cruisers. It was a formidable squadron of warships that should have been able to handle these three smaller ships. Miles glanced at the sensor data along the side of the holo display. It provided what specs and information it could about the vessels approaching them, and judging by the length of these ships, Miles would venture a guess they were somewhere between the size of a Republic frigate and a heavy cruiser.

Then, before he knew it, the Altairian commander fired first, the *Berkimon* battleship scoring multiple hits against the closest vessel with several hits from its primary turbo lasers before firing a volley of plasma torpedoes. In fractions of a second, the display lit up with ships on both sides now tearing into each other. Miles looked on in horror as he watched one of these strange vessels fire on a Republic heavy cruiser. A beam of light bored into the ship, the laser cutting through the vessel in seconds—the Republic warship exploding moments later.

"Geez, would you look at how fast those ships were able to close the distance against our ships?" Fran said aloud, aghast at what she was seeing.

Wiyrkomi nodded in agreement. "Indeed, Admiral McKee. We call these vessels Slashers. They are incredibly quick and formidable adversaries."

Miles barely heard what Wiyrkomi had said as he felt his jaw drop agape when the Altairian battleship scored the alliance's first kill against the ship it had fired on at the outset of the battle. A bright flash occurred. Miles averted his eyes briefly, then looked to see what had blown up. It only took a moment for him to spot the wreckage of a Republic heavy cruiser—RNS *Antalya*. The screen flashed again, then a third and fourth time as one of the Slashers tore through the Altairian frigates like they were nothing.

"Watch this next part," Wiyrkomi cautioned, alerting Miles and Fran that something was about to happen. The ship that had just torn through a quartet of frigates had pivoted away from the remaining alliance ships as it darted back to the Orbot Collector ship that had hung back from the fight. Then he saw something strange—almost like a shimmering effect like what they saw appear in the center of the stargate as a ship would pass through it.

One second, Miles saw the Collector ship. The next, it was gone. Then, the remaining two Slashers disappeared as quickly as they had arrived. "Whoa—did I just see that? Those ships, they created their wormholes—their own bridge back to their space?"

"Yes, Viceroy, that is exactly what they did," Wiyrkomi confirmed. "I finished reading the report while you two watched the video. It would seem the Collector ship, along with its trio of Slashers for escorts, moved swiftly through the conquered Orbot systems, transmitting a kill signal to any and all remaining Orbots still in the system. They killed them. It would appear the only system they failed to reach and transmit this signal to was the Tau Sagittarii system. That squadron of ships that Altairian *Berkimon* managed to rally at the gate looks to have saved what Orbots remain."

Miles looked away as the video stopped. He couldn't believe what had just happened. *Somehow, someway, Legion managed to find and link up with an Orbot Collector ship that either we missed during our postwar searches or that Legion already had in reserve for such a moment as this.* In either case, only a single system of Orbots appeared to have survived this lightning attack.

"Admiral Wiyrkomi, we need to dispatch whatever reinforcements you think are prudent to the Tau Sagittarii system. At this point, it appears that the system may hold the only Orbots left alive. Perhaps with that knowledge, knowing what Legion has just done to the rest of their people, we can get them to elaborate more on what their relationship is with Legion and perhaps provide us with some intelligence about them that might prove useful," directed Miles, pushing the alliance into high gear, their first official encounter with Legion ending with them withdrawing.

Chapter Thirty
A Chancellor Is Chosen

January 7, 2114
Chancellor's Residence
New Cambria, New Eden
Rhea System

Aimes Morgan, the man who had defied the odds and emerged victorious in the race for the Chancellorship, sat on the sofa in the library of his new home, his wife, Nancy, nestled against his chest. He savored the tranquility of the moment, a brief respite before the weight of his new responsibilities descended upon him. Tomorrow, he would be sworn in as the second Chancellor of the Republic, a position he had never imagined he would hold when he'd first announced his candidacy a year ago.

The path to this moment had been a tumultuous one. In the wake of the devastating Zodark attack, Senator Charles "Chuck" Walhoon, the most senior elected official to have survived, had been sworn in as the Chancellor Pro Tempore. He was to serve until a general election could be held on December 31 of the following year. When Aimes declared his intention to run, many had scoffed at the idea of an unknown like him challenging the formidable Senator Walhoon, a man with decades of political experience and a reputation for competently steering the Republic through the aftermath of the crisis.

As the field of candidates swelled to thirteen, Aimes found himself in the midst of a grueling electoral process. The candidates had just six months to campaign across the vast expanse of the Republic before the first run-off election would narrow the field to five. Aimes, against all expectations, secured a spot in the top three, igniting a spark of belief within him that victory might just be within reach.

With just four months until the general election, Aimes faced the monumental task of introducing himself to a nation that knew little of him. As he strategized with his campaign team, an unexpected call from Eddy Knowles, the candidate he had narrowly edged out for third place, changed the trajectory of his campaign. Knowles's endorsement, followed by a surge in fundraising and the backing of the Union of Fellow Shipbuilders, provided Aimes with the resources to campaign across Earth, Alpha Centauri, Sumer, and New Eden, and the numerous moons and other outposts the citizens of the Republic had set up.

As the weeks ticked by and the debates unfolded, Aimes went out of his way to distinguish himself from his opponents. While Walhoon touted his sixty-two years of government experience, Aimes focused on the future, asking voters to consider who they wanted to lead the Republic through these uncertain times. Did they want a career politician or a political outsider with the mind of an engineer?

In the final debate, just three days before the election, Aimes delivered a bold closing statement that resonated with the electorate. When the polls closed and the votes were tallied, Aimes emerged victorious with forty-two percent of the vote. As Senator Walhoon conceded, Aimes finally allowed the reality to sink in—he would now bear the responsibility of leading the Republic into the future.

As he sat with Nancy in the quiet of the library, Aimes reflected on the challenges that lay ahead. He knew that the road would not be easy, but he was determined to build a brighter tomorrow for the people of the Republic. With the support of those who had believed in him and the strength of his own convictions, he would strive to create a legacy worthy of the trust the nation had placed in him.

"Are you ready for tomorrow, Mr. Chancellor?" Nancy asked, her voice soft as the warm glow of the late-afternoon sun filtered through the floor-to-ceiling windows of their new residence.

Aimes drew in a deep breath, his gaze fixed on the horizon. "I think so," he replied, his tone contemplative. "If I'm honest, I think I'm still in shock that I won." It had been eight days since the election—eight days since a retired Navy captain had defied the odds and defeated the Chancellor Pro Tempore, Chuck Walhoon.

Nancy pulled away, her eyes meeting his with fierce intensity. "You won, my dear, because you had better ideas and a better vision for the Republic than that creature of the Senate. You won because you inspired the people with what the future could hold and what it will take for us to achieve it."

A smile tugged at Aimes's lips as he leaned in to kiss her. "And they say I'm the one who's good at this realpolitik stuff. It's you who wins people over and draws their support."

Nancy's laugh echoed through the room. "Oh, I think it's a team effort for sure." She turned her gaze to the windows, taking in the breathtaking view. "Just look at this—it's beautiful. The contrast between the snowcapped peaks of the mountains and the azure sky above, the tall pines and spruce trees descending the slopes. It's a sight to behold."

Aimes nodded, his eyes following hers. "This is a new beginning, not just for us but for the entire Republic. Until Mountain Home and many of the other cities destroyed in the attack are rebuilt, New Cambria will represent the hope of a nation, a desire for a time of peace, a time to enjoy our hard-fought victory. We will rebuild, and we will overcome this."

Nancy rested her head on his shoulder, her voice a whisper. "And you, my love, will be at the forefront of it all. Chancellor Aimes Morgan. It has a nice ring to it, don't you think?"

Aimes felt a wave of emotion wash over him, the memories of their lost children still fresh in his mind. "They would be so proud of you," Nancy murmured, her own eyes glistening with unshed tears. "Just as I am. You've always been a leader, Aimes. Whether it was as a captain in the Navy or as a father to our children. The Republic couldn't have chosen a better person to lead them through these challenging times."

He drew in a deep breath, the weight of responsibility settling on his shoulders. "I just hope I can live up to their expectations. Tomorrow's swearing-in ceremony, meeting all the new government officials—it's a lot to take in."

Nancy shifted, turning to face him fully. "You've faced far greater challenges, my dear. You've fought in wars, lost loved ones, and still found the strength to carry on. This is just another mission, one that you are more than capable of handling."

Aimes met her gaze, finding solace in the unwavering love and support he saw in her eyes. "With you by my side, I feel like I can take on anything."

"And I'll always be here," Nancy promised, sealing her words with a soft kiss. "Now, let's take a moment to enjoy this view and the peace it brings. Tomorrow will be a big day, but right now, it's just you and me and the beauty of this new world we're building together."

As they settled back into the sofa, arms wrapped around each other, Aimes allowed himself to relax, to soak in the tranquility of the moment. The challenges that lay ahead were daunting, but with Nancy's love and the support of the Republic, he knew he could face them head-on. A new chapter was beginning, and Aimes Morgan was ready to lead the way, his unwavering determination and vision guiding the Republic toward a brighter future.

Chapter Thirty-One
Warrior Diplomats

Camp Shadowrins
Gurista Prime

Drew was anxious to speak with Colonel Mateo Barton. For the last four months, the Delta commander had been in charge of multiple training camps, as well as ensuring that the indigenous forces who had volunteered were properly trained by his Deltas and the newly arrived team of Gallentine Special Forces who were tasked with supporting this effort.

For secrecy and compartmentalization, Colonel Barton had divided the training into separate camps—that way, no single recruit would know about anything other than the camp they were at. Barton had shared the location of Camp Shadowrins for this particular rendezvous, though, which included the Gallentine advisor Third Soldier Silvaran JaxVen—Drew's right-hand man when it came to military matters.

"So how many camps are there?" asked Drew after they'd finished the necessary niceties. "And what skills are you training for?"

Barton smirked. "Cutting to the chase—I like that about you. Well, we have four different camps training basic infantry skills: Camp Felgors Alpha, Camp Felgors Bravo, Camp Felgors Charlie, and Camp Felgors Delta. Each group is receiving instruction on weapons skills, ambush and counterambush, assault and counterassault, and basic first aid."

Drew nodded. "Go on."

"At Camp Tigrians, we're going over radio communications. So they're learning hand signal communications, weapons skills, basic infantry skills, and basic first aid.

"Camp Vulkors trains on heavy weapons in addition to the standardized infantry training and first aid everyone is taught. The primary difference between their training and what we call 'grunt training' is the heavy weapons they're learning to become experts on. This includes the Republic machine guns like the M90, M91, and the M12 multipurpose guided missile launcher."

"Sounds like a good time," said Drew with a wink.

"I like the way you think, Drew," replied Colonel Barton jovially.

Silvaran gave them a side-eyed glance. The Gallentines were not much for humor.

"That leaves Camp Shadowrins, which is where we are now," Drew observed. "Why don't you tell me more about what goes on here?"

"Well, I thought it might be more fun if we joined the group for a little while," said Colonel Barton. "Here, I have some PPE for you before we do."

Barton pointed over to some high-impact suits and helmets, causing Drew to smile. He knew right away this camp covered explosive training, but for the colonel's sake, and for the added amusement of seeing Silvaran in this getup, he went along with it.

With their gear on, Drew and Silvaran joined a class that was meeting in a sort of shack with a roof but no walls, allowing for air to flow. There was a table in the front, three tables in the back for the students, and several chairs. Other than that, the only thing there was a large metal storage box.

"Who can remind me what the five components of an IED are?" asked the instructor, a hulk of a man who couldn't have been shorter than six foot six. A few people raised their hands, and one student was selected.

"The switch, a fuse, a container or body, a charge, and a power source," said the trainee.

"Excellent. Today, we are going to create IEDs that will camouflage into the available surroundings," the instructor explained. "Each one of you has different supplies in front of you. At the end of this session, you will all have working IEDs, despite the variety of appearances."

Drew looked around. One student had a bowl with what looked like papier-mâché and some dirt and leaves to cover their creation with. Another had a taqaffa cup from one of the popular chain shops nearby. A third had a rock collected from the surrounding area, and he had quickly begun drilling a hole so that he could put a pipe inside it. One soldier was 3-D printing an artificial houseplant that looked incredibly realistic, and one was even deconstructing a P2. Drew found himself impressed with the variety.

Colonel Barton escorted them past another group, which was learning how to construct pressure plate mines. These were nasty contraptions. The pressure plates would get buried in dirt or covered with something, until an unsuspecting person eventually stepped on it.

Boom! Drew envisioned the explosion.

Colonel Barton smiled with mischievous glee. "This is the session I really wanted you to see," he announced.

Another wall-less shelter housed a few tables and chairs. Drew saw quickly that each student here had a microdrone in front of them. But there were also a lot of other miniature drones behind the instructor.

What do they have up their sleeves here? Drew wondered.

The female instructor held up one of the microdrones, which was similar in appearance to a dragonfly. The group scoffed quietly. "You've seen small drones before—that's nothing new," she began. "However, this tiny, lightweight mechanism contains a .32-caliber explosive bullet."

There was a murmur among the group, and one person even mumbled aloud, "How is that possible?"

The instructor wasn't fazed. "This drone has four hours of flight time, and up to seventy-two hours of semidormant passive battery mode, so it can sit in a tree branch and…well, I think it's time I just show you what this thing is capable of."

She led the group to a clearing in the trees, which had been set up with mannequins standing about.

What the hell is this? Drew asked himself. He noticed that each of the dummies that had been placed here had a unique face, which was a bit odd. He really didn't know what was coming next.

The female instructor held up one of the drones. "So you want to see what these babies can do?" she asked with a twinkle in her eye.

The anticipation was palpable.

She held up a tablet, which displayed the image of one of the mannequin's faces, overlaid with a grid that emphasized the different facial features. Drew had seen this type of setup for biometric scanning of human faces before, only in this instance, they were plastic faces. "Each one of these microdrones has a camera with AI facial recognition." She flipped through a few of the mannequins' images until she settled on one. "First, we assign a target. Then we activate the drone, and…"

The drone nearest her levitated into the air, then flew about among the crowd, scanning faces. As it did, the screen on the instructor's tablet showed a small window with the images of each face the drone had scanned. Each image capture happened so fast that Drew didn't even notice the drone pausing or stopping at all as it continued its flight pattern. Then, the drone found the matching mannequin. The images on the tablet briefly flashed in red, with a notice that said, "Target acquired." The drone dove down with lightning speed.

Boom!

The sudden blast caused Drew to jump. He hadn't been expecting that, at least not so quickly. When he turned back to the mannequin, it had a hole right in the middle of its forehead.

"Once the bullet is released, the rest of the microdrone self-detonates, leaving no evidence behind. These drones are going to be amazing for targeted assassinations," the instructor remarked. "We can feed entire rosters into the system and, with a swarm of these devices, take them all down in one fell swoop."

Drew was impressed. Technology like this had been in development for a long time, but these were so accurate, so compact, and they had so many of them. As they took off their protective suits, Drew thought he even detected a smile from Silvaran.

"Having a good time?" Drew teased.

Silvaran tilted his head, definitely smiling now. "Don't let it go to your head," he replied.

Drew laughed. If the Gallentine was having fun, that was a good sign.

The two of them reconvened with Colonel Barton. "All right, Colonel. We've had some fun here, but I guess we should finish up with the business portion of the meeting," said Drew. "Where do we stand in terms of numbers trained so far?"

"At this point, we've trained a total of forty, twelve-man insurgent teams and two battalions of three-hundred-and-fifty-person insurgent infantry units," Barton replied. "We also have a total of one thousand, one hundred and eighty Guristas, all fully equipped with Republic weapons and basic infantry body armor and uniform setups."

"So, Silvaran, you've been pretty quiet today, but I have a question for you now," said Drew.

"Ask away," Silvaran responded.

"Do you think we're ready to move forward with the coup—take the government down and sever their ties to the Zodarks?"

"Yes, so long as the Republic is ready to dispatch a force once the coup is underway. If days or weeks go by without their appearance, the Zodarks will likely have enough time to rally a force large enough to put down our insurrection," the Gallentine advisor answered dryly.

Drew locked eyes with Colonel Barton, who gave him a little nod. That was all the affirmation that he needed.

****

Emek Brews
Gurista Prime

Drew handed Ashurina a cup of taqaffa. Although she had been raised on this particular hot drink, Drew knew that after her time in Sol, she had definitely come to favor coffee, the Republic equivalent. However, there were no coffee shops here on Gurista Prime, so this would have to do. This shop, which had a name that roughly translated into "valley," operated as a hidden corner where the resistance was freely welcomed.

"So, Drew, what's going on?" asked Ashurina coldly after the first sip.

"What, can't a guy try and have a conversation over some coffee with a work colleague?" Drew replied cheekily.

"I have never known you to 'chew the fat' unless you had a reason for it," Ashurina insisted. "Are you trying to butter me up for something?"

"No, not exactly," said Drew. He recalibrated his approach. "Ashurina…do you think your father is ready to become the leader of a free Gurista society?" he asked.

"Oh," Ashurina replied. She took a few sips of the drink that had been handed to her, a pensive look on her face. "I do have my concerns, honestly," she admitted. "I know my father is prepared for this role, but I am not entirely certain that the people will accept him as the leader following a coup. I'm still not sure how people will respond to the coup."

"Is there any way for us to gauge the pulse of the public's attitude before the coup?" asked Drew.

"I think this would be very dangerous," Ashurina responded. "The Gurista society runs on gossip; it is a part of our cultural DNA. You put out 'feelers' and word is going to get around very quickly."

"Let me put it to you another way," said Drew. "You know your people and your culture better than anyone in the Republic." He smacked his hand down on the counter, not enough to draw the attention of the other patrons, but enough to make her startle. "Not thinking, just responding from instinct—which way do *you* think it will go?"

Ashurina took one more sip of taqaffa, then blurted out, "I think once the Zodarks are really gone, and the people realize that we are free, the Guristas will want to keep that taste of independence."

"Good," said Drew. "I was hoping that was what you would say."

****

Nannar Nightclub
Gurista Prime

The strobe lights and loud music frankly drove Dakkuri crazy, but it was one of the easier locations for him to meet with Drew in plain sight. He grabbed a drink and tried to blend in, but he was nervous.

Drew appeared behind him, facing the opposite direction. If anyone were to see them, it would not have appeared that the two men had come there to meet each other. "Man, you've got to loosen up," he said. "Try and act like you want to be here a little."

Dakkuri realized he'd been stiff as a board and tried to allow his body to move with the music a bit more.

"So, why don't you tell me what's on your mind?" asked Drew.

"It seems like there are a lot of shifting sands happening with the Groff and the greater Zodark society in the wake of their failed invasion of Earth," Dakkuri began. He ran his fingers through his hair. "I believe my time of discovery may not be far off."

"Is this a general impression, or do you have more specific intel?" Drew inquired.

"The Groff is purging anyone they suspect may be a spy," Dakkuri explained. "I've shielded my presence on Gurista Prime, but I'm not sure how much longer that will last."

Drew danced silently for a moment, apparently mulling that over. "If we execute the coup now, would it succeed?" he asked.

Dakkuri calculated in his mind. "It depends on if the new Gurista Army and Navy stay neutral, or if they come down on the side of the Zodarks."

"What would tip the scales in our favor?" Drew inquired.

"The key to making the coup work would be the elimination of as many of the current Zodark military advisors as possible, I think," Dakkuri replied. "Then we would need to make an offer to the remaining Gurista military leaders and soldiers."

"What kind of an offer?" Drew pressed, sounding a little irritated.

"Not a bribe or anything, if that's what you were thinking," Dakkuri assured. "I mean, the offer is for a better life and society. If they side with Ashurina's father, and this other human society called the Republic, then this Republic will bring the Guristas under their protection and defend them against the Zodarks. They can actually be truly free."

Drew's dance moves shifted; he seemed uncertain. "It's still a gamble, though, right?" he said. "I mean, they have to wait and hope the Republic does send warships to hold up their end of the deal—to prove the military support is real and not made up."

Dakkuri wasn't completely convinced it would work either, if he was being honest with himself. "The thing is, Drew, I don't see another option. I say we do what we can to make this successful, then go for it before we get discovered."

Drew didn't say anything; he just downed the rest of his drink. He walked the glass back to the bar. As he turned, he caught eye contact with Dakkuri for a split second and then gave him a tiny nod before he walked out of the nightclub.

******

Ekur Eninnu Hotel, Eleventh Floor
Gurista Prime

Catalina's heels clicked along the polished basalt floor, and she stopped at the ornate desk, inlaid with gold and precious stones, intentionally leaning forward a bit more than necessary so as to draw attention to her cleavage. She pulled forward a lookbook with images of several very attractive women printed inside it. This type of business steered clear of P2s and went strictly "old school."

"So what do you fancy this evening?" Catalina asked with a wry smile. Her red lipstick made her even more alluring, and the man in front of her ogled her with a look that said he'd take her if she were on the menu.

She hid her personal feelings of disgust. Catalina found the business of prostitution to be horribly degrading, and she had never imagined that she would end up being a madam. The culture on Gurista Prime was entirely different from what she was used to, though. Here, polygamy and polyamory were rather common, and the women that she had recruited for this little mission were all fully aware of what they were getting into. Not only had they assured Catalina that they fully consented to this type of work, but they were proud to do it because they wanted to be a part of the resistance.

Honeypot traps were as old as espionage itself. Men often said things they were not supposed to disclose when they became emotionally involved with someone. It was a great intel-gathering arrangement. However, while Catalina's women were reporting important information to her, their real job was a type of slow inception, planting thoughts, questions, and suggestive ideas along the way. They would make seemingly innocent statements like, "I wonder what life would be like without the Zodarks." Then as things progressed, they might ask a repeat customer what they thought of some of these "Free Gurista" marches and activists. Depending on how that client responded, they might say that some of the messages they were advocating for made sense. "Wouldn't a society free to evolve and develop without the ever-present Zodarks having to approve everything we do be a positive thing?" Basically, it was their job to plant seeds of doubt about the "good intentions" of their "benefactors," the Zodarks, and hopefully cause them to question their loyalty. It was psyops at its finest.

Utu had stopped drooling over Catalina long enough to make his selection. "Excellent choice, Utu. I'm quite certain that Eresh will make you very happy. Before we go over our different packages, I want to let you know that because you were referred by Nidaba, you will get a discount on your first visit with us. And if you refer more of your friends, then you will receive another price reduction."

It was a brilliant system they had worked out. Ekur Eninnu Hotel was near the capital district and amenable to the idea of an entire floor being rented out on a continuous basis. The decor was appropriately lavish to bring in their upper-class clientele. Several months ago, they had planted a few of their girls in the bar of this hotel, scouting out anyone who worked for the government. Once they had a few men hooked, they utilized their referral system, and the whole gravy train just kept rolling from there. At this point, they were nearly at capacity.

Catalina showed Utu to his room, which was decorated with what appeared to be finely woven tapestries but were actually digital fabrics with changeable patterns. Eresh sat atop a bed adorned with silken sheets and pillows, her long black hair flowing slightly from the fan in the room. She smiled seductively at her customer.

"Eresh, this is Utu. He's signed up for package number three," said Catalina.

"Sure thing," Eresh replied, grabbing a bottle of massage oil as she stood, her long, athletic legs showing their best features in her dress, which had two very high slits for this purpose.

"If you all need anything, there's a buzzer on the nightstand. Otherwise, we'll see you in a couple of hours."

"Thanks," Utu muttered before Catalina closed the door.

She let out a sigh. One more down. It was almost time to change shifts. Jess would be in soon to relieve her, and then Catalina could go back to the safe house and cleanse her mind of the experience. She knew way too much about all the inner workings of the personal lives of the government workers on Gurista Prime at this point.

Catalina heard some moaning from room three and did a double take. *Am I hearing things?* she wondered. No one was supposed to be in that room. Only the Kites had the master codes to the doors and the elevators, and the lobby didn't let anyone up unless they were accompanied by Catalina or Jess.

She put her ear against the door. Definitely moaning, she confirmed. Catalina was about to bust into the room when her brain suddenly identified the two voices within. She stopped herself flat. Her mind was already making mental images, and she didn't need real ones.

Catalina walked back to the desk and took a seat. She barely stopped herself from laughing out loud. She smiled slyly and waited...

Several minutes later, Jess emerged from room three, her dress a bit askew and her hair looking somewhat windblown.

"So...you might want to grab a mirror and touch up before the next client," Catalina said with a wink.

Jess's cheeks turned bright red, and she rushed to pull a mirror out of the drawer in the front desk. She frantically fiddled with her hair until it looked intentionally tousled.

"You know?" asked Jess.

"You weren't exactly quiet," Catalina teased. "So how was it?" she asked.

Jess's cheeks went from crimson to beet red. "Honestly, it was electric."

"I wondered for a while if you two would ever leave the friend zone," Catalina remarked. "I think you can tell him to come out now."

Jess didn't say anything aloud, but Catalina knew she was using her neurolink to communicate. Thirty seconds later, a sheepish Somchai emerged from the room.

Way to go, brother, Catalina told him through the neurolink. It was like the silent version of a high five.

"Maybe we could keep this between the three of us, just for now?" Jess asked meekly.

Catalina put her hands up in mock surrender. "Of course! Who am I to complicate a new love story?"

At the mention of the word *love*, Somchai and Jess looked at each other as if realizing that they were in fact in love for the first time.

"Take your time," Catalina said. "I'm happy for you. Now if only we could somehow find a match for Amir."

"I think he's kind of content being a bachelor," Somchai mused.

"He thinks that now," Catalina replied, "but when the heart meets its match, it is very hard to resist."

Chapter Thirty-Two
Weight of the World

January 2114
Office of the Chancellor
New Cambria, New Eden
Rhea System

Aimes Morgan looked up as the door to his office opened; Amelia, his executive assistant, walked in. "Good morning, Chancellor," she declared, then asked, "Would you like me to have an assortment of freshly baked pastries and coffee brought to your office for your nine o'clock meeting or just go with coffee?"

He smiled at the energy she brought to the room when she entered. "Morning, Amelia. This might be a combustible meeting. Let's go with coffee and the freshly baked pastries—you know their favorites."

"Yes, I do. I'll let the kitchen know," she replied, then exited as quickly as she had entered.

I hope this won't be a contentious meeting, he thought.

Aimes Morgan had been sworn in as the new Chancellor two weeks ago. It had taken him nearly that long just to absorb a portion of the challenges facing the Republic. It was like drinking from a firehose as he tried to grasp the information. Despite nearly eighteen months since the attack on Earth, the repairs and reconstruction efforts were nowhere close to being done. The damage alone to the critical infrastructure across much of the planet had been wrecked hard. Trying to reconnect cities, states, and regions was proving to be a monumental task. Just the number of refugees and displaced persons was close to one in fifteen of the survivors.

One of the very first executive orders Aimes had signed during his first week in office was a modified prioritization order between Space Command, the Republic government, and Walburg Industries. When Senator Walhoon was sworn in as the temporary Chancellor, he had gone along with Admiral Bailey and Viceroy Hunt's recommendation to prioritize the delivery of the C100, C200, and C300 Advanced Combat Synthetic Soldiers for the military ahead of commercial interests. This meant for each noncombat Synth produced for the commercial sector, there were eight produced for the military.

With the loss of so many people from the attack, there was an acute shortage of manpower available to keep broad swaths of the economy running, let alone the enormous task of clearing debris so the reconstruction efforts could begin. All of that would soon change as his EO was about to upend that ratio.

****

Space Command Headquarters
New Cambria, New Eden
Rhea System

"Chester, what's up with Ripley's Raiders?" asked Miles. "I thought we had an agreement. Raids and reconnaissance into the Gravaxia system are fine," he said, then pointed to the holographic report hovering between them. "This, however, is not what I would call a reconnaissance or cross-border raid—four frigates, two heavy cruisers, and a battleship—the *Mars* was a new *Victory*-class battleship, for God's sake."

"I get it, Miles," said Chester, throwing his hands up in mock surrender. "He bit off more than he could chew. In fairness to Ripley, it was a clever ambush—one lesser officers would have escaped from." He paused. "I hope you read the rest of his report—especially the part about them destroying a large-scale Zodark mining and fuel storage facility. That was in addition to the eighteen enemy ships they destroyed, four of them Zodark battleships."

Miles sighed as Chester pointed out the likely tactical victory Ripley had scored for them in his "unauthorized" border excursion. He knew Chester was right. It just hurt losing one of their newest battleships and a pair of heavy cruisers. They were short on trained crews, ships, and time. The only thing he felt he could control was potential ship losses, by not fighting battles that didn't need to be fought—at least not yet.

"Moving on, what are your thoughts on Chancellor Morgan's EO regarding Walburg production quotas?" asked Miles, changing topics. "We meet with him in an hour."

Chester shrugged. "He's not wrong, Miles. Timing sucks, sure. But when else is going to be a good time to readjust priorities?"

"After we've defeated the Zodarks?" Miles shot back.

Chester scoffed. "Miles, let me ask you something. Defeating the Zodarks could be several years off. What should the Chancellor tell the hundreds of millions of survivors still without a home? We have one in ten of our citizens on Earth still living in refugee camps and temporary housing. Without the quantity of skilled labor necessary to remove rubble and restore critical infrastructure to the damaged areas, reconstruction efforts in many of these hard-hit areas can't even begin.

"Miles, right now, as leaders held in high esteem across the Republic, we have a duty to our people beyond just protecting them. We cannot be the entire reason why the government is unable to adequately provide the most basic of human needs—shelter. I'm not saying the production of combat synthetic soldiers isn't important or a priority—it is. We just can't allow it to be prioritized above providing our private industrial sector the necessary supplies and materials and the qualified and skilled labor needed to rapidly rebuild these destroyed communities," Chester concluded.

The explanation caught Miles off guard. *How have I missed this?* he thought to himself. It was perhaps the first time he had heard the consequences of the series of decisions he had pushed, maybe coerced, Chancellor Pro Tempore Walhoon into agreeing to. Walburg had of course protested the arrangement, making the same arguments the new Chancellor had echoed when he'd announced the EO last week.

Miles brushed aside the holo display between them and leaned forward. "Chester, you speak the truth—I was wrong. I allowed myself to become so narrowly focused on defeating this threat to our existence that I failed to realize what we are sacrificing so much for—our people. At the end of the day, if our priorities stay devoted to our quest to build the force necessary to defeat the Zodarks and this deprives our people of their ability to live, then our eventual victory will be stained forever with the unnecessary sacrifice of our people."

Chester smiled softly.

"You know, before we had this conversation, I was planning to play hardball with Chancellor Morgan," Miles said. "I would have agreed to modify the requirement by half. I don't know what specifically it was about what you said—maybe it was our failure as leaders to look after those we're charged with protecting. I see the error we made in the immediate aftermath of the attacks. I wish I had seen it sooner. I see it

now, and you're right—we should work with the Chancellor to fix it. Come, let us head over to the Chancellery and find a way to fix this."
****

Three Hours Later
Office of the Chancellor

Chancellor Aimes Morgan finished his lunch. He couldn't have been more surprised at how well things seemed to be going during his first official policy meeting as Chancellor with the head of his armed forces and the alliance Viceroy. He had spent a lot of time preparing stats and arguments to convince his former ship captain, now the Viceroy, to recognize the need to change the previous agreement that the Chancellor Pro Tempore had saddled him with.

It wasn't that Aimes didn't recognize the persistent threat the Pharaonis and Zodarks still posed to the Republic. He likely understood the threat better than Chancellor Luca or even Senator Walhoon. He had, after all, served thirty-six years in the Navy before he was injured and given a medical retirement. What he couldn't allow, now that he had the power to do something about it, was for the government to continue to fail at taking care of its people. The industrial capacity of the Republic could not continue to focus solely on supporting the war while leaving nothing of substance to rebuild following the Zodark attack.

When the group finished lunch, they returned to the conference room adjacent to the Chancellor's office to resume their talks. For the afternoon session, Admiral Bailey's staff was going to brief him on the status of the war effort against the Pharaonis. This would be followed by a status update on the preparations underway to deal once and for all with the persistent threat posed by the Zodark Empire. At the same time, Aimes was looking forward to receiving the unvarnished truth about how these military campaigns were really doing. It was the last meeting of the day that intrigued him the most—the one with Viceroy Miles Hunt, who had just returned from another meeting with the Humtar President, Gudea, to continue their discussions about technology transfers the Humtars might be willing to make separately with the Republic versus the alliance.

The Humtars had shared their advanced quantum beam communication technology with the Republic and the alliance, which had already proven invaluable in aiding the coordination of alliance logistics and ongoing offensive campaigns. It wouldn't be long now before they would have essentially real-time communications between Republic colonial worlds such as Alpha Centauri, Earth, New Eden, Sumer, and even the Interstellar Irish Republic's home world, Éire, would eventually be looped into this quantum communication system.

By the time Admiral Bailey's staff had finished bringing him up to speed on the status of the Pharaonis campaign, Aimes couldn't help but wonder what was still happening in the Orbot-occupied territories, especially after the official sighting of Legion in their territory. When he interrupted to ask questions about this societal kill code that a previously unknown Alpha unit had apparently issued, it left him with more questions than answers. From the limited usable information they had obtained from questioning the senior-ranking Alpha Orbot that hadn't received the kill code, it sounded like a decision had been made somewhere along the line with Legion to evacuate the Orbot consciousnesses and relocate them to a safer location. In Aimes's mind, the Orbots didn't seem all that different from Legion—but having never faced Legion, he was speculating at best.

Once the admiral's staff had finished briefing him on the activities of Task Force 28, the Republic task force meant to reinforce the Pfeinstgard system, the daylong ordeal of death by holograph was mercifully over. It wasn't that Aimes found the briefings boring or lacking in detail. On the contrary, the amount of data being dumped on him was overwhelming.

The admiral's staff collected their materials and exited the conference room. With just the three of them in the room, Aimes commented, "Chester, that was a lot of information. Perhaps the intent was to overwhelm me with it. I suppose if I have questions, I'll have to follow up with your office."

"It can be a lot to take in, Chancellor. My office is here to help answer questions and interpret whatever data you have," Chester replied.

Aimes nodded, then turned to Miles. "I guess it's your turn, Miles. How was the meeting with President Gudea? Was he receptive to our question about any kind of support they might be able to provide to aid in our recovery efforts on Earth? Do they seem open to potentially allowing us to acquire any sort of advanced technologies they believe might help our society?"

****

Miles was glad the military portion of today's briefings had finished. They had met with Chancellor Morgan a few times during the past couple of weeks following his official swearing-in. Today, however, was the first time they had been able to provide him with a comprehensive picture of the Republic's role in the ongoing war. Miles knew the perception was that the Republic had been the one bearing the brunt or even the lion's share of the alliance casualties and ship losses during the First Zodark War and now this one. In his role and position as the Viceroy of the alliance, he knew the truth, and the truth was every race was paying a price during these wars.

"Miles, you've spent time with the Humtar leader. What do you think of President Gudea?" asked the Chancellor.

Miles realized his mind had wandered while the Chancellor was speaking. Feeling his cheeks flush, he attempted to recover. "Gudea is the most unique and interesting person I've ever met. I know his visits to Earth and New Eden were short and tightly packed, especially once Emperor Tibus and King Grigdolly arrived. Unfortunately, that didn't leave much of an opportunity for you to speak with him."

Miles leaned back and stroked his chin. "What do I think of the Humtar leader?" he asked, as if speaking his thoughts aloud. "Let me explain it this way—if there were such a thing as an ideal human being, a human whose DNA is near to perfect, having never been exposed to toxic materials or radiation that might alter it—President Gudea and the other Humtars I met would be it. They were by far the most perfect-looking humans I've met," Miles explained.

He leaned forward, his tone hushed. "I would never say this to Lilly—even the Humtar women...my goodness," Miles explained. "I don't know what it is about these people—genetically, they appear in all regards to be flawless. Perhaps they've achieved a standard of medical science we don't understand. Maybe that's something I can speak to them about sharing with us, their medical knowledge."

"Hmm, that sounds like it might be useful, especially in our continued recovery efforts on Earth. Heck, I have to imagine their medical science would be a huge value aboard our ships and the C200 medical Synths deployed with our troops. Maybe it could help us save more of our injured soldiers," Chancellor Morgan replied.

Chapter Thirty-Three
Maximum Pressure

Headquarters
Republic Third Expeditionary Army
Astrionis, Tau Sagittarii

Standing alone in the room, next to the conference room table with the holographic display showing the star system Pyrallis. Vice Admiral William "Willie" Rosentreter stared at the next objective in Operation Orion's Hammer. The Pyrallis system had a K-type orange dwarf star with four uninhabitable planets, a dozen or more uninhabitable moons, and the crown jewels of the system—a pair of habitable planets and a moon in the orbit of one of them.

The first habitable planet was called Drakontas. It was mostly an arid desert planet with minimal surface water. What little water the planet held was largely found in the form of mini-oceans and giant rivers and tributaries that wrapped around the planet's equator and didn't deviate too far to either side of it. Intelligence had learned the Pharaonis cities were mostly underground, in giant caverns left over from past mining activity. Apparently, the planet was rich in fluxionite crystals— a unique crystal the Republic had only just learned of as they battled against the Pharaonis.

The crystals were deep blue, almost black in color with a core that pulsed with a silver light when energy was conducted through them. He'd read a report from the Altairians, who had a long history of encounters with the Pharaonis. There was something strange about its molecular structure that allowed it to not only conduct but exponentially amplify any form of energy that passed through it, making it critical in boosting the power outputs of their engines and weapons systems.

With large caverns carved beneath the surface, the Pharaonis had developed vast underground cities—in contrast to the handful of larger cities on the planet's surface. Rosentreter knew if there was going to be a fight on this planet, it would eventually turn into an underground nightmare the RA would eventually have to fight their way through. The thought of fighting these ant-like creatures underground sent shivers down his spine. A fight like this could chew through an army quickly. That was something he couldn't allow.

He turned to the other habitable planet, Naiadon—the polar opposite of the arid deserts of Drakontas. Naiadon was mostly covered in water. It had deep oceans and large underwater cities near the planet's small continents and patches of land.

With the scarcity of buildable land, the Pharaonis had built several interconnected megacities and industrial centers that looked to have been constructed around dozens of small to medium space-based naval shipyards. The Altairian intelligence report on the planet detailed a series of materials the Pharaonis mined from the seafloor at varying depths. Materials like plasmiron, and titanexium alloy—a highly durable and lightweight material composed primarily of titanium and an exotic element called xenium. Materials science wasn't exactly a field Rosentreter had excelled in during his days at the academy. All he knew was it was mined in massive quantities from asteroid belts, moons with rich metal deposits, and apparently the seabed of Naiadon.

What really caught his interest was the moon Caligo, in orbit around the planet. Unlike Drakontas, Naiadon had multiple space elevators connected to large orbital platforms with large industrial factories and shipyards. Even Caligo had a space elevator connecting it to not just an orbital station but a shipyard with no less than forty-two slips, each with the hull of a warship in various stages of construction. What the intelligence report left out, or more likely those drafting it didn't know, was what kind of defensive weapons were affixed to the platforms or floated near it. If it was anything like the Republic naval shipyard between Luna and Mars, it was likely bristling with weapons.

He tapped his finger on Caligo and the holo display expanded the moon, providing a bevy of information and technical details to either side of the moon floating in the center of the display. The moon was habitable, which was unique. The intelligence summary said it had a thick, misty atmosphere that contributed to the planet's low visibility; from orbit, most of the surface could not be seen. Despite the lack of visibility from space, the moon boasted multiple megacities with a vast industrial center that connected it to the space elevator and the shipyards in orbit.

Lost in thought, he hadn't realized someone had walked into the room and was practically standing next to him.

"There you are, Admiral. I thought I might find you in here" came the voice of the Primord admiral, Thorvald Eirikson. "Already thinking about the next system we have to conquer?"

Rosentreter turned slightly to face his comrade. "I would be lying if I said otherwise. This battle to seize this moon Serenea, Thorvald—it's taking much longer than I had anticipated. That series of interlocking fortresses the Pharaonis built—wrapping around the equator. Damn if that hasn't proven to be challenging to overcome." As Rosentreter spoke, he changed the display to show Serenea. He then highlighted one of the Pharaonis forts to emphasize his point.

"We still do not fully control the high ground, the moon's orbit—not so long as they retain control of these four equatorial forts and those three supporting forts here, here, and that last one here. You remember what happened when Pandolly ordered one of his *Berkimon* battleships to attack it head-on, don't you?" Rosentreter asked.

Thorvald grunted at the question. "Of course—how could I forget? He nearly lost a battleship."

"Exactly, and after what happened with that surprise Orbot Collector ship and those vessels from Legion, the Viceroy wants us to finish this campaign as swiftly as possible and be prepared should Legion reappear in either Orbot or now Pharaonis space," Rosentreter replied uncomfortably. He then shifted the conversation back to the recent changes in their orders. "I don't know, Thorvald. Perhaps the Viceroy is right. Instead of sticking to our original planet-hopping campaign, striking at the heart of the enemy—their home world, their capital city— we might bring a swifter end to this fight and maybe—maybe for the Pharaonis like the Orbots—force them into capitulating."

The Primord admiral listened to him but stayed silent for a moment as he tinkered with the holo display, cycling through the different star systems under Pharaonis control.

He then pointed to the Zanthea system. "This planet, Eurysa. According to Altairian and Gallentine intelligence, this planet is the Pharaonis home world—their capital planet. It may not be the industrial heart of their empire, like the Pyrallis system you were just looking at. But if the Viceroy wants us to essentially ignore all other planets— forgoing this planet-hopping campaign we have planned out—I suggest we have Pandolly's ship generate a bridge for us from Tau Sagittarii directly into the Zanthea system—right on top of their home world.

"If we muster everything we have—if we can get the *Freedom* to join us—we could smash whatever remaining warships they have defending the planet and system, bypassing these other systems entirely. I highly doubt they have the same kind of planetary defensive system we are encountering right now on Serenea. Once we have cleared the system of warships and orbital defenses around the planet, we can start bombarding their cities and industrial centers until they surrender—or until there is nothing left," explained Thorvald as the holo display illustrated his plan.

For a moment, no one said anything. Rosentreter canted his head to the side, as if looking at the plan from a different angle. He nodded a few times, then commented, "Huh, OK. Let's walk this plan out a bit. What about our ground force? Do we pound the cities from orbit a certain amount of time and then drop the Army near the capital to see if they'll quit or need a little more persuading?"

Thorvald looked at Rosentreter, or rather he appeared to be looking through him, his eyes running scenarios over in his mind. "Yes, I think that is exactly what we should do," he concluded matter-of-factly.

Rosentreter bit his lower lip in thought, then nodded in agreement. "OK, I think we have a workable plan here. Let me run this past Admiral McKee and see what she thinks. Then we can pitch the idea to the Viceroy and see about getting the *Freedom* to join us."

Chapter Thirty-Four
I Am Spartacus

11th Spartacus Armored Regiment
FOB Yankee, Serenea
IVO Torquato Tuga Ridge

Colonel Steve Thomas sighed to himself, his frustration growing by the minute. It was taking his regiment longer than normal to exit Forward Operating Base Yankee. With eighteen tanks to a company and six companies to a regiment, his command consisted of 108 Yeti tanks—they were the armored fist of the Republic. But right now, in moments like this, his frustration was reaching a boiling point.

Why is it taking so long to exit the damn base? he wondered.

"Sir, if I'm not mistaken, I believe the regiment's overhead ISR drone is deployed and loitered above us," said Staff Sergeant Joe Wilson, his tank gunner. "You could check it out and see what the delay is," he offered.

"You know what, Wilson? That's a good idea," Colonel Thomas said, tapping on the controls. He found the drone ID and selected it. A moment later, the drone's real-time video showed him why and where his tanks were getting bogged down.

The military police or MPs had erected a series of barriers along the road leading to and exiting the ECP, forcing the vehicles to navigate their way around multiple barriers aimed at slowing the vehicle traffic heading into the base. While he appreciated the attention paid to better protect the base, he didn't appreciate how much slower it would take them to get off it.

"Damn, who would have thunk placing barriers every twenty feet would cause a slight traffic problem when vehicles like, I don't know, *tanks* have to navigate their way through them? Maybe we should just run them over," Wilson commented as they watched the drone footage of the Yeti tanks clumsily trying to navigate their way around the obstacles.

"Yeah, it wasn't the smartest idea to gum up the exit like this. You would think they would have a way of easily moving the obstacles to the side when a regiment like ours is trying to exit," Thomas countered, his frustration easing now that he knew what was going on.

He understood the reasoning behind the multilayered entrance control points—it didn't mean he liked it.

Thirty freaking minutes to snake our way off the damn FOB, he thought angrily. They were officially behind schedule and for a commander with OCD, it annoyed the hell out of him.

As he continued watching the overhead drone footage on the monitor, the dull gray Serenean landscape stretched before him, pockmarked with craters from the relentless artillery barrages that had characterized the months of bitter fighting.

I can't believe how long we've been stuck on this godforsaken moon, he reflected grimly.

"Ah, come on, sir. It's not so bad—we could be fighting Zodarks," Wilson said, trying to cheer him up.

"Yeah, I suppose you're right, Wilson. At least we got replacements the other day. We'll be attacking at one hundred percent," Thomas replied.

They drove on in silence for a bit. Each man was lost in his own thoughts. The front lines had moved a few kilometers forward since the regiment had cycled off the front for a break. At times, they'd run into a heavily fortified area that might take them the better part of a month to clear. Other times, they got lucky and punched a hole through the enemy line, turning the flanks and forcing the enemy into a haphazard retreat to the next defensive position.

Thomas's regiment, the 11th Spartacus Armor, had been at the forefront of the action since rolling off the ramp of the T-92 Starlifter that had brought them to the surface. During the past ninety-two days, the regiment had been deployed to the surface. He had lost twelve percent of his troops—men and women who were now on an eternal patrol of no return. It was a sobering figure that weighed heavily on his mind, especially after all the letters he had written to the families. He had wanted to provide a final account of how and why each of their loved ones had died and to tell them how their death wasn't in vain. He'd told each one how their sacrifice had helped to maintain the freedom and security necessary to safeguard the Republic.

"Colonel, we just received an update from the 21st Mech—the Sumerian regiment is alerting us to the presence of the 23rd Mech. Once we merge onto the highway, the 23rd will be parked on the left side of the highway. The message said the 23rd is going to be our infantry support for the attack," relayed Wilson, who was also the comms NCO in addition to his role as gunner.

"Acknowledged. Thanks, Wilson. It's good to know we'll have infantry support," Thomas replied before adding, "Those Pharaonis have a way of bum-rushing our tanks, then climbing on top to tear apart anything that's not permanently attached to the hull."

"Yeah, no joke. Hopefully, they'll do a better job than the last unit that accompanied us—oh, before I forget, weapon checks are good. All systems nominal."

Thomas acknowledged with a curt nod. He liked working with Wilson. He was a damn fine gunner, steady under pressure, and he knew how to employ the tank's full lethality. From the tank's 155mm magnetic railgun to the dual-barreled blasters mounted above the commander's hatch to the antidrone microwave and laser defense weapons, Wilson was a master gunner he had come to rely on and greatly respect. They'd been through crucibles together that had forged an unbreakable bond of trust and camaraderie.

Thomas watched the drone feed as it showed the convoy stretched out behind them, a serpentine column of armored might. The 23rd Texas Mechanized Infantry Regiment brought up the rear, their IFVs bristling with energy blasters and antitank missiles. They were a formidable combined-arms team, honed to a razor's edge by the unforgiving rigors of combat.

As the armored column turned onto the highway, Thomas admired the engineering prowess of the Pharaonis. The road was a marvel of alien construction, a six-lane artery that intel had suggested led directly to the heart of the enemy's fortifications, a complex network of interlocking trenches and bastions centered around the planetary defensive weapons—the ion cannons at the heart of the enemy forts they had been battling against since they'd landed.

Those cannons were the key to everything. As long as they remained operational, the Pharaonis could continue to contest Republic orbital supremacy, threatening the fragile supply lines that were the lifeblood of the invasion force. Taking them out would be a turning point, a decisive blow that could finally break the stalemate and secure a foothold in this hostile world.

The kilometers ticked by as the armored column pressed onwards, the thrum of powerful engines and the clatter of tracks on pavement filling the air. Thomas scanned the horizon, searching for any sign of the enemy. The Pharaonis were crafty adversaries, masters of camouflage and concealment. They could be anywhere, waiting in ambush with their fearsome energy weapons and biotechnological terrors.

When they reached fifteen kilometers from the current allied positions, Colonel Thomas ordered the regiment to halt and regroup. He wanted his reconnaissance unit to deploy their drones and scout a path toward friendly lines and identify potential lanes of attack they could pursue as they approached the line of contact. He also needed them to look for mines, tagging their locations for the regiment's sapper units to disable or destroy before they had a chance to ruin his tanks.

This waypoint would likely be their last chance to take a moment to stretch their legs and take a bio break before the action started. When Thomas exited his tank, he stood on the turret, smiling at the sight of drivers doing equipment checks, gunners making their weapons ready, and tank commanders helping when needed and looking after their troops.

"Bloody moon dust gets everywhere, Colonel," Sergeant Wilson grumbled as he clambered down from the tank, his face streaked with grime. "I'll be coughing this crap up for weeks. It's murder on the respiratory system."

Thomas chuckled mirthlessly. "Ha, just add it to the list of things the VA will say weren't service-related when they deny your appeal for the fifth time. Mark my words, Sergeant. This crap will haunt us for years after this war is over."

"Damn, Colonel, aren't you the Debbie Downer today," teased Sergeant Wilson. "Here I thought I was trying to be positive."

Colonel Thomas shrugged. Standing on top of the Yeti, he looked out over his regiment, a ragtag assembly of battered machines and weary soldiers held together by guts, spit, and sheer willpower. They'd been through hell together, and there was more to come before it ended. Thomas knew he could count on them, down to the last man and woman if necessary. They were the Spartacus Division, and they'd see this war through to its bitter end.

Craning his head to the side, Thomas listened to a soft droning noise approaching. He heard a chirp on his Qpad, an alert letting him know their drones had returned. Their reconnaissance painted a grim picture of the road ahead—enemy fortifications loomed on the horizon, a brutal gauntlet of interlocking fields of fire and dense minefields. The Pharaonis were dug in deep, ready and waiting for the assault they knew was coming.

Thomas steeled himself, a cold knot of anticipation tightening in his gut. This was it. The line of contact, the razor's edge between life and death. He keyed his comm, his voice steady and resolute as it echoed across the regimental net.

"All right, Spartacus. This is it. Our objective lies ahead, and the enemy is waiting for us. But I'll be damned if we're going to give them the satisfaction of an easy fight. We're going to hit them hard and hit them fast, with everything we've got. Today, we're going to blast through their lines, kick down their doors, and shove our guns right down their damned throats. The Spartacus regiment leads the way, and we'll not stop until that ion cannon is nothing but a smoking pile of rubble. Mount up and get ready to give 'em hell. Thomas out."

As the regiment roared back to life, engines growling and weapons priming, Colonel Steve Thomas climbed back into the armored cocoon of his command tank. The road to victory lay ahead, a crucible of fire and blood that would test them all to the limits of endurance. But they were ready, and they would not fail.

****

Bravo Company, 23rd Texas Mechanized Infantry Regiment
Line of Contact

"Contact front! Engage, engage!" Captain Chris Dausch barked into the comms as the Linebacker jolted forward, reactor whining. The line of contact was a seething maelstrom of fire and fury. The Pharaonis were well fortified and not lacking in alien weaponry.

"Gunner, target those emplacements! Flush the bastards out!" Dausch gripped the edge of the holo display, eyes flicking over the tactical overlay. The 11th Armored was pushing ahead, their Yeti tanks shrugging off enemy fire as they advanced inexorably toward the trenches.

The Linebacker's twin-barrel laser blaster opened up, searing beams of light stabbing out at the enemy positions. Microwave pulses crackled, seeking out the telltale emissions of Pharaonic drones. Missiles whooshed from the launcher, arcing over the battlefield to detonate in thunderous explosions among the enemy fortifications.

"Bravo Company, advance!" Dausch ordered, his voice cutting through the chaos. "Stay tight on the tanks. Watch your spacing. We're going in!"

The Linebackers surged forward, a phalanx of armored might. Overhead, artillery shells screamed down from the heavens, plowing into the enemy lines with devastating force. The ground shook, a relentless drumbeat of destruction.

Dausch's eyes narrowed as a swarm of alien infantry emerged from the shattered trenches, their chitinous exoskeletons glinting in the harsh Serenean sunlight.

"Gunner, light 'em up!" he snarled.

The laser blaster thrummed, sweeping the enemy ranks with deadly precision. The Pharaonis soldiers exploded, their carapaces bursting like overripe fruit.

"Keep pushing! Don't let up!" Dausch urged his company forward. The Linebackers were grinding over the ruined earth, crushing enemy carcasses beneath their treads. The Pharaonic line was buckling, the tanks of the 11th Armored thrusting deep into their defenses like a spear being thrust into flesh—breaking through the enemy lines.

But the enemy was far from defeated, and the enemy always got a vote in a fight. Bright flashes of plasma fire stitched across the air like bolts of energy, making a sizzling noise as they slammed against the Linebackers' armor. Some of the infantry fighting vehicles exploded when the energy bolts pierced their armor. Others were merely left with molten scars on their hulls, a reminder of the near-death experience for their occupants.

BOOM!

Dausch's Linebacker shook hard from the nearby explosion. When the right external camera readjusted, Dausch saw the vehicle to his right had taken a direct hit, exploding in a fireball of shredded metal and vaporized flesh.

"Damn it! Return fire, return fire—keep the pressure on!" he roared.

BAM!

The Linebacker in front of them exploded into a giant fireball— the armored hull of the vehicle bursting outward as if there had been an bomb within the vehicle. Dausch knew from experience this was typically what happened when a Pharaonis plasma cannon penetrated a vehicle's armor.

As their own vehicle raced forward, their driver jinked to the right and left periodically to avoid being hit. They inadvertently careened into the burning wreck with their own vehicle, jostling Dausch and his crew inside. "Take that, you bastards!" Corporal Jackie Walkup, his gunner, shouted as he swiveled the blaster to the right.

Dausch watched on the monitor as his gunner targeted the enemy bunker the plasma cannon had fired from. The Linebacker's blaster cannon fired a blistering barrage that ripped into the enemy position, silencing the plasma cannon in a bout of flame.

"I got him! That bunker is toast!" Walkup whooped excitedly.

The battle raged on, a swirling frenzy of chaos and destruction happening around them. Dausch gritted his teeth, his mind racing as he coordinated the movements of his company, directing fire and maneuvering his vehicles to support the advancing tanks. They were making progress and had punched through the first line of defense, but the cost was high. The Pharaonis were tenacious, fighting with a ferocity born of desperation and alien fury that was difficult to describe.

"Whoa! Would you look at that!" Walkup shouted.

A Talon fighter bomber raced overtop the fortifications as a series of small, elongated objects fell from beneath its wings. The air ignited in flames, the ferocity of the fire consuming the bunkers and trenches.

Moments after the fuel-air explosive bombs had gone off, the tanks leading them forward lurched once again toward the enemy, their main guns firing into the bunkers they could still see.

"Captain, they're through!" Walkup shouted excitedly.

They watched the first Yeti burst through the final layer of the enemy lines. "They did it. They found us a way through! I can't believe it—it's a straight shot to the ion cannons now!"

Dausch allowed himself a tight smile. The Spartacus regiment had done it. Now, they were turning the flanks, ripping the hole in the lines into a multikilometer gash. With their success, it was up to the infantry to exploit the gap, to rush through the opening and mop up the remaining resistance.

Depressing the talk button, Dausch shouted, "Bravo Company, rally on my vehicle! We're pressing forward into the breach—it's time we finish this fight!"

Excited acknowledgment rolled in from his platoon and squad leaders. His vehicle surged forward like a tide of armored wrath as it washed over the top of the enemy positions. While Dausch was excited, he steeled himself for the fight still to come—clearing the trenches and destroying the ion cannons. This fight might be coming to an end, but this war, this invasion of the Pharaonis—this was just the first planet of many to come.

****

Second Platoon, Bravo Company, 23rd Mechanized
Line of Contact

The world exploded around Master Sergeant Jackie Walkup. There was a searing flash of light and then a thunderous roar slammed him against the restraints of his seat. The Linebacker rocked violently, alarms shrieking as systems overloaded and failed.

"We're hit! We're hit!" someone screamed over the din, voice laced with pain and fear. Walkup shook his head, his ears ringing as he tried to clear the spots from his vision. The interior of the infantry fighting vehicle had become a smoke-filled death trap. Inside the chaos, sparks cascaded from ruptured power cords and shattered displays.

We have to get out of the vehicle now before it blows!

"Out! Everyone out!" Walkup roared, his training taking over. He slammed his fist against the emergency release, the rear hatch blowing open as emergency charges built into the hinges blew the hatch open.

"Go, go, go!" he shouted, shoving soldiers out the hatch and free of the vehicle.

As the soldiers stumbled to their feet, they found themselves and their destroyed Linebacker on the edge of a blast crater, not far from the enemy positions. When Walkup peered around the corner of their smoldering IFV, a surreal scene unfolded before him. Multicolored laser fire crisscrossed the battlefield, zipping with blinding speed as the beams of energy seared the air and scorched the earth.

Then he saw Pharaonis warriors swarming overtop the trenches. The sounds of their alien war cries rose into a fury across the plain.

Ah, damn it. Here they come, he thought to himself.

Walkup turned to the squad of soldiers behind him. "Everyone spread out along the edge of the crater and start laying down suppressive fire!" he ordered. "Higgins, get the M12 set up right there—Dixson, start tossing frags while Higgins gets the machine gun set up!"

Walkup aimed at the charging horde, fixing a Pharaonis warrior in his sights. The creature was a nightmarish fusion of insect and machine, its exoskeleton bristling with cybernetic enhancements. He squeezed the trigger. The rifle kicked against his shoulder as a burst of high energy erupted from the muzzle. He watched as it hit the enemy.

The left upper shoulder of the Pharaonis exploded in a spray of purplish biomass and shattered armor, its momentum carrying it forward to crumple just meters in front of Walkup's feet. But there was no time to celebrate the kill. More of the aliens were closing in, their weapons spitting death.

"Frag out!" Dixson shouted to Walkup's right, hurling a grenade into the enemy's midst.

For the briefest of moments, Walkup saw the fragmentation grenade arc its way through the air before it detonated in a blinding flash overtop the enemy. The Pharaonis warriors shrieked in pain as hot shards of shrapnel tore into their exposed flesh, injuring many of them.

Ratatat, ratatat..., came the quick reports from Higgins's machine gun, spraying the Pharaonis with .338 magnetic railgun slugs.

Still, the Pharaonis continued to charge heedless of their casualties—crawling over dead comrades to get at them. All Walkup and his soldiers could do right now was grit their teeth and continue firing into the onrushing horde. His soldiers were fighting with grim determination, their weapons blazing away as they sought to hold their position.

Bam! Bam!

Walkup felt the ground shake beneath their feet. Artillery rounds burst in the air over the enemy, a remorseless drumbeat of explosions as dozens of Pharaonis disappeared into mists of purplish biomass.

"Thank God for artillery," Walkup muttered to himself as he watched the shells obliterate entire ranks of enemy soldiers.

Suddenly, a shadow fell across him from his left. As he turned, Walkup looked up to see a Pharaonis warrior looming over him, its clawed appendages raised to strike. Moving on instinct at a blinding speed he didn't know he possessed, Walkup drove the butt of his rifle up into the creature's face. He heard and felt the exoskeleton crack beneath the butt of his rifle as it splintered, fluid spraying from the ruined mandibles.

The Pharaonis staggered back, shocked from the violent hit to its face. Walkup pressed the advantage, leveling his rifle and firing a burst point-blank into its thorax.

The warrior crumpled to the ground, its protective outer shell smoking in a couple of places. "Hot damn, that was close," Walkup said to himself as he kicked the corpse aside, scanning the battlefield for his next target.

Somehow, in the midst of the fight, his squad had spread out too much, fighting desperate individual battles against the relentless Pharaonis onslaught.

"Second Platoon! Rally on me!" he shouted, his voice cutting through the chaos. "Come on; we need to form a perimeter. We've got to support those tanks!"

The soldiers of Second Platoon fought their way to his side, their weapons blazing. They eventually formed a ragged circle, their backs to the burning wreckage of the Linebacker. Plasma fire sizzled around them, the air becoming thick with the stench of ozone and charred flesh.

In the distance, Walkup could see the lumbering forms of the Yeti tanks, their railguns flashing as they dueled with Pharaonic emplacements. The ground shook with each titanic impact, the very air seeming to shiver with the violence of the exchange.

"We have to hold the line!" Walkup roared, his voice becoming hoarse from shouting. "We hold until relieved! Not one step back!"

And so they fought, a handful of human soldiers against a tide of alien warriors. Laser fire and plasma bolts continued to crisscross the battlefield, searing the flesh of his soldiers and shattering the chitin of enemy armor. The battle continued to rage, the soil of Serenea becoming slick with the blood and fluids of the Pharaonis, a hellish slurry of biomass goo that clung to their boots and fouled their weapons.

Walkup turned to his left, the mechanical sound of tanks approaching. A light breeze touched his face, brushing aside the black smoke of charred vehicles. Yeti tanks emerged from the smoke. He smiled at the sight of them.

The tanks pushed past the remains of the enemy line. What few Pharaonis remained attempted to retreat, the guns of the tanks cutting them down like cords of wood. Sighing, Walkup allowed his body to rest against the side of a charred Yeti. He had survived, and so had most of his soldiers. He counted that a win.

Chapter Thirty-Five
Wait, Where Am I?

Task Force 28
RNS *Cassiopeia*
En Route to New Eden

Blake "Coop" Cooper entered one of *Cassi*'s small medical bays. The space was cramped due to its location deep within the bowels of the Republic flagship. A tinge of antiseptic stung his nostrils as a hospital room's door slid open with a soft hiss. The muted lighting sent shadows across a bank of monitoring equipment lining one bulkhead.

A pair of med techs fussed over the lone patient lying on the solitary bed—Anaya "Rogue" Singh. Her face appeared gaunt, with dark circles under her eyes. Tubes and wires snaked from beneath the thin sheet draped over her, connected to various machines measuring her vitals. She had been in a medically induced coma for a while now, but Coop had received word that she might be ready to regain consciousness soon.

One of the techs noticed Coop right away. "Commander," said the tech. Coop straightened, offering a nod. "We don't know exactly how this will go," he explained. "She's stable, but still critical, even after all this time. There were a lot of internal injuries from the crash. The surgeons worked some miracles, but we can't be sure of the outcomes until she wakes up."

Coop nodded soberly. He approached the bedside, studying Rogue's pallid features. A purplish bruise marred her left cheek while a bacta-patch covered a gash along her jaw. The advanced medicine was unable to fully heal the trauma. He wondered what other horrors her body had endured in the crash. Anger twisted inside him, but he pushed it away quickly. She should've followed orders and broken off her attack run. Maybe then she wouldn't be lying here, fighting for her life.

Rogue's eyelids fluttered open. Her gaze found Coop's face. A ghost of a smile tugged at her cracked lips. "I... I'm sorry... Coop." Her voice cracked, hoarse and faint.

"Save your strength, Captain," a tech said. She checked one of Rogue's monitors and injected some type of clear liquid into her IV line. "The commander will debrief you once you've recovered."

Rogue's eyes slid shut again as she drifted back into unconsciousness.

"Will she make it?" Coop asked. His throat tightened. He couldn't bear the thought of losing a great pilot like her, especially one that had become a true friend.

The tech offered a reassuring nod. "Her will to live is strong. As long as she keeps fighting, her chances improve every day."

Relief washed over Coop. The holographic display hovering above Rogue's bed pulsed with her vitals in a soft blue glow.

"We'll leave you alone with her," a tech said, and both of the medical officers exited the room. The door shut behind them.

Sinking into the chair beside her bed, Coop went to reach for Rogue's hand, careful to avoid jostling the tubes snaking from her arm. As he was about to touch her fingers, he shook his head. What was he doing? He was a pilot, and other than a high five and a pat on the back every so often, they didn't really engage in physical contact.

He forcefully exhaled. About a dozen of his pilots had died over the last few years during combat, and it had started to wear on him. He squeezed his own fingers.

With nothing else to do but wait, Coop bowed his head. He closed his eyes as silent prayers tumbled from his lips—prayers for her recovery, for her strength to pull through this latest brush with death. He prayed that this war would end soon, so no more pilots would suffer like Rogue or meet their end like Pronto.

His murmurs faded as the room's hush enveloped him once more, broken only by the steady beeps of the machines monitoring her vitals.

Coop's mind drifted to the battered leather-bound book he'd brought with him—his great-great-grandfather Presley Paul Cooper's World War II journal. He thumbed open the worn cover, pages crinkling as he flipped through the entries detailing Presley's harrowing missions over Europe. One passage in particular stuck out. They were words Coop had read dozens of times over the years.

During Presley's thirtieth mission, as he and his comrade had flown their WWII fighter planes over Germany, flak suddenly tore through his comrade's fuselage. Moments later, Presley's own plane took a major hit as well. With their aircraft severely damaged, they had no choice but to eject. They both went down in a blaze of glory, parachuting to safety during the moonless night. After landing in soft snow, Presley searched for his friend in the cold darkness but couldn't locate him. Finally, he found the young man half-buried in a snowy field, barely clinging to life. It turned out that on the way down, a stray bullet had struck the man in the chest and left him critically wounded.

As Coop continued reminiscing over his great-great-grandfather's journal entry, the words etched into his memory effortlessly formed on his lips, and he mouthed the words he knew by heart:

"Knelt in that frozen wasteland, I prayed over Jackson like I never had before. I called on the Almighty to spare his life and bring him home to his folks back in Arkansas. By some divine miracle, and I don't know to this day how it happened, a German doctor found us, someone who sympathized with our cause, and whisked Jackson off for treatment in a farmhouse. For days we stayed there, and for days this brave man worked on my friend and fed us, kept us warm, and gave us whatever else we needed. I don't know how Jackson pulled through those injuries or how that nice doctor found us, but I'm convinced those prayers had something to do with it."

Rogue stirred. She blinked groggily. "Hey, Commander." Her voice was slurred, likely an aftereffect of the injection administered by the med tech before Rogue had drifted back into a deep slumber. "Nice to see... you here."

Coop grinned. "It's good to see you awake again, Rogue."

"Did we...?" She winced. "Did we complete the mission?"

He nodded. "Thanks to your flying skills, we crippled that mining facility. We couldn't have done it without you leading the charge."

A tired yet beaming smile spread across her face. "Just doing my duty, sir." She crinkled her brow. "Didn't I go against...orders?" She chuckled like she was drunk.

"You did. We'll talk about that later. I just want you to get better."

"But I did it for a good reason." She rolled her eyes. "I'm in trouble, aren't I?" She began to slur her words more intensely.

"You're not in trouble. That's not how I—"

"And Pronto?" Rogue interrupted. "Did he ma-ma-make it back OK?"

278

Coop stood. Whatever cocktail the tech had given Rogue was making her loopy. This wasn't like Rogue at all. She would never interrupt or be so careless with her words, let alone say the things she was saying now. It was clear that the medication was affecting her judgment and causing her to speak erratically. "You should rest right now and not worry about anything else, OK?"

"Hell no." She went to sit up, then cringed. "I, I think... think you're right about the resting thing." She lay back down. "About Pronto, though. Is he all good? He's such a great pilot, you know?"

"He is." Coop hesitated. He didn't want to disappoint her with the truth—that Pronto had been killed when his Valkyrie took a direct hit during their bombing run. Coop forced a reassuring look. "I'm sure he's fine. Like you said, he's a great pilot."

"That's an understatement. Like, one of the best...ever...pilots." She started to sound loopier. "I was starting to think..." Her voice trailed off as exhaustion overtook her once more. Within moments, she drifted back into a deep sleep, her chest rising and falling in a steady rhythm.

Coop watched Rogue for a long moment before sitting back down, his mind turning back to the diary. Maybe, just maybe, those old prayers his great-great-grandfather had written about so long ago would work their magic once more.

He prayed a second time.

Rogue shifted, her movements stiff. She turned toward Coop, eyes like saucers, her expression wide awake. "Why are you talking to yourself?"

Coop hadn't realized he was saying his prayer out loud. "Oh, no reason."

"You... you're crazy."

Perhaps they gave her the wrong meds? he wondered. "I think I should get going," Coop said aloud.

"You know, I can't wait to get back planetside. To New Eden. Yep, to New Eden. Gonna be per... per... perfecto. I got me some family to hang out with, you know? I miss them more than anything."

Coop's left eyebrow rose in surprise. In all the years he'd known Rogue, she'd never mentioned having any family or deep ties beyond the starfighter corps. Or perhaps he didn't truly know her. Maybe he should erase that checkmark beside her name in the metaphorical friend box he thought she occupied in his life. He'd always assumed she was unattached, dedicated solely to the Republic's cause like him. "Oh? You have some big plans once we return to New Eden? Your husband—"

"Husband? You dope. No hubby here, buddy." A grin played across her chapped lips. "I can only wish. No, I was hoping to get some leave approved so I can visit my parents. It's been too long since I've seen them." She lazily touched her nose. "Why does my face hurt? Did something happen? Did I get into an accident? Or did someone overpower me during hand-to-hand combat training?"

"You were in an accident." Coop blinked, his assumptions about Rogue's lone wolf status crumbling. "Your mom and dad live on New Eden?"

She gave a slight nod, grimacing at the motion. "Yeah, just a couple hours outside the main base in the capital city. A nice little homestead out in the countryside." She raised her arms and dropped them when pain took over. "I gotta stop moving, eh? I'm talking fast, aren't I?"

Truth was, she was talking slowly, her words very slurred.

"That's really great, Rogue. As soon as we enter New Eden's sector, I'll put in for some well-deserved downtime. You've more than earned a chance to spend time with your parents after that flying you pulled off."

"Oh, yes, I crashed during a mission." She made a pouty face. "But you're mad at me."

"Mad?" Coop shook his head. "When you're all rested and feeling better, we'll speak about what happened. Until then, just get some good shut-eye, all right?"

"Thanks, Coop. You're swell. I'd really appreciate that. Anyway, my parents worry about me enough as it is when I'm out here taking on the Zodarks' best. It'll mean so much to see them again in person, you know?"

Coop had to lean in to understand everything she said. "Of course. We'll make sure you get that family visit lined up. You just focus on resting up and getting back on your feet, OK?" He stood to leave. "I'll see you soon."

Rogue's eyelids grew heavy once more. "You got it, sir. Can't wait to see the old-timers again."

"Old-timers?"

"My parents. It's what I call 'em." She paused, looking Coop up and down. "You know…" Her words were mixed, barely understandable. "The other squadrons think you're kind of an arrogant hotshot. They say you strut around like you own the place and never listen to orders."

Coop raised his brows. He'd never heard her speak so bluntly. He opened his mouth to respond, but Rogue barreled on.

"They say you overestimate your abilities sometimes and take too many risks. Butt-blade, Burn-blade, Bum-butt, or whatever his name is, was telling me just the other day how you disobeyed command and went after Zodark fighters alone during the second battle at New Eden so many years ago." She let out a snort of laughter. "But we all know that's just 'cause you're so good, Coop. You're the best pilot I've ever flown with, even better than Pronto. I used to study the holos on your flying vids before I even met you… before I even enlisted."

Coop rubbed the back of his neck. He took a step to leave. "I'm going to bid you farewell, OK, Rogue?"

"Gotta say, though…" Rogue's eyes drifted down in an obvious leer. "You do have a real nice tushy for a—"

"Rogue." Coop cut her off. "You're not yourself right now and you don't know what you're saying. I'll leave you to rest up, all right?"

She rested her head back against the pillow. "What did I say? Oh, anyway, those other squads are just jealous of your skills. That's all."

"Listen…" He turned and bent slightly forward, gently patting her arm. "Why don't I go ask a med tech to lower your dosage, huh? We don't need you saying anything too crazy while you're still recovering."

Rogue opened her mouth—likely to protest—but Coop had already headed for the exit before she could respond. "See you soon, Rogue."

The door shut behind him as he headed for his quarters, his shoulders stooping a little. It was time to write Pronto's parents a letter, one that would take everything he had to write without shedding a tear.

Chapter Thirty-Six
You Saved Lives

Republic Navy Headquarters
New Cambria, New Eden
Rhea System

It'd been one hell of a day, and an even worse week.

Ripley Willis Lee paced toward the office of Admiral Fran McKee, head of Space Command Operations. Everything felt wrong. His mind was a train wreck. Life would never be the same after this day— not that he judged what Admiral McKee would soon say to him, and in fact, he would accept it as truth. He had failed, miserably.

Almost a day ago, the *Cassiopeia* had emerged from FTL jump. The rest of Lee's fleet had followed close behind as they approached Paradise Station, in geosynchronous orbit above Emerald City, New Eden. A mixture of dread and relief had swept over Lee at the sight of the sprawling docks. In some strange way, this planet usually felt like home to him, but the weight of his decisions during their last campaign pressed down on him hard. So, in a paradoxical moment, nothing felt familiar or comforting.

He clenched his jaw as he walked, the dull ache in his temples reminding him of the lack of sleep he'd had. Lee had been agonizing over the tactical missteps that had cost his fleet so dearly. Ships had been lost, lives snuffed out—all because of him.

Lee knew the repercussions were inevitable. A demotion loomed. The axe was soon to fall at the hands of Admiral McKee, who had commanded him to embark on this very mission, one now tarnishing his incredible record.

Did I act too brashly? Did I push my forces too hard in pursuit of victory? The reverberations of those lost haunted him, their voices a chorus of accusation drowning out any attempt at justification. Lee understood the truth; his hubris had blinded him to the consequences of his actions.

Lee's boots echoed on the floor while he held his Qpad firmly in his hand. Earlier, he'd sent the same version of the contact report through the holo channels to Admiral McKee. By now, she would have read it, and no doubt she'd be disappointed.

The polished floor reflected the overhead lights. When he neared the imposing double doors leading to Admiral McKee's office, a knot of apprehension tightened in his gut. Lee could almost hear her sharp tongue lashing out, each word a scathing rebuke. The losses they'd suffered, the strategic missteps, the sheer audacity of his actions—all would be laid bare before her withering gaze.

He paused outside the doors, his free hand hovering over the entry panel. A bead of sweat trickled down his temple. He wiped it off.

With a steadying breath, Lee pressed his palm against the panel. Through the speaker, an assistant's soft voice announced, "You may enter, Admiral Lee."

The doors opened and Lee squared his shoulders, schooling his features into a mask of stoic professionalism as he stepped into the anteroom.

McKee's aide looked up from her desk, her expression betraying nothing as she gestured for him to proceed. Lee gave a curt nod and strode forward. The doors to the inner office stood before him like the maw of some great beast, ready to swallow him whole.

As he reached for the handle, he realized this meeting would seal his fate—one way or another. He would have to face the reckoning head-on. Lee grasped the handle, pushed open the door and stepped into the lioness's den.

Lee stood ramrod straight, his boots planted firmly on the plush crimson carpet as he faced Admiral Fran McKee's imposing desk. On the desktop, two holo frames stood side by side. One depicted the familiar continents of Earth, while the other showcased the unique landmasses of New Eden. Diagonally behind McKee, a holographic display table occupied one corner of the room. Its surface pulsed with real-time data on fleet movements and strategic operations.

The walls were adorned with McKee's numerous accolades, each framed and arranged with perfection. Among them were her Distinguished Service Medal, awarded for her exemplary leadership, her Interstellar Campaign Medal, and her admiral's stars, signifying her rank as one of the highest-ranking officers in the Republic Navy.

On the opposite side of her, a flag of the Republic Navy hung proudly. Beside it and on a table sat a collection of antique nautical instruments, including a cross-staff, a mariner's compass, and a massive hourglass standing a meter high. All around, bookshelves lined the walls, filled with volumes on military history, strategy, and leadership.

To be exact, the office was a study in austere grandeur. With floor-to-ceiling windows, the view outside offered a breathtaking panorama of one of Emerald City's gorgeous forests that the capital building butted up against. Trees swayed in the wind. A critter scurried up a vine and to a branch. The sun shone through the gaps in the forest's canopy and brightened various spots where flowers grew tall and vibrant from the soil.

In front of Lee, McKee sat behind the expansive desk. Her features were cast in sharp relief to the glowing Qpad she held in her hands. She scribbled something with a stylus, her brow wrinkled in concentration.

After a tense moment, she looked up. She steeled her gaze on Lee. "At ease, Admiral."

Lee shifted his stance, clasping his hands behind his back as he met her unblinking stare. "Admiral McKee."

With a quick nod, McKee set down the Qpad and motioned toward the chair opposite her desk. "Please, have a seat."

Lee complied and perched himself on the edge of an upholstered chair.

McKee regarded him with a stern expression. Her lips were pressed into a thin line. "Admiral Lee, in light of your recent actions and the losses incurred…I have no choice but to promote you." Her words hung in the air, heavy and unexpected.

Lee blinked, certain he had misheard. "I… beg your pardon, ma'am? After the debacle in the Velos Belt?"

"Disaster though it may have been, it showcased your strengths—your judgment under fire."

"Judgment, ma'am?"

"Yes. You held fire until the precise moment necessary. Those initial commands you gave? Calculated and effective."

Lee dipped his head. *Didn't she read that I sent my armada into a surprise attack?*

"When your task force took hits from the unexpected ambush, you pivoted immediately," McKee continued as if reading his mind. "Most would have frozen at the moment, at least for a minute, maybe two. Not you, Admiral Lee. You acted fast. You showed decisiveness.

You may think you lost lives, but your immediate decisions saved many more."

"I... I made a call, that was all." Lee kept his chin held high, though he wanted to lower it and eye the carpet for his mistakes. "I allowed us to be lured into their trap, ma'am."

McKee stood and pressed her palms on her desk, leaning forward. "Listen, the majority of commanding officers and flag ranks would have navigated their task force into the same operational hazard. All Zodark maneuvers, coupled with faulty reconnaissance data from drone sensors and visual feeds, indicated a lack of awareness regarding our presence in that sector. You executed the operation at the opportune moment according to the established timeline. Furthermore, you demonstrated commendable poise and leadership capabilities while engaged in asymmetric combat conditions against a numerically superior adversary."

"Thank you, Admiral. I was just trying to keep us in one piece."

"I'm not done. Now, you called for a full tactical withdrawal at the crucial moment. By now, I hope you realize how important that was. At that specific time, you minimized our losses and ensured the survival of the fleet, something only a true leader could have accomplished under such dire circumstances. A much larger Zodark fleet jumped in shortly after you left the sector. Did you know that, Admiral?"

"I did."

"Your decisive actions diminished the hostile Zodark fleet's strength by over fifty percent while our forces sustained minimal vessel casualties," McKee continued. "This success is attributed to your precise relaying of sector coordinates for targeted fire missions. Furthermore, you demonstrated tactical awareness by leveraging the stargate's strategic positioning for an efficient fleet extraction."

"It was our only option, though we lost good ships... and friends," Lee said, his voice choking.

McKee stood straighter and folded her arms. "War demands such sacrifices. Yet you never lost sight of the objective, and you preserved the core of Task Force 28. Ultimately, this mission was an overwhelming success. This is why we need you in a new position, hence your promotion."

"May I ask what position, Admiral?" Lee inquired.

"I will get to that soon. And I know you will do well wherever I put you."

Lee sat straighter, the situation starting to sink in. "I appreciate your confidence in me, Admiral," he said. "I won't let you down."

"I know you won't, Lee. You are hereby awarded a second star and given command of an expanded fleet." McKee tapped a few commands into her Qpad, and a holographic display flickered to life between them, showing the schematics of a formidable armada—battleships, cruisers, flak frigates, and more. Over a hundred in all.

"These ships," McKee continued, "are fresh from the shipyards and training grounds, and they will be under your leadership." Her tone brooked no argument. "Your new orders are to prepare this fleet for the invasion of the Zodark Empire once our campaign against the Pharaonis is complete."

Lee's mind reeled, struggling to process the information. A promotion? An expanded fleet? The implications were staggering, and he found himself at a rare loss for words.

Outwardly, he maintained his composure, his face a mask of professionalism. Inwardly, a maelstrom of emotions swirled—shock, disbelief, and a hint of trepidation at the weight of the responsibility now resting squarely on his shoulders.

"Understood, Admiral," Lee said. "We will succeed."

McKee's expression softened, just a fraction. "Yes, see that you do, Admiral Lee. Now, I know your record has been exemplary, but before you're dismissed, I wanted to ask about your family."

"My family, ma'am?" *Why would she ask about them?*

"Have you spoken to them lately?" she asked.

Lee held his breath for a moment at the unexpected query. "No, ma'am. I haven't spoken to my parents or siblings in years. Maybe a decade, actually."

"I see." A flicker of sympathy crossed McKee's features. "Family is important, even in our line of work. If you don't mind me asking, why haven't you reached out to them?"

Lee hesitated, his mind drifting back to that fateful day when he had told his parents of his decision to enlist in the military.

His mother's tear-streaked face swam into focus. Her voice had trembled with anguish. "But the military... violence... it goes against everything we believe in, Ripley. How can you turn your back on our faith, on God's teachings of peace and love?"

Lee had tried to reason with them, to explain his sense of duty and desire to protect humanity. They couldn't be swayed. In the end, his decision had proven too much for them to bear. Their communication had grown strained, then ceased entirely over the years as the gulf between them widened.

Pulled from his reverie by McKee's expectant gaze, Lee remained expressionless. "It's... personal, Admiral—a difference in beliefs and values that proved irreconcilable."

She gave a solemn nod. "I understand, Admiral. Family rifts can cut deep. But I hope one day you'll be able to mend that divide. We need our loved ones, even in this life we've chosen."

"Ma'am, may I ask why you asked about my family?"

"The way you command, Admiral Lee. It's as if they're your family. If you don't have close ties to your own blood relatives, now I understand. It's a benefit, and yet another reason to add on reasons for your promotion and the expansion of your fleet."

"I see."

"I hope you do." Her expression softened more. "You're dismissed, Admiral."

Lee rose from his chair, his legs like lead weights. As he exited the office, his mind raced, already strategizing and planning for the monumental task lying ahead.

In minutes, he found himself outside. The warmth of the New Eden sun felt good on his face. While he took slow strides down the bustling promenade, the towers of Emerald City loomed overhead. Their mirrored surfaces reflected the sunlight.

Despite the throngs of people milling about, Lee barely registered their presence. His mind was a whirlwind of thoughts and emotions, a tempest raging beneath his outwardly composed demeanor.

As he walked, his pace quickened. The steady rhythm of his footfalls matched the pounding of his heart. He needed space.

Up ahead, the verdant expanse of a public park beckoned. It was an oasis amidst the gleaming spires of metal and glass.

The park was relatively empty as the few occupants scattered across the sprawling lawns and winding paths. Lee was immediately drawn to a gnarled old tree, its thick branches sending cool shadows across a secluded bench.

He made a beeline for the shaded refuge and sank onto the weatherworn seat. Immediately, the tension in his shoulders eased. Closing his eyes, he inhaled deeply, filling his lungs with the crisp, earthy scent of the park.

The respite was fleeting. For no sooner had he begun to relax than the memories came crashing down upon him like a tidal wave.

The recent battle replayed in vivid detail. Each strategic misstep, each costly mistake etched into his mind's eye and seared with clarity. He could almost taste the acrid smoke, could almost hear the screams of the dying as his fleet's ships were torn asunder by the enemy's relentless onslaught.

A tremor rippled through Lee's battle-hardened frame as the weight of his strategic failure threatened to crush him. How could Admiral McKee promote him after such a catastrophic loss of life and resources? Although McKee insisted that even the most skilled officers would have led their armada down the same treacherous path, how could he have missed the blatant signs of an impending ambush?

The truth was, he hadn't. He had sensed the trap before ever entering the Gravaxia system. The nagging suspicion had gnawed at him relentlessly, even before his task force had emerged through the stargate and into the perilous Velos Belt. Every intelligence report, every surveillance feed—they all silently pointed to a meticulously laid ambush if one read it all just right, and he had. Still, he'd marched his forces straight into the crosshairs. It was like a seasoned poker player going all-in, risking everything on a desperate gambit and clinging to the slim hope that his gut instincts were wrong.

In poker, he understood this was called "going for the dream." It referred to when a player had a strong hand, but that player felt or sensed their opponent might have an even better hand. Despite this doubt, the player would then decide to stay in the hand and keep betting anyway, clinging to the "dream" their hand would ultimately be the winner.

Lee clenched his fists. His nails dug into his palms as he forced his eyes open. Before him, a group of children inspected well-cut brush full of blue flowers. To the right, a family laid down a blanket on a vibrant purple-and-green manicured grass bed. Off in the distance, two kids laughed as they chased a butterfly-like insect around the foliage.

He slowly calmed down as everything came into focus. All of this, everything around him, was what he fought for.

In that moment, a single, crystalline thought pierced through the fog of self-doubt: he would not squander this second chance to keep humanity safe. He would learn from his mistakes, grow stronger, and lead his new fleet to victory against the enemy empire, no matter the cost.

It was what leaders did. It was what his mentor would have done.

Lee stood from the bench and smiled at the children, who grinned in return. He took a step forward and down a brick trail, his stride once again imbued with purpose. Though the path ahead was fraught with violence and loss, he steadied himself, resolute in his purpose to protect humanity.

Lee stepped out of the park and into the cityscape surrounding him. Towering skyscrapers pierced the heavens, their exteriors adorned with mesmerizing holographic advertisements painting the bustling streets below in an array of colors. The sidewalks teemed with pedestrians, some greeting others or walking into restaurants. A mother, father, and daughter held hands just up ahead as they walked across the street.

While he took in the scene, Lee was reminded of the immense responsibility he carried as a member of the military. These were the people he had sworn to defend, the civilians who placed their trust—their very lives—in the military's ability to safeguard their future.

He would marshal every resource at his disposal, would push his officers and crew to their limits and beyond if necessary. There could be no half measures, no room for mercy or compromise. The Zodarks understood only the language of overwhelming force, and Lee intended to become fluent.

Chapter Thirty-Seven
Operation Gurista Freedom

March 2114
Paradise Station
New Eden, Rhea System

Admiral Amy Dobbs glanced sideways at Brigadier General Brian Royce as Lieutenant General William "Wild Bill" Hackworth and Admiral Fran McKee took turns briefing their portions of Operation Gurista Freedom. The more Amy listened, the more she began to doubt the feasibility of such a bold plan.

This brought to mind a recollection from years past when she'd served as the tactical action officer aboard the RNS *Rook*, under the command of Viceroy Miles Hunt during their second encounter with the Zodarks. He had said, "Dobbs, the more intricate a plan becomes, the more it relies on variables beyond your control, increasing the likelihood of failure. Conversely, a simpler plan with fewer variables offers better prospects for success."

"Amy, you still with us?" asked Admiral McKee as she paused.

Amy realized she had missed part of the conversation. Feeling her cheeks redden, she answered, "Sorry about that, Admiral. Thinking about this coup reminded me of something Viceroy Miles Hunt used to tell us junior officers aboard the *Rook*. If a plan is complicated, it probably won't work. In contrast, he used to stress the term KISS—keep it simple, stupid."

"We have something similar in the Deltas, except we call it Semper Gumby," interrupted Brigadier General Brian Royce. "You aren't wrong about this being, how shall we put it—complicated. This isn't to say we don't have a few surprises of our own that will greatly aid in our effort."

"Oh really? And when was everyone going to share that tidbit of knowledge with me?" asked Amy, a bit of a mischievous smile beginning to form at the corners of her mouth.

McKee asserted her control of the briefing as she placed her Qpad on the table. A floating image of a Gallentine covert ops ship grabbed their attention. "Amy, if we were attempting to do this ourselves...it probably *would* fail," she admitted. "Fortunately, we are not doing this alone. The Viceroy managed to convince Fleet Admiral Nirex TanGol to provide one of their *Vraxerian* stealth corvettes along with its crew and a pair of Aurion Shadows—that's Gallentine Special Forces—to assist us in pulling this off.

"What no one is aware of, Amy, is this operation started eighteen months ago, not last week or a few months ago. Meaning we have been working toward this for some time. In fact, I am sure General Royce will be able to attest. We currently have eighteen, twelve-man Operational Detachment Alpha teams already on Gurista Prime, training insurgent forces that will aid our operatives from Republic Intelligence when it comes time to initiate the coup," McKee explained, pausing long enough for General Hackworth to join the conversation.

"Basically, this is how it's going to work, Amy," the grizzled Special Forces officer began casually in his Southern twang. "You and a group of badass warships are going to move to the dark side of Tigris— out of sight, out of mind. You'll hang out doing whatever it is you spacers do while you wait for our guy on Gurista Prime to contact your ship. When he does—the only words you need to hear from our guy are 'the pigeons have landed,' or 'honey badger don't care—'"

"Wait a second, come on, you can't be serious—your guy? Who is this *guy* you're speaking of?" interrupted Amy, unsure if this SF general they called Wild Bill was joking with her or something else was going on.

Undeterred by her interruption, Will Bill continued to explain without missing a beat. "As I was in the middle of saying"—he then winked at her before smiling as he elbowed Brian Royce, whispering something before he resumed speaking—"our guy, Drew, after he has contacted you, he might say something that will use the words *the pigeons have landed*—which means the coup failed. If you hear that, Amy, then there's a good chance Drew is going to relay further instructions, likely requesting immediate assistance in evacuating Republic forces from the surface of Gurista Prime. Should that happen, the Gallentine stealth corvette, GN *Vraxerian's Dagger*, will open a bridge connecting the Rhea system to Orinda—in case you didn't know, that's the star system Gurista Prime is located in."

Amy furrowed her brow, unsure how mad or put off she should feel right now. Deciding to play along, she commented, "Wow, OK, so if this Drew character tells us the rats with wings have landed, it means things went to crap—now he wants a ride out before the locals decide to string up? Do I have that about right?"

Bill laughed hard at her question, tapping the table a couple of times. "You were right, Brian. This admiral chick is cool—that's twenty credits I owe you."

By now, Fran let out an exasperated grunt, her head shaking from side to side in frustration. "Come on, Bill. Stop dicking around and wasting my time. Cut to the chase and tell her what she needs to know. I've got a mountain of work and I've given you about as much time as can."

Appearing hurt, Bill clutched at his chest before holding his hands up in mock surrender as Fran stared daggers at him. "OK, OK, I can see everyone is a little serious—OK, maybe a lot serious. So, I'll just wrap it up by adding this final thought on the matter." Bill leaned forward, his grayish-blue eyes now piercing into Amy's as he explained, "All kidding aside, Drew's our senior operative on the ground and the person running the show. If he uses the phrase 'honey badger don't care,' it means the coup worked—or at least it's holding for now.

"The moment the *Vraxerian's Dagger* opens a bridge to the Orinda system, your ships must cross ASAP and move to destroy whatever Zodark ships happen to be in the system, if there are any. The latest intelligence we have is from the *Dagger*'s sister ship—*Vraxerian's Shadow*—which has been operating within the Orinda system from the beginning. The most recent intel we have is from six hours ago when the *Shadow* sent their daily update. As of now, there are no Zodark warships, transports, or other ships in the system. That's not to say some ships won't show up after you arrive, but at the moment, the system is empty.

"Now FYI, the system the Zodarks have set the Guristas up in is basically on the fringe of their territory but absolutely nowhere close to alliance territory. Once your force arrives in the systems, Amy, if there are any enemy ships, you have to clear 'em out of the system and assert control over it. Should there be any holdouts or skeptics on the surface, the sight of your warships in low orbit should convince them that we control the system—that they have been cleaved from the clutches of the Zodark Empire and are free," Bill finished explaining, the meeting coming to an end on a high note.

Chapter Thirty-Eight
Fracturing an Empire

Zon Private Study
High Council Building
Drokanis, Zinconia
Zodark Home World

Zon Otro looked at the intelligence report with frustration. "Is this the best the Groff can do?" he muttered to himself, trying to piece together what was really happening in the Gravaxia system. For months, the Malvari had imposed a quarantine across the system, and now, they were even going as far as denying ships the ability to dock at orbital facilities or land at the spaceports across the various settlements and mining facilities. Although the Malvari weren't blockading ships from transiting between the stargates, the quarantine was undermining their ability to defend the system from a steady increase in cross-border raids by Republic and Primord ships in the neighboring system, Pfeinstgard.

Months had passed, and still, the source of the illness remained a mystery. Was it a natural occurrence, or was there something more sinister at play? If it was the latter, who could be behind it? The Republic, or the Groff, seeking to undermine his rule as Zon? The pieces of the puzzle didn't fit, and the answers he sought seemed to elude him.

Zon Otro's gaze shifted from the report to the walls, adorned with symbols of his past military triumphs. A wave of nostalgia washed over him, a yearning for the days when his only duty was to fight the Empire's enemies. He longed for the simplicity of those times, before the Republic's interference on the planet Clovis and the subsequent war ignited by the actions of T'Tock on that fateful day.

"What do I do now, Lindow?" he muttered softly, staring at the two-meter-tall golden statue of the Zodark who had united the clans and led them into the stars, becoming the god they now prayed to.

Just then, the door to his study slid open silently as NOS Vorun Talvex, his trusted advisor, entered.

"Zon, NOS Tarvox Nilkar and Mavkah Griglag are here to see you," Vorun announced, reminding him of his afternoon meeting.

Otro felt momentarily foolish. He'd forgotten all about this meeting with the Malvari. Griglag had requested an audience ahead of the Council meeting a few days from now. "Excellent, please show them in and see to it some refreshments are brought. Join me—I may need your counsel if I am right about what Griglag wants to discuss."

"Yes, very well, Zon," Vorun replied as he exited the room as quickly as he had entered.

A few moments later, the head of the Malvari and his deputy walked into his study, their faces grim as they approached his desk, bowing slightly.

"My Zon, we come to you with grave information," began Mavkah Griglag. "The path forward is a decision only the Zon or the Council can render."

Otro nodded, motioning for them to sit at the nearby table. Vorun reentered the room, taking a seat next to Otro. As Vorun and Otro exchanged pleasantries with Griglag and his deputy, Tarvox, a pair of human slaves entered the room—each carrying a tray with glasses made from horns and plates from the bones of a Talish, a giant bearlike predator hunted by young Zodark males during their rite of passage into adulthood. Once the drinks and refreshments were placed on the table, the slaves quickly exited to return to the kitchen.

Griglag spoke first. "Zon, this quarantine in Gravaxia needs to end so we can properly defend the system and fortify its defenses. The attacks by the Republic continue to escalate. We suspect they will launch an invasion soon. Its capture would place the Republic and their allies next to Tueblets. If we lose Tueblets, we could lose the Empire.

"Meanwhile, the Groff continues to ignore our requests for information on what is making our warriors sick and killing them. I can't deploy soldiers to the surface or dispatch additional fighter and bomber squadrons to our bases if they will just become sick or die shortly after arriving," Griglag explained.

Tarvox asserted himself at this point. "Zon Otro, we need your intervention with the Groff if we are to defend the system successfully. We cannot fight with our hands tied behind our backs. The Groff needs to share what they know of this sickness that plagues our people before it spreads to—"

"Has the illness spread beyond Gravaxia?" Otro interrupted, a sense of fear washing over him.

"No, no, nothing like that, my Zon," Griglag quickly assured him, shooting his deputy a disappointing look. "We are not aware of this sickness spreading beyond the Gravaxia system."

Otro breathed a sigh of relief, then turned serious. "I grow frustrated with the Groff and their lack of transparency in this matter. I will summon Director Vak'Atioth to speak with me before the Council meeting. In the meantime, with this growing civil unrest on the planet Shwani, I would like the Malvari to keep more soldiers prepared to intervene. The Groff should never have allowed this unrest to grow into what it has. This discontent now spreads beyond Shwani—it threatens the Empire at a time when we need to remain unified to withstand the likely invasion of our territory."

Griglag and Tarvox nodded in agreement, assuring Otro that the Malvari was prepared to intervene should it come to that. Ending the meeting, Otro had a message sent to the Groff—he was summoning Vak'Atioth to discuss urgent matters of state.

****

Three Days Later
Zon Private Study
High Council Building
Drokanis, Zinconia
Zodark Home World

Heltet stood there, grimacing as Zon Otro tore into the Groff for what he perceived as a personal slight. Otro had summoned Director Vak'Atioth, but Vak'Atioth had sent Heltet in his stead, forcing him to endure the beratement the Zon leveled against his agency. Heltet knew of Zon Otro before he had become Zon—when he had been the Mavkah of the Malvari. The feud between the Zodark military and the intelligence agency was long-running and notoriously vitriolic. Heltet wasn't particularly sure why the relationship had developed into what it had become. He suspected it was the Council or the Zons who had stoked the flames of fury over the years. It wasn't uncommon to play two powerful organizations against each other in a way that allowed neither of them to become powerful enough to challenge the Council or the Zon for control of the Empire.

"Don't just stand there like a statue! Say something!" Otro shouted at him.

Heltet suddenly realized he had missed whatever it was the Zon had asked him. Searching for what to say, he offered, "I am sorry, my Zon. It is the Director who is leading the investigation and the one with the answers you seek. I can share what little I know if that would be of help?"

Zon Otro walked closer to him, his face inches from his own, his eyes boring into his. "Then speak—share what you know, and I shall determine what help it was."

"At first, we struggled to learn where the virus started—"

"Wait, you said *virus*. Does the Groff now believe that's what this is?" Zon Otro interrupted, a fleeting look of fear crossing his face before he suppressed it. "Has the Groff determined if this sickness is a natural occurrence, something that jumped species, perhaps, or does it appear to be engineered, created with a purpose—like what we're witnessing in the Gravaxia system?"

The question lingered uncomfortably in the air as Heltet searched for what to say. Had he already said too much? Had he just made a mistake by alluding to the virus theory still being argued within hushed circles of the Groff?

"Vak'Atioth is not here, Heltet—he cannot silence you from answering my questions. What say you, Heltet? What is Director Vak afraid of the Council discovering?" growled Otro, his voice barely audible.

Heltet glanced briefly at NOS Zarun, who leaned forward in his chair, waiting for him to speak. "Don't worry about Zarun, Heltet. I see you looking at him," insisted Zon Otro, his eyes narrowing as he studied Heltet's eyes and facial expressions.

Just speak the truth, and you have nothing to fear, Heltet reminded himself.

"Forgive me, my Zon, I misspoke. There is no consensus yet within the Groff that this…illness…is anything more than something natural—"

"Do not lie to me!" roared Zon Otro.

Heltet fought the urge to step back from Otro shouting in his face. He was not used to being chastised in front of someone, let alone by the Zon himself. "Apologies, my Zon. As I stated earlier, Director

Vak is managing this investigation directly. He is the one with the answers to the questions you have. What little information I have was gained from conversations I overheard, and bits and pieces others have shared with me. The majority of the investigators believe this illness is something natural, something that occurred on the moon Lunakor, in orbit of the planet Torvulkis. However, within the Groff, some of our scientists who have examined samples—blood, saliva, etcetera—believe it to be engineered, possibly a biological weapon of unknown origin."

Heltet saw fear momentarily return to the eyes of the Zon before being suppressed.

"My Zon, I must stress that this idea, this potential engineering of a virus—it is not widely supported by the majority of the Groff's scientists, researchers, and intelligence analysts. It is a minority view for the moment," Heltet tried to emphasize before Zon Otro could reply further.

"And why is that, Heltet? Does the Director lack confidence in the scientists of the Groff?"

Heltet shook his head. "No, it is not like that, my Zon. The Vhalkar Protocols of the Treaty of Yanooth are clearly outlined in the Rules of War. The use of genetically engineered biological weapons and the temporary or permanent irradiation of habitable planets is strictly prohibited. The penalties for violating the Vhalkar Protocols are expulsion from their alliance and a one-hundred-year ban from rejoining any Yanooth Treaty alliance.

"Beyond the obvious punishment for violating the Vhalkar, our analysts and researchers do not believe the Republic or anyone else possesses the technological capabilities required to produce a genetically engineered weapon such as this. Therefore, it must be a naturally occurring illness," explained Heltet, who legitimately believed this to be true.

Zon Otro stared at him a moment longer, then seemed to accept what Heltet had said as he turned to walk back to his desk, sitting in his chair as he nodded his head in acceptance of his response. With nothing more to be said, he dismissed Heltet, who eagerly left the room.
****

A Few Days Later
High Council Building

High Council Chambers
Drokanis, Zinconia
Zodark Home World

Heltet's voice cut in, his tone bitter. "Vak's investigation has been going for dekwikas[4] and still nothing—we are no closer than when we started."

Vak'Atioth's eyes flashed with annoyance, but he kept his tone measured. "It is true that my investigators arrived in the Gravaxia system ten weeks ago to begin investigating the origins of this illness. Unfortunately, they became infected themselves. Like many others who contracted this strange illness, they died. The percentage of those who have died from it has risen to sixty-three percent. Of those who recovered, half report that they still do not feel that they have returned to full health after two months."

Mavkah Griglag's face reddened with anger, his fists clenched. "So not only have you failed to identify the source of this illness, but your own investigators have succumbed to it as well? This is beyond incompetence, Vak. We don't even know if this illness is indigenous to the Gravaxia system or if it's been introduced by an external force. If the Republic and their alliance decide to attack now, our forces in Gravaxia are compromised. We won't have healthy soldiers ready to defend the planets and moons in the system."

Vak bristled at the accusation. "We are doing everything we can, Mavkah. The situation is unprecedented."

Griglag's voice rose, cutting through Vak's words. "Unprecedented or not, we are on the brink of losing the Gravaxia system. If that happens, Republic forces will be positioned right next to Tueblets, the most critical system and stargate hub that ties our entire Empire together. We cannot afford to lose Gravaxia."

Otro watched the heated exchange, his frustration growing. The stakes were clear, and the implications of failure were catastrophic. The room fell silent as the gravity of the situation settled over the Council members.

---

[4] Dek is the Zodark word for ten. Wika is the Zodark word for week. Dekwikas is ten weeks.

"We need solutions, not excuses," Otro said finally, his voice hard. "Vak, I want a new team sent to Gravaxia immediately. Ensure they are equipped to handle this illness. Heltet, coordinate with Griglag to tighten security and reinforce our defenses in the system. We cannot allow the Republic to exploit this weakness."

Vak and Heltet exchanged a wary glance but nodded in agreement. "Understood, Zon," Vak said, his tone resigned.

Heltet's response was equally firm. "We'll secure Gravaxia, Zon."

Otro leaned back, his gaze piercing. "This is our priority. Failure is not an option. This council is adjourned. We will reconvene in three days to review your progress. Do not disappoint me."

As the Council members filed out, the tension in the room remained thick, lingering like a storm cloud. Vak'Atioth and Heltet left in opposite directions, their animosity clear. Griglag lingered for a moment, his eyes meeting Otro's.

"We'll get through this, Zon," he said quietly. "But we need unity, not division."

Otro nodded, his gaze hard. "Unity, indeed. But first, we need results."

The room emptied, leaving Otro alone with his thoughts. The challenges ahead were daunting, but he was determined to steer his people through this crisis. The fate of the Zodark Empire depended on it.
****

Later That Evening
Zon's Private Residence
Narixian Haven Neighborhood
Drokanis, Zinconia
Zodark Home World

Zon Otro stood by the grand entrance of his palatial residence, the evening air carrying the scent of the meticulously maintained gardens. The mansion was a testament to his success and power, an opulent estate nestled in the wealthy Narixian Haven neighborhood of Drokanis. Tonight, he was hosting a gathering of significant importance, but for now, he awaited the arrival of his close friend, Mavkah Griglag.

The imposing double doors swung open as Griglag approached, his eyes widening slightly at the sight of the estate. "Mavkah, welcome," Otro greeted him, extending his hand.

"Zon," Griglag replied, grasping Otro's upper-right hand firmly. "This place is even more impressive than I imagined." This was the first time Griglag had seen the inside of his friend's home since he'd moved to the Zon's private residence.

Otro smiled, motioning for Griglag to follow him. "Come, let me show you around. I've had the place remodeled since my promotion. No more sleeping on warships for me."

They stepped into the grand foyer, where marble floors gleamed under the soft light of ornate candlelit chandeliers made from the antlers of Beardogta beasts. "This is the entrance hall," Otro began. "The marble was imported from the mines of Shwani. Exquisite, isn't it?"

Griglag nodded, his gaze sweeping over the intricate mosaics and high ceilings. "Impressive craftsmanship. It's a far cry from the barracks we used to call home."

Otro chuckled, leading Griglag into the next room. "Indeed. This is the Great Hall. We host many of our formal gatherings here." The hall was expansive, with towering columns and walls adorned with tapestries depicting Zodark victories. The centerpiece was a massive fireplace, above which hung the mounted head of a fearsome beast Otro had slain in single combat.

"Ah, I remember that fight," Griglag said, a hint of nostalgia in his voice. "You nearly lost an arm bringing that beast down."

"But I didn't," Otro replied with a grin. "And it makes for a fine trophy, doesn't it?"

They moved through several other rooms, each more lavish than the last. The dining hall, with its long table set for an extravagant meal, and the armory, a personal museum showcasing Otro's vast collection of weapons and armor from his many campaigns.

"Here we are," Otro said, pushing open the heavy doors to his study and library. The room was a masterpiece of craftsmanship, with intricately carved wood, animal bones, and other materials forming the floor-to-ceiling bookshelves. The shelves were filled with volumes on Zodark history, the founding clans, Lindow, philosophy, and extensive military writings.

Griglag whistled softly. "This is incredible, Otro. You've outdone yourself."

Otro nodded, pride evident in his eyes. "This room holds a special place for me. It's where I come to think, to plan. The history of our people surrounds me here."

They moved to a seating area by the fireplace, where plush chairs awaited. Otro poured them both a glass of fine Budarian wine. "To the battles we've fought, and those yet to come," he toasted.

Griglag raised his glass. "To the old days, when we were young and dumb."

They shared a laugh, the memories of their youth and the battles they had fought together flooding back. It was a simpler time, when their only concerns were the enemy before them and the comrades beside them.

As they sipped their wine, the door to the study opened, and Otro's house manager stepped in. "Zon, your guests have arrived."

Otro set down his glass and stood. "Thank you. Show them in."

Griglag rose as well, straightening his uniform. "Time to get back to business."

Otro nodded, his expression hardening. "Indeed. Let's see what tonight brings."
****

After the extravagant dinner, the group moved into Otro's study. The air was thick with the aroma of smoking pipes and wine. As they settled into the plush chairs around the fireplace, the mood shifted from the camaraderie of old friends to the gravity of state affairs.

Otro leaned back, his gaze sweeping the room. "All right, let's get down to it. I want to hear your thoughts on the civil unrest spreading across the Empire. We need to handle this decisively."

Mavkah Griglag, the first to speak, took a drag from his pipe. "Vak and the Groff continue to fail in their job to end the upheaval. If you ask me, they are letting this unrest spread like a virus. If they don't stamp it out, it'll continue to spread and undermine everything we've built."

Zarun Falkor, ever the keen observer, shook his head. "That's easier said than done, Mavkah. We have to decide what we are going to do with the Groff—with Vak'Atioth. He is the one pulling the strings and holding his agency back from doing their jobs and restoring order."

Griglag, the seasoned warrior, looked angry as he leaned forward. "We have faced much worse in the past—but we have never faced a threat from within coming directly from the Groff itself, from its very leader. We have to solve this problem before our enemies turn their attention to us."

Otro nodded thoughtfully, knowing that tough decisions faced him. The sooner he decided what to do, the sooner action could be taken. "Vorun, you know what's happening with Vak. What do *you* think we should do with the Groff?"

Vorun Talvex, his trusted advisor and childhood friend, took a sip of his wine before speaking. "I agree with Griglag. Vak has taken things too far. His whisper campaign against you, Zon, is undermining your authority and the authority of the Council. I mean no disrespect when I say this—Zon Utulf would not have tolerated this. He would have ended it sooner; you should end it now before this cancer cements itself into these soft minds."

Otro considered this; he knew they were right. He needed to stamp this out—he needed to replace Vak as the Groff Director. He turned his attention to the next pressing issue that still hadn't been solved. "Your opinions of the Groff and Vak in particular have been heard. I am still formulating how to handle Vak—how to replace him without going to war with the Groff. Now let us discuss what to do about the Gravaxia system. We all know the Republic and their alliance is getting bolder. How do we defend the system and the Empire?"

NOS Harvox, captain of the battleship *Nayi Akat*, spoke up. "We need more ships in the sector. Our forces are stretched thin. When the Republic eventually invades, we need to be ready to respond with overwhelming force."

Griglag nodded. "Agreed. But we also need to ensure our soldiers are healthy. The strange illness in Gravaxia has been a wild card we can't ignore. However, it seems to be tapering off. Once we are sure there are no new cases, we can start reinforcing and rebuilding the system again. We will be ready for the Republic when they come."

Otro sighed, the weight of leadership pressing heavily on him. "We have multiple threats facing the Empire. We need to be smart about our resources and our strategies to defeat them. This illness, the unrest, the imminent invasion—they're all connected. We have to deal with them simultaneously."

Harvox leaned forward, his face determined. "We need to handle the Groff and Vak'Atioth before the Republic invades. We cannot fight ourselves and the enemy at the same time. We must sort out our own house now while we have time."

Vorun added, "If we move against Vak, we better take him out fast. We do not want him to flee to some safe place where he can rally people to his side and attempt to split the Empire."

Otro stood, his presence commanding. "Then it's settled; we remove Vak from the Groff. Zarun, contact Heltet and find out if a move against his boss were to happen, what side would he come down on? Can we count on him to help us, or will he side with Vak? We will meet again once Zarun has a decision from Heltet. Mavkah, I want you to reposition additional Sparrow and Axe units to Shwani. When it comes time to move against Vak, we will need to be prepared to fight the Groff's security units if necessary."

"Yes, Zon, it'll be done," Griglag assured him as the meeting came to an end.

The room buzzed with the sound of chairs scraping and low murmurs as the guests stood to leave. Otro's mind was already racing ahead, plotting their next moves. The fate of the Empire hung in the balance, and failure was not an option.

As his guests departed, Otro lingered by the fire, staring into the flames. The challenges were immense, but he was determined to see his people through this crisis. The future of the Zodark Empire depended on it.

Chapter Thirty-Nine
A Coup D'État

May 2114
Resistance Safe House
Gurista Prime

Drew was known for being extremely cool and collected under pressure, at least to the world around him. However, on the inside right now, it felt like he was being chased by a train and unable to get off the tracks. Everything had been culminating up to this, and there was a lot riding on what happened in the next few days. The Spartan surroundings of this safe house felt like they were closing in on him.

Just as Drew was about to start pacing the room, Tammuz opened the door quietly and sat down at the minimalist kitchen table where Drew was seated.

"You're late," Drew remarked.

"Sorry, I thought I might have a tail," said Tammuz. "And before you ask—yes, I followed the protocol to the letter. You might remember that I am also highly trained myself."

"I didn't say anything," Drew replied.

"No, but you were thinking it, and I could tell," Tammuz shot back.

Drew smiled. He wondered if he was going to be like Tammuz when he "grew up"—still a spy, but with definite sassy old man vibes.

"The coup is going to happen in twenty-four hours," Drew informed him. "We've determined that you're ready to take charge once the current leader and his immediate followers are neutralized."

He slid forward a folder. "These are speeches we've drafted up for you," Drew explained. "Each one is to be given at specified intervals during specific situations that will occur within the first twenty-four hours of the coup. I want you to study them and internalize them."

Tammuz took the speeches and nodded. "I will do what needs to be done," he replied.

Drew looked the man over. He was confident but had shown himself to be a servant of the people he worked with. He was intelligent but capable of speaking in a manner that anyone could understand. He was good-looking but not vain. He was exactly the kind of person they needed at this moment.

I sure hope everyone else sees what I see, Drew thought to himself.

****

Capitol Palace Building
Zidara, Gurista Prime

It was 0330 hours and pitch black. David had received confirmation from all the insurgent teams that they were in place, scattered among critical locations they had identified across the city and planet, ready to execute the moment David and the Kites gave their signal.

David took a deep breath and let it out. His mind calculated all possible paths. *Send it*, he told Somchai.

The line at the palace gate tower was very light at this time of night. Only two vehicles were waiting in line to show the guard their credentials. Who knew what those individuals were there for, but they were in the wrong place at the wrong time.

A high-speed vehicle approached the checkpoint at maximum velocity. The guard, probably tired from working overnight, didn't immediately realize what was happening, and by the time he did, it was too late. He fired his weapon at the driver's seat, only to realize that there was no driver. This car had been programmed for this mission.

Metal crunched as the vehicle slammed into the two stationary cars, killing the drivers on impact. The gate guard wouldn't be so lucky. He tried to get out of the way, but as if in slow motion, the heaps of metal kept rushing toward him until he was trapped between the structure of the guard tower and the heaping wreck, his lower extremities crushed.

The crash and subsequent fire drew the attention of the nearby guards. It was exactly the kind of chaos they wanted.

Go, go, go! David ordered.

Clad in their black lightweight armored suits that masked their heat signatures from infrared cameras, David and Amir ran up behind the three security guards that had been stationed at the front of the building. Using a knife, each of them slit the throat of one guard in a swift and all-but-silent motion. They lowered the bodies quietly to the ground. The third guard, who had been unaware of his colleagues' demise, turned around.

"We have to secure the perimeter!" he directed—only his fellow guards were down.

Stunned, he hesitated for half a second before attempting to draw his weapon. It was just enough time for Amir to come behind him and stab him in the back, exactly where his heart was located. The guard was paralyzed by pain and terror. Amir took the knife out and sliced the man's neck, finishing the job.

Somchai, Jess, and Catalina were stationed at the side entrances of the palace, taking care of the outer guards there. One by one, each of them checked in that their sector was cleared.

Catalina, make sure our guy inside held up his end of the bargain, David directed.

Normally, in a situation like this, the palace QRF would have responded immediately. However, the head of palace security happened to be one of the many clients that Catalina's women had been whispering to, and he was quite interested in retaining a position in a new government.

She sent a quick message via her P2, and just a moment later she received a positive response.

On course, Catalina confirmed. *The QRF is being told there is a security drill happening at the palace—they are to turn the cameras off while the drill is underway.*

Each group approached the entrances without any resistance. Somchai had hacked into the biometric database at the palace and added each of their fingerprints, retina scans, and facial recognition patterns into the system as "approved," granting them unfettered access to any and all rooms throughout the palace. Other than any human intervention, they were going to have green lights all the way.

Not only had their inside man caused the palace QRF to stand down, but he had also given the Kites a highly detailed explanation of how many guards were in the palace, where they would be and at what times they would be there. This allowed them to travel the path of least resistance.

David and Amir stacked up next to the stairwell on the right of the main entrance. At most, it would be protected by one guard, which would be easy work for the Kites.

Using their neurolinks, they confirmed they were ready, then opened the door, weapons drawn. They had drilled this kind of thing until it was literally second nature.

I think the guard is on break, Amir commented.

Maybe, but he could also be at the top of the landing. Stay frosty, said David.

****

Nippur Military Base
Outside Zidara, Gurista Prime

While the palace QRF might not have responded to the attack at the capitol palace gate, the explosion near the guard tower triggered an automatic warning to the military base just outside the city. Alarms blared. Soldiers ran about in a flurry of organized chaos, grabbing weapons, putting on body armor, and loading up into the three armored personnel carriers the QRF would respond with.

Each vehicle carried five soldiers, fully kitted out. These fifteen members of the Gurista military were highly trained individuals who were always looking for an adrenaline rush. If anything could be said of the Guristas, it was that they were certainly not afraid of a fight.

****

Near Nippur Military Base

Staff Sergeant Otieno Wekesa saw the vehicles exiting the base through his scope and alerted his team, a mix of Deltas and the local insurgent teams they had trained. He could tell from the tenor of their response that they were excited to get this show on the road.

Sergeant Wekesa might not have had the most exciting job, surveilling from a hide position far from the action. But an op like this required a sniper who could provide an overwatch for the team that was going to conduct the attack. From his location, he could spot dangers they couldn't, and he had the rifle to stealthily deal with it depending on whether it was a person or a vehicle.

Vehicle one is approaching kill box three, Wekesa announced over the neurolink. *Vehicle two has crossed kill box three…vehicle one is approaching the mark...fifty yards...forty...twenty yards...he's turning the corner...execute!*

Boom! Boom! Boom!

As soon as all three Gurista APCs rounded the bend past a convenience store, the IEDs erupted in a brilliant flash of fiery flames, washing over the intended vehicles as the force of the blast tossed them onto their sides like a child's play toy fractions of a second after the blast. Wekesa heard the thundering boom from the explosions and watched the vehicles scrape to a halt against the side of the road.

He watched as the rest of his Delta team and their local insurgent partners leaped to their feet to encircle the damaged vehicles quickly. He couldn't hear the words exactly, but he knew they were shouting for the occupants to step slowly out of the vehicles and surrender if they wanted to live. They had been intentional in the design of the IEDs for this attack—ensuring enough explosives were used to upturn the vehicles but not destroy them outright. They wanted prisoners—or rather they wanted to give the occupants the opportunity to surrender. If bloodshed could be avoided, they would avoid it.

****

Outside Nippur Military Base
Gurista Prime

Varian of the House KelVor turned to his Gallentine SF counterpart, Torian.

"Is everything ready?" Varian prodded.

Torian managed a half smile, an enthusiastic reaction for a Gallentine. "All set for Operation Chaos."

Phase One involved the use of stealth drones, virtually undetectable until they magnetically attached their plasma charges to their targets. Each one of the stealth drones had been very specifically programmed; key infrastructure such as vehicle charging stations and weapons stores were first, then the gate and the road out of the base. A chaotic cluster of explosions and mayhem erupted. Fires caused secondary explosions. Even from their vantage point, Varian heard screaming.

With all their stealth drones deployed, Varian moved to Phase Two. All around the base, he and Torian had placed devices that would employ sonic resonance bombs. The Gallentines had studied the construction materials of the Guristas very carefully, and they had worked out a particular sound frequency with a very beneficial effect, at least for the Republic.

The wall surrounding the base and the attached guard towers suddenly shook violently. As the sonic waves continued to resonate with the components that made up their structure, the shaking turned into the spontaneous collapse of the entire outer defense system for the base.

Varian looked at him and said, "I think that's enough now, don't you?"

Torian agreed. It was time to wait and see if their inside man would contact them.

They didn't have to wait very long. Soon, a military commander, a client at Catalina and Jess's establishment, reached out. He had the base under his control. It was time for the attacks to stop.
****

Capitol Palace Building
Zidara, Gurista Prime

David and Amir stealthily advanced up the stairs, barely making a sound, guns at the ready. When they reached the third floor, Amir pulled a small, thin disk from the pack he had with him.

Ready? Amir asked.

David did one last suit check to make sure all systems were go. *Ready.*

Amir slid the disk under the door, then activated it using a switch.

Thump, thump…thump.

They waited a few seconds, then opened the door. A fine mist was wafting through the air, which would have knocked them out if they had taken off their helmets. They rapidly put restraints on the guards so that if they woke up, there wouldn't be any surprises.

Somchai, Jess, and Catalina had been assigned to different areas to take out other key leaders who lived in the palace, but David and Amir were taking out the head honcho. They tiptoed down to the fourth door and silently opened it.

There, in an ornate bed that was at least twelve feet wide, lay a very overweight man, surrounded by four of his wives. The way he was snoring indicated that he clearly had untreated sleep apnea, which surprised David, given the medical advancements of the Guristas. Only pride would have allowed that.

One by one, David and Amir injected each of the sleepers with a medicine that would keep them unconscious for the next part. It wasn't done out of mercy—they just really wanted to avoid drawing attention with a lot of noise.

The Zodarks liked to decapitate their victims and pull out their hearts. It was cultural and a grotesque intimidation tactic. But since they intended to send a message to the Zodarks today, that was exactly what they did to the former leader of Gurista Prime. They collected their photographic evidence and sent it over to Drew. The wives were taken into custody. The Kites' work here was done.

****

Resistance Safe House
Gurista Prime

Dakkuri was having a very busy day. From the safety of one of the resistance safe houses, he had coordinated with Republic Delta Special Forces units all over the planet to decapitate many members of the upper echelon of the Mukhabarat on Gurista Prime. At the same time, mini-drone swarms had been sent to every known Zodark outpost and every other known location of the giant blue beasts on Gurista Prime and any other Gurista planets. Those tiny devices proved very effective in wiping out the threat of any of their overlords attacking them during the coup or bringing rapid help from outside Zodark ships.

Once Dakkuri had confirmed that all teams had been successful in eliminating their targets, he breathed a huge sigh of relief. The more immediate threats to his existence had been neutralized.

Now the real work would commence. Dakkuri, heavily guarded by teams of Delta SF, walked into the headquarters of what was left of the Mukhabarat. With the top dogs gone, he drummed up a meeting of the middle managers and field agents who happened to be present.

"Let me lay out the facts to you," Dakkuri began. "The Zodarks have not been our protectors or our benefactors. They use our people as

310

their cannon fodder to further their territorial ambitions at the expense of our blood—those days are over."

He slid forward folders that had images of Zodarks killing, abusing, and torturing Guristas, including babies. Each image had the type of documentation that a Mukhabarat would expect in order to prove that the picture was legitimate. Dakkuri walked them through in painstaking detail how the Zodarks had taken advantage of the Guristas economically, and how they had lied to them in any number of ways to control them. All of this was backed up by the research.

"We have a new opportunity today," Dakkuri continued. "All across the planet, we have been liberated from the Zodarks. Every outpost has been cleared. We do not have to submit to their control ever again. Today is the day that we can become a free Gurista society—able to control our own destinies. Instead of fighting for them, for the first time, we can fight for our own people."

Dakkuri took time to answer any questions they might have and then met with each of them individually. At the end of the day, only ten percent of the remaining Mukhabarat wanted to remain loyal to the Zodarks, and they were put in holding cells until a more formal procedure could be established. The other ninety percent were swayed by the copious amount of undeniable evidence they had been provided and were willing to fight for their own people.
****

Capitol Palace Building
Zidara, Gurista Prime

The sun had risen now. Tammuz climbed up the steps of the palace and waited for the cameraman to tell him he was ready. What he was about to say would be broadcast to every owner of a P2 throughout Gurista Prime and the surrounding Gurista planets. It was the first time something like this had been attempted, and it had certainly helped having an insider at Enlil Labs.

The cameraman stopped fiddling with the lights and the angle and started counting down. Tammuz took a deep breath and looked directly into the lens in front of him.

"Fellow Gurista people, I am Tammuz Zidan, the clan elder and leader of Clan Zidan. I had devoted my life to working closely with the

311

Zodarks, believing it was for the benefit of our people. However, since the discovery of a human society beyond the Zodarks' influence, it has become evident that we have been deceived and manipulated for generations. What has been kept hidden from us and our Sumerian ancestors is that we are actually descendants of another human society called the Republic. This society is from a star system known as Sol and a planet they call Earth. This Republic, as it is called, is part of a greater alliance with other alien races—an alliance that is at war with the Zodarks.

"I know what you have heard is a lot to take in. I have shared this with you because this Republic, this alliance they are a part of—they have offered for us to join, to break free of these Zodark 'benefactors' who in reality only seek to use us. They want to keep us divided, like how they separated us from Sumer and perpetuated this annual culling of that society. We have been offered a chance to become a free society, a free people to choose our own path, our own destiny.

"Last night, while the people of our nation slept, brave patriots from the Free Gurista movement worked in collaboration with soldiers of the Republic to liberate our people. As of four o'clock this morning, all Zodark overseers, advisors, and soldiers were eliminated. For those of you now serving the Gurista Navy and Land Forces—you must choose a side. Will you support and defend a free Gurista society, or will you choose to capitulate to a race that sees us as nothing more than cattle, cannon fodder for their wars of expansion? I ask you to side with *us*, to join with us, the free Gurista people—I ask you to now be our defenders, our soldiers, the protectors of our realm. Will you join your people...or will you subjugate them?"

He paused for a moment to let his words sink in, glancing down as he collected his thoughts. He then looked at the camera as he spoke. "I envision life and a bright future for our new free Gurista society: a world where we are able to make our own rules, where our taxes go only to support our own people. Even now, this human society, the Republic, has dispatched a military force to aid our efforts in remaining free from the Zodarks should they attempt to reclaim control over us. I've come to learn that the Republic is not our enemy—in fact, the Earthers are just like us. We are the same race—same DNA, same blood.

"I call upon our military forces and all of you to renounce any loyalty you may feel to the Zodarks. Instead, join me in fighting to remain free, and we will rebuild our society based on our values and who we are, not the Zodarks. We are free—now help us stay that way!" Tammuz gave the cameraman the signal to end the recording.

When he saw the camera stop recording, he breathed a sigh of relief. He could finally wipe the sweat from his brow and run his fingers nervously through his hair. He had held up his end of the bargain. He had delivered the message they had crafted. He had conveyed what needed to be shared. Now it was a matter of how many people would accept the gift of free will.

Following his message would be a series of instructions for citizens, a request for them to remain home—to shelter in place for the next couple of days until it was known which side the military would choose.

****

A Few Hours Later
Free Gurista Training Camp
GN *Vraxerian's Shadow*

Drew walked toward the Gallentine stealth corvette as he looked for Third Officer Seraphel Tavon. It was time to contact the Republic and let them know they had initiated the coup and so far, it had succeeded. They had removed the Zodark puppet government and replaced him with their guy—Tammuz. With no Zodark ships currently in the system, now was the best time for the Republic to bridge into the system and establish control over the stargate.

It was time to send ground reinforcements and ensure the Zodarks couldn't return to the system and restore order even if they tried. The longer the Zodarks were gone—no longer able to exert influence or control over the Guristas—the harder it would be to restore the old order. That was why the Republic needed to be able to send a strong enough force to repel whatever attempts the Zodarks might make.

"Ah, Drew, there you are. I listened to the speech Tammuz gave," said Tavon as he exited the ship, walking toward Drew.

"It was a good speech," replied Drew as he approached Tavon. "Now that Tammuz has given delivered his message, it's time to crack open that new comms gear Space Command gave us during your last trip to New Eden."

During the last supply run to New Eden before they'd initiated the coup, Space Command had given them a new communication system they would use to communicate directly with Admiral Dobbs's ship and Space Command Headquarters. It was a piece of new Humtar technology that had been shared with the Republic to help solve the communication latency issue they'd previously experienced when sending messages between star systems and ships. While Drew knew nothing about how the Quantum Beamlink communication system worked, he immediately recognized the value of being able to connect in near-real-time with Admiral Dobbs or Space Command, especially during an operation like the overthrow of a foreign government.

The portability of the system made it even easier to use and integrate into a ship's existing comms system or a field kit. Being no larger than the size of a carry-on piece of luggage, it was perfect. It was powered by some sort of power source Drew had never heard of, but once they turned it on and entered a security code, it activated a smallish rectangular antenna, which reoriented in the direction of where the signal would be sent. While quantum entanglement was a foreign subject to him, being able to communicate in real-time wasn't. He knew it worked, and it would allow him to send a message to an address that would alert Space Command that it was time to open a wormhole bridge and send whatever force they were going to use to secure the system and keep the Zodarks from returning.

Tavon had the QB system set up in no time and confirmed it was ready to transmit as he gave Drew a comms device to transmit his message. Recalling the call signs and code words they were supposed to use, Drew sent his portion of the message and was now waiting for confirmation.

"How long do you think it'll take before some ships arrive?" Tavon asked.

Drew shrugged. "Not sure. Hopefully, it won't be long. Maybe we'll get lucky and there will be one of your ships nearby that can open a bridge."

The Gallentine nodded. He was about to respond when the QB device came to life, having received a response. Drew and Tavon looked at it and laughed.

"It's vague. You would think they would be more specific," Tavon said matter-of-factly.

Drew tried not to laugh. The message was all of three letters: O.O.W., shorthand for On Our Way.

Chapter Forty
Operation Gurista Freedom

Same Day
Task Force Freedom Fourteen
RNS *Maximus*
Tigris, Rhea System

Brigadier General Brian Royce savored the aroma of the freshly brewed cup of Death Wish coffee as he stood near one of the observation windows aboard the giant heavy orbital assault ship RNS *Maximus*, breathing in the steam rising from the heavily caffeinated nectar of the gods. The moment he took the first sip, he could taste the subtle notes of dark chocolate and black cherry-infused arabica beans carefully roasted to deliver that extra kick of caffeine his body craved. He looked into the bitter, potent brew, which seemed to match his mood of the moment as he turned his gaze out toward the desolate landscape of Tigris, the closer of the pair of moons in orbit of New Eden.

For the past forty-eight hours, the *Maximus* and its two sister ships, the *MacArthur* and *Eisenhower,* had lingered in orbit while they waited for the pair of *Jupiter*-class troop transports coming from Earth to link up with them before the start of Operation Gurista Freedom. During the planning of the operation, Royce had been told if things went according to plan, the ground contingent wouldn't be needed for active combat but would serve in more of a peacekeeping or advisory role to the new government. If it did come down to fighting, then two divisions' worth of orbital assault troops, a division of Rangers, and a JSOC contingent should be enough combat power to handle whatever resistance they might encounter. This was in addition to the four *Saturn*-class fleet replenishment support ships that would supply the Fleet, along with the 67,720 Republic soldiers accompanying the mission.

Lifting the coffee to his lips, Royce savored the chance to have as many hot, fresh cups of his favorite brew as he could. Once he was dirtside, the opportunities to brew a fresh pot or an insta-cup would be few and far between. For now, he was going to enjoy every drop he could.

"Never thought I'd see this place again," he muttered, more to himself than anyone else.

The volcanic surface of Tigris stretched out below, a stark contrast of jagged black rocks and glowing rivers of molten lava. The barely breathable atmosphere lent the moon an eerie perpetual twilight, broken only by the occasional flares of volcanic eruptions.

Royce's eyes followed the winding paths of the lava flows, tracing their fiery trails across the barren landscape. "Looks like hell down there," he said, taking another sip. "Can't imagine why anyone would want to mine this rock."

A junior officer, Lieutenant Harris, stepped up beside him, glancing out the window. "They say the minerals are worth the risk, sir. High-grade ore, rare elements. Makes it worth dealing with the heat and the gas."

Royce grunted in response. "I suppose. Still, it's a damn inhospitable place. Perfect for training, though. Nothing builds character like surviving on the edge of a volcano."

Harris nodded, his eyes wide as he took in the scene. "It's hard to believe anyone trains down there. How do they even breathe?"

"They manage," Royce replied, his voice tinged with a mix of respect and weariness. "Barely. They've got rebreathers, special suits— it's not easy, but it weeds out the weak."

The observation window offered a panoramic view of the moon, its surface marred by scars from both natural volcanic activity and the impact craters from long-forgotten skirmishes. In the distance, faint lights from the mining operations flickered like beacons of life in an otherwise lifeless landscape.

Royce turned his gaze away from the moon and looked at the vast expanse of space beyond. "All this waiting," he said, almost to himself. "You'd think I'd be used to it by now."

Harris glanced at him, sensing the deeper meaning in his words. "It's the calm before the storm, sir. Once we move out, there won't be much time for reflection."

Royce nodded slowly. "True enough. Just hope this time, it's worth the cost."

He took another sip of his coffee, the bitter taste grounding him as he stared out at Tigris. The moon was a harsh reminder of the challenges they faced, both from the environment and their enemies. But it was also a testament to their resilience, their ability to endure and adapt.

"Here's to hoping," Royce said quietly, lifting his mug slightly in a mock toast to the volatile world below. "And to surviving whatever comes next."

****

RNS *Aquila*
IVO Tigris
Rhea System

Rear Admiral Amy Dobbs stood on the observation deck of the RNS *Aquila*, the newest jewel in the Republic's naval crown. At 2,700 meters in length, the star carrier was a marvel of engineering and firepower. Her gaze swept over the vast expanse of the main bridge below, where the crew moved with disciplined efficiency. The hum of activity was a constant reminder of the ship's readiness for Operation Gurista Freedom.

Dobbs took a moment to appreciate the formidable array of weaponry the *Aquila* boasted. Twenty-four twin-barreled antiship turbo lasers and twenty-two twin-barreled twenty-four-inch magrail turrets lined the flanks. Five missile pods, each armed with fifty antiship missiles, and an array of sixty point-defense guns stood ready to protect the carrier from enemy attacks. The antifighter missile pods, each carrying fifty missiles, ensured a formidable defense against enemy fighters.

The RNS *Aquila*, the battleships RNS *Defiant* and *Triumph*, the four battle cruisers RNS *Invincible*, *Resolute*, *Dauntless*, and *Valiant*, and the six heavy cruisers RNS *Thunder*, *Havoc*, *Warlord*, *Reaper*, *Vortex*, *Dominion*, and *Guardian* stood ready to begin their mission. To round out the remaining escort vessels, the task force had six flak frigates for antimissile, antifighter defense along with eight escort frigates and ten corvettes.

The support vessels for her ground force contingent consisted of the RNS *Maximus*, *MacArthur*, and *Eisenhower*, supported with two *Jupiter*-class troop transports, RNS *Ganymede* and *Thebe*, and five *Saturn*-class fleet replenishment ships: RNS *Titan*, *Enceladus*, *Dione*, *Tethys*, and *Iapetus*. Last but not least were the RNS *Bechtel* and *Skanska*. These last two ships were the Fleet's newest expeditionary base construction platforms. In her case, the two ships were ferrying a total of forty Sentry II defensive towers they would deploy near the stargates leading into the Orinda System, the home system of Gurista Prime, along with placing some 240 antiship proximity mines. This would round out the noncombat ships Dobbs's task force would have to defend should the Zodarks return to the Orinda system looking for a fight.

Dobbs's attention shifted to the two fighter wings housed within the *Aquila*. Each wing consisted of three fighter groups, each group comprising four squadrons of sixteen fighters or bombers. In total, the *Aquila* carried 384 fighters and bombers, a testament to its role as the flagship of Task Force Freedom Fourteen.

Despite the number of ships and the size of her disciplined crew, Dobbs had a sinking feeling in the pit of her stomach. They were spread too thin. *I just don't know if it's going to be enough*, she bemoaned. She took a deep breath and sighed. *It is what it is*, she told herself.

The observation deck offered a commanding view, and Dobbs found herself admiring the precision with which the crew operated. Her second-in-command, Captain Pavel Marik, was down on the main bridge, overseeing the final preparations.

The intercom crackled to life, and a young ensign's voice filled the room. "Admiral Dobbs, all systems are green. The fleet is in position, awaiting your command."

Dobbs nodded to herself, feeling the weight of responsibility settle on her shoulders. "Thank you, Ensign. Maintain readiness. We're on standby until we receive the code word."

She turned her attention back to the vastness of space outside the observation window. The Orinda system lay ahead, a critical stronghold in Gurista territory. The upcoming invasion was a bold move, one that required perfect coordination and unwavering resolve.

Captain Marik's voice came through her personal comm unit. "Admiral, the crew is ready. How's the view from up there?"

Dobbs allowed herself a small smile. "Breathtaking, Pavel. The *Aquila* is a fine ship, and the crew is performing admirably."

Marik chuckled. "She's a beauty, all right. Only the fourth of her kind, and the first two were lost in battle. We're making history, Admiral."

"We are," Dobbs agreed, her tone becoming more serious. "But let's make sure it's the kind of history we can be proud of. This operation is critical. The Orinda system is vital for both strategic and symbolic reasons."

Dobbs glanced at the tactical display, showing the positions of the other ships in Task Force Freedom Fourteen. Each vessel, from the mighty *Victory*-class battleships to the agile corvettes, had a role to play in the upcoming assault.

Her thoughts drifted back to the briefings and strategy sessions that had led to this moment. Intelligence reports, battle plans, and contingency scenarios had been pored over endlessly. Now, it was time to execute.

The silence on the observation deck was punctuated by the soft beeping of instruments and the occasional murmur from the crew below. Dobbs felt a surge of pride for the men and women under her command. They were ready, and so was she.

Her communications specialist broke her wistful reverie. "Ma'am, we're receiving a transmission over the new quantum beam communication system the Humtars gave us," he announced.

"What do you have?" asked Dobbs, walking over.

"It says, 'Honey badger don't care.'"

Admiral Dobbs smiled. This was the signal that everything was working out and that they should come on over. Had they wanted them to turn around, they would have sent a message saying, "The pigeons have landed."

She turned to Captain Marik. "We are a go," she confirmed. "You know what to do."

****

Hours Later

Admiral Amy Dobbs stood on the observation deck of the RNS *Aquila*, her eyes fixed on the Gallentine ship, the GNS *Vraxerian's Dagger*, positioned at the edge of the fleet. This ship was unlike any other in the task force, equipped with technology that could create a temporary wormhole, a bridge between star systems. The anticipation in the air was palpable as the final preparations for Operation Gurista Freedom were underway.

The Gallentine vessel began its complex maneuvers, aligning with precise coordinates. Dobbs watched as the ship's massive energy

320

arrays started to glow, a brilliant blue light that pulsed rhythmically, growing in intensity. The observation deck offered a panoramic view, and Dobbs could see the other ships in her fleet aligning themselves, ready to follow her lead.

"All ships, prepare for transit," she commanded over the fleet-wide comm channel, her voice steady and authoritative. The hum of activity increased as the crew on the bridge executed their final checks.

The *Vraxerian's Dagger*'s energy arrays reached a blinding luminescence. Then, with a sudden, almost imperceptible shift, the space between the two star systems began to warp. It was as if the fabric of reality was being folded, the stars distorting and bending around an unseen point. A swirling vortex formed at the center, expanding outward with a mesmerizing, almost hypnotic motion.

Dobbs's breath caught in her throat as she witnessed the wormhole's birth. The swirling colors of the vortex, a mix of blues, purples, and shimmering whites, created a kaleidoscopic tunnel that stretched into infinity. It was both beautiful and terrifying, a raw display of power and technology.

"By the stars," she whispered, unable to tear her eyes away from the sight.

"Admiral, the wormhole is stable," Captain Marik's voice came through the comm. "All systems are green. We're ready to proceed."

Dobbs nodded, her resolve hardening. "Understood, Captain. All ships, prepare to move through the bridge."

The fleet began to advance, the massive bulk of the *Aquila* leading the way. The closer they got to the wormhole, the more intense the distortion of space became. The *Aquila*'s hull vibrated slightly as it crossed the event horizon, the transition smooth but deeply unsettling.

Dobbs could feel the eyes of her crew on her, their faith in her leadership evident. She kept her gaze fixed on the vortex, the swirling colors reflecting off the observation window.

"Steady as she goes," she murmured. "We'll get through this."

As the *Aquila* entered the wormhole, the sensation of movement became both disorienting and exhilarating. The stars outside blurred into streaks of light, the ship seemingly suspended between two points in space and time. Dobbs felt a strange, almost weightless sensation, as if the boundaries of reality were momentarily suspended.

"Status report," she ordered, her voice cutting through the surreal atmosphere.

"All systems normal," Marik replied. "Fleet is maintaining formation. Transition is stable."

Dobbs allowed herself a moment of relief. The technology was holding, and the fleet was on course. She watched as the other ships followed, each one swallowed by the shimmering vortex, disappearing into the tunnel of light.

"We're almost through," Marik said, his voice calm and reassuring.

Dobbs nodded, feeling the familiar surge of adrenaline that came with leading a mission. "Prepare for reentry. All hands, brace for exit."

The end of the wormhole approached, the swirling colors giving way to the dark expanse of the Orinda system. The transition was seamless, the *Aquila* emerging into the new star system with a slight jolt. One by one, the rest of the fleet appeared, the wormhole closing behind them with a final burst of light.

"All ships accounted for," Marik confirmed. "We've made it."

Dobbs took a deep breath, her eyes scanning the new surroundings. The Orinda system lay before them, a mix of anticipation and tension hanging in the air.

"XO, now that the Fleet is through the bridge, I want all ships to set Condition One, battle stations," Dobbs ordered. "Helm, set course for Gurista Prime. Bring our engines to fifty percent power and form defensive position Charlie Four—I want a pair of those corvettes and frigates to push out from the Fleet and conduct a deep reconnaissance of the system," she continued, speaking with urgency. "Let's get a move on, people. Ops, TAO, EW—what do we have in system? Any threats identified yet that I need to know about?"

"Negative, Admiral," responded Commander Waldman from his electronic warfare station. "The threat board is clear—we are not detecting any known communication frequencies between Zodark or Orbot vessels."

For the next few minutes, the ship and the fleet itself continued to move forward, closer to the planet. The longer they were in the system, the more their sensors picked up. A clearer picture of the system, its planets and moons was developing.

"Captain Marik, it seems we have gotten lucky; looks like we're alone in the system," Dobbs remarked. "Let's try and capitalize on that and get those sentry towers anchored around the stargate. Send a message to the *Bechtel* and *Skanska* to set course for the stargate and get to work," she ordered. She wanted to get the system secured and locked down as soon as possible.

"Aye, Admiral," said Marik. "May I suggest we dispatch a few escorts, just in case the Zodarks happen to show up?" he asked.

That's not a bad idea, Dobbs thought to herself. "OK, what do you have in mind?" she asked.

Marik smiled. "Well, since the task force is going to be near Gurista Prime, I suggest we send a strong enough force that should any Zodark ships jump into the system, we can immediately engage them and take them out before they can attempt to flee the system back through the gate. I'd recommend we send the battlecruiser *Resolute*, along with the heavy cruisers *Thunder*, *Havoc*, and *Warlord*, to support them and help provide some anti-fighter support. I'd also include a few frigates and corvettes. This should provide enough support to protect the *Bechtel* and *Skanska* while we focus on supporting whatever needs Republic Intelligence have for us on Gurista Prime."

"Huh, you don't think that's a little overkill?" Dobbs asked skeptically.

Marik was about to respond when a blip near the stargate appeared on the tactical action map or TAMs near the TAO station. The ship's AI system responded loudly, announcing, "*Alert—New Contact— Alert—New Contact.*" The crew responded to the automated alert with practiced precision, honed from years of experience and war.

"Commander Hill, get me a SITREP on that contact! We need to know what kind of ship that is and if they are the only ones that jumped through. Do not lose track of that ship!" Captain Marik instructed.

Admiral Dobbs couldn't believe what she was seeing. They had just arrived in the system themselves—they still hadn't made contact with Republic Intelligence on the planet surface. Pushing aside the anger and frustration she felt building inside her, she turned to Lieutenant Luther, her Comms specialist. "Lieutenant, order the battlecruiser *Resolute*, along the heavy cruisers *Thunder*, *Havoc*, and *Warlord*, to advance at maximum speed toward the stargate to engage and destroy that enemy ship and any others they may encounter!"

"Aye, Admiral. Sending the orders now," replied Lieutenant Luther, immediately contacting the ships in question.

"Captain Marik has the bridge," exclaimed Dobbs, making sure the bridge crew knew he was in charge.

Dobbs looked Marik square in the eyes. "I need you to fight the ship," she told him. "I have to establish communications with Republic Intelligence and complete the other part of our mission. Don't forget to employ our space wings if necessary, and whatever you do—do not let them leave the system."

"Yes, Admiral. We're on it," Marik confirmed.

While Captain Marik was fighting the ship and directing the other ships in the battle, Lieutenant Luther waved his hands to get Dobbs's attention. As she walked toward him, he announced, "Admiral, I've finally got them—the Republic Intelligence operative, Drew—he's on the line along with a person named Tammuz…they're asking to speak to you."

Dobbs exhaled in relief, not realizing she'd been holding her breath. "Thank God. Put them through; display it on my personal screen," she ordered before returning to her seat, adjusting her monitor as the call transferred to it.

A moment later, she heard a voice as an image appeared of a man who was easily in his seventies, maybe even early eighties. His face was weathered, his eyes sharp but disarming. "Admiral Dobbs, it is a pleasure to make your acquaintance. My name is Tammuz, of the Clan Zidar. I have been chosen by my people to be their representative." He sounded very relieved to be speaking with her.

Dobbs could hear another voice nearby, probably Drew. He was the Republic Intelligence operative working alongside the soldiers already on the planet.

She returned Tammuz's smile. "It is a pleasure to meet you as well, Tammuz," she replied. She took only half a breath before she explained, "Look, I don't mean to be hasty, but given the circumstances and the fact that our sensor just detected a ship entering the system via the stargate, I don't think you'll be offended if I skip the niceties and we go straight to the point and get you officially recognized as a sovereign power."

Tammuz's face briefly betrayed his concern at her comment, but then he appeared to shrug off whatever he had just felt, bowing his head slightly to acquiesce to her request.

"Is the Free Gurista Society ready for official recognition?" she asked.

Tammuz and Drew, who now appeared on the screen next to Tammuz, answered in unison, "Yes, it is."

"Excellent," Dobbs replied. "Well, Tammuz, while your nation begins your application to join our alliance, I am authorized by Chancellor Aimes Morgan, elected leader of the Republic, to formally recognize your government as the official and legitimate government of the Gurista people. I have also been authorized by the Chancellor and Viceroy Miles Hunt, the appointed leader of our alliance—the Galactic Empire—to offer your government whatever military and economic support you may request to help ensure your government and people remain free of the Zodark Empire and its control. Tammuz, would you like to accept the offer of support from the Republic and our alliance?"

"Yes, we would be most gracious in accepting whatever kind of support and assistance your force can provide to aid in our quest to remain a free—"

Boom!

Suddenly, there were shouts in the background as the Guristas with Tammuz and Drew seemed to be shouting before a loud explosion ended the transmission.

"What the hell was that?" asked Admiral Dobbs, looking at the communications specialist, who was frantically checking through different screens at his workstation.

"Ma'am, I don't know what that was, but an explosion of some kind terminated our connection."

Damn it! thought Dobbs. *What just happened?*

****

RNS *Maximus*
Approaching Gurista Prime
Orinda System

General Brian Royce stood in the bustling operations center of the RNS *Maximus*, his eyes fixed on the holographic display that

325

dominated the room. The *Maximus* was moving in formation with the rest of the fleet, advancing toward Gurista Prime. The planet loomed large on the screen, its surface dotted with the strategic markers of their upcoming assault.

The operations center was a hive of activity, with officers and technicians moving with purpose, coordinating the various elements of the invasion. Royce's attention was drawn to a small element of Republic warships advancing to engage a trio of Zodark corvettes, two frigates, and six giant freighters—the contacts that they had recently identified as entering the system via the stargate.

"Captain, status report on those ships," Royce commanded, his voice cutting through the din.

Captain Ellis, the *Maximus*'s tactical officer, looked up from her console. "Our ships are engaging the Zodark corvettes and frigates. It looks as if the enemy is attempting to use the freighters as cover while one or more of them is burning out their engines to reach the gate and try to jump through it."

Royce nodded, satisfied with the answer. "Good. Keep me updated on any changes or if one of them manages to escape. In the meantime, let's focus on our mission at hand."

As the *Maximus* continued its approach to Gurista Prime, the ship's quantum beam communication system came to life, a pulsating blue light indicating the establishment of a secure link. A second later, data streams flowed into their computers, displaying real-time information from Republic Intelligence and Special Forces units already on the planet's surface.

Royce stepped closer to the main console, his eyes scanning the influx of data. Reports from the Special Operations Forces units detailed their progress in destabilizing the Zodark puppet regime that had controlled Gurista Prime. The holographic map of the planet showed various hotspots where the locals, with SOF assistance, had taken control of key installations.

"General, we have a secure line with Colonel Mateo Barton on the ground," said Lieutenant Harris, the communications officer. "He's ready to brief you on their current status."

Royce nodded, tapping a control to bring up the live feed. Colonel Barton's face appeared on the screen, a backdrop of makeshift command center behind him.

"General Royce, good to see you," Barton began, his voice steady as he began to relay his report of the situation on the ground. "Our operations here have been highly effective—frankly, the initial twenty-four hours of the coup went smoother than expected. The speed with which we struck the Zodark and Gurista security elements left them paralyzed, at least at first. We've managed to rally significant local support and have successfully deposed the Zodark puppet regime. The Guristas are excited to take back their home world."

"This almost seems too good to be true," said Royce.

"Well, now that we're starting the third day post-coup, the remnants of the Zodark cadre we didn't kill yet have begun to organize a resistance," Barton explained. "Whatever Gurista Army, Navy and other security elements didn't immediately switch sides are now coordinating a more serious effort against us. As of nine hours ago, they were launching attacks against my own units, trying to regain control over certain critical areas of the capital, like the spaceport."

Royce did a mental inventory of his available resources. "Colonel Barton, I'd like to send a regiment of orbital assault troopers and dispatch them to the spaceport to help you retake it or restore order. It's a significant piece of infrastructure. Then we can send you more troops and equipment to help suppress the recent uprising and hold down the capital until the remainder of the Republic ground force can be brought to the surface."

"Excellent, General Royce, that—" His voice cut off as an aide came over and spoke in hushed tones.

"Pardon the interruption," said Barton. "Royce, we've just confirmed a multipronged attack happening against the governing palace where Tammuz and several newly appointed members of the government are operating."

He pulled himself to the side to speak with the aide further, then turned back to Royce. "Our information is spotty, incomplete, but I do know that Deltas are locked in a fierce battle around the palace, and I need to rally what forces I can to come assist them."

The urgency of the situation was not lost on Royce. "Before you go, Colonel, I just want you to know that the moment we're in orbit and can deploy, I'll lead a regiment of Rangers and Deltas myself to conduct an orbital HALO insertion overtop the palace…hang on, Colonel, help is on the way."

****

From the Author

Miranda and I hope you have enjoyed this book. If you are ready to continue the action, the preorder for the next book in the series, *Into the Inferno*, is already live. Simply sign up on Amazon to preorder your copy.

If you would like to stay up-to-date on new releases and receive emails about any special pricing deals we may make available, please sign up for our email distribution list. Simply go to https://www.frontlinepublishinginc.com/ and sign up.

If you enjoy audiobooks, we have a great selection that has been created for your listening pleasure. Our entire Red Storm series and our Falling Empire series have been recorded, and several books in our Rise of the Republic series and our Monroe Doctrine series are now available. Please see below for a complete listing.

As independent authors, reviews are very important to us and make a huge difference to other prospective readers. If you enjoyed this book, we humbly ask you to write up a positive review on Amazon and Goodreads. We sincerely appreciate each person that takes the time to write one.

We have really valued connecting with our readers via social media, especially on our Facebook page https://www.facebook.com/RosoneandWatson/. Sometimes we ask for help from our readers as we write future books—we love to draw upon all your different areas of expertise. We also have a group of beta readers who get to look at the books before they are officially published and help us fine-tune last-minute adjustments. If you would like to be a part of this team, please go to our author website, and send us a message through the "Contact" tab.

You may also enjoy some of our other works. A full list can be found below:

Nonfiction:
Iraq Memoir 2006–2007 Troop Surge
Interview with a Terrorist

Fiction:

The Monroe Doctrine Series

Volume One
Volume Two
Volume Three
Volume Four
Volume Five
Volume Six
Volume Seven
Volume Eight

Rise of the Republic Series

Into the Stars
Into the Battle
Into the War
Into the Chaos
Into the Fire
Into the Calm
Into the Breach
Into the Terror
Into the Uncertain
Into the Reckoning

Crisis in the Desert Series (co-authored with Matt Jackson)

Project 19
Desert Shield
Desert Storm

Falling Empires Series

Rigged
Peacekeepers
Invasion
Vengeance
Retribution

Red Storm Series

Battlefield Ukraine

Battlefield Korea
Battlefield Taiwan
Battlefield Pacific
Battlefield Russia
Battlefield China

Michael Stone Series
Traitors Within

World War III Series
Prelude to World War III: The Rise of the Islamic Republic and the Rebirth of America
Operation Red Dragon and the Unthinkable
Operation Red Dawn and the Siege of Europe
Cyber Warfare and the New World Order

Children's Books:
My Daddy has PTSD
My Mommy has PTSD

Abbreviation Key

ALCON	All Concerned
AMA	Against Medical Advice
APC	Armored Personnel Carrier
BDA	Bomb Damage Assessment
BLUF	Bottom Line Up Front
CAR	Combat Aviation Regiment
CIC	Combat Information Center
CO	Commanding Officer
COB	Chief of Boat
CSB	Combat Support Base
CSH	Combat Support Hospital
DZ	Drop Zone
ECCM	Electronic Counter-Countermeasures
ECM	Electronic Countermeasures
EMCON	Emission Control (electronic silence)
EO	Executive Order
ETA	Estimated Time of Arrival
EWO	Electronic Warfare Officer
FRAGO	Fragmentary Order
FTL	Faster-than-Light
G2	Intelligence Staff
HALO	High Altitude, Low Orbit
HQ	Headquarter
HUD	Heads-Up Display
ID	Infantry Division
IED	Improvised Explosive Device
IF1	Ice Fire One
IFV	Infantry Fighting Vehicle
IVO	In the Vicinity of
JATM	Joint Advanced Tactical Missiles
JSOC	Joint Special Operations Command
LSR	Logistic Support Regiment
LST	Logistic Support Transports
LZ	Landing Zone
MPL	Multipurpose Launcher
MRE	Meals Ready to Eat

MWR	Morale, Welfare, and Recreation
NCO	Noncommissioned Officer
NDA	Nondisclosure Agreement
NOFORN	Not Releasable to Foreign Nationals (an intelligence classification)
NOS	Zodark leadership
ODA	Operation Detachment Alpha (team of Deltas)
OIC	Officer in Charge
OOW	On Our Way
OSA	Omni-Spectral Array
P2	Priority Pad
PCU	Prepacked Cargo Units
PDG	Point Defense Gun
PELS	Pulsar Echo Location System
PPE	Personal Protective Equipment
QB	Quantum Beamlink
QRF	Quick Reaction Force
R&R	Rest and Recreation
RA	Republic Army
RNS	Republic Naval Ship
RTB	Return to Base
SCIF	Sensitive Compartmented Information Facility
SITREP	Situation Report
SOCOM	Special Operations Command
SOF	Special Operations Forces
T2	Troop Transporter
TAM	Tactical Action Map
TAO	Tactical Action Officer
TEUs	Standard Twenty-Foot Shipping Containers
TF	Task Force

THE END